PRAISE FOR
Groupies

"Priscus's audacious debut totally ro[...]
story of groupies, and the young wom[...]
as she is with grabbing her own star[...]
story about the cost of fame, desire, a[...]
nothing short of superstar."

—Caroline Leavitt, *New York Times* bestselling
author of *With or Without You*

"This dark, absorbing coming-of-age tale, set in the folk-rock scene of the 1970s, captivated me from the very first sentence. With deep intelligence and massive heart, Sarah Priscus captures both the allure of fame and its dangers. I loved her thorny heroine, Faun, and I loved this novel." —Joanna Rakoff, internationally bestselling author of *My Salinger Year* and *A Fortunate Age*

"What a thrill it is to read Sarah Priscus's '70s rock, California-dreaming *Groupies*. This shimmering debut is packed with tenderness and awe against a backdrop of drugs, sex, rock stars, and high drama. Faun is a lovable, believable, and wonderfully drawn character who will remain in my heart and mind for a very, very long time."

—Jessica Anya Blau, author of *Mary Jane*

"A luscious glimpse into the '70s L.A. music scene—in all its exhilarating, destructive glory. A love letter to a lost time and a lost innocence, Sarah Priscus's dark, glittering debut is irresistible."

—Robin Wasserman, author of
Mother Daughter Widow Wife and *Girls on Fire*

"The rock star '70s as seen through the eyes of the wild and reckless girls eager to live in the shadow of fame—and the trouble that comes when they try to claim a place in the spotlight for themselves. Gripping, vivid, and perceptive, *Groupies* swept me into a darkly glittering world I didn't want to leave."

—Natalie Standiford, author of *Astrid Sees All*

"I devoured *Groupies*—a gritty, glamorous novel that shines a spotlight on the iconic women behind the male rock legend and asks the question 'What happens to girls who love too much?'"

—Emma Brodie, author of *Songs in Ursa Major*

Groupies

Groupies

A NOVEL

Sarah Priscus

wm

WILLIAM MORROW
An Imprint of HarperCollins*Publishers*

GROUPIES. Copyright © 2022 by Sarah Priscus. All rights reserved. Printed in Canada. No part of this book may be used or reproduced in any manner whatsoever without written permission except in the case of brief quotations embodied in critical articles and reviews. For information, address HarperCollins Publishers, 195 Broadway, New York, NY 10007.

HarperCollins books may be purchased for educational, business, or sales promotional use. For information, please email the Special Markets Department at SPsales@harper collins.com.

A hardcover edition of this book was published in 2022 by William Morrow, an imprint of HarperCollins Publishers.

FIRST WILLIAM MORROW PAPERBACK EDITION PUBLISHED 2023.

Art courtesy of dannyburn/Adobe, Inc., BMCL /Shutterstock, Inc., and Yuriy Seleznev/ Shutterstock, Inc.

Library of Congress Cataloging-in-Publication Data has been applied for.

ISBN 978-0-06-321802-4

23 24 25 26 27 LBC 5 4 3 2 1

For the girls who love hard, who love recklessly, who love too much

1.

JOSIE, WHO'D BE COVERED IN BLOOD ON BATHROOM TILES IN nine months' time, met me at the Greyhound station.

She sprung up as soon as she caught sight of me, burying my face in the jasmine-scented fabric of her white fur coat. Faint streaks of glitter sat on her cheeks—ghostly remnants of nights past. Josie clasped my fingers tight, turning them red. "Oh, Faun," she said. "It's about time you got here." She held my hand, guiding me over grimy tiles and through travel-weary crowds to a metal bench. We were always linking our pinkies together in unnamed promises. Above our heads, houseflies burned to death on the bulb of an incandescent light.

I unclasped my Polaroid bag, which I'd embarrassingly hand-embroidered with Carpenters lyrics. Josie smiled before I asked, ignoring the travelers milling past as she posed.

I snapped the photo.

For a millisecond, when the flash went off, the heaviness of her makeup was clear. Clearer was how under layers of cover-up, a purple-blue bruise was blooming on her tanned cheek. She kept smiling as the photo started developing.

Josie's face burst with sunny remembrance. "I've got a surprise for you," she said, reaching into her tote bag. "Don't peek!"

I put my hands over my face, leaning against the bench. The see-no-evil monkey.

Josie poked my side with thin cardboard and said, "Here!" I opened my eyes as she handed me a pristine copy of Holiday Sun's 1970 debut album. We'd spun it endlessly when it came out, spending our junior year huddled in Josie's family's den weaving fantasies about the band's four dreamy members. Even now, in 1977, years after we memorized their breakout hit "Sheila," I could still recite it. Holiday Sun had grown, finding their place between Aerosmith and the Eagles on rock radio. Despite my ensuing slip into the sphere of folk and Americana, having a Holiday Sun record in my hands still thrilled.

I traced the embossed leaves on the cover. "Thank you," I said, meaning it. "This is a Faun-and-Josie *classic*. It looks brand-new." The covers of the records I'd sold before hopping on the bus had been coffee-stained or bent at the corners.

"Flip it over," Josie said.

There, in cursive swirls, was Cal Holiday's signature. "How did you get this?" I asked, eyes wide.

It was the question Josie had been waiting for. I pictured her staring into her compact mirror, rehearsing the elegant ways she could play sheepish about answering it. "Well," she said, "Cal and I *happen* to be dating." She paused. Her coy facade slipped, and she burst into laughter.

"No!" I cried. "No way!"

"I know you were always in love with folksy little Harry Carling, but —"

"No," I said, insistent. Sure, Harry Carling was the handsome folk singer of my dreams, but I couldn't deny the remarkability of Holiday Sun. They were huge—they were *everywhere*—and Josie was dating their front man. "No, no, no way! How? What's he like? In real life?"

"He's everything," Josie said, with an affected sigh. "He's different than I imagined. He's better, I mean."

We laughed together in mystified glee until Josie settled into a prideful smile. I tried to reconcile the Josie in front of me with the one I knew from high school. Her once-mousy hair was now peroxide blond, puffed in a half-fallen perm. She had left for California to get a psychology degree, but I doubted she'd graduated. I couldn't picture her as a cardiganed coed, considering her current outfit: braless in a lace blouse and gold shorts. Just as well—I'd dropped out, too. We weren't so different.

Still, Josie wasn't as placeless as I was. She seemed happy here without me.

The Polaroid finished developing and we admired it together. I dared to ask, "What happened with that, uh, bruise you've got?"

Josie laughed. "Oh, that? I was at the Forum and got elbowed right in the face trying to get to the front."

I believed it.

She brought me up to speed on her life, telling hazy concert stories about screaming toward amplifiers and bathing in the heat of strangers' bodies. I listened incredulously, holding her hand to make up for the past distance.

In high school, lifetimes ago, we were inseparable. Our classmates called us "Faun-and-Josie" the same way you'd say "peaches-and-cream." You could have one without the other, but it wouldn't be as sweet. We'd both kissed older boys in borrowed cars' back seats, but I never had the nerve to reject the ones I didn't like. Josie, though, had scoffed at more offers of class pins and promise rings than I could count. I helped with all her reckless schemes—sneaking out, secret dates, stealing from liquor cabinets and corner stores—and enjoyed it. She'd let me borrow her clothes when I begged to. I thought if I put on her miniskirts, I could emulate her in other ways, too.

I borrowed one of her countless tiny dresses for our high school graduation. We suffered side by side for an hour of speeches, whispering commentary and laughing loud enough to draw dirty looks from our classmates. When it came time to shake the principal's hand, Josie went first, because "Norfolk" comes before "Novak." That half minute when the auditorium seat beside me was empty was the loneliest moment of my life. I watched Josie strut across the stage in heels she didn't need thanks to her five-seven stature. When she took her diploma, she let her graduation robe slip open to reveal an impossibly short red skirt. She winked to the crowd as boys and fathers wolf-whistled. I barely recognized her. She was older, suddenly. Freed from little-girl headbands and uniform knee socks. We split up for college. I headed an hour away to my Seven Sisters school of choice and Josie headed west.

But under the Los Angeles bus station's flickering lights, Josie was as familiar as ever. Despite the layers of decadence she draped herself in, sparkling California hadn't swallowed her completely.

"How about you?" Josie asked. "How have you been?"

"Well," I said, "all things considered, I'm all right." My mother had a heart attack in March. The paperboy, peering through the distorted glass of our front door, had spied her body, stiff and lifeless on the linoleum. She'd been a few years retired from her secretary job and was only hosting the occasional Tupperware party to make ends meet. No one noticed her absence from society for days. Not even me. I'd been away from home, renting a room in Springfield and taking the bus every few days to work odd jobs. I spent all summer meeting with the bank, seeing distant relatives, and moping in a Wrentham motel room. The problem with having a self-imposed hermit for a mother is that when she dies, there is no one to help you.

Josie and I were consistent pen pals when we split apart after high school, but soon she stopped writing as often. Scared of seeming overeager, I slowed, too. By the time I was done taking care of my mother's affairs, it was early September and ten months since any communication with Josie. I'd had to dig through past letters to find her telephone number. I told her the news and asked if I could come stay with her. I worried she'd forgotten about me, but she said she'd missed me. I bought my bus ticket the next day and left without double-checking what was in my suitcases. I knew that if I hesitated for even a second, I'd chicken out and never get on the bus.

If I didn't do this one thing, I'd never do anything at all.

Since leaving school, photography had become my half-job-half-hobby, but all there was to photograph in little New England towns were kindergarten classes on picture day and family Christmas cards. There was no reason to stay in the land of no opportunity and rot in anonymity. Like my mother.

"Good," Josie said, genuine. "I'm glad you're all right."

She called a taxi, holding the pay phone receiver three inches from her ear, muttering about germs despite having just told me a story about kissing three strangers in one hour. I stretched, wondering if anyone else in the darkening bus station knew how practically famous Josie was.

I tucked the Holiday Sun record under my arm. Cal Holiday had not only touched it, he'd personally inscribed his name on it. For me. *Of course* Josie had wheedled her way into the life of a celebrity. Her charm would have been wasted on anyone who didn't have at least two platinum records. Any charm I'd once developed had fizzled away in college and afterward while I tried to be true and professional and boring.

Sweat pooled in the small of my back as we waited outside for the taxi. I'd spent most of the unseasonably cool Massachusetts summer indoors. The arid heat here was alien. Josie, in her thick coat, was unfazed. The ride to her apartment felt longer than half an hour as I carefully gawked at every neon light and vintage facade.

I fiddled with the four hundred dollars in cash I'd tucked into my jeans pocket, wondering who had bought my mother's house after the bank foreclosed. I couldn't pay off the mortgage when she died and she had no estate to speak of, unless you were counting ceiling-high stacks of Perry Como records and shattered dessert plates. I'd spent most of my so-called inheritance on my bus ticket and funeral costs, but $400 was enough to carry me through until my photographs made a splash. Or, if I couldn't manage right away, a midway job as a waitress or stenographer would do. Even that would be better here than in Massachusetts. I stared at every high-rise balcony, imagining the breeze atop them. You could see the ocean from that high up. Maybe the pull of the Pacific dragged me to California. A watery girl always aches to watch the sea, and I was all liquid by then.

Josie tapped my shoulder every time she spotted something she thought might be of interest to me. The best secondhand stores. The best hitchhiking and pot-buying corners. The best places to get a late-night submarine sandwich.

I worked up the nerve to ask the driver to turn up the radio, if it wouldn't be too much trouble. Josie lit a cigarette without glancing at him for approval. He said nothing, rolling down his own window. Smoke billowed around Josie's face, clouding her in a marble haze. She used to call smoking a "yucky, icky" thing to do. Now she did it with such expertise that I was more jealous than dismayed.

When we arrived on Fairfax, the cab driver bid us a quiet wish of good luck. I knew I'd need it, but how did *he*? Was I completely starry-eyed? Was I embarrassing Josie?

She didn't seem to mind helping me drag my bags up the two flights of stairs leading to her smoky apartment that sat above a magic shop. I trailed her as she entered the living room, pausing to wave her hands and declare, in an impression of *Young Frankenstein*'s Igor, "Well, here it is—home." She laughed at herself and asked, self-indulgently, "Oh, isn't Gene Wilder a *babe*?"

I nodded, distracted by the explosion of impulse purchases across every surface: strings of beads, purple votive candles, and novelty ashtrays shaped like Dalmatians and go-go boots. The coffee table was fingerprinted glass, and empty vodka bottles stuffed with semi-wilted orchids and carnations lined the windowsills. The flower petals waved in the breeze.

"There's no balcony, but if you stick your head outside, it's almost the same," Josie explained, throwing her coat over a pile of high-heeled shoes on the floor. I put my bags to the side of the futon. She lit a candle and inhaled its waxy scent. Two glossy modeling shots, in teakwood frames, stared at us from across the room. One featured

Josie lying across the floor in a window-curtain dress, and the other showed her cupping her own exposed breasts, affecting mock surprise.

"You're a model?" I asked.

"Mmhm," Josie said, brushing the dust off her TV set with an outstretched finger. "I'm breaking into the biz, as they say. Soon Cal won't have to pay my rent anymore." She laughed.

I leaned over one of her bookshelves, scanning the titles and wondering why she needed two copies of *Lady Oracle*. Josie snapped her fingers behind me, and I realized she'd made her way to her bedroom door. She moved so easily that you never noticed her until she wanted you to. She winked on cue, as if she could read my mind.

She gave a practiced tour of her bedroom, pointing out every exciting artifact. A replica of a NURSES DO IT BETTER shirt she and a friend named Yvonne had seen Robert Plant wear up in Oakland. A crushed can of Dr Pepper she said Steve Miller had discarded. A pair of gold-plated necklaces from Cal Holiday. Signed posters decked the walls. Little love notes on napkins and notepad pages were scattered on her vanity between Estée Lauder lipsticks and kohl pencils.

I crossed my arms, wishing I was half as interesting as the gems around me. Josie fluffed her hair in the mirror so I mimicked her, even though my brown hair was frizzy already. She studied me and decided to pat bronzer on my pale cheeks.

Josie fancied herself a rock-and-roll muse, a fact made clearer as she pulled open the closet door and revealed three leather jackets, four silk skirts, and seven pairs of platform boots. I nearly tripped on a velvet dress shoved underneath the crooked shag rug. "There you are!" she cooed to the garment, then turned to me and explained. "This is the prettiest thing you'll *ever* touch. It's 1940s vintage. I saw Jerry Hall wear something like it."

She tried the dress on for me and I clapped. I wanted to be her so badly I felt like I would burst. I tried on some of her clothes. They made me feel expensive, but I couldn't button any of the leather pants she coaxed me into.

"We'll take you shopping," Josie said, "and get you all gussied up, as the old ladies say."

I rambled about needing a job and new rain boots and bedsheets and film and pantyhose because my good pair had a run right up the left thigh.

Josie laughed. "God, take a breath! It'll work out. You don't need rain boots in L.A. And you don't need a job. I barely have one and I get by fine. Don't act so lame. You used to be fun, Faun."

I wanted to regale her with tales of my rebellions and exploits to prove I was still fun, but I had nothing akin to her wild stories. Just sad anecdotes about days spent surrounded by moving boxes and mouse-traps. I wondered if I'd ever been fun. Josie and I became friends by default. She'd been a ninth grader with a bad reputation, overdeveloped and unfazed, and I'd been the new girl in class wanting someone to talk to. With all her new California friends, Josie might have no use for the person who'd once been her *only* friend. All I said was "I didn't come here to sit on my ass all day."

"I understand," Josie said vaguely. Her eyes drifted around the room to all her shiny tchotchkes. "You must have had a tough few months." She lit another candle.

It was hard to put words to my feelings. I didn't want to mentally return to my struggling summer—I was already so far away from it. All I wanted was ease. I shrugged and sat beside her on the bed. "I'm really fine. I don't want you to worry about me. I just wanted to get away from it all." Josie looked skeptical, so I added, "I'm happy to be so far away from home. It's boring there. There's—there's nothing there." Not anymore.

She nodded sympathetically, touched my unreceptive arm, and moved on. She started brushing her hair, counting each stroke. "So I guess Mount Holyoke was a bust?" she asked between numbers. Before I answered, she whispered, "It's okay. I failed out of UCLA after a few semesters."

"I didn't *fail* out. Well, I was *failing* so I left on my own," I clarified. I had convinced myself I couldn't pass my final year of classes. I didn't think I was smart enough, good enough, worthy enough. I thought the working world would be better, but the feeling of inadequacy hadn't left.

Josie smiled, her white teeth shiny in the candlelight. "Failing, dropping, falling into an academic void, whatever—all you need to know is that it's way more fun to be here."

"I hope so," I said. "I'm a photographer now, you know. I did it professionally for a bit and I'm hoping to pick it up again here." That was half true. Taking school portraits was paid, albeit uncreative, work.

"What a sneak you are"—she laughed—"using your inheritance to run away to Hollywood. It's oh-so-very-cinematic. Your mother would crucify you!"

Josie was done pretending to be sad about my mother's death. My mother blamed all my shortcomings on Josie's rebellious influence. When Josie would come over to watch *Petticoat Junction* or do homework, my mother pointed out how unladylike everything Josie did was. How Josie would speak loudly and snap gum and unbutton too much of her blouse. By eleventh grade, Josie had taken to calling my mother "Dictatress Novak."

I laughed at the absurdity, liking that my mother would hate I was here and not fully understanding why.

Josie took a phone call, and I began to unpack in the living room. That NYC sketch show, *Laugh Riot,* was on TV, the host-of-the-week futzing around while I refolded my blouses and smoothed the creases on my jeans. I tucked my camera into the top drawer of the empty dresser, nestling it in a mound of socks. I was about to ask if there was a Laundromat nearby when Josie burst back into the living room, nervous joy ablaze in her eyes.

"You're staying for good with me, aren't you?" she asked. Her mouth sat open.

When my silence seemed to sadden her, I said, "Of course. Where else would I ever want to go?"

She beamed. "Perfect. You know, I really flipped out when you said you wanted to come down here," Josie said. "I missed you tons and tons. I always tell people about you." She stuck her hands into my half-unpacked luggage and pulled out a pair of "Tuesday" panties. "Is this day-of-the-week underwear?" She cackled. "You are so *cute*! You'll fit right in with everybody; I know you will!"

"Fit in with who?" I asked.

Josie smoothed a lock of blond hair, and asked, ignoring my question, "Do you wanna come to a concert tomorrow?"

I said yes on instinct. I said yes like it was breathing. On the TV, the live audience cheered.

One Photo

Josie smiling expertly, angelically, under the bus station's
incandescent lights.

2.

JOSIE STARTED SINGING "GOOD MORNING STARSHINE" AT SIX
A.M. She wasn't up early—she had never gone to bed. She'd crept out
before midnight, the clack of her high-heeled boots echoing in the
small hallway and waking me. I didn't mention it, out of respect for a
woman who sneaks out of her own home.

"You ever hear a song so beautiful you cry?" Josie asked once I
got up from the pile of sheets I'd curled into.

I folded up the futon and smoothed myself out, listening to a metal
spatula scratch Josie's cast-iron pan. "Maybe," I said. "A couple times."

Two years ago, when I came home for our two-person Christmas,
my mother lent me her good headphones and I listened to Simon &
Garfunkel's *Wednesday Morning, 3 A.M.* in the dark. I started crying
during "Bleecker Street" and didn't stop until the needle lifted from
side B. It wasn't sad—it was the kind of unfathomable prettiness that
made you want to scream because you hadn't made it yourself, and no
matter how much you wanted, you could never own it. That was why
I was a photographer. Photography gave you the ability to possess a
moment—it solidified the ineffable. It was concrete and abstract at
once.

"I love crying," Josie said, spitting out a piece of overcooked
omelet and wincing. "It's very freeing."

I stopped myself from asking if she'd cried when she'd gotten that
bruise on her face.

We ate off napkins and pretended the eggs tasted good. Josie said
she'd get a second key cut for the apartment as soon as she tracked
down her own. Until then, the door would remain unlocked. Before I

could object, Josie insisted it was safe, saying if I wanted to live with her, I had to live like her, too. Open and unafraid.

I kept forgetting where I was while brushing my teeth or pulling a new T-shirt over my head. Part of me kept becoming convinced each passing hour was just a second in a dream and that I wasn't really here at all. But I *was* here, and, I remembered, jobless. Worries of starving on the streets flooded me until I insisted to Josie that I head out immediately and beg for work.

"I told you Cal pays our rent. You don't have to pay. You don't have to worry," she said, picking dust bunnies off the carpet like there wasn't food and clothing and water bills and insurance to worry about. She moved on. "Why did you come here?" she asked, drawing out her words. "Really? I know you want to kick-start your Annie Leibovitz fantasy, but you could do that back home. You could have gone to Boston." Her Beantown-adjacent accent slipped out on the last word. "But something brought you here, to little old me."

I gave her the answer she wanted, which was maybe the answer I wanted, too. I wasn't sure if it was true. "To have fun." To be someone new, I added privately—someone vivid and breathless, who didn't shirk away from anything. Who didn't care about grades or hair frizz or weather forecasts. Someone else.

Josie smiled all-knowingly. "We'll buy you the cutest little concert outfit," she squealed. She chucked her collection of dust bunnies out the window and leaned against the back of a wicker chair, resting her cheek in her hand. "Oh, aren't you excited? The tickets say the show starts at seven, so we'll get there nice and early, seven fifteen. We'll walk around, I'll get you free drinks, and you can see Cal and the gang in action."

I blushed. "And afterwards, do I get to, um—I mean, if it's okay, could I meet Cal? And all of them?"

"Of course! You can take oodles of photos. The whole band loves getting their photo taken." She laughed.

"Far out," I said in a way I hoped sounded blasé. Lynyrd Skynyrd were on the radio. I decided I could be a free bird, too.

I'd been molded into fearfulness from a young age. My never-married parents split up when I was six, my father returning to either Philadelphia or Pittsburgh (my mother was never sure) to his real wife. My mother always said he'd betrayed her, that he was proof that the world was dark and unfeeling. That I should watch out for people like him, who make promises they never intend to keep. That I should watch out for the world. She didn't hate Josie because Josie wasn't lady-like. She hated Josie because she wasn't scared and never had been.

Josie and I set out into the broad world, her basking in the sunlight as I squinted. Three men in madras shirts waved from the stoop of a barbershop as we strutted toward a Goodwill. I waved back but Josie swatted my hand down.

"No one should realize you see them seeing you," she said. "That way, they think you're effortlessly lovely."

I mentally jotted down the note. When Josie told me to jaywalk, I did, laughing as my Mary Janes slammed onto the pavement. When she told me to wait on the curb, I did, patiently. I smiled and frowned whenever she did. At the discount store, I'd hold up a creped blouse or plaid skirt and wait, like a hungry dog, for Josie's opinion. We rifled through the secondhand clothes together, pointing out food stains and hand-sewn seams until we found an appropriately sparkly top for me to swirl on the dance floor in. I spotted my reflection in its silver sequins, blinking and wondering when I'd feel carefree. I was too nervous to try it on. If it didn't fit, it'd be a sign of terrible luck. Josie told me to take a gamble. We sought a pair of bottoms, and I made a beeline to the jeans. Denim was rock and roll, right? I picked a pair of pale Levi's.

Josie snapped her gum, the smell of peppermint flooding from her mouth. "Well, we could cut them into shorts."

"Sure," I said, not registering what she said. She'd said it. It had to be right. I would have gouged my own eyes out if Josie said it would make me cool. In tenth grade she convinced me to let her cousin, a motorcycle-fixing delinquent, build his tattooing portfolio by stabbing a crooked, coin-size turtle onto my left hip. It stung, but Josie said that I'd be the talk of our class if I got inked up. I'd lain back, closed my eyes, and breathed in the motor oil fumes, repeating "slow and steady" under my breath. (Hiding it from my mother wasn't hard; she didn't let me wear low-rise anything.)

Josie had looked at me after her cousin finished stabbing me with ink, then said, "That's what I like about you—you'll do anything."

I hadn't been sure if I agreed, but I said thank you anyway.

I made my purchase, while Josie encouraged me and flirted with the cashier, and slung the THANK YOU, COME AGAIN bag over my shoulder. My Mary Janes were still loud on the sidewalk, but I liked the extra inch of height they gave me. A few blocks later, Josie suddenly looked like she'd been hit by lightning and announced she had to make a phone call to someone whose name sounded familiar. She blew me a kiss and dashed home.

I hated running errands on my own. I always thought I was being looked at—bored into by every pair of eyes—but I told myself to be brave like Josie.

I knew I ought to stock up on film if I was telling the truth to myself about taking photography seriously. I'd need at least two packs of instant film for the concert, and two more for whatever Josie had hinted would ensue after it. I wandered down the sidewalk, daydreaming about showing managers and editors my portfolio. Life was unsure and washing in and out of focus, but tonight wouldn't be. My Polaroid would make permanent its impermanence.

It took three blocks to track down Garter Photo Hut. Its white-brick facade had yellowed with age—it wasn't glamorous, therefore hopefully inexpensive. It was one of those cluttered, cavernous places built into another older building, with tape securing the front windows and a film of grime on every surface. Outside it was scorching, with thick, dry wind, but in that half-dead camera shop, the air sat in musty clouds. The rusted fan by the cash register rattled over the T. Rex song blasting from the overhead speakers but did nothing to alleviate the stagnation.

I scoured a corkboard for photography jobs. One, seeking a portrait-studio assistant, had promise. I tied my hair into a pony-tail, catching the attention of the stubby man puttering behind the counter. He couldn't have been older than thirty, with a pit-stained Led Zeppelin tee and jeans hanging too low to be flattering. His red muttonchops bristled as he asked, "Hot enough for you out there?," then laughed for half a minute.

A comedian. "That's funny," I said. I walked toward the counter, traced the checkerboard pattern with my fingers, and mumbled, "Could I get four packs of Polaroid film?"

"What?" he asked. He leaned close to my face, canned tuna on his breath.

"Polaroid film," I repeated, a little louder. "Four packs. Please."

He looked at the camera slung around my neck, nodded, then plucked the packs off the wall and slid them toward me. I paid him and tucked my purchase into my purse.

He cocked his head and pointed to the speakers. "Do you know what song this is?"

I shook my head no. When he laughed, my stomach burned, righteous and acidic. I tilted my head, imitating his pretentious pose, and asked if he had heard of Cal Holiday.

He nodded, slow and condescending. "Holiday Sun aren't exactly underground. Obviously I know him."

I tried to smirk and lied, "He's a close, intimate friend of mine. I know the whole band. In fact, I'm seeing them tonight. You wouldn't believe all the funny little *underground* secrets I know about them. I'm practically their personal photographer."

He squinted and said, "Take some pictures of them, then. Come back here and show me, sweetheart. I want to see them, as long as you'll be the one bringing them to me." He added, his baritone voice wavering, "My name's Otis."

I thought of those pastel teen-advice columns I'd scoured for wisdom when I was freshly fourteen. While the boys in my grade joked about sending *Penthouse* letters about their English teacher's panty lines, I pored over the answers to immortal questions like "How do I get my gym teacher to let me sit out during my women's troubles?" and "Will I be flat-chested if my T-shirts fit too tightly?" The innocent and absurd worries of girls who would rather consult an anonymous source than their own mother for pubescent advice. My mother was never any good for questions like those. She'd click her tongue, saying she'd tell me all I needed to know and that any additional inquiries were uncouth.

I never sent in any questions of my own, but if I had, maybe I would have known the answer to what I wondered now: *If a man calls me "sweetheart" and asks me to show him pictures of the rock band I not-so-accidentally declared I was intimately acquainted with, is he trying to leech off me or flirt with me?*

I agreed to his offer, unsure why I needed to prove myself to a man I'd just met. On my way out, I took down the address from the photo studio poster and asked an elderly couple on the street for directions.

A few minutes later, I found Coswell's, a mom-and-pop department store pretending to be franchised, no doubt sweating under burgeoning pressure from big chains like Sears and Macy's. Gold paint chipped onto my hands from the art deco doors. I wandered through cosmetics, coughing in perfumed clouds sprayed by manicured women with pageboy 'dos, through menswear, and through ladies' intimates until I found Foto Fantasy, the portrait studio operating next to the service elevators.

I hesitated. Josie said I didn't need a job. But that was only because *she* lived off Cal and her sporadic modeling. All my life, I'd been bolstered by my mother, then by Josie, then by my mother again. It was time for independence.

I pushed open the glass door, chimes twinkling above my head, and sank into the plush carpet. Children crying in church clothes and dance costumes crowded the floor, their parents trying in vain to wipe away chocolate stains or spit dribbles before it was their turn in front of the camera. Mothers clutched flyer-clipped coupons, waving them at anyone who looked like they could offer a deal. Barry Manilow played low. I cleared my throat to get the attention of the middle-aged man indolently sorting checks behind the front desk. He grunted.

I said, "I saw you're hiring."

"Yep," he said. His red-striped uniform was baggy on his arms, too-short sleeves revealing tufts of dark body hair. His name tag was on sideways. "You've got experience taking photos?"

"Uh," I said. "Yes. I've taken classes in it. I take lots of pictures. I'm new in town, but I took some family and school portraits back home, in Massachusetts. Professionally. I mean, I know this is an assistant job. But it would be a great start, if you'll have me." I stuck out my hand for him to shake. He didn't.

He signed the back of a check, dripping ink onto his thumb. From the corner, two kids in Scout uniforms laughed, saying something about *The Flintstones*. A baby screamed.

"You look like a hardy girl," he said. "We pay minimum wage, $2.30 an hour. Can you start tomorrow at nine?"

I nodded quicker than I thought I could. Quicker than I said yes to Josie. The man introduced himself as Enzio and gave me a starchy uniform and a name tag reading DONNA.

"Oh," I said. "My name's Faun Novak, actually."

Enzio shrugged. "It doesn't matter if your real name's on it. This is the only spare one I've got, unless you want to be 'Buford.'" He pulled another name tag out of the drawer and showed it to me.

I said I understood and thanked him too much. I dashed home, exhilarated. Everything was falling into place. I was a working girl in the big city.

Josie was blasting Tom Petty loud enough to hear it from the street below. The music grew louder as I climbed the metal back-hallway stairs. She was spinning in her underwear in the living room when I burst through the door. She didn't notice me until she completed her slow twirl. "One moment, my dear!" she shrieked as she ducked into her bedroom. As she dipped away, I caught sight of a greenish-brown mark on her ribs. I opened my mouth to ask about it but didn't, figuring that it was another battle-wound bruise from a rough concert crowd.

She reemerged in a bathrobe with a warm bottle of wine in each hand—one red and one white, both freshly opened. I fetched two glasses. We people-watched through the open windows, sipping away. I couldn't tell if the wine was good, but it didn't make me gag, so I swallowed it in full-mouthed gulps.

"I got a job today," I said, proud, "at a photo studio."

Josie winced. "Sounds boring." It *did* sound boring. When she realized she hurt my feelings, she added, "Well, it's a good start. I bet it makes tons of money."

I didn't tell her it was minimum wage. My ultimate ambitions now seemed far-fetched and impossible. I didn't confirm to Josie that I only meant the Foto Fantasy job to be a jumping-off point. What if I'd be coaxing toddlers into looking at cameras and mopping spit-up until I died?

Josie poured me another glass of wine. I drank with gratitude as she talked up my confidence for the concert. Soon, she was straightening my hair with a clothes iron, almost burning my ears and begging to hear about my misadventures at Mount Holyoke. When I explained it was a women's college, so most of my time was spent in the company of the same sex, she groaned and said, "You *have* to tell me you at least got in with some of the Dartmouth boys!"

I shrugged, afraid to move too much because of my head's precarious position on the fold-up ironing board. "Um," I said, "I went to a sorority party. Well, it was a disaster-relief fundraiser. It was fun. Uh, once I tried to smoke a joint with my friend Beulah. The smoke alarm went off, so we gave up." As soon as Beulah passed the joint to me, I pictured my mother shaking her head in solemn disappointment. Beulah pulled the alarm off the ceiling, shutting it up, but I had already changed my mind and let her have the whole joint to herself.

"Ooh," Josie said, really trying. "That sounds exciting." After my hair was sufficiently crisped, Josie reinspected the clothes I'd bought. She liked the fit of the blouse well enough, but when I tried on the jeans, she gagged. They weren't bell-bottoms on me so much as they were baggy. Josie laughed until I removed them. I hopped onto the couch in nothing but butterfly-print underwear and watched her take a pair of kitchen scissors to the jeans, cropping them so they were shorter than wide. I stared dumbfounded.

"I could never," I said, trying to form a thought that made sense while staring at the raw hems. "I mean, my *mother* would hate to see me in something like that."

"God bless her and all that, but her ghost is not going to haunt you for wearing cutoffs. Besides, you don't belong to her. Not anymore. Not ever. You don't have to do what she would have wanted," Josie said, then added, after a small pause, "You can just be yourself."

I didn't want to be myself, a speck drifting aimlessly in the ether. I wanted my dreams to come true. Now. I asked Josie to do my makeup how she thought would look best.

She slathered red lipstick onto me, noting how the bright color made my thin lips look plumper. I felt almost pretty. I smiled at my reflection, touching my cheek, and asked, "Do they put on a good show? The band?"

I knew Josie would sugarcoat her answer. I just wanted to hear her talk.

"Of course they do!" she said, practically drooling. "They finished their tour about two months ago, so they've had time to perfect everything. They're playing a gig tonight, and then next week, and I think the week after that at the Troubadour again."

Holiday Sun had been famous for seven years, which felt like ten, which felt like forever. They became California staples with lives pinned to the Golden State. Cal Holiday, although British, became a naturalized U.S. citizen amid fanfare a few years earlier. I thought I'd outgrown them and their predictable brand of radio-ready rock, but the idea of seeing them live made me reconsider. I nodded so she'd keep going.

"Everybody says their next album is going to be amazing," she said. "Cal played me some new songs and they were incredible. Really. Oh, he's so good—they're all good—and you'll love it. Now let's toast!" She realized her wineglass was empty, so she grabbed a bottle and held it up in the air. I grabbed the other bottle and did the same. "To having a good time."

"Cheers," I said. The bottles clinked in a delicate harmony, and we drank them down faster than we should have.

ONCE WE WERE drunk and dolled up, Josie tucked our tickets into her purse and we set out. By the end of the concert, the sky would have blackened, but now, it was only beginning to turn a misty pink. We took the bus partway there, walking the last fifteen minutes. Josie said it helped make an entrance—hopping off a greasy bus would never give the same impression as stepping around a brick-walled corner. She towered above me, bouncing along on shimmery six-inch heels. "It's going to be a dream."

"I hope so," I said.

At the booth we gave our tickets to the clerk and Josie said, "Listen, I haven't actually told Cal you're coming tonight, but don't worry. It'll be a fun little surprise. We'll watch the show together and then zip our way backstage. You've gotta go out the alley and around the building." Josie pulled a laminated lanyard from her front pocket. The backstage pass sat comfortably around her neck. My camera strap was already chafing.

"Do I get a pass, too?" I asked.

"So," Josie said, "I don't have an extra, but you *really* don't need one. I'll get you in."

I trusted her. She batted her angel eyes and beckoned me into the darkness of the Troubadour. I was swept into a cauldron of bodies and breaths, where every word melted into a gurgling, transcendent hum. I forgot how vulnerable my bare legs made me. The mess of anonymous limbs stirring in the crowd transfixed me. We had missed the opening act, Careful Kiss, which Josie said was hardly a tragedy because they were too green to sway a crowd.

The audience knit itself together too tightly for us to be able to squeeze through, but Josie knew to slide past the bar and against the soundproofed wall until we reached a slight platform. She waved hello to a woman leaning against the front of the stage. The woman waved back, then mimed a handgun suicide. Josie laughed, and I did, too, not knowing why.

We could see straight to the stage from our pedestal. The instruments lying in wait were mere feet away.

The lights dimmed and Josie clutched my arm, shaking. My heartbeat pulsed in every inch of my skin. The crowd screamed and so did we, so loudly we hurt our own ears. Life burst into bright colors. Shouts blared. Hands clapped. The electric liturgy had begun.

Holiday Sun's entrance was pure, lucid melodrama. A cloud of smoke billowed into the room and once the members of the band began to emerge, the crowd roared even more. I blinked and blinked, expecting them to disappear, but they didn't. Holiday Sun, the legends, stood ten feet away. They were real-live-actual people.

Cal Holiday stepped toward the microphone. The rings on his left hand glimmered under the stage lights as he said, his Manchester accent molasses thick, "Hello, L.A., you really are the City of Angels, aren't you?"

The crowd screamed, replying *yes,* yes, they *were*.

"We're happy to be home," he said.

The crowd screamed again. Cal Holiday could have said he had a rash and everyone would have gone crazy. His face fell into a permanent smirk, every inch of him oozing cocky magnetism. It was easy to adore him. The rest of the band shone brightly, too, all practiced at being beautiful and wild in front of a crowd. Kent Pearce twirled his drumsticks to the delight of anyone who dared look. Howie Guerrero blew a kiss to someone in the crowd, drawing an overjoyed yelp from the receiver. Scott Sutherland, more aloof but just as charming, pointed to the balcony, waving. They strung the room together, telling us we belonged there—more than that, they *needed* us to be there. I hadn't outgrown Holiday Sun—how could I have? I was a fan. I was a lucky fan, to be here, to be about to meet them.

Without any visible cue, they erupted in song, banging out the first few chords of "Sheila." I stared, moony-eyed and blinded, as the lights flashed and Cal Holiday sang:

Oh, she's got the passion, she's got the dream
She's caught in twisting lies, enough to make you scream
Sheila's a commander, Sheila's indiscreet
Don't pull her hair or kiss her lips
'Cause Sheila's loving me.

Josie called out, "I love you!"

Cal replied to the faceless mass of men and women and girls and boys in front of him, "Thank you."

During a slight lull after a few more songs, Josie pointed to Cal and whispered, "Isn't he the most?"

I snapped photos, but they were all blurred or overexposed. Either I was too caught up in the moment to pay attention or I wasn't as effortlessly good as I thought. Both, maybe.

Josie fetched me Styrofoam cup after Styrofoam cup full of cheap beer, which I sipped, swaying to the music in between clicks of my camera. I appreciated her generosity, but my bladder didn't, so I crept off near the end of the gig to find the restroom. Josie barely noticed me go—all she left me with was "If I'm not here afterwards, I'll be backstage. But I'm sure I *will* be here." Her eyes were trained on the slick way Cal's fingers fell across his Fender Telecaster.

I weaved through the crowd, making use of my bony elbows, and tracked down the washroom.

There were four stalls, only one of which had a door. I didn't want to relieve myself in plain view of the room, even if it was empty. I knocked on the shut stall, getting no response. I pressed my ear to the graffitied door and heard faint heaving noises. I knocked again, harder.

"Fuck off!" the voice inside called.

"Are you all right in there?" I asked. I pushed open the unlocked door and was met with a frowning, freckled teenager. Snot and tears ran down her baby face, her fingers toying with the rips in her fishnets. She heaved a final time toward the toilet but nothing came out. I shut the door, hoping to afford her some privacy but unwilling to leave her alone for too long. The band was still playing. The music sounded different a room away. Without the shriek of the crowd, the songs were just fun. Hummable. Not quite miraculous. Oh, but who cared? I tried to figure out what song was playing as I shuffled across the tiles, my shoes sticking to the beer-soaked floor. I peed quickly in an open stall and washed my hands. The girl grumbled before flushing the toilet's vomit-contents down. She emerged.

"Can I get you anything?" I asked.

She looked to her side. "You got any blow?"

I shook my head. "Are you with your—your mom or something?"

She looked at me like I was the biggest idiot in the world. "No," she replied. "I'm here with my boyfriend."

"Let me go get him for you," I suggested. "Where was he in the crowd?"

She laughed. "He's onstage. Kent? Like, he's the drummer?"

"How old are you?" I asked, afraid of the answer. I did weak math in my head, calculating Kent Pearce and the rest of the band to be in the early-thirties range.

"None of your beeswax." Her face twisted defensively as she stood up tall. She reapplied her lipstick, her thick lips glossy. Not as effortlessly cool as Josie, but cooler than me. She sighed and turned to me. "How old are you, huh? Ancient?"

Oh. I tousled my hair in the mirror, trying to think of a good, cool, casual comment. I settled on "Far out! How long have you two been together?"

"Long enough," she said, her eyes narrowing. "What are you, a fucking cop?"

The crowd cheered outside, and people streamed into the restroom. The show was over and the girl rolled her eyes at herself. I asked if she knew Josie, hoping that having a connection to Cal Holiday's girlfriend would win me some points.

She wobbled, smoothed her tube top, and said, "Obviously. Who doesn't? Are you her friend Dawn?"

"*Faun,*" I corrected softly.

"Aces," she slurred, "you're not that bad, Faun, you just act so old. You're pretty. Do you like Fleetwood Mac? I do. My name is Kitty. Or Itty-Bitty Kitty. Whatever you prefer is, like, fine with me."

She was a disaster, but harmless enough.

I wiped Kitty's face with a piece of toilet paper, pressing against her skin in gentle circles. She smelled like Love's Baby Soft perfume, the scent trailing around us as she guided me out of the bathroom, talking nonsense about her boyfriend and her best friend and her mother. I asked her to wait by the door to the theater while I did a once-over of the floor for Josie.

The theater had already started to empty, its patrons taking advantage of the warm autumn night to shout on Santa Monica and stroll to the Sunset Strip. A sweep of the room revealed no sign of Josie's bopping blond head. I should have known better than to expect otherwise. Josie didn't like to wait.

I stepped closer to the stage, crushing a plastic cup with my feet, trying to reconcile the garbage-covered floor with the neon dreamscape it had been before. Broad-shouldered men were already onstage twisting cords and sweeping, disassembling Holiday Sun's setup. I slipped between a group of teenage boys and a young couple and wandered until I was close enough to the stage for a *good* Polaroid after all my mid-show flops. It might have been my last chance to document a sliver of the Troubadour. I snapped it quickly, hoping the roadies wouldn't notice. When it faded in, I realized a pair of them, one with a Santa Claus beard and the other big-eyed and barefaced, had blown kisses. I laughed, tucking the picture into my purse.

Kitty was gone from the door when I returned. Flightiness was the only thing anyone in this city seemed to know. If I had to go it alone, I would—I hated it, but I would.

I tied up my blouse and stepped out into the orange glow of the night, wishing for rain to wash the sweat off my skin. Josie had let me borrow an old perfume, but now I just smelled like wet dog.

I took a deep breath and accidentally inhaled a thick cloud of expelled cigarette smoke. I turned the corner and delved down an alleyway, walking along until I spotted a smattering of cars and small trucks. Excitement bubbled in my chest, and I had the urge to hiccup it out.

I approached the stage door and scoured it for a doorbell. When I couldn't find one, I banged my fist against it, loud enough for the noise to echo along the backstreet. I waited for a rock-and-roll Saint Peter to let me in.

A middle-aged man in a checkered shirt opened the door, looked me up and down, and said, "Nope." He pulled the door shut, and as soon as he did, I knocked again. He didn't realize I had no other options.

When he opened the door again, I said, "I'm a photographer. I'm meant to be here." I looked down at my chest and lied, "I, uh, lost my press pass." The doorman shook his head and before he could shut the door on me again, I held my hands out, pleading. "Please wait, please—my friend Josie Norfolk is inside and I need to see her. Could you grab her for me? Please?" I peered over his shoulder, searching for wonderous things hiding in the theater.

He sighed. "No. Damn groupies."

Was I a groupie? I'd never met a groupie, but I could picture them: hungry-eyed, eager, and unafraid. It wouldn't be so bad to be that way. Maybe it wasn't the perfect insult the doorman thought it was. Was Josie a groupie? If she was, I wanted to be one, too. If it meant I could meet Holiday Sun, I'd be anything at all.

He ducked into the wood-walled caverns of backstage. Before the door shut, I stuck my foot against its frame to keep it propped open. He didn't look back. This was serendipity. Luck. Blind nerve. I watched as he began to disappear down the narrow hallway, then slipped inside.

Fluorescent lights buzzed. So did my heart. I looked into every open door, hoping I'd spot Josie. I tried to evoke secret-agent silence, but my hard-soled Mary Janes betrayed me and the doorman turned around. Desperate, I crouched behind a cart of electrical supplies, my pulse beating in my throat. He scanned the hall, then turned back around, leaving me alone.

I inched forward, blinking hard to make sure I was really there. Footsteps sounded from around the corner. Shit. I searched for a hiding place again, thinking of excuses to explain my presence, worried I'd ruin Josie's night.

A man with a clipboard turned the corner and I froze, ashamed. I caught his attention and he stared, his eyes beady behind round eyeglasses. His bolo tie swung as he walked toward me. "No," he said, pointing his finger in unspecified accusations. "Who are you? Who let you in? Where's your photo pass for that camera?"

A lanyard bounced around his neck, but I couldn't read it as I stumbled backward, spewing apologies.

He turned red, and as his eyebrows furrowed, I burst into nervous laughter. *Oh God, help me.* He grabbed my arm, twisting my skin, until a voice called over from the end of the hall.

"Hold on, Stanley," the voice said. Wait—I knew that accent. I knew that slow, lovely lilt. Was it really him? I turned around slowly, squinting like someone was shining a light in my eyes. It was Cal Holiday himself, holding out his hand. "I know her. She's harmless. She's a friend."

He didn't know me. I was about to say as much, dumbly truthful, but Cal Holiday winked so I stayed silent. Stanley released my arm, muttering about having important business to take care of, his Brooklyn accent more pronounced with every frazzled word. He shuffled down the hallway, grumbling all the while.

Cal Holiday took a step toward me, smiling. "Don't worry about Stanley. He's just our tour manager." He was beautiful and strange, exactly and nothing like I'd imagined. His face was cast with slight age lines and his hair, deep brown, was overgrown—less perfect than on his album covers, but more intriguing. A denim jacket covered with motor-company patches and pins stretched across his broad shoulders. He pointed at the camera on my chest.

I looked down, too, suddenly aware of how the fabric straps pressed between my breasts, tracing their small curve. I clutched the camera, lifting it off my torso.

"What's that?" he asked.

"A camera," I said, struck stupid. I took shallow, nervous breaths. I looked into his eyes and away again.

Cal signaled for me to keep going, rolling his fingers in a circle, but I didn't. He spoke for me: "Are you a photographer?"

I nodded. "Yes." My brain worked for a brief flash before melting into a fan freak-out again. "Can I take your photo?"

"Of course," he said. He smiled for the camera, posing perfectly.

He was used to the click and the flash, recharged in its light. How was he real? How was he Josie's? How was he here in front of me? He laughed a bit. "What's got you scared?"

I cleared my throat. "I'm not scared. I'm looking for Josie. I'm her friend Faun." I grabbed the Polaroid as the camera spat it out.

Cal's face lit up and I fluttered, unable to believe the recognition he apparently felt at my name. "Come here, Faun."

I nodded, moving at double-speed toward his outstretched hand, my legs wobbling. Bambi on the ice.

"Pleasure," he said, shaking my hand. My palm brushed across a scab on his knuckles. "I'm Cal. But you might have known that."

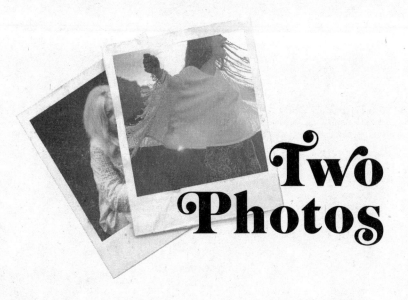

Two Photos

Holiday Sun, mouths open mid-song, sparkling under stage lights, blurry.

Floyd and another roadie, sweeping garbage off the stage, blowing kisses.

3.

CAL WAS TOO WARM, LIKE A STOVETOP ELEMENT TURNED OFF but still burning with residual heat. I didn't know what to say, so I shook his hand for as long as I could, melting. A laugh rose from around the corner, high like wind chimes. I looked over his shoulder, afraid to look directly at him. He was like the sun. I could only take daunted, blinking glimpses lest I burn my eyes out.

He glowed.

"Thank you," I said, "for helping me out. I know I'm not *supposed* to be here, but——" He shook his head, but I wanted to keep thanking him. Stanley could have kicked me out easily—he would have a million excuses to—but Cal stopped him before he knew I was Josie's pal. Did he see something good within me? I dissolved into unending gratitude. "Thank you."

"Faun," he said, my name sweet on his tongue. "Did you enjoy the show?"

"Yes," I said, my voice catching. I swallowed hard, trying to be brave. "It was amazing. You were amazing." Was it wrong for my heart to beat this fast, when he was Josie's? I didn't want him in the way Josie had him. It was enough for a star like him to say my name. For him to know it. "Thank you," I said again.

Cal tried to stifle a laugh. He pointed to a musty dressing room. "Could you wait in there while I get Josie for you?"

"Yes, of course." I shuffled inside, resisting the urge to keep thanking him. Too wobbly to stand, I perched on a desk, fantasizing about which celebrities might have sat in this room before and unable to fathom how I'd lucked out into inhabiting it now. A pair of initials were carved into one of the dark walls (*DD* + *SS*) and I traced their form, considering whose paparazzi-photographed hands had etched it. A cave painting discovery. A miracle.

Laughter echoed down the hall and I laughed along into the empty air. I swung my legs. A kid on the swings.

Before Cal could return with Josie, a woman appeared in the doorway. Old Hollywood beauty marks clustered in colonies on her dark skin, and her hair fell in tight, twisting curls over her exposed shoulders. The flared legs of her jumpsuit swayed in a nonexistent wind. Was I imagining it, or was she floating half an inch above the ground? Silent power radiated from her fingers, her nails long and perfect. She wasn't famous, but she seemed more than a fan like me. "Hello," she said, her voice flat. "What are you doing here?"

"Oh, hi," I said. "Cal let me—"

"I don't care." She gestured for me to stand. I slid off the desk, almost tripping over my own feet. She continued her assessment, stepping closer. A feather woven into a lock of hair fell over her face and she blew it away before it could stick to her glossy lips. "You could be a liar. There's a lot of liars trying to get back here."

I searched my purse for the Polaroid I'd taken of Cal. I held it out. The woman inspected it, watching Cal's face fade in, fuzzy as a ghost, onto the photo paper.

Stanley, the tour manager, popped his round head into the room. He pointed to me like gesturing to gum on a shoe. "Yvonne?" he asked. "What's the scoop on this one?"

The woman—Yvonne—searched for something in my face, cocking her head. I smiled, bleeding desperation. After a secondary glance at the photo I took of Cal, she said, "She's cool, Stanley. Now shoo."

Relief pooled like a bathtub filling with water.

She leaned close and whispered, drawing out her words, "Confess your sins."

"What?" I asked.

"Who are you?" Yvonne asked, plainer this time.

"Faun Novak. I'm here with Josie Norfolk."

"Who cares? Tell me something awful you've done."

I laughed. She didn't. Where was Josie now? I couldn't think of anything good to confess, so I pointed to my Polaroid and asked instead, "Can I take your photo? I'm a photographer."

"Without a press pass?"

"Mmhm."

"I think you're a groupie. We're at groupie capacity tonight."

"What are you, then?" I asked.

She squinted, offended. She raised fingers as she counted. "I am a promoter. I am a muse. I am Howie Guerrero's acting manager. I'm a lot of things."

"Oh."

She stared at me.

I said nothing.

"You're a terrible sport. If you can't play along, you don't belong here," she said, beads rattling on her wrist. An old straight scar peeked out from below her clacking bracelets, running all the way from her left wrist to the crook of her elbow. She noticed my staring and asked, "What? You've never seen a cat scratch before?"

I knew she was lying, and she seemed to know I knew, but neither of us said anything more.

She said, "Take the photo, then."

I snapped the flash and said, "It's nice to meet you."

She almost smiled. She held out her hand for me to grab and I did, letting her lead me into the hall. Her skin was cold. Medusa.

Jim Morrison's ghost-voice grew louder as we walked toward the source of the Doors song blasting through the hallway. Josie had always loved them, so I taught myself to love them, too. When Jim Morrison died, we mourned on milk crates in her parents' garage listening to "Love Her Madly" on a loop. I felt fraudulent back then, seventeen and pretending I was cool enough to weep for a musician I barely listened to.

I didn't feel like a fraud anymore. I felt *real*. My ears still rang from the live music an hour ago and I craved more. The concert had been punchy and proud—things I'd never been but, soundtracked by Holiday Sun's brash guitars and thumping bass, I thought I could be. No, these weren't the artsy, deep-and-brooding moody tunes I'd grown accustomed to in college, but in a way this was better. I felt invincible.

It was all so unbelievable and unplanned. I took note of every scratch on the floor and poster on the wall, trying to commit the backstage world to memory. Yvonne and I turned a corner, finding the party in all its drunken glory. I *was* real. I was here.

The band, sans Cal, was scattered across the backstage area, engaged in various acts of refined debauchery. Kitty was there, too, jumping along to the Doors' "Wild Child" against a theatrical curtain. I couldn't spot Josie. Holiday Sun was flanked by unfamiliar, beautiful women. Or were they girls? They prodded each other, giggling and gasping for air, fiddling with their baubles and beads, but every time someone from the band spoke, their faces focused in devout attention. All the women were different strange, slinky silhouettes wearing rare colors, but they all held an identical desperation to please. Worker bees. I kept swallowing the sour spit pooling in my mouth, worried I was about to vomit from nerves. I stared at the band, all of them so handsome and nearby, pinching my bare thighs to make sure this wasn't a dream.

"Go, go," Yvonne said. "If Cal let you back here, like you said, then I'm *sure* you'll be just fine on your own." She rolled her eyes and slinked over to Howie Guerrero, the bassist.

Kitty yelped a greeting to me. Kent Pearce, the drummer, grabbed her waist. Kitty touched his head, his light brown hair looking impossibly soft under her lucky fingers. "Hiya, Faun!" she called. She turned to her drummer and said, "Kent, this is that girl from the bathroom."

I wandered toward the pair. I still questioned Kitty's age, mulling over possibilities in my mind and pushing away the uncomfortable ones—maybe she just had one of those young faces, the kind women curse in their twenties but yearn for beyond. That would explain her defensiveness. I lost the thought as Kent Pearce offered me his hand and I shook it too hard. "Nice to meet you," I said.

He patted me on the shoulder, smiling absently. He fidgeted his jaw, running his tongue along his teeth and humming. His forehead dripped with sweat, residual from his legendarily wild drum set. His face was boyish, with round cheeks and wide eyes, but there was a patch of stubble across his chin. "Thanks."

"Oh, oh, tell her about your good idea," Kitty said, jumping and prodding Kent's side. "Tell her!"

Kent was blank for a moment, then his eyes lit up. "Hydraulics," he said. Kitty and I both nodded so he'd go on. "I want my drum kit on hydraulic lifts. I want to lift off the ground like Jesus fucking Christ. Or John Bonham. Both."

Kitty gasped. "That would be so far out. You have, like, the best ideas. Faun, doesn't he have the best ideas?"

Was the idea good? Did it matter, when I was a lucky enough fan to be hearing it? "Yeah, for sure," I said, fiddling with the collar of my shirt. "Do either of you know where Josie is?" If I could find her, I could feel purposeful. I could be told what to do and how to do it.

Kitty didn't know, but suggested I ask the women sitting across the room at Scott Sutherland's feet. I made my way forward, my feet slowing with each step as I worried I'd blurt something stupid and ruinous. Scott Sutherland, the guitarist, was an aloof bad-boy type with baby-blond hair and a look of constant distance. He did most of the songwriting, and his pale head was always tilted, silently composing more hits. Nothing seemed to satisfy him—not the girls, or the crowd, or the coke one of the women at his feet held for him on a heart-shaped mirror. He offered her a line and she accepted. I wondered how it felt. How it felt for him to offer it to you.

The woman—girl, probably, with her acned skin—sucked on a Tootsie Pop. When she laughed, her metal fillings glinted in the light. She pointed to me with a wobbling finger and asked, "Who are you?"

Before I had time to answer, she stood, introducing herself with a minute-long handshake as "Clementine Cleopatra Tuesday Guinevere Scooby-Doo Blue."

"Right on," I said, trying not to overanalyze her obviously fake name. Was anything real here? Did it matter? "Do you know where Josie Norfolk is?"

"Hm," Clementine said, considering. She crunched down on her lollipop, wincing at the noise. "I think she's in Cal's dressing room. She said she'd be back soon. Sorry if I'm slow, I took so many Quaaludes that my face is about to fall off. You want one?"

Scott Sutherland whacked me on the arm, not quite gently. He pointed to the mirror Clementine held. "You wanna hit the slopes?"

"Uh," I said, "that's a really nice offer. I, um, might, but—"

A light bulb smashed from the corner. Scott laughed. I did, too, grateful for a distraction. I turned to see one of the roadies I'd taken a photo of standing over a pile of broken glass, shaking his head at his own misfortune. "You're a fuckup, Floyd!" Scott Sutherland called over.

"Go fuck your mother!" the roadie—Floyd—yelled back. His rapport with the band was genuine. He smirked, self-aware and semi-charming, as he began to sweep up his mess. He caught my eye for a second and I looked away, blushing, to the opening act, Careful Kiss. They were helping a sweating member of the backstage crew load equipment into a road case. An older roadie hunched over in a corner, playing with the guitars while pretending to tune them.

Yvonne, who'd drifted up beside me, elbowed me in the side hard enough to bruise. "Quit gawking," she said.

"I wasn't," I said, then corrected myself. "Sorry." How could I *not* gawk here? No fan fantasy could have come close to the reality in front of me.

We both looked to Scott as he wiped off his reddened nostrils and sniffled. Yvonne sighed, then said low enough for only me to hear, "I always tell Darlene that Scott looks like an albino rat."

I didn't know who Darlene was but said, "Oh, right. I think he's handsome, though."

"I didn't say he wasn't. Come meet Howie." She grabbed the short sleeve of my blouse and pulled me toward the bassist. If Kent was the wild one, and Scott was the moody one, then Howie Guerrero was the romantic, with round dark eyes and full lips. He was the handsomest, turning back and forth, admiring every angle of his clean-shaven brown face in the pink mirror Scott had used for the coke. Howie smiled at Yvonne and her hard exterior dissolved, her grip loosening on my hand.

Yvonne slid over, still dragging me, and said to Howie, "Right when I thought you were too old to be good, you surprised me. I was at the front. Turns out I still know all the words after all." She lit a cigarette.

I didn't know what to do. I was so close to Howie—so close to Scott, too—and my mouth was speechless and gummy. I didn't have to speak because Howie only wanted to talk to Yvonne. His face warmed and he waved for her to come even closer. Yvonne dropped my hand and did as she was asked.

Howie said, his voice low, almost growling, "Of course I saw you, Miss Yvonne. You're impossible to ignore."

"Sycophant," she said.

I stepped back from the pair and held my camera up, snapping a photo. It developed with a blur where Yvonne had moved her hand in gesticulation, but it caught the true-blue-illusionary way Howie Guerrero gazed up at her. His magic.

He continued to Yvonne, "What does that make *you*?" Like he couldn't help himself, he added, "You are the loveliest."

"I brought you Kahlúa. I left it with Kent, though, so we'll see if there's any left." After a long pause, she looked toward Scott Sutherland and said, "You were good tonight."

In an instant, Howie and Scott's flock of girls erupted in praise.

A girl dressed all in pink down to the polish on her toenails said, "You were *more* than good, you were *amazing,* you were life-changing!"

A girl with two Baby Ruth bars said, "It was the best show of my entire life, and I've seen Queen twice."

A girl in metallic pants so tight they looked painful said, "You guys are incredible. You guys are everything."

Clementine moaned, "I almost creamed my fucking jeans when you came onstage."

They turned to me, and I caught on. I felt the adoration the other women did, but every way I tried to phrase it felt trite. I couldn't blow this moment. I stuttered out, "It was—was—so very . . . very good. It was very good." I gave a pageant-queen smile and wished I could sink into the floor.

My blushing was interrupted by a delighted scream rising from my left. Josie called my name and I turned, dashing toward her in the hallway's entrance, grateful for some fragment of familiarity.

Josie smothered me, whispering words I couldn't understand. Maybe they weren't words at all. Maybe she was just buzzing in my ear to make me feel fuzzier or speaking in tongues. All I knew was that she was *there,* in a mass of frightening wonderment, and she was the most wonderful part of it all. "It all worked out!" Josie cried, reading my mind. It *had.* It didn't matter if she'd disappeared on me because when she reappeared, we were backstage in our own personal dreamland.

I whispered that Yvonne had been weird.

"She's a 'nowhere woman,'" Josie said. "That's what she calls it. She flies all over."

"She said she's Howie's manager? His acting manager?"

Josie burst into laughter. A sinewy hand landed on Josie's shoulder and we both looked up, facing Cal Holiday. His fingers burrowed into Josie's white coat. She slung her arm around his back and said, "Faun, this is Cal."

"We've met," I said, smiling at Josie, then sheepishly at Cal. "He saved me from the wrath of Stanley."

"It was my pleasure," Cal said.

The room took notice of Cal, all conversation pausing, as if anticipating something unplaceable. Cal raised his hand and said, "Great show tonight, everybody. Big energy. Big fun. Big love. What do you say we leave in half an hour?"

The rest of the band agreed. The girls and roadies did, too.

Cal put his hand down, letting the room breathe, and turned back to me and Josie. He and Josie swayed like tall twin trees. I thought I remembered something my mother had told me after she came in from the yard, gardening gloves still on her hands, about saplings suffering when they're planted too close together.

Josie wandered to a table brimming with bottles, all funny shapes and colors like pieces of sea glass. She winced, taking a swig from a bottle of coconut rum, but went back for a second taste. Cal plucked the bottle from her hands, then asked me if I wanted anything.

I said, "I drink wine," which was not an answer.

"We have gin," Cal said, pouring me a glass of something that smelled like bathroom cleaner.

I downed it, gagging as Josie winked at me. The bitter taste trickled down my throat, eventually warming within my stomach.

"Is Faun coming to the after-party?" Cal asked, looking at me but speaking to Josie.

Josie didn't answer, so I said, "I'd love to. Say, um"—I pointed to my Polaroid—"you're a beautiful couple. I take pictures. Could I— maybe?"

They both nodded. I took two photos, letting the flash illuminate every inch of their faces, and when I finished and began shaking the dual printouts, Josie muttered, "I think I blinked in the last one."

Cal said, "I'm not taking another one. Flash is too bright."

"I'm *joking*," she said.

"Anyways," I said, searching the ink for the emerging images, "where's the party gonna be?"

Across the room, Kitty insisted she could swallow an extension cable, then pull it back up her throat. Kent begged her to try. Scott, taking it further, suggested she swallow it down so someone could pull it out her asshole. She giggled a refusal, so they turned their attention to something else.

"We're renting out a favorite bar of ours," Cal said, grabbing my attention again. "It's called Witching Hour. Very cool spot."

I said something about that being very cool indeed. Josie bid me a temporary goodbye. She and Cal made their rounds across the room. I was alone but with a perfect opportunity to glean more pictures from the night. I took a photo of nothing in particular, imagining all the secrets I could unearth within it once it faded in.

We hung around as the roadies finished their disassembly. Kitty demonstrated a cheerleading move, which Kent followed up with a "cool karate kick" that knocked two wine bottles onto the floor. Everyone laughed, groaned, and ignored poor Floyd, who had to sweep up the mess. I waved to him, shrugging sympathetically. He shrugged back. Kent carried Kitty on his back, bouncing from wall to wall, looking cherubic and deadly at once.

A whisper filled the room and Scott forced Clementine to evacuate the real estate she had started occupying on his lap. She pulled a piece of red licorice out of her overalls pocket and hopped onto a stool. Scott smoothed his jeans and took a meditative breath, eyes focused on the smudges on the floor, saying something to Howie about "his lady."

I inched over to Josie and asked, "Who's Scott talking about?"

"Oh," Josie said, genuinely surprised I didn't know. "His wife. Darlene. Darlene Dear? Have you heard of her?"

"I think so," I said, remembering something Yvonne had said. I turned to catch a glimpse of this apparent legend.

Darlene's red hair floated in gravity-defying curls above her head. A lit match. Josie told me that Darlene was known for having good coke and beautiful doll eyes (the color of which you could rarely see, because of the good coke). She was from rural Georgia and was a wannabe mystic. She carried a deck of battered tarot cards everywhere she went, and once held up the band's tour bus for an hour because she drew the Ten of Swords—a terrible omen.

The room erupted in coos over the toddler bouncing in Darlene's arms, a round-cheeked girl in a zebra-print bonnet. Darlene set the child down and pried open her alligator-skin purse. "Hey, y'all!" she cried. Darlene was a witchy woman, like in that Eagles song. A fortune-teller bringing good times and high spirits. The girl at her feet was her familiar. Her miniature. Scott blew a kiss to Darlene and its softness made me realize I would do anything to be in her place. Darlene yelled, "Has everyone met little Wendy yet? She's so damn cute. We slept all day long so we could be up tonight, didn't we, baby girl?"

Darlene raised two plastic bags of cocaine into the air, their white color glinting like shooting stars. I should have been scandalized, but all the years of unenacted rebellion inside me were desperate to emerge.

Clementine, a lady-in-waiting, held up Wendy so everyone could see. We all said, "Aw," then Wendy started bawling, so Scott gestured for Clementine to hand her over.

Scott wiped the tears off his daughter's face with the collar of his T-shirt, the white fabric losing its shape. He whispered something to Wendy and she smiled, babbling contentedly. She had Scott's blue eyes and swatted at nothing, giggling. I took a photo of them together, not realizing that one day Wendy would be a real person. An adult. Not a prop, but a whole human being born to a rock star. Wendy was too young to understand whom any of the people surrounding her were—all she seemed to know was Mama and Dada. Everyone else was just a funny, too-chattery face.

Stanley said Wendy was a liability and Scott replied, "All she does is puke and cry. It's like having a second Kent around."

Wendy hiccupped in apparent agreement, muttering, "Dada sleepy?"

Scott answered, "No, Dad's wide-awake. Are you sleepy?"

Wendy shook her head and yelled, "Awake!," as Darlene dipped into the cocaine.

Once the equipment was ready to go, the groupies helped the band pack their personal artifacts. They stuffed sweated-through silk shirts and cravats into suitcases, sorted dollar bills from fives, and fetched cigarettes whenever Cal or Howie complained they were dying for a smoke. Josie asked me to grab Cal's jacket from the chair he'd left it on. I carried it back slowly, almighty with its power on my hands. Josie kissed me on the cheek and started rambling incoherent mush about Cal. Her adulation was intense and vibrant and difficult to believe because of all the contradictions. He was soft but sturdy; he was observant but easy to surprise; he was bold but bashful.

She kept helping Cal, and I had nothing to do but watch as girls wiped the band's brows, mixed last-minute drinks, and spewed praise. I tried to preen and fawn, too, unsure how—I kept imagining sideways glances and confused laughs directed my way. I'd never been good at flirting or being flirted with. My speech always turned stilted, my eyes cast sideways. Most of my high school dates were double dates by Josie's side—controlled environments with no space for silences. I'd kissed any boy who was willing to kiss me, then three men in college, and one woman while drunk. Each time, the fear was the same. It all had felt terrifying and wrong, and each time someone had kissed me, I'd thought they were mocking me somehow.

But it didn't have to be that way here.

Soon the Troubadour's backstage would be tidied and groomed, emptied of all excess and grime. No trace would be left of Holiday Sun except a stray Miller High Life bottle or a permanent marker signature on the wall. It was tragic.

Darlene scooped Wendy off the floor, pulled a candy wrapper out of her mouth, and plopped her down on the couch beside me, letting Wendy play with her hair. I didn't look at Darlene but instead stared at the water pipes on the ceiling.

"Honey," she said gently. When I didn't reply, she repeated, "Honey, look me in the eyeball." She propped her head on her hand, daring me with doe eyes to glance her way. I turned slowly, my Polaroid swaying across my chest, and stared at the twitching face a few inches from mine. Wendy sucked on a piece of Darlene's dyed hair.

I looked into Darlene's eyes and saw my own reflection. Her pupils swallowed her irises.

"There," she said. "Not so scary, right?"

"You're not scary," I said quietly, unsure if I meant it.

"Damn right." She cackled, then adjusted Wendy's frilly socks, asking me, "Did they tell you I can whistle through the gap in my teeth? I figured that out 'bout a week ago and fuckin' near flipped." She demonstrated, asking me to guess the song and pouting when I couldn't tell it was "Ring of Fire." Darlene continued, "I wanna add the whistling to the next song I lay down."

"You make music?" I asked.

"I *try*," she said. "It's experimental. Scott hooked me up with a producer who likes my whole thing. Wendy even made it onto a song, didn't you, Wendy?"

Wendy nodded and said, "Singer!" Darlene cuddled Wendy close to her chest. Madonna and child.

I asked, "Could I snap a photo of you two?"

"Are you a photographer? Professionally?" Darlene asked, eager.

I considered for a moment, then said, deliberately, "Yes."

I took their photo, framing it beautifully with a potted plant sprouting winglike from Wendy's back. Darlene ogled it as it developed. She smiled at the faded image and that was all I needed. Acting like a big-shot photographer was the same as pretending to be anything else. Did the band do that, too? Or did we pretend for them? When Kent scraped his ankle, Kitty pretended to be a wartime nurse and fixed him up. When Howie plucked out a bass riff that was average at best, three girls at his feet pretended he had cured cancer.

Half-truths. Lifelike nothings. Who cared about truth, about an-alyzing, about anything, in a place as good as this? I smiled so hard my cheeks ached.

The nervous hollow in my chest closed when Darlene said I was "damn good" and ordered the girl who'd been eating two Baby Ruths to make us piña coladas. I sipped mine graciously and took pictures of anyone who would let me as the party prepared to shuffle out onto the street.

We stepped out of the concrete shell of the theater and into the starlit night. The early autumn air brushed against my bare arms. I took two photos of Kitty and Kent kissing with more tongue than I thought possible, then hustled along the sidewalk toward Witching Hour, a few paces behind Josie and Cal, feeling all-important.

Taking the photographs was easy because everyone *wanted* them to be taken. It was a game of prettifying and perfecting—they'd gussy themselves up in paisley ties or mesh shirts or dot on their eye makeup or home-perm their hair in the hopes someone would find them worthy of documentation. That could be my job: documenting those worth preserving. I laughed at every joke and smiled at every face, doing everything I could but outright *beg* to belong. Everyone had started beaming at me and I was beaming back. Josie and Cal walked in front of the crowd, staring at each other like they were made of gold. At the end of the pack were Kitty and Kent, scream-ing into the sky in sacred celebration of every inch of hedonism the human body could handle. Groupies and roadies traveled in swarms, hovering around the band.

A hand tapped my shoulder and I jumped, unready but excited for touch. It was the roadie—Floyd—who'd shattered the light. "Whoa, whoa, be still." He laughed.

"You spooked me," I said, blushing a little. "I, um, took your photo earlier when you were onstage—I don't know if you noticed."

"I noticed." He laughed again.

"Sorry," I mumbled, then added, "I'm Faun. I'm friends with Josie, if you know her."

"Oh yeah," he said, then rolled up the sleeves of his black T-shirt. "I'm Floyd. Like Pink. But not." The storefront lights made his brown skin look coppery, as if he were a sun-soaked statue. He offered me a flask and I paused with it in my hand. Suddenly, I remembered—my first shift at Foto Fantasy was at nine tomorrow. It was midnight now. I almost turned around and bolted home to bed, but Floyd's smile stopped me. It wasn't like I knew the way back. It wasn't like I really *wanted* to go either.

I said, voice lost in the cacophony, "Thank you."

"You gonna drink it or hold it?" he asked.

I was such a drag, hesitating while Floyd stared at me, growing more and more confused. Everyone else was sloppy drunk. I hovered somewhere between tipsy and sober. A teen magazine question: *Does peer pressure exist after school, and if so, am I allowed to cave to it?*

Here goes nothing, I thought. Here goes nothing to stop *being* nothing. I'd been half wild by Josie's side once. I could do it again. I could do it better. "Fuck it," I said, the words odd on my tongue, "I'm here to have a good time." I could make it to work even if I stayed up late, right? I could still count change and hang backdrops hungover. I'd set an alarm clock. Easy. I was sure Josie had one.

Floyd laughed as I swallowed down three sips of cheap vodka. My stomach gurgled and I laughed, too, thrilled at my own courage. He took his flask back and I paid attention to every step I took. Reeling from everything, I stumbled and nearly burst into tears when Floyd caught me.

"Watch out, good-time girl," he said, teasing. "You almost fell right into the street."

"Thanks," I said, then asked, my brain not filtering my thoughts properly, "Can we touch each other like everyone else is touching?"

He slung his arm around me. He asked if I would have caught him if he'd fallen toward the late-night traffic, too. I said I would. I would have tried.

Darlene, walking backward, yelled that she liked my hair. I yelled a thank-you back, which made Yvonne glance toward me. Her fingers were intertwined with Howie's, and her face twisted strangely when she saw Floyd's arm around me. I didn't care what she thought, not then, because Floyd's hand was the softest thing in the world.

We arrived at Witching Hour and life was delicious and candy-apple sweet. Midnight was a time of magic, and as we stood outside, I searched for supernaturality in every face I saw.

Although Holiday Sun had rented out the whole bar, the bouncer was still hesitant to let in the wild group of ambiguously aged girls the band had amassed. It was smart of him to worry—sensible—but no one else was thinking straight, and instead complained about how inconvenient it was he didn't want fifteen-year-olds in the bar. Stanley said something to the bouncer about contractual obligations and social expectations, and soon anyone with the band, whether or not they could produce a valid ID, was let inside. The bouncer was meant to keep out the common rabble, and no one who had walked all the way to Sunset with the band was common.

Inside, the lights were dimmed to an orange hue. Cal began to greet everyone who had already arrived, and Josie took me in the opposite direction to help me make introductions. Floyd hung by the bar with some other roadies, who spoke with Stanley and another managerial type, trying to seem important. Darlene, ordering a bourbon on the rocks, took offense to Stanley's suggestion that she take Wendy home. She argued the cultured environment of the bar would be excellent for Wendy's social development and stuck her tongue out. Josie left a trail of smoke behind us as we walked around the mural-walled room.

We were all only half conscious of reality, the world a delightful, dark-lit dream. Howie Guerrero said I looked "lovely," and I dissolved. He was perfect, so golden-eyed and gleaming. I fell in love with everything. With the band. With the party. With myself, in a way.

I thought of the other fans in the concert crowd, how they all would have died to be in my place—how they'd look green-eyed at me with jealousy—and smiled.

Friends and a few lucky handpicked fans slid through the doors of the bar until Witching Hour bubbled at capacity with famous patrons. Each face held such promise and I wanted to document them all. I tried to be selective with my photos, but, drunk on everything, I snapped away until I was all out of film.

The night unfolded in Dionysian flashes.

I sat with Josie, Cal, Howie, and Yvonne for a while, all of them making me take sips from their drinks. I watched, enraptured and repulsed, as Scott gave his shirt to a chilly Darlene, leaving his sweating skin naked and sticky against his vinyl chair. Wendy toddled beneath us, barefoot and wide-awake.

Floyd took my hand and we danced to the music, shouting lyrics into each other's mouths as we half kissed, half sang. I didn't realize we were kissing until thirty seconds in, but didn't mind. After all, any mouth at a party like this was a mouth worth kissing, wasn't it? When Floyd stepped outside, Yvonne told me a roadie—even if he was a lighting designer—wasn't a "choice cut" in terms of someone to romance.

Kitty moped around the bar, complaining about personal drama and all the ways she thought her mother was out to get her. Tequila Sunrise in hand, she asked Kent, "I've got class real early tomorrow. Would it be, like, awful if I didn't go?"

He answered, "Do whatever you want, baby."

When he called her baby, it seemed too true. Could she mean college classes? Floyd kissed me again and my discomfort was readily forgotten. Already I was an expert at looking the other way.

Late in the night, I semiconsciously trailed Josie outside, standing beside her like a pet while she made a pay phone call. I didn't know who she was talking to, nor did I wonder. After she was done speaking and I was done stargazing, she grabbed my cheek, blinked hard, and said something about Cal I couldn't hear over the drone coming from the bar's open door. She went back inside and I showed a handful of Polaroids to Howie, who was smoking pot on the curb with two roadies.

He nodded gently at the pictures. I smiled. I told him he was wonderful, and he smiled back.

I sat with them, swelling with pride every time a passerby glanced over with recognition on their face, until Kitty ended up outside, too. She tried in vain to hail a cab back to her suburb of origin, which Kent would surely have to pay for, but got cold feet every time a car would pull up to the curb. She gave up. Before she could venture back inside, no doubt in search of Kent to cling to, I called her over.

"You're having fun," she said. She yawned, stretching her arms, Doublemint gum falling out of her mouth.

"Are you?" I asked. Before she answered, I said, "Oh, you're so cool. You're so little."

"I am *not*," she said. "Who are you to decide that, anyways?"

I laughed. She huffed and got up, but I caught her hands, standing before she could sulk away from rudeness I hadn't realized I'd spoken. I reeled where I suddenly stood and my stomach churned. "I'm sorry," I said. "You're old. Is that—isn't that—better? It is, right?"

Kitty narrowed her eyes and said, "You're so *bizarre*."

"I'm sorry."

"No, like," she said, playing with her bangs, "it's not a bad thing. You could fit in."

I beckoned her to hug me and she did. She patted my hair and Howie said, "Aw," from the curb. A car honked.

Letting go of her, I said, "Hey, do you know that song—by Mick Fleetwood—Fleetwood Mac—where the bass goes 'bum . . . bum, bum, bum, bum, bum-bum-bum-bum'?"

She said yes, she loved that song, and wasn't Lindsey Buckingham a stone fox?

I turned and vomited into a rosebush.

I was having the time of my life.

Six Photos

Yvonne, crossing her arms and beautiful, unsure of whether to trust the camera or the person behind it.

Josie and Cal hand in hand backstage, smiling straight at the camera.

A family portrait of Darlene and Wendy on a leather couch, both freshly napped and seeking different kinds of adventure.

Josie with her tongue out and skirt off, the white fabric of her underwear glowing under the bar lights.

Kitty with chunks of pink vomit stuck to her chin, smiling widely.

Cal and Kent flipping off the camera, beers in hand and halo lights above their heads. Yvonne's hair creeps into the corner of the frame, but if you hadn't been there, you'd just think it was an anonymous curled tuft.

4.

I SLEPT SOUNDLY, TOO TUCKERED OUT BY DANCE FLOORS AND tequila to obey an internal alarm, and awoke swaddled in a quilt and yesterday's clothes. The makeup Josie had done for me was still on my face, and I didn't wash it, hoping it could sink in and stay. Josie snored from the bedroom, her exhales steady and deep.

I looked at the cat-shaped wall clock, its eyes lolling side to side. Ten A.M.

My shift at Foto Fantasy was supposed to start an hour ago. I'd been foolish and reckless and stupid and now I was paying for it. I cursed myself as I pulled on my dry-cleaned uniform and clipped on the DONNA name tag, running out the door to the department store.

I burst through the Coswell's door half an hour later, unkempt and panting. The other shopgirls I scurried past on my way to the photo studio were tight-lipped and stiff, held together by layers of hair spray and spritzes of Rive Gauche. The shopgirls working in menswear were smoother, leaner, affecting a careless air as they pointed customers to polyester ties and suit jackets. Finally, I reached Foto Fantasy and tried to steady my breath before giving Enzio what I hoped was a winning smile. My smile fell, and I said, "I'm so sorry. I'm so sorry. Please, I promise, I won't be late again."

"Not impressed," he said, then grunted, pointing for me to start polishing lenses. "You go to college?"

"Well," I said, "I used to."

"I'm surprised they let in a girl who apparently can't tell time."

My sweat dried and I got to work tilting mirrors and wiping counters. I resigned myself to a half-hearted sense of duty at Foto Fantasy, hoping one day my customer-service smile would turn real.

My teeth grew dry from the openmouthed grinning, my arms sore from bouncing plush versions of Daisy Duck and Mickey above my head to trick children into smiling. Every mother made me say their children were the most beautiful ones. I obliged, confused by their casual familial bliss. Their unprompted love. I'd never known that. My mother had taken us for portraits only once, and I'd been barred from smiling because I'd lost my front teeth the week before.

I worked overtime at Foto Fantasy that evening without being asked, proving my hardiness to Enzio, who would scan me sporadically for signs of weakness. I never talked back to his snide comments. He was my boss, and if he wanted to tell me I was sloppy, I thought I was supposed to let him.

The studio camera's flash was brighter than my Polaroid's but made me itch to take pictures of my own. I was forbidden from touching the expensive equipment until my probation (which was of unspecified length and possibly eternal) ended. As I walked home after that first day at the studio, I thought of the Scouts and five-sibling families at Foto Fantasy, unsure if I wanted to have a round-cheeked child or be one.

I took a shower first thing, rinsing off grime that had sat too long on my skin, then changed clothes and massaged Josie's cucumber-scented lotion onto my sore limbs, trying to relax. On my way to the couch, I tripped on my camera, which laid in a mess of dust and crumbs on the carpet. I inspected it to make sure it wasn't broken, then went to take a look at last night's Polaroids. I searched my jeans pockets. Nothing in the front two except for three Dubble Bubble gum wrappers and a bitten-off cigarette filter. Nothing in the back left but two dollars in quarters, and nothing but lint in the back right. Nothing in my purse but my wallet and someone else's Maybelline Kissing Stick.

Shit.

Stupid, careless Faun. What a "professional" I was—losing all my photos. Almost breaking my only camera. Working minimum wage dusting the darkroom in a department store. I had so little and here I was, apparently indifferent if I lost what remained. How could I lose all solid proof of the wonder of last night? Maybe I hadn't deserved to be there—it should have been a fan who'd take better care. I circled the living room, hoping the stack of pictures would jump out or call my name. I brushed my teeth. I stewed. I peed. I stewed some more.

I put my head out the window for a breath of fresh air, almost sticking my head up Josie's flowing skirt.

"Modesty, my darling!" She laughed. She was perched on the roof, her legs dangling, nibbling a piece of raisin bread straight from the bag and watching the clouds.

"Have you seen my pictures? The ones I took last night?" I asked, leaning to the far left of the window, my back against its hot frame.

Josie looked down at my bobbing head and said, "Before I sent you home in the cab you gave them to me 'for safekeeping.'"

I didn't remember it at all, but I trusted Josie more than I trusted my own blacked-out memories. A hint of guilt coursed through me, but Josie insisted she'd kept the pictures as pristine as possible. No harm done.

Josie picked up the raisin bread and asked if I wanted some. I pulled myself onto the roof. The sun-faded tiles were stiff underneath me, giving me a balance that was precarious in the best way. "Easy, breezy," Josie said, and we were. Light and careless. What a change it was for me to feel genuinely relaxed under the clear, perfect sun.

I chewed a piece of raisin bread as Josie covered a yawn with the back of her hand, the same way my mother used to.

Everything always came back to my mother. It always comes back to the person who gave you water when you cried. I hated her and loved her, even now. My mother liked to watch *Sonny & Cher* and sunbathe on our fenced-in back porch, so close to normalcy I barely noticed how overbearing she was. She cared so much it terrified her every time I was late coming home from school or Josie's place. I'd walk in the door as the sun was setting to see her weeping at the dinner table, heaving so hard the blood vessels in her eyes burst. I'd apologize and she'd tell me she thought I'd gotten killed.

I hid all of my and Josie's exploits, lying through my teeth most weekends about where I was going, and cursing myself all the while. I was a good daughter, and I grew good at being scared. Once Josie left for California, I promised my mother I wouldn't get into any more "nonsense" at Mount Holyoke. She liked that Josie wasn't there, saying maybe now I'd "go straight" and be a "good girl." I thought I *was* good. I tried so hard to be good for her. I passed all my classes (until my final year's uncertain dread crept in), did all my readings, and even went to a sorority recruitment or two.

My mother had warned me a couple years earlier, as we were baking our weekly cinnamon rolls, that I ought to be more "tactful" in conversation. She'd seen me out with my friends, she'd said, and I'd been talking so passionately I'd been spitting. "It looked dirty," she said. "It looked . . . embarrassing." I hadn't meant to embarrass her but I *had*, and that was enough to hurt me. I ate my roll in silence and moped all night long, resolving to be more careful. To be more like my mother.

I asked Josie if I'd embarrassed her when we were out with the band.

"God, no! You were excited. The band loves that," she said, like it was the most obvious thing. Like they were the only ones I'd ever have to impress. "I showed them your photos; I hope that's all right. They thought they were precious. Gorgeous. I couldn't get Cal to look at too many, but Kent just adored them. Especially the one with Yvonne's tits out." She laughed and I did, too, unable to believe how absurdly sublime last night had been. "They think you're something special."

Special. I'd only ever been a half-interesting plain Jane. But with Josie guiding me, I was becoming special. I took a sharp breath. "I'd like to see the band again. I'd like to . . . meet them again and take more pictures." My chest contracted as I asserted myself.

Josie lit up, bouncing in place. "There's a party at Howie's house tomorrow."

"What are they celebrating?"

Josie shrugged. "Tuesday."

A celebrity party—at a celebrity's house! I was the luckiest fan in the world to be invited, and the unluckiest one, too, as soon as I realized attending would be unwise. "You know what? I probably shouldn't," I said grimly. I had another shift at Foto Fantasy tomorrow, although it was supposed to end at five. Saying no was the right thing to do—going to another party with the band would be too wonderful, and I'd come to distrust anything that promised overabundant joy. "I'll be tired from work. I don't get paid until Friday. The world's not free."

"If you really want to let Foto Fantasy stop you, then fine," Josie said.

Goddamn Foto Fantasy, with its papery uniform and its boss who acted like I couldn't count to ten. Where nothing was good enough. Good at all. A musty studio wasn't the place to make my name. Holiday Sun's world, however, was ripe with connections and bright opportunities.

"Please say you'll have some fun," Josie added. Oh, to be as breathlessly careless as her. Then she said something I didn't understand: "I don't want to have to go everywhere alone anymore."

She balled up a piece of bread and chucked it into the street. It bounced along the sidewalk and rolled under a moving truck, sliding against its road-worn tires. She pulled two twenty-dollar bills out of her bra and pressed them into my palm, insisting I take them. "A payment," she said, "for yesterday's excellent work as Holiday Sun's photo girl." How could I argue?

I said yes to Josie and myself, ready to mill about people who looked like angels and catalog models again. Ready to be near the band. Ready to be important.

Josie's thin arm brushed my back as she pulled me into a hug. I

breathed in deep as she held me, loving how she smelled like cigarettes and Christmastime cinnamon.

WE CLIMBED BACK indoors when my calves started to sunburn. Josie
briefly flipped to the six o'clock news, wanting to see if Mary Tyler
Moore had won an Emmy in last night's ceremony. She shrugged,
too impatient to wait past the weather, and put on a record. I took a
Polaroid of the view from the window. Josie cranked the record until
the glass in her picture frames shook in minuscule earthquakes. She
said she'd never heard music loud enough until L.A. Only when she
was pressed right against the speakers at a Holiday Sun show could
she truly *hear* it.

I agreed, remembering the magic of seeing Cal Holiday form familiar lyrics right in front of me. My youth had been spent listening to
everything at a sensible level, lest my mother warn me my eardrums
would explode or I'd lose my hearing by thirty. She pestered me until
I learned to prefer a low warble. Now, I thought it would be criminal
to listen to anything that didn't rattle my skull. It would be better
to have the bass pounding in my bones and go bleeding-ear deaf for
something worthwhile than to keep perfect hearing without ever *really* hearing at all.

Josie returned my stack of photos, which she'd neatly tied together
with a hair ribbon. Shyly, she asked me to show them to her and nar-
rate the stories they told. She had very little interest in the ones of
her and Cal and gravitated to ones of her by herself. I pointed out
the details I'd tried to incorporate, using semi-correct language lifted
from critiques my old photography professor had given and phrases
I'd come across in *Modern Photography*. The one of Yvonne and Howie
was overexposed but "purposeful." A shot of an off-balance Kitty was
centered by the "necessarily square aspect ratio" of the Polaroid form.

Josie nodded thoughtfully. "You're very educated."

We both laughed.

Once we exhausted all of last night's pictures, Josie said she had another modeling shoot booked up for a "bottom-tier" soft porn mag.

I said I was proud of her.

"Even though I don't get paid much, I'm getting lots of exposure," she said. "Cal got me my first job—that was just for a catalog—but all the rest, I've gotten by myself."

"How?" I asked.

"If you want something, you get it. I get what I want," she said. A second later she laughed. "I'm so dramatic, aren't I?"

I laughed, too, but she was right. She got anything she wanted. So what did I want? How could I get it?

THAT EVENING, WE ventured out in knit sweaters to get some cheap dinner and wound up in the corner booth of a Chinese restaurant. We sipped bitter tea and ate packets of white sugar. Josie blotted her forehead with a paper napkin. The slow foot traffic of a Monday night drifted past the restaurant's dirty windows, and the tangerine glow of the decorative lanterns bathed Josie and me in delicate warmth.

Josie flirted with the waiter as I slurped soup.

"Liquid foods are good for your figure," she said wisely.

"Oh," I said, "good." I wiped a drop off my chin and reached toward one of our sharing plates.

"That's what Yvonne says, at least. I don't know how much to trust her, because sometimes she eats cotton balls so she doesn't get hungry. Don't tell her I told you that."

"That's sad."

Josie shrugged and popped a forkful of moo shu pork into her mouth. It was nice to be alone with her—with no one watching. I bit my nails.

I asked Josie how she met Cal (a question I had been privately pondering for as long as I'd been in L.A.) and she obliged. I knew I'd be getting a practiced story, but I wanted it anyway.

"Oh, it was absolutely romantic." She sighed. "Sophomore year. Was that seventy-two? December, I think, 'cause I was flipping my wig over my final exams. I dropped out in January, 'cause I failed those exams. Guess I should have flipped out a bit more. My roommate at the time, Leslie, and I were just walking to dinner. We were going to this hot dog place which I've really gotta take you to since it's super famous. Anyways, we were walking along Santa Monica Boulevard, and up to the curb pulled this big old limo. So Leslie and I hung back for a second, 'cause it's always fun to see who's inside them. One time I saw Peter Fonda. Or maybe it was Robert Redford. Either way, it was really cool.

"But anyways, the back window of the limousine rolled down and out poked the head of a funny-nosed long-haired guy. For a second, I didn't recognize him, and then I did—it was Cal, obviously—and I tried my hardest not to melt on the spot. I said hi and he said hi back. He asked if we wanted to come to a party. Leslie was a real wet blanket, with these big clunky glasses. She said no. Can you believe that? Who could say no to Cal fucking Holiday? You know? I said I'd go to the party and Leslie looked at me like I was nuts, which just, you know, made me want to go even more.

"Leslie grumbled a little bit and left. I walked right up to the window of the limo and looked dead into Cal's eyes. He looked right at mine. Then I asked him, real coy, 'Shouldn't we get going, then? We don't want to be late.' He nodded and let me into the car. The party was in Westwood. We stayed together all night long. It was very romantic. Afterwards, you know, I went to school for a while, but it was too hard. And boring. Compared to the kinds of things Cal brought me to see, everything was boring."

All I could say was "Wow."

"I *know*," Josie said. She popped a chicken ball into her mouth, chewing in a way that was somehow dainty. I grabbed one, too, finishing off our shared plate. "Do you want anything else?" Josie asked. "To eat, I mean?"

I shook my head. "I don't want it to be too expensive."

"It's okay, I told you I'll pay," she said. "As long as we can stay here a bit longer."

The sky turned dark outside as we spent the rest of the evening talking perfectly about nothing. We went home and watched *Monday Night Baseball* until we fell asleep.

THE NEXT MORNING, Josie reminded me I was invited to a party. *The* party, Howie Guerrero's, the beautiful-talented-wonderful-famous bassist's, party. I set off on my errands—the Laundromat, the drugstore, and finally, the camera shop—early before my shift at Foto Fantasy, hoping to leave lots of time to get ready once it ended. Dressing up was half the fun of going out—becoming a new person in front of the mirror and practicing all the pretty ways you'll turn your head when someone says hello to you. Floyd—mysterious, hardworking, softly indulgent Floyd—would be in attendance. I rehearsed my "Oh, I didn't see you there" and "You again? How nice!" while waiting to cross the road, mouthing the words.

I walked everywhere, worried bus fare might be too pricey, winding up at Garter Photo Hut around ten. There was an old man hunched over at the counter, running red-painted fingernails over telephoto lenses. The man muttered something about his daughter's regional production of *Brigadoon*, trying to impress Otis, who slouched so severely that he seemed to be dissolving. He picked dandruff out of his hair, not listening to anything the customer said. The old man bought his lens and left. Then, it was my turn to try to impress the man I had no reason to want to impress.

Otis took a swig from a can of Hi-C and slipped a five-dollar bill into his jeans pocket. He nodded slowly when I approached. "She's back."

"Hi," I said carefully.

Otis nodded, waiting for more.

"Do you want to see some photos?" I asked. I spread the Polaroids out on the counter like tarot, thinking about how Darlene could read it. If you drew Josie-Laughing-Shirtless or Cal-Winking you'd have good fortune. If you drew Kitty-Licking-Yvonne's-Face, you had a storm coming.

Otis prodded at the photos with one stubby finger, leaving smudges on the dark colors. He lingered for a minute over a picture of Josie. She was always the most enthralling. He looked back to the ones of the band and said, "I could sell the ones with Cal Holiday in them for about three hundred dollars. The Kent Pearce ones are good, too."

I threw my hands over the pictures instinctually, then said, quietly, "I don't want to sell them."

"You don't?"

The photos found their way back into my hands, falling into a pile. "No," I explained. "They're art. Not tabloid fodder."

"Aw, poor sweetheart's worried she'd get in trouble for selling her friends out."

"I am *not*," I said. I was, a little. To shatter a barely built professional relationship for quick cash wasn't worth it. I was in this for the long haul. I reconsidered, slowing repacking my purse, trying to brush off the fingerprints Otis had left on the photos. It *was* a lot of money, and I did need it. But I didn't want to contribute to some gossip rag. These pictures were too important to end up there. I ran through Otis's words again, realizing he'd called Holiday Sun my friends—were they? I'd die if they were—I'd die to make people *think* they were. I put on an affectation Josie would have made fun of me for. "I suppose you wouldn't know much about artistic integrity, but to us professionals it matters a great deal."

"Suit yourself," he said. "If you change your mind, I've got connections."

"Really?"

"I can tell you about them. Over dinner. Tonight?"

I shook my head, pulling the strap of my purse taut over my shoulder. My mind was made up. "I'm busy."

He threw his hands in the air, then softened when I said I wanted to buy five packs of film.

I KEPT MY purse close the whole walk to work, feeling its weight to make sure it was still there. In every quiet second at Foto Fantasy, my mind drifted, imagining what incredible, impossible things might happen at the party. I dropped a box of negatives on the floor. They shone like black ice. I picked them up before Enzio could reprimand me. I hummed catchy Holiday Sun songs as I folded backdrops and swept, remembering that pleasure was possible beyond the beige confines of Foto Fantasy. A Holiday Sun song ("Bright Cadet") played on the store radio and I thrilled. Secret superiority carried me through the day. I'd wondered if Holiday Sun's music was truly good, but the band was so good to me that it didn't matter. They could have recorded Tibetan chants and I would have still bought a copy, knowing they could consider me an acquaintance. An ally.

When my shift ended, I changed out of my uniform into a ratty tank top and the cutoffs Josie made for me. I whirled through the perfume section, asking the shopgirls for samples and dotting them randomly behind my ears. I hitched a ride home in a businesswoman's Ford, trying out my thumb for the first time. She tugged at her pearl necklace as I gave directions home.

The businesswoman dropped me off in front of our building, parking behind a dirty Oldsmobile.

"Faun!" Josie called from the second floor, waving to me.

Kitty stuck her head out the window and meowed.

I barreled up the stairs, kicked off my shoes, and said hello to Kitty, who was straining to remember the name of the Steely Dan song on the radio. I hung my purse on its hook and transferred the Polaroids to a drawer. Josie was half dressed, her tan lines revealing her East Coast roots.

Kitty said, "So, Faun, we've seen each other puke and today's only our third day of knowing each other. Isn't that, like, wild?" In the sunlight, it was obvious she was teenaged. Not young faced, not immature, but decidedly underage. I wasn't sure how to feel—I wondered what Josie felt and decided to feel however she did.

"Very wild," I said. "Is that your car outside?"

"My mom's car," she said. "But I'm borrowing it. She'll let me borrow anything if I say I need it for drama club. She's, you know, a little dim. No offense or anything."

Josie called Cal, whisper-screaming into the receiver about God knows what. Kitty killed a joint and declared she was going to recall her whole life story, just for me. She adjusted the sleeve of her milkmaid top, pushing it off her freckled shoulders, pouting about teenage troubles and family holidays. She rolled another joint and passed it to me. I took her picture.

Kitty said her mother was a seamstress whose penchant for glitter and keeping secrets granted her the favor of many of L.A.'s 1960s semi-stars. There was a trio of velvet wiggle dresses sewn by her mother pictured on the cover of the Opalines' 1962 debut, *Baby, Remember Me Always*. Kitty's fascination with her mother's job—and her mother's friends—began when she started accompanying her to some lower-profile costume fittings. Having a wide-eyed kid around was so novel that Kitty became a celebrity in her own right. When Kitty was absent from a fitting, she'd be asked about. She'd be worried about.

Kitty thought it was sensational. She turned pubescent under the careless eyes of half the artists in town.

In '74, her mother sewed floral vests for the Goodnews Brothers, a folk-rock duo whose music was not nearly as excellent as their name. The brothers invited Kitty to their album release party and her mother dropped her off at Francis Goodnews's Brentwood home. Kitty tried to look older than she was and had her first drink (well, her first seven). Paul Goodnews told her she was mature and interesting and different, and she believed it. He took her virginity on quilted sheets, and an hour later her mother picked her up and drove her home, none the wiser. Kitty was thirteen.

Every sentence was punctuated by a half giggle, like she wanted you to believe it might have been a joke. There was nothing to laugh at. Kitty told me it was a wonderful time, but an hour later remarked, "Nothing good ever happens in Brentwood."

Kitty met Kent Pearce last December at a bar, a month before her sixteenth birthday and a week before Holiday Sun set off on tour. She spent Christmas break on the band's tour bus and in February Kent asked her to be his girlfriend. Kitty "said yes so quickly, you, like, wouldn't believe it."

"Wow," I replied. I spun rationalizations like thread on a loom, trying to weave a version of Kitty in my mind that didn't make my skin itch. *Sixteen was mature, wasn't it? She could have been an early bloomer. Some people get married at sixteen.*

Who was I kidding?

Josie slammed the phone down in the next room.

Kitty sighed, her eyes batting. There should have been bluebirds perched on her shoulders for how romantically she said, "So divine, right?"

Everything about her screamed faux maturity, from the flick of her eye makeup to her platform sandals. I loved her immediately because I feared no one else did. She was still pink-cheeked at sixteen.

I fake-smiled, somehow cursing my mother for not allowing me such a reckless life—wondering why I hadn't been plucked up and declared a pretty young thing. Wondering why I wanted that at all. It wasn't right to want it. It wasn't right to be jealous of someone I also pitied.

Josie barged out of her bedroom in the slinkiest outfit she owned. "It's time to go," she said. "Cal's being an ass. We've got to show up early. I've got a cab coming."

I scrambled to get ready, dousing myself in more perfume and painting on thick streaks of eyeshadow. Josie and Kitty argued about what I should wear, so I tied up the baby pink tank top I was already in, hoping that if my stomach was showing, I'd seem chic. I needed more time to look perfect but what I had on would have to do. I stuck a lipstick in my pocket to apply in the taxi.

Kitty plucked a bottle of wine from the fridge as we followed Josie out the door. We left for Howie's house in the taxi, leaving Kitty's mother's Oldsmobile to sit in the street. Kitty turned around in the taxi's passenger seat, twisting her arms around the headrest. The cab driver pushed her hip, adjusting her body so he could see out the rearview mirror. Kitty told me a story about a groupie before my time named Starla Night-Light, who'd painted exquisite portraits of male musicians' genitalia.

Josie said, bobbing to the radio, "I liked her. No one else did."

"She was ridiculous!" Kitty cried. She took a swig from the bottle of wine and offered some to the cab driver. He shook his head and pushed her hip away again. "She thought she was, like, so above it all. Above the band. She was always putting them down, telling them to stop having fun, basically. A real snooze."

I took a sip from Kitty's bottle of wine and asked, "Where'd she go?"

Kitty's eyes went wide with scandal. "I heard she got *deported*. She was Hungarian, you see."

"Awfully convenient," Josie said, a laugh twinkling behind her words.

"The band did *not* have anything to do with that," Kitty snapped.

Josie shrugged, playing innocent. "You've got to admit that it's a lot nicer without her whining all the time. I maintain that *I* liked her, though. She had spunk."

Josie and Kitty moved on, but I worried that I might make the same mistakes as Starla Night-Light. Had she been overconfident? Too at ease? I was neither. Starla had been a complainer, and I couldn't fathom ever having something to complain about when Holiday Sun were letting you into their world. Then again, there were inklings of doubt—insecurity in the band's sincerity or stability. Kitty's young age, for one thing. Her youthful lips blabbed compulsive gossip and

I almost asked Josie if having a high schooler in the band's world rubbed her the wrong way.

The wind tousled my hair through the open windows, and I felt cool and shiny. A new penny. If only Otis could see me now, I thought. If only everyone could, then they'd understand I belonged here. I was one of the special ones.

Kitty asked if I could keep a secret, and I said yes. She didn't tell me one. She was testing me out, she said. Making sure.

The wind in my hair got colder. I rolled the window up.

While Kitty was rambling to the cab driver, Josie asked what I was thinking about.

I tried to form a question about why I was worried about, and captivated by, and frightened by, Kitty all at the same time. All I could say was "Do people think it's strange she's so young?"

Josie whispered back, "Don't think so. I mean, we oughta let others make their own mistakes. Right?" She added, seemingly more to herself, "I mean, it's not like she's thirteen or something . . ."

Two Photos

The view from Josie's apartment. Low-rise L.A. bathed in golden afternoon sun, stretching until it disappears at the horizon.

Kitty clouded in pot smoke, telling a story, trying to smile, mid-remembrance of who she was at thirteen.

5.

WE RATTLED OUR FISTS AGAINST THE DOOR OF HOWIE GUERRE-
ro's Holmby Hills home. Flower petals and condom wrappers littered
the ground. Party crumbs, untidied from a previous celebration.

Howie opened the door with a woman at his side I recognized.
Brooke Hwang, I think, from a cable comedy about a drive-in theater. Onscreen she was wacky, doing pratfalls and zipping around on
cherry-red roller skates. Here, she was pin-straight in a green floral
blouse, the skin on her face tight and hollow. Her connection to Howie
confused me, but I pretended I understood it. I half smiled, politely,
trying not to stare at her famous face. Had she been at the Emmy ceremony Josie had caught up on? I reeled at the idea.

Brooke stretched out a stiff hand, which we shook. She held a stack
of polka-dotted party hats in the other, her long fingers pressing
against the cones' tip. She said, "Happy Tuesday to you. Aren't we
early?"

Howie said, "These girls are always on time."

Brooke handed me a hat. I snapped the transparent elastic under
my chin, adjusting the paper cone over my hair.

Howie leaned close to me, smelling sweet and perfumed, and
asked, "How are you tonight, Faun?"

I blushed, despite myself. "I'm excited." I pointed to my camera.
"I'm sure there'll be lots to photograph."

"Of course!" Howie stepped aside, letting us in.

We looked like children's party castoffs, but the hats showed we
were willing to play along.

The string dug into my neck as Brooke pointed us down the dimly
lit entrance hallway. I pulled the hat off as soon as she looked away,

trying to toss it onto a potted plant, but Josie said to put it back on, so I did. She walked like a water skimmer toward the living room. Kitty darted beside her, and I followed a half step behind. Kitty muttered something about Kent and pulled another joint out of her purse, tucking it behind her ear. Josie threw her hair behind her shoulders, Marcia Brady style, and I felt entirely Jan behind her.

We paused before the main section of the oversize living room. Oh, the sweetness of a party's start—the fall into ritual madness, the relief from the day's stress. Hands outstretched, begging you to drop your coat and stay awhile, saying that there's always a later bus or another cab. The break from normalcy. The twinkle of specialness that made you want to hang around. Or if you left, come back. Remolding yourself into the demanded form, never unsettled by the shift but as comfortable as hot, runny glue.

Brooke surveyed the room as Howie passed by her, giving her a precise nod. She gave one back as she left to mingle. He made a kissy face, laughing, and hooked his arm around a singer named Linda Lessinger's shoulders. His eyes were gorgeous and hungry.

"True love," Kitty said.

"Really?" I asked.

Kitty and Josie erupted in laughter.

"No, no," Josie said, her back flat against the frame of the living room's archway. "Well, yes. But no." Before she could explain further, she saw Cal and dashed toward him.

Darlene sat on her husband Scott's lap, nibbling on his ear. A few roadies and crew members, including Floyd, were among the blessed few to be invited. Half the guests were famous and the other half were pretending to be, complimenting each other's designer clothes and smelling glasses of wine for two minutes at a time. It was hard to eke out where to sit, how to act, who to talk to. Everyone here was important, and I was once again the lucked-out fan with the wide eyes. I wallflowered.

The famous faces were interesting to watch. Trixie Childs, a pretend punk singer whose songs found airplay on college radio; Linda Lessinger, a wannabe Emmylou Harris with skunk-stripe brown roots; Jed Tooley, a waifish rocker with navy tattoos. A TV bit player here, a newscaster there—the room brimmed with people I knew who didn't know me. I scoured for magazine writers or editors—those who could grant me an in to my desired sphere. I considered talking to Brian Lee Gagneau, a journalist who I'd read was starting his own mag after quitting *Circus,* but his handlebar mustache and crossed arms intimidated me. Everyone looked so perfect on Howie's shag carpets and olive-green couches. The delicate wash of sunset turned the whole room into an oil painting: warm, impossible, and fuzzy. Josie broke away from Cal, moving toward the windows. She invited me to come stand with her away from the walls. I did, stepping onto the carpet, the evening sun kissing my skin through the casements.

I looked to Brooke and Howie, who seemed more like business partners than lovers. Josie explained that was exactly what they were. "Everyone was saying Howie got a girl from Tacoma pregnant—it was a dirty lie, of course, but she went to the magazines about it—so their manager hooked him up with a tidy fake girlfriend," Josie said. "Cleaned up his image."

"What does she get out of it?" I asked.

Brooke, answering my question, pressed her lips against her girlfriend's, a thick-thighed blonde. Howie was free to be with any girl he wanted, and Brooke was free to be with a girl.

"It's a good arrangement. She's a little famous," Josie said, considering. "Plus, it helps that she's filthy fucking rich, with her dad owning those hotels and all."

I nodded slowly, staring at Howie, smiling with his tongue pressed against his pearly teeth. He clinked glasses with Davey Rosenstein, the dewy main character of a TV drama about old Southern money and murder. I leaned to Josie and asked, remembering Yvonne's comment, "Howie acts, doesn't he?"

A memory I didn't share flashed across Josie's face. "He's giving it a try. He wants to diversify. I don't see why, because Holiday Sun keeps him busy enough, but we can't look down upon a dreamer, can we? He's gotten some little parts. Yvonne's his 'acting manager' or so she decided a few months ago."

"Is he good?" I asked.

"Well, he's handsome." She caught herself. "Of course he's good." Josie told me to have some fun, then made a beeline for a roadie I'd seen for a second at Witching Hour.

She brushed his shoulder to say hello and he jumped, not noticing her approach. Josie was always a welcome shock. She laughed, then he laughed, and all looked mellow between them.

Kitty grabbed my waist from behind and said, her bubblegum breath hot in my ear, "Stick with me for a second?"

I nodded.

Kitty waved to Yvonne and Darlene, and Yvonne gestured for us to follow her. We did, and the four of us left the living room to drift into the study, which was filled with nearly empty bookshelves and piles of snapped guitar strings. Yvonne shut the door with her hip and cracked open a can of orange soda. Kitty lit the joint she'd stashed behind her ear. Darlene pulled out her left breast and rubbed a smudge of red lipstick onto her nipple.

Yvonne stared, unblinking, the fizz of her drink crackling over the drift of noise. "So you're back."

"I guess." I measured my words and said, "It's good to see you again." I picked at the skin around my thumbnail, peeling it off in stinging strips.

She circled me, her long shawl sweeping through the air. A vulture's wing. After making a full rotation, she looked to Darlene, who had the manners to at least pretend she wasn't inspecting me. Kitty was distracted by a copy of the *Kama Sutra* sticking out of a chestnut desk's top drawer, flipping to the dog-eared pages and giggling. Yvonne leaned close to my face and held still. Then, when they couldn't take it anymore, Kitty and Darlene burst into laughter. I looked to my feet, my heart in my throat. Yvonne didn't care—she touched my chin and commanded me to pay attention. "Being here is a privilege."

"I know," I said.

Yvonne laughed. Darlene rolled her eyes, plucking the joint out of Kitty's fingers and taking a hit. Yvonne paced the study, her face as solemn as a shuttered cave. "I understand you're Josie's gal pal. I understand she brought you to the gig on Sunday and she brought you tonight. But just because you're here doesn't mean you can stay here. It's a privilege to party here."

"I don't follow," I said. I thought of Starla Night-Light, wondering how she would have fit into the motley crew surrounding me. Wondering if I fit into them.

"Holiday Sun likes you. They like your little camera, and they like your face, or your tits, or whatever." Yvonne finished off the orange soda and crushed the can, its tin bending willingly. "I've met a lot of girls like you. Girls with a dream about being a photographer or a dancer or a singer." Or a manager, I added in my head. She continued, "You're not one in a million. But Darlene and Kitty like you, so I might be seeing more of you." She chucked her can onto the floor, its lopsided body rolling past my feet. "Will you let me help you?"

Yvonne, cryptic queen supreme of all things band worship, was offering advice. I'd be a fool to turn it down. If I could be close to her, I could be close to the band. If she was the gatekeeper, I'd beg her for entry. "Sure," I said.

Yvonne perched on the desk, rising a foot above me, ready to give her crash course. "First off, if you're going to be friends with us, you need to respect us. We're not a sacred circle of sisterhood, but I expect common decency from everyone I hang around with." She crossed her legs. "You've got to commit to the band. You need to pay attention to them and tell them they're good. They need us. Without us, there's no music because there's no inspiration. You've got to prioritize them. Go to their gigs, go to their parties, buy their albums, and make all your friends buy their albums. Finally, you've got to care. Not too much—

not so much it hurts—but enough. Some girls say the way to enjoy life with a band is to be ice cold. That doesn't make any sense. If you don't care—if I don't care—then what the fuck are we doing here? Huh?"

"You've gotta give it all to them," Kitty added, trying to be helpful. "Your whole heart."

"No," Yvonne said, holding out her finger. Kitty sighed. "You never give them everything. You keep something, and you ask for something back."

"That makes sense," I said. It did. I was thrilled to be let into the band's circle, placed so close to significance and celebrity as an elevated fan. Still, I'd try to hold parts of my heart back. Caring about the band was well and good but I didn't want to dive into an arrangement where all I'd do was dote. My mother had done that with my father, and it left her alone with an unhappy little life and an unhappy little girl.

"If you care about them enough, they care about you," she said. It was symbiosis. "They help you." They could do a lot for dreamer girls. Yvonne sat silent for a moment, absorbing her own words. Maybe convincing herself. I decided to adopt her rules as my own, trusting Yvonne's years of experience. Love the band, support the band, be kind to your friends, and care just enough—easy rules. Especially compared to the two-page typewritten document of employee instructions Enzio had given me at Foto Fantasy. "Is this groupie school?" I laughed.

"You think this is so simple," Yvonne said, standing up. "But it's not. There's groupies, there's friends, there's muses, and there's girlfriends—"

"And wives," Darlene chimed in.

"Sure," Yvonne said, her patience thinning. She said those words were labels that did nothing to truly encompass our wealth of duty. Groupies weren't fans—they were more, they were different, they were rare. *Groupie* was a collective brush used to paint every woman seeking closeness to the band. Some, like Clementine, flickered into one band's world before bursting into another's, thrilled by the chase. Others, like Darlene, were in a band's world for life, bound by marriage or promise or blood pact. Yvonne was undecided about claiming the title. "It's a dirty word," Yvonne said, "but when someone calls me a groupie, I say 'thank you very much.' No one sneers and says 'groupie' unless they wish they were one."

Kitty spoke up, teasing. "Yvonne, I thought you'd been doing lots of reading. *Feminist* reading." She giggled. "Boring."

"I've been doing research," Yvonne snapped. "It doesn't hurt to be well-rounded. One copy of *Ms*. won't kill you."

Darlene played with her lipstick, pushing the waxy color all the way up to peer at the tube's mechanics. "I'm too busy for women's lib, girls. I've got the baby and all."

Women's lib was a mystery to me. I didn't know anything about Gloria Steinem or Angela Davis or Kate Millett other than their names. I knew the lyrics to "I Am Woman," but that hardly counted as education. Girls in college would talk about women's lib but the books they read were dense and abstract. I convinced myself I was too behind to catch up. I stuck to my *Cosmopolitan* and thought I was revolutionary for sometimes not wearing pantyhose.

Yvonne walked up and leaned close, shifting the focus of the room to me again. Another routine inspection. She smelled like strawberries. "What do you say? Will you follow the rules?"

"I promise," I said. If it meant I could keep taking pictures of this party's population, I'd agree to anything. Yvonne nodded sharply. Darlene rubbed the top of my head as Kitty goaded me into taking shot-size swigs from an ancient bottle of rye whiskey on the study's bookshelves.

"It'll be good to have another friend," Kitty said.

BY TEN, THE party had grown loud and vibrant.

For a while, Josie and I sipped from the same bottle of wine. She told me about her favorite roadie, Rajiv, the one she'd spoken to earlier. "You know how the Beatles had their India phase?" she asked, then explained, "Maybe it's time for mine." She pointed him out and gushed about how kind he was and how his accent made her flutter.

Her exotification of Rajiv made me squirm, but I struggled to express it. "Isn't that a little . . . I don't know, simplistic?" I didn't have the right phrasing. Was Josie shallow and clinging to obvious differences, bored with the monotony of her rock-star boyfriend? That seemed impossible. A person wasn't meant to be a novelty. But wasn't that what the band was to me? No, there was a difference, I told myself. I couldn't place it, but I knew it existed.

"Big words, baby." Josie laughed. She said she was obsessed, but as soon as I mentioned Cal, her conversation turned to how obsessed she was with *him*. I told her I was nervous and she asked why. I couldn't answer. I always was.

Thirsty for something nonalcoholic, I left the living room (where a horde of people stood elbow to elbow heckling late-night TV, and Kitty and Kent sucked face on the couch) and found the kitchen.

I turned on the sink, surprised when jewels didn't start flowing from the faucet. The water was cool in my mouth as Yvonne tapped my shoulder.

"Hello," she said, her tone lighter than before.

I hopped up onto the counter, gaining an inch on her considerable height, and she leaned to my right. The kitchen led into a great room, where a makeshift dance floor had been assembled.

Her stomach grumbled and I laughed. After a second, she did, too.

"Listen," she said, "I didn't mean to be a bitch. I just take this very seriously."

"Of course," I said, thinking if I agreed with everything she said, she'd learn to like me.

Yvonne stared absently through the archway at Howie dancing with a bleached-blond runway model. "Howie and I have something special. I'm helping him with his career." She liked to repeat herself. She was drunk and slurring, and continued, "I mean, shit, girl, I knew them before they made it. They need me. That's what Howie says."

Was she right? At that party, I believed it. For months, I believed it. Maybe I still do. But I also believed—I also knew—*we* needed the band. We needed something to nurture, and they needed nurturing. Constant attention made you need it even more. The band never learned to be alone and neither did we. But if they were starved for attention and we were, too, didn't we make a perfect pair?

Yvonne left to use the restroom.

Scott slid into the kitchen and, heart pumping, I reached to touch his shoulder. He was the first member of Holiday Sun I touched that closely. The fact I remember this so clearly is both embarrassing and a testament to how miraculous it felt to be near the band. The brushed leather of Scott's jacket was summer soft, and I stared at him in awe, thinking of how he reminded me of sainthood and sunflowers. I blushed but met his eyes. "Hey, dollface," he said. "You were there on Sunday, right?" His round cheeks were extra pale under the kitchen lights, but I thought he was smooth and clean as a marble figure.

"Yes," I said, "I was. It was amazing. I've been a fan of you since I-don't-know-when. High school."

He liked this. "You ever have a poster of us in your room?"

I didn't—my childhood bedroom was painted a tasteful beige and adorned only by a framed Harry Carling album cover and my sixth-grade class photo. The rest of the house was filled with clutter, but I preferred my private space tidy. Clean but not clinical. Josie's high school room was spackled with posters of every semi-relevant band, including Holiday Sun. I pretended Josie's room was mine and said, "Of course I did. You practically watched me sleep every night."

He laughed. "I don't mind you."

I would have done anything to tell him he was wonderful. I would have scaled walls and swum oceans to thank him for a good show. I loosed a torrent of compliments, but nothing I said seemed enough, so I kept trying and trying, over and over. He leaned close.

There was a lipstick kiss on his cheek. Darlene's color. I didn't back away, speaking slower as he came closer. A lone deer in the forest. Yvonne said I should make the band happy, and that would include kissing them, but didn't that contradict the rule about respecting my friends? I could see the pores on his nose, tiny pinpoints, but he didn't kiss me. He asked if I wanted to go outside for a smoke.

I shook my head, sputtering an excuse, but he pressed his hand to my lower back and led me out toward the porch anyway.

"Come outside," he insisted, pushing me along. "Don't be boring," he teased, but I couldn't help but feel he meant it.

We stepped into the night. The backyard was broad but mostly empty, with just a white-tiled swimming pool sloshing under the moonlight. A handful of people clustered under a porch light like moths.

I craved the quiet nighttime I used to find on my mother's porch. Sometimes I'd tote out my portable radio and listen to the fuzz of faraway stations, trying to make out magic words or a secret code. I'd curl my legs up on the painted wood and stare out at the forest behind the house. It went on forever. That's what I told myself. I knew eventually the trees ended and the human world took over again, but I liked to believe I lived at the end of civilization—at the edge of the world. It felt good to imagine things like that. To imagine I was a different person.

Now, I wished for Josie, because she was familiar. Stop being ungrateful, I told myself—millions of other fans would have died to be here. Maybe I wasn't committed enough. Maybe I had to try harder.

Scott made a small noise and the others outside turned to look, their faces cast with his light. A fly zipped past my nose. Scott's hand warmed my back, reminding me that I had a place here after all.

A girl from Sunday's show—Clementine—waved and said, "Hey, Scott, I've been looking for you all night!"

Kitty clung to her shoulder and gave a broad wave.

He scoffed. "You weren't looking too hard. You guys met this girl?" He gestured to me with a nod.

"I'm Faun," I said, both to the crowd and to him.

"Who wants to join our threesome?" he asked.

"What?" I asked, my tongue tangling in my mouth.

He said, ruffling my hair, "I'm joking. I've got a lady and a baby."

Clementine laughed. "But she'd do it. Wouldn't you, Faun? I'd do it."

Another test. I nodded and said, "Yeah. Obviously. Anyways, does anyone here want their photo taken?"

Everyone did. I snapped Polaroids of the back-porch crowd in various arrangements, all of them vying for documentation of their presence. Darlene came outside, saying the moon's vibrations were calling to her. Scott danced with her to silent music under the porch lights, swirling on the wood, feeling things I'd never understand. He grabbed a guitar from the living room. They sang "Don't Think Twice, It's All Right" while dipping their legs in the pool. Kitty, Clementine, and I sat cross-legged on the porch, passing a joint back and forth. Clementine drove Kitty nuts name-dropping, but I didn't mind. I watched Scott and Darlene reveal their secret sweetheart selves in the saltwater pool, wondering if rock-star love felt different than regular love. Wondering what regular love felt like, too. I wondered if Floyd had even noticed I was at the party.

Scott drowned the guitar, its wooden body floating into the middle of the pool.

AT ONE, CAL stood by the living room archway and rattled a spoon against a champagne glass, the noise bright and sharp through the hazy air. Floyd wedged himself next to me on the carpet. His shirt was too tight, so I encouraged him to unbutton it. Our knees touched but our hands didn't, both of us nervous in a grade-school way, inching closer but refusing to admit we were. He snuck an arm around me as Cal cleared his throat, quieting the crowd for a speech.

The room settled. Cal wore his denim jacket with the sleeves rolled up, the veins in his hands tensing as he spoke. "Now, I don't want to upstage our friend Howie at his own home, but I had to say—I've had the best bloody time tonight with all of you. Holiday Sun's been on the road for so long that I've forgotten what a good party in a real home can feel like. So I'd like to thank you all for coming tonight, and I hope you're all having as good of a time as I am."

I thought Cal would have had something more profound to say but I joined everyone else in clapping for him with eager hands. As I'd come to find, his speeches were usually short, which made each word valuable. A few girls wolf-whistled and the party returned to its decadent bustle.

Floyd slid closer to me and asked, "Are you a permanent party fixture now?"

"Maybe," I said, glad to be flirted with but not sure how to flirt back. "Who'll take pictures if I'm not?"

"Where are you from?"

"Massachusetts," I muttered, then tried to sound more exciting by adding, "But I've been all over, really."

"Right," he said. He picked up a fireplace poker and rattled the hearth's coals. "Where are you going after this?"

I shrugged. "Anywhere. Home. I don't know."

"There's a twenty-four-hour diner on the way back to my apartment. Well, actually there are about twenty."

"So I'm going there?"

He feigned naivete. "If you *want*."

It was an easy choice. I liked his voice and his face, but his proximity to the band was my main motivation for agreeing. That didn't feel right but ethics didn't seem to matter. I was an almost virgin and equal parts terrified and thrilled.

Across the room, Josie took off her shirt playing strip poker with Cal, Howie, and a couple others. The room erupted in so many hollers you'd think no one there had ever seen a tit before. Men gawked at her, open-mouthed, and Josie climbed onto a table to dance. I snapped a photo of her and her adoring crowd.

With a wave of her hand, Josie captured the room in a magic act. Sweat dripped on her forehead but she smiled anyway. Something told me she'd rather die than have anyone realize how necessary her personal performance was. Every time someone started to look away, she would sway back and forth or flip her hair. Rajiv was in charge of the music, and he cranked it up.

Cal clapped his hands every so often but didn't cheer with the rest of the crowd. He fiddled with his rings and spun one of them around on his middle finger. He stared at Josie with a strange blankness, his nose twitching, his eyes just about to squint.

Josie's attention grab ended and she slipped her shirt back over her torso.

Rajiv approached her and she leaned toward his ear, whispering something with a Mona Lisa smile. So maybe he wasn't an experience to Josie. He was a plaything, which was no better.

He laughed and brushed her waist. Josie leaned close to Rajiv's face and giggled. She put her hand on his shoulder and he brushed her waist again.

Cal stood up.

Floyd said my name, asking what I was looking at, but I didn't answer. The music still blasted, but it was an unwelcome soundtrack as Cal shoved Rajiv so hard he nearly toppled into a crowd of party-goers.

"What the fuck are you doing?" Cal asked him. The emotionless look he'd given Josie was now how he looked at Rajiv.

Josie crossed her arms. "Oh, relax," she said.

Rajiv steadied himself and Cal pushed him again, his fingers crumpling the striped fabric of his T-shirt. "You like touching my girl?"

"Take it easy, man," Rajiv groaned. "I didn't do anything to your girl. Honest."

"I see you touch her. I see how you look at her."

"She's the one touching me."

Cal looked back at Josie, who wouldn't meet his eyes. Rajiv was right, wasn't he? "She's the one touching you?" Cal asked sarcastically, still staring at Josie. I thought he wanted her to look. He wanted her to watch him.

"Man," Rajiv said, backing away, his eyes wide and confused. "I don't know—"

Cal threw his fist at Rajiv and smacked him, his rings digging into his cheek. Blood gushed from Rajiv's face. "You know what I'm talking about," Cal said, examining the damage.

Rajiv grabbed his cheek. "What are you *doing*?"

Cal punched him again, so violently I imagined Rajiv's brain bursting. More blood dripped from where Cal's jewelry had left claw-like gashes. I clenched my jaw. Josie thought Rajiv was a pawn and Cal thought Rajiv was disposable. I looked to Floyd beside me, wondering if Cal would mindlessly smack him the same way if he did something wrong.

We all gawked at the fight like we had at Josie's table dance, but there were no cheers. The room flipped into a stunned silence— the hairs on the back of my neck prickled. I worried if anyone said anything, they'd be gored, too. Instead of interjecting, sixty or so people, including me, all watched as Cal Holiday, the charming British front man of Holiday Sun, smashed his roadie's face in. Those partying in other rooms seemed to hear the noise and found their way over. Nearly every guest was peering around corners or staring openly.

Rajiv got a few smacks back, but Cal was bigger and stronger despite his relative thinness. Josie was the only one to beg for a reprieve of the violence, but apparently her dramatic cries went unnoticed.

Brooke turned up her nose. Howie called, "Don't get blood on the carpet!"

Cal shoved Rajiv too hard and he fell to the ground, pulling Cal down with him by his shirt collar. Cal positioned himself over Rajiv's waist and continued smacking and smashing until it looked like he was molding putty on Rajiv's face.

A few stood up to get a better view.

Rajiv whimpered and so did Josie from her position on the sidelines. After a few more seconds (or was it hours?), Stanley burst forward and yanked Cal off Rajiv.

"This is a lawsuit about to happen, Cal," Stanley said.

Cal stood at last, admiring the carnage. He had a few scratches, but nothing in comparison to the gore we could spot on Rajiv's face and neck in quick flashes through the crowd. Josie's face was sullen.

Stanley called for two men to help Rajiv, then turned to Cal. "You can't do this," he said. "Are you all right?"

"Pretty sure I broke my hand." Cal laughed.

"Poor baby," Josie said, without any sense of falsity. She gestured for Cal to show her his hand and he did. He muttered something and Josie, in her perfect delicate way, peeled off her white top once more and wrapped it around Cal's bleeding hand. Blood soaked the white fabric. Spilled ink on paper. She doted on him and didn't cry. A wannabe Florence Nightingale. Howie began talking to Stanley, gesturing wildly at the carpet. Darlene was asleep. Josie put on someone else's cardigan and buttoned it up.

The room breathed. Chatter arose and right as it did, I took two pictures. They weren't the best—I couldn't exactly curate them— but they still caught Rajiv's bloodied face and Cal standing near him. They looked fake. Now that Rajiv was being hustled out of the room and to the hospital, equilibrium was restored. Everyone could return to their heartless, happy debauchery. I held my photos and watched them develop.

"What are you doing?" Floyd whispered.

I said, unsure, "I like remembering things."

"You," Floyd said. He wiped a slick of sweat off his nose. I thought he looked pretty. For a second, his eyes fluttered to Cal and Josie, then he looked back at me. "You don't have to remember this part."

I didn't have to, but I wanted to. No one else would, content instead with willful blindness. Was it more fun that way? I considered how sour I'd feel if I spent all night mulling over the way Cal's fist smacked against Rajiv's face. I didn't know the full story, really——I was too far away to have caught the conversation in full. I borrowed a lighter from Floyd and toyed with it, watching its flame flicker into existence.

I looked at the pictures, still developing, and lit one on fire. It burned quickly, tiny sparks fluttering into confetti before I threw it into the fireplace. I went to light the other one but couldn't bear it. I tucked it into my pocket.

Floyd asked me to stay but I got up, pressing toward Josie and Cal. They sat on a wicker couch as people greeted them, wishing Cal good luck healing.

Josie's eyes went wide when I approached. She kept a vacant smile as her face tensed. She jolted from her place at Cal's broken right hand and grabbed me, pulling me aside. She pushed up the sleeves of her borrowed cardigan and said, "Can you believe Rajiv did that?"

"What do you mean?" I asked, half whispering. "Cal just—he just started whacking at him. Like it didn't even matter."

Josie shook her head fast. "No," she said, her face flat and un-changing. "Rajiv started it. Didn't you see?"

Word spread that Rajiv had provoked Cal until the whole party agreed, settling into an easy explanation. I supposed I might have seen wrong. Bodies had obscured my vision, and all I'd seen of the fight were quick, blurred glimpses. It had all happened so fast. It was easy to make a mistake about it. Wasn't it? My hesitation to believe it was pushed aside by the fear of winding up like Starla Night-Light, tossed away and replaced with someone more agreeable . . . if that was what had happened to her at all.

Floyd and I got ready to leave, both of us long hungry for greasy food and each other. I said goodbye to Josie and Cal on the way out, taking their photo. Cal held up his bloodied hand, laughing a bit at the stiff, sticky skin. Josie leaned into him, smiling. The flash reflected off her white teeth. I gave Josie the picture to keep.

"Did you have a good night?" Cal asked, his face bent with exaggerated concern.

I nodded. "Absolutely." I glanced quickly at his hand and said, "You oughta get that looked at."

"Thank you, I appreciate that," he said, soft, then turned to Josie. "Listen, Jo, you should bring Faun to our recording session. Faun, we're starting a new album in a couple weeks."

Josie nodded. "Of course I'll bring her."

Floyd rubbed his stomach, gesturing comic starvation. I laughed.

Josie gave me a peck on the cheek and leaned close to my ear. "See you at home." She corrected herself, winking, "See you *tomorrow*."

Three Photos

Howie Guerrero with Brooke on one arm (hand around her waist) and Yvonne on the other (hand on her ass).

Josie proposing a toast. You can't tell what she's saying, but the bubbles in her champagne glass seem to sparkle.

Cal looming over bloody-faced Rajiv, unfocused yet still too clear.

6.

THE PARTY AT HOWIE'S HOUSE DRIFTED TO AN EMPTY CONCLU-
sion, with taxis rolling along the road every few minutes. It was two
hours to sunrise. I was growing sick of the night's cover.

Floyd held my hand as we wandered toward his car. I rubbed my
thumb back and forth on his skin, making sure he wasn't about to
melt away. The hum of crickets echoed down the mansion-laden
roads. Beautifully barren. The sudden quiet was peaceful—there
was no one around us, no one to look at for approval or worry about
appeasing.

Floyd wasn't the band, but at least he wasn't going to start any
fistfights. Yvonne had whispered, giggling to Kitty, when we passed
her on the way to the car. She was spoiled by years of celebrity attention. I'd never had any attention at all, and Floyd's kind words were
blissful. To the other girls, he was a blip on the band's long-running
radar, but I'd known him for as long as I'd known the band. He felt
just as forever as Holiday Sun, even if his last show with them was
apparently over.

Both of us were cold sober now, sludge-brained and sleepy but
clear enough to muse about what color the sky might be when the sun
rose. He drove me to a diner as promised, taking me out of Holmby
Hills and through the city to Koreatown. I mourned the party, but it
had to end for another one to ever start. There was something just
as nice about sitting in the passenger seat of Floyd's rental car. He
popped in a folk-rock tape, and I smiled. He liked what I liked. He
laughed when I laughed. Our maternal grandmothers had the same
name (Lena). The glow of the Qwik-Eats sign greeted us as we approached, its blue neon making the whole street look underwater.

Floyd held my hand as we stepped through the diner doors, my chest contracting with uncertain fears. In the crowd of the party, I could feign confidence—find comfort in knowing there were a hundred other people talking at the same time. There were no such distractions here for Floyd. Just me, a maybe groupie in a late-night diner with a man I barely knew. Me, who'd grown so prudish that my college roommate joked my wash-faded Wrangler's were a chastity belt. Me, whose freshman-year first time with that same college roommate's older brother had ended with a pat on the head and no kiss goodbye. We'd found each other outside a community center sorority event, both complaining of a headache. He lived nearby, took me to his apartment, scared of waking his roommates as he rushed through foreplay and came too quick. His name was Harold. He didn't call me, although I asked him to. I spent two months trying to understand what I did wrong, never coming to the idea that maybe it was nothing at all.

Floyd and I ordered twin hamburgers and waited for the middle-aged waitress to bring them. She did her eye makeup the same way I did mine and had a splatter of carrot soup staining her uniform.

Either Beethoven or Brahms played quietly from the speakers. Our food arrived after ten minutes of Floyd flipping through my pictures and me attempting to explain them. I pointed to one I took of Darlene and Scott soaking in the pool and said, "This one turned out, um, a little too dark. It was a gamble, 'cause they were outside, but I think it worked. The lights from the kitchen kind of reflected onto the pool."

"It looks like a dream."

"Thank you."

The waitress came by and chucked the burgers onto the table, the plates rattling like rolled dice. We dug into our food and, with hamburger meat falling out of my mouth, I asked, "So, what do you do?"

Floyd nodded. "Lights, mostly. I move things. I tune things. I do whatever they ask me to. Assembling the set takes up most of my time but lights are my focus. My goal. That sounds stupid."

"It doesn't."

Floyd squirted ketchup across his plate. "It's not my job because I'm in love with lighting design. It's my job because of the people. I worked in a shipyard for a while. That was way back. I dropped out of high school when I was sixteen, and I started working then. I'm twenty-six now. Um, I've done some driving. But this job is the only one that feels special. Does that make sense? The people you meet . . . shit, Faun, it's the coolest thing in the world."

I realized, watching him ramble in the restaurant lights, that Floyd and I wanted the same thing. We wanted the specialness that only comes from having someone special like you. Roadies built up the sets and groupies built up the band.

Floyd continued, "I don't think I'll do it forever. Or maybe I will. I don't know. All I know is I enjoy it. I'm pretty good at lighting design, or so people tell me. I used to just drift."

My nerves grew worse, my pulse so fast I could feel its vibrations where my neck met my jaw. I was spiraling now. God help me. "So," I asked, "do you, uh, watch TV?"

"Yeah," he said.

"I like *All in the Family*. That episode where Archie thinks he's gonna die of botulism is—it's good."

"Yeah." He looked at me and I sighed at myself.

What to say? I searched my mind for something interesting but only managed "Did you know you're the first Black person I've ever kissed?" Why did I say that? Jesus Christ, where had my brain gone? "That was weird. I didn't say that. I'm sorry. I didn't mean that's *why* I wanted to kiss you." Did that help or hurt? "I mean, it had no effect. On my desire. For you." Desire? Ew.

Floyd laughed, squinting and smiling faintly. "It's okay. I think I understand." He stole a french fry off my plate. "You're strange," he said.

"Am I?" God, I'd ruined everything, hadn't I? I sang a few lines of "People Are Strange" by the Doors, which was meant to alleviate the awkward tension but probably made it worse.

"I mean, you're just so nervous," he said. "It's sweet. You care. I can tell."

"I can tell you care, too," I said quietly.

We finished our food and paid our split check. Floyd paid in change.

"You'll have a bitchin' time here," he said as we headed back to the car. "This city's always fun, even when it's not. Do you want me to drive you home?"

His eyes were so dark and so big. I couldn't think properly. "Don't you live near here?" I asked. "That might be closer."

He brought me back to his apartment. It was cramped and unmaintained, but I excused it since he said he was rarely home to keep it up. It was a sublease, he said, rented month to month in case he went on tour with a band. A bare mattress laid on his floor, covered with a crocheted blanket and two throw pillows. A sneaker sat on his dining table, next to a stiff, empty takeout container. Two pine air fresheners dangled from his doorway like mistletoe. I liked it.

We slept together. I made more nervous jokes, but he laughed at them and played along. He was good to me. He was patient. He was fast, but that was fine. I didn't tell him he was only my second because I didn't want to know what number I was to him. It was better to enjoy it for what it was, without past-and-future history to concern myself with.

Afterward, I worried Yvonne would be disappointed with me because he was just a roadie and not in the band. Then I felt selfish and stupid—stop thinking of people as titles, I told myself, and think of them as people.

I couldn't stop. I traced the floral pattern of Floyd's bare mattress as I narrated the romantic tryst of Groupie and Roadie in my mind.

When he left to shower off the remnants of the night, I sat up, overheating, and glanced around his place. Car horns shrieked outside, the sound dripping in through the open window. Floyd's apartment had no toaster or curtains, but it *did* have a signed print of Willie Nelson pinned to the wall and crate upon crate of first-release records. I didn't care anymore what Yvonne thought. *I* thought Floyd was important.

I wasn't lonely when I was with him. He had been so close to me and would be again soon. I wanted to beg him to return. Was I starved for touch? Was I desperate for adoration? All I knew was Floyd, with his round eyes and chapped lips, had just taken up a heavy spot in my mind.

He came out of the bathroom, his tight curls still wet from the shower, and all I could think to do was do my best Chico impression, saying, "Look-ing goo-ood." Then, embarrassed, "I'm so sorry."

He ignored it. Thank God. "So your first Hollywood house party," he said. "Was it fun?"

"How do you know it was my first?"

Floyd pulled the towel off, exposing his wide shoulders. We were both naked, I never having re-dressed. It was strange but not bad. "Well," he said, tossing me a T-shirt from his laundry pile to put on, "you—you looked at everything like it was a miracle."

He sat beside me on the mattress, crossing his legs and leaning in. I took a Polaroid so close to his face it didn't focus. It didn't turn out right—too dim to capture his features—so I turned on the bedside lamp and tried again. He needed more light.

Then I showered, too, trying to step around the mold growing in the grout. I wasn't quite as disgusted as I should have been. I returned when Floyd was half asleep, so I curled beside him and listened to him breathe. He scooped up my head and kissed me carefully.

"Do you want to see me again?" I asked.

Floyd muttered a yes. "I'll be busy soon because Harry Carling's playing the Bowl. I'm working it."

Harry Carling? Harry Carling, the golden-haired, golden-voiced, guitar-strumming dream? Harry Carling, the folk-pop-crossover king? "Oh, cool," I said, internally flipping out. Was my voice wavering? "Maybe I'll come see the lights." I wondered if Floyd could help me meet Harry Carling. I wondered if he'd like me.

Floyd tucked his arm underneath me and we slept until mid-morning.

THE NEXT FEW times I saw the band were in passing, in savored moments that I milked. They wanted to focus their energy on writing music before their scheduled recording session. Cal flaunted the cast installed on his right hand, all of us glad he had come away relatively unscathed from what gossip decided was a life-or-death match for Josie's honor. I didn't see Rajiv again. Floyd told me, on a semi-date we took to the beach, that Rajiv had been "dishonorably discharged" from any roadie duties. I asked if Floyd would miss him, but he said they were never close. Holiday Sun's crew seemed to cycle faster than others.

Josie had me take modeling shots of her to send out to agencies and began to get a few responses back. We patted cover-up over a pair of little bruises on her upper arm. Josie muttered that she might be anemic, with all these mystery marks. She pressed toward independence but fell into Cal's arms every time he called her up. She got a gig in a minor jeans campaign, photographed bent over backward and caressing her own legs.

She showed me the proofs after the campaign shoot. They were beautiful, and when I pushed the pictures back to her, I chanced to ask, "So, that stuff with Cal and Rajiv was nuts. I know you said it was Rajiv's fault, and I believe you." Did I? "But, um, I just want to make sure—Cal doesn't . . . he doesn't do stuff like that to you, right?"

Josie's jaw dropped. "God, no!" She shook her head back and forth. "Absolutely not."

A week later, she received her $900 check in the mail. We celebrated with a night on the town, where two girls toting fake IDs recognized her as Cal Holiday's glittery girlfriend. I asked how they knew who she was. Josie said she once made it into a photoshoot of his. It was back when they'd first started dating, back when they were crazy in love and starry-eyed.

EVERY PART-TIME SHIFT at Foto Fantasy played out the same way, in menial, animatronic motions. I swore I could feel my soul slipping away with every industrial flash and identical mother-daughter portrait I set up. The customers were cold and unappreciative, but did I do anything worthy of appreciation? Enzio glared at me for twenty hours a week, so I ignored him, drifting into complex daydreams about Holiday Sun. Daydreams where they told me they loved my photos and thought I was worthy of the whole goddamn world.

I wished every hour on the clock away but reminded myself I needed the money. Not that it was much. I stayed poor; $2.30 an hour didn't make a difference when I spent three times that a night. I spent an hour crying after lending Darlene $20 for God knows what. I snatched dollar bills at parties after people finished using them to snort coke. No one seemed to mind, but I felt guilty anyway.

Cal had seen me weeping on a balcony and asked what was wrong. I told him, snot dripping out of my nose, sniffling and sick-looking but unable to care. "Poor girl," he said. "I'll lend you some. I'll give you some. Would that help?"

I nodded, wiping my tears away. He rubbed my shoulders, but no matter how hard he pressed, my tension didn't dissolve.

Cal handed me a stack of bills and I told him he was an angel.

Fall faded into almost winter, and Josie said her white fur coat was finally comfortable in the weather.

Two Photos

Floyd on his bare mattress, looking straight through the camera, looking at me.

A test shot of Josie against a brick wall, posing professionally, practicing all the ways she could look serious and sell jeans.

7.

SCOTT SAID THE DRUMS ON THE SONGS FOR THE NEW ALBUM, *Outfield Flowers,* sounded like shit, so Kent locked himself in his Corvette and refused to leave until he got an apology. Scott, who had rolled in half an hour late with bloodshot eyes and two cigarettes in his mouth, in turn refused to apologize.

Josie's eyes glazed as she rubbed Cal's shoulders, then crossed her legs and sat straight on the stained couch. Cal glowered around the studio, peering over a technician's shoulder to examine the soundboard. Howie slipped on a pair of headphones and asked to hear the drum track. He was always hunched over and focused, wearing dark shades to act as blinders lest he catch a peek of Yvonne's thigh or some other girl's cleavage.

I was put in charge of personal photography after half pleading for the title. Sometimes someone would hand me an SLR, a single-lens reflex camera, but having to wait for your photos was no fun. The Polaroid had immediacy. There was no time to regret a picture or wish it away. I tried to impress the band with my quick camera flashes, wanting them to love me as much as I loved them.

Stanley took charge, demanding the band lay down "Miss Springtime," an acoustic track, in Kent's absence. Stanley was hopped up on power, promoted from tour manager to regular manager after Holiday Sun got into a screaming match with their previous one. I wasn't sure what the fight was about. Everybody gave different answers.

Stanley delegated me to stop taking pictures and placate Kent. I took to my task eagerly. Years of playing with dolls left me with the required skills.

In the parking lot, I knocked on Kent's window, murmuring compliments. He rolled the window down, whining that no one took him seriously. He kicked at the cigarette butts and half-eaten Caramilks littering the carpet of his brand-new car. I lured him back into the studio with the promise I'd call for Kitty to come support him. He punted rocks around the parking lot as I phony-phone-called Kitty's high school secretary and got her out of class. It wasn't a moral act, and I would have admitted as much. But it was necessary. Kent returned to the studio hand in hand with Kitty and got to work recording what was set to be the lead single: "Bee Sting."

Each recording session went the same way. The band would run behind schedule and start to bicker, unburying hatchets and nitpicking personal minutiae. The majority of my time was spent resolving mistakes on behalf of their makers. I rushed to glue together the band's casing before it broke. I was honored and terrified that without my care, Holiday Sun would wilt. I skipped too many Foto Fantasy shifts to spend more time with the band. I'd look up Enzio's number in the phone book and call him an hour before my shifts, coughing into the phone and complaining of stomach pains.

Most days, Josie and I rolled up together in taxis. She'd groan, anticipating all the nothing arguments that would inevitably ensue. She wanted to have *fun*, she said, and watching Holiday Sun bad-mouth each other had grown old.

The music was still thrilling to Josie, but when the band spent an hour debating whether or not to double the backing vocals, all she could do was drift and pick at orange peels, wait for Cal to offer her blow, or pretend she wasn't yawning. At least I had my camera to fall back on.

The band liked my photos, which was a semi-shock. My first-year Photography 120 professor—Minskoff—at Mount Holyoke had tried to convince me most of what I did was "uninspired" and "reductive." He'd entered every class by tossing his wide-brimmed hat onto his desk and frowning. When I fumbled with the lens of the camera the school lent me, he would whack the back of my chair so I fumbled it further. Despite the forty female faces looking up at his podium, he only lectured on Ansel Adams and Karsh and Helmut Newton. Never Diane Arbus. Even new male faces that the class found inspiration in, like Brian Duffy, were too "fruity" and informal for him.

My classmates liked my work. We'd huddle in the darkroom together and coo over the beauty of each other's slowly developing pictures. But it didn't matter—it was Minskoff handing out the grades.

There were no grades here. Just kind words and insistence I was doing a far-out job. With Holiday Sun, I was untouchable. I was proud. After years of reducing myself, I found no fault in a slight swelling of my ego.

In between recording studio adventures and photo studio slumps, I saw Floyd. Our interactions were growing sparser because of Harry Carling's big-time comeback benefit show. I was proud of Floyd and how he'd be helping my favorite singer save the trees or whatever, but I missed spending whole evenings barely clothed and giggling, playing house in his empty apartment. I tried to make him a quiche once, but it baked wrong and was egg soup in the middle. He choked down half a piece, then smiled and asked if I'd like to order pizza and pretend we made it. I'd said yes, asking him to tell me more road stories while we waited. He asked me about my photos sometimes. Not enough, but being asked at all was still novel.

ON HOLIDAY SUN'S last day of recording, the studio overflowed with friends of friends who wanted to catch musical magic in the making. The band gave jolly smiles to their visitors, pretending they hadn't spent the last six weeks uttering half-serious threats to each other and punching walls. Kitty had skipped her last two classes in order to support her boyfriend, which we all thought was charming.

I laughed as she told me she was failing English. "It's just not, like, something I'm passionate about," Kitty said. She pulled a copy of *Animal Farm* from her canvas backpack and flipped through it. "I have to read this. It's not even about anything real," she said. "The characters are thoroughly, like, undeveloped. They're all dumb. They do whatever the pigs tell them."

While the band was busy bantering about songwriting credits, I sat with Kitty on an oversize vinyl chair and tried to help her eke out the meaning of the book. She yawned, but she listened.

Yvonne arrived late and gave her own kind of lecture to Kitty. Kitty sat alert as Yvonne described April 1972, when she lived in the Chelsea Hotel and rubbed shoulders with everyone from Andy Warhol to Marianne Faithfull. Later, she would claim she meant 1970, and insert a fictionalized Jim Morrison into her rock-and-roll fairy tale. Yvonne's stories were so good they didn't need to be real.

Kitty asked, "Were you in New York last year? The guys always talk about how you disappeared."

Yvonne beamed. That was what she wanted, wasn't it? To be talked about when she wasn't there? She dropped the smile and said, "No, I wasn't in New York." She gave no alternate answer, leaving the mystery hanging thickly in the air.

"Why'd you come back to L.A., then?" I asked.

"I missed it," she said simply. "All of it. All of *this*." She paused for a second, then called out to the room, "Who's up for some dancing tonight? I want to barf my guts out."

Half an hour later, we all cheered as Kent drummed violently in the sound booth, his arms flailing like Animal from *The Muppet Show*. Once he finished, we erupted in applause, celebrating the grand finale of the weeks-long recording session.

The songs on this album were richer and broader than the past ones, filled with vibrant metaphors that made little sense when you thought about them too hard. It didn't matter if there was real meaning, because it all *sounded* like anthems and battle cries. Sometimes I'd whisper the lyrics to myself, or sing them like hymns when I was alone, awed that I was one of the lucky few to have heard the songs before their release.

I wasn't talking myself into feeling important. The band was doing that. Every so often, Howie or Cal would tell me they were *so* glad I was there. Didn't they know how indebted I felt to them?

Holiday Sun popped a few bottles of champagne and we girls waited for whatever it was we were waiting for.

We could glean from glances out the studio's hallway windows that night was falling, so we began the grand transition into party mode. Darlene arrived (sans Wendy) in time to sip from a glass of bubbly, saying she had done some recording of her own earlier. She spoke highly of herself, but Josie clued me in that Darlene's endeavors were restricted to Zappa-meets-Ono experimentation.

I secretly gave Darlene the benefit of the doubt. After Minskoff's class, I'd submitted photographs for consideration in a local art show. They were of my college chums in billowy dresses, standing soaked in creeks or swaying in a harsh wind, holding figurines of fairies or bundles of lavender I bought at the grocer's. The collection was meant to be a statement about fairy tales and regression and emotion, but the curator called them "cute" and sent me on my way.

Brooke, Howie's fake girlfriend, arrived at the studio, her white blouse straining at her neck and her upturned nose dotted with fake freckles. Stanley guided her in, linking her arm in his. Howie waved to her as she perched on the arm of a leather couch. Yvonne was sprawled on the same piece of furniture, legs up in a position Scott made a handful of awful jokes about.

Howie paid Brooke minimal attention, paying Yvonne a bit more. His eyes darted from the two of them to other women—any others— at random, as if he were watching an ill-organized tennis match.

Brooke yawned, already tired. An assistant handed her a cup of coffee and she turned it down. She snapped a few photos with Howie, telling him where to put his hands, then left as quickly as she came. Her duty was done for the day.

Stanley hustled in and out of the rented studio space, muttering and checking his watch. I'd never seen him nervous before. Kitty and

I giggled at how the back of his neck had turned bright red because he kept rubbing it. "He said nine fifteen on the dot. Nine fifteen. It's nine forty-five now and he's not here and the limos are booked for ten thirty," Stanley said.

I paid little attention and toasted to Wendy's good health with Darlene and Scott.

Ten minutes later, Stanley returned, doubly frazzled and doubly red, and called to the band, "All right, gentlemen! Ridley Dagg is here! He's waiting for you in room 105A. Let's get a move on and get this interview done."

"What a good mood you're in," Josie said, rolling her eyes before glugging down half a bottle of champagne. Cal slapped her ass on his way out the door.

Stanley nodded. "I'll stay in a good mood if you girls stay quiet. It's not a good look having you lingering about."

Stanley shut the door behind him and Holiday Sun. The session musicians and producers gathered by the mixing board to do serious work. And we, the groupies, yapped about everything and nothing. Like children left alone while the teacher runs a document down the hall, we stood on the furniture and broke every rule we could remember. We liked to sparkle, to glimmer, to gleam. Josie had taken to wearing her most shameless, slinky outfits to the studio. She liked the way Cal couldn't focus when she was in view—how he'd fumble the lyrics after a glance at her low neckline or skintight pants. He was unamused by her wiles, however, asking her once why she needed to wear a bikini top in mid-November like a "regular whore."

"It's the only thing I had clean," she'd said, and they'd both laughed.

Josie took another swig from her bottle of champagne and passed it off to Darlene, who finished it, listening to Yvonne ramble about the "aggressive tendencies of North American men." Josie countered by saying not all men were aggressive, that some were gentle and true-hearted. Yvonne laughed. "Oh, yeah?" Yvonne asked. "Like who?"

Josie considered for a moment. The fact she had to think at all said everything. "Floyd's very nice to Faun."

Yvonne snorted. "Sure, our knockoff Quincy Jones and *Mod Squad* Peggy are really perfect."

"What's that mean?" I asked.

Josie stood up and crossed her arms, pretending to inspect the recording equipment. "If you hate men so much, Yvonne, then why are you here cheerleading with the rest of us?"

Yvonne shrugged, expressionless.

Darlene was bouncing her legs up and down as she sat on the floor, running her hands across the knit rug. She threw up in her mouth and swallowed it back down. I said nothing except to tell her she needed a piece of gum to hide the smell.

"Let's go see the guys," she kept saying, "I wanna talk to Scott. Let's talk to Scott. Faun, come with me."

Josie said, aside, to me, "She goes nuts when she's on speed. It's very unbecoming, in my opinion."

"They're being interviewed for a big magazine or something," I said, grabbing Darlene's twitching arm. "We shouldn't interrupt."

Yvonne laughed a little strangely. "Let's all go see them." She pretended she didn't care about Howie or about the band, but she did. She wouldn't have come back from wherever she'd disappeared to if she didn't.

So, we reapplied our lipstick, downed our drinks, and trickled toward the sound of laughter coming from room 105A. A parade of brightly colored girls pretending they hated attention while seeking it out. I snapped a picture of all the girls walking down the hall, the backs of their heads shimmering under the overhead lights.

Josie took the lead and knocked on the door Stanley had slammed shut behind him. Nobody answered, so she turned the handle and asked, blinking slowly and sweetly as she stepped into a casual lounge, "Oh, please don't say we're interrupting?"

Ridley Dagg nodded to Josie, allowing her to step into the room, while Stanley shot daggers her way. The rest of us, with me last, followed, finding arms of chairs and floor pillows to perch on. Ridley Dagg was a young forty years old, with thinning brown hair and a suit that looked flannel but probably wasn't. A woman beside him, with a flushed face and pigtails, clutched a tape recorder. She pointed to Josie, then to the rest of the groupies, whispering something to Ridley Dagg.

He shook his head, saying, "It's all right, Rhoda."

He had a photographer with him, too, whose denim shirt was stained at the armpits. I tried to catch his eye and point to the Polaroid around my own neck. He had an SLR, its hulking mirrored body shining. A satchel bag sat at his feet. I rushed to open my own stuffed purse. I had about twenty pictures with me, ones I carried because they were too beautiful or dangerous to leave alone. I ran my index finger across their slick white borders and picked them up, holding them to my chest. They were tokens of memories, reminders of glee and gasping. The photographer glanced at me for a moment, then looked away.

Patience.

Ridley Dagg scribbled and asked the band about musical processes and inspirations, insisting he was different from all the other suits at the *Asking* magazine office.

The band gave answers emphasizing their "collaborative roots" and "early influences."

Josie hopped on Cal's lap and held her hand out for Ridley Dagg to shake.

"This is my girlfriend, Josephine Norfolk," Cal said, as Ridley Dagg greeted her. "She's a model." Josie ran her hands through Cal's unwashed hair. He shifted, unsure of whether or not to let her touch him.

I pressed against the wall, counting my breaths.

Josie was too at home in this room she didn't belong in. Even as she stroked Cal's hair, she looked straight at Ridley Dagg. She dipped her finger in someone's drink and slowly brought the digit to her mouth, then sucked off the alcohol, never breaking eye contact.

The formal interview ended and the room erupted in conversation. Everyone kept throwing questions at Ridley Dagg, hoping he'd catch them and respond. He was mega-famous, at least in rock circles. Even the band was falling prey to celebrity. The photographer snapped a few candid shots. They were mostly of the band, but Kitty crept into a solo shot of Kent and bragged about it for ten minutes.

Kitty waved at Ridley Dagg and asked, half yelling across the room, "Have you ever met anyone cool?"

"I've met 'em all." Ridley Dagg laughed, his chest puffing.

"You're so lucky," Josie breathed.

Stanley frowned at his watch, Ridley Dagg's cue to go. He opened the door and started out into the hallway, his assistant and photographer trailing a half step behind him. The girls hollered goodbyes, watching him slide away.

The photographer asked, pointing to Holiday Sun, "A few more shots, misters? A few more shots for the magazine?" The band posed graciously, even cracking a few smiles. I held my breath.

Kitty shook hands with the assistant, wishing her luck in "any future endeavors and efforts." She tapped the assistant's nose.

I shook hands with her, too, considering her a surrogate for Ridley Dagg, who himself was a surrogate for other celebrities. An intense chain of connections I sought a link in. "Really cool to meet you," I said.

"Nice to meet you, too," she said quickly. "My name's Rhoda Weaver. I'm an intern reporter. How do you know the band?"

I shrugged. "I take photographs for them. It's my gig, or whatever."

"Far out," Rhoda said lightly. She looked to Ridley Dagg's photographer, who held his camera more confidently than I held mine. She pointed to him. "You should talk to Nikolai."

"You think I should?" I said, then corrected myself. "Of course I will." Be professional, I told myself. Be serious. Nikolai finished snapping shots of Holiday Sun, tucked his SLR into its bag, and scratched his nose, shifting the frame of his aviators. I tapped him on the shoulder and he turned around. He looked down at my chest.

"Hi, there," I said. "I'm a photographer, too."

"Cute," he said.

"I've got lots of really great photos of Holiday Sun. And of other stuff, too," I said. "Would you want to—would you like to see them? Maybe you could help me find an outlet for them? You could even put them in the magazine."

He looked at me, almost laughing. "Girly," he said, "no offense, but, uh, no one's going to buy groupie shots. No one wants little Polaroids of guys you fucked. Even if they're famous." Rhoda opened her mouth to say something but didn't. She flipped through her notebook and glanced down the hall.

"Oh," I said.

"Groupie shots" were worthless. Anything I had was worthless. That was why Rhoda had been so gentle with me. Why nobody had cared we had waltzed into the interview room. Because we would never do anything worthy of respect. How easy it was to flutter around the band and look pretty and pretend you matter, when no one really cared about you.

I could blather on all day about nothing, but I couldn't think of anything to say that would convince the photographer I had something valuable to share. Sure, the band would let me take my photos and say they were good, but when it came to magazines or real jobs or the real world, my Polaroids were useless. *I* was useless.

I went to the bathroom and cried in the single stall. How empty it was there. How lonesome and lifeless. My cheeks stung with hot tears. I didn't know why I'd even tried. Why I'd spent so much time believing my photos were worth *anything*.

My Polaroid swung at my side. I imagined picking it up and smashing it against the concrete walls. I wanted it to break. I wanted to see all its parts splayed out. Clutching it in my hands, I pulled the strap off my neck and prepared for the act, but I couldn't do it. I brought the camera to my chest and hugged it. A coward till the end.

Well, whatever, I told myself. *Whatever* was a mantra. *Whatever* meant nothing could hurt you, because nothing meant anything.

I whispered it, like a continuous prayer, as I wiped the runny streaks of mascara off my face. My smile was grotesque in the mirror. I'd been full of hope just minutes ago. All those compliments from the band and all that encouragement from Josie and Floyd and Rhoda Weaver— was that all meaningless? I couldn't let one cut bleed me out. A little wound clots easily. Nikolai didn't believe in me? I could prove him wrong. This didn't have to be like it was with Minskoff. With Enzio. With myself, a moment before. No time for tears. Brush it off.

Whatever.

I tracked Nikolai down in the recording studio lobby. He was about to start dialing the pay phone, but I called his name and the dimes in his palm tumbled to the carpeted floor.

"Hey, Nikolai!" I yelped. I felt like my heart was exploding. Still, I pressed on, running on emotional fumes. "Let me show you some photos. They're good. They are. Just take a look."

"Fine," Nikolai said. "Let me call my cab first." He dialed for his ride, then leaned down toward me. "Ten minutes, girly."

"Right," I said. "Here." I revealed my stack of photos and cleared my throat. The first one I showed was tame—a smiling shot of Cal and Scott with their arms around each other.

Nikolai hummed absently. "That's sweet."

Sweet wasn't what I wanted. Sweet was the same as cute. I pulled another Polaroid, this one of Scott flipping off the camera (or me) with one hand and hoisting a naked girl (possibly Clementine, but maybe Darlene, judging from the shape of her ass) over his shoulder.

Nikolai snorted, his eyes widening. "Depraved. That's aces."

Depraved was better. Depraved was interesting. Depraved was what he wanted, so I gave it to him, flipping through endless shots of Holiday Sun and the groupies engaging in acts of consummate degeneracy.

"These are cool. These are good. Maybe I'll give you the number of my guy—my editor."

I could have died right then. I beamed so hard my face went numb. What could take that *maybe* away? What could flip the switch to *yes*? I swallowed hard and tabbed through the photos until I chanced upon the photo of Cal looming over bloodied Rajiv. "What do you think of this one?" I asked. "It's of Cal Holiday and a roadie. He smashed his face right in."

Nikolai grabbed it out of my hands. "No *way*."

I giggled, flipping my hair back just in time to see Stanley's disapproving face emerge from the darkened entry hallway.

Smiling a winning smile was no good, because he snapped his fingers at me. He said, "Faun. Come here. With me. Now."

I snatched the photo out of Nikolai's hands, shoving it back with its pile into my purse. "Another time," I said to him.

Stanley grabbed my elbow, yanking me across the lobby and into the parking lot. His loafers crunched the gravel, the sound like gnashing teeth. The lobby light and streetlamps cast clouds of yellow light across the pavement. November in L.A. was mellow and pale, with lazy gusts blowing out of boredom. Nothing felt mellow now, though. I crossed my arms, twiddling my fingers. Stanley's face was barely visible in the dark. All I could make out were his cheekbones and his shoulders.

"What do you want?" I asked, drawing my words into an immature whine. I might as well have stomped my high-heeled feet.

"You cannot be showing people those photos," he said. "You can't even be taking those photos! And you especially cannot be selling them. Absolutely not." He ran a hand through his hair, catching on a tangle.

I said nothing.

"Faun," he said, a bit softer, "pictures like the one of Cal with Rajiv could devastate the band's career."

"I won't sell them," I said.

"You better not."

I had an idea—the gutsiest one I had ever had. I almost couldn't bear to say it, but I did. "You've gotta give me something in return if I help you out like this."

Stanley stuck his hands on his pudgy hips and turned to the side. "Fine. What?"

I considered.

"Well?"

"I'm thinking," I said. Then, "Let me shoot the album cover."

"I don't decide who does that," he said.

"Then find who does and tell them the band wants me to do it. I want to do it. And I want to get paid." I puffed up. "I know they haven't picked anyone yet." I was bigger than Stanley now, even though he towered above my five-foot frame.

Stanley agreed, his face sunken.

I blew him a kiss, already preparing to deliver my resignation to Enzio. I was leaving my soulless, useless job for a *real* job. A job I deserved. Enzio was hardly scheduling me anymore anyway—he tossed most of the shifts to the dependable high schoolers he also employed.

We returned to the band in the studio, but not before Stanley muttered, "Selfish girl."

Was I selfish? The night was full of self-interest. Why shouldn't it have been? It was foolish to forget other people could feel, but I still did it. I was twenty-three and always a little drunk. I was proud and pretty and beaming. I'd just talked my way into a dream job. I was making people *like* me. If that sprung from vanity, then I wanted to continue.

The line between selfishness and self-improvement was so thin and everything I saw was blurry anyway.

The band had rented out a club to celebrate the completion of *Outfield Flowers*. We barreled into two limos, conversations overflowing with congratulatory bleating. We ended up stuck in traffic, delayed by a car crash or construction—the eternal pauses of Los Angeles.

Josie said I seemed a little blue.

"Me?" I asked. "Oh, no," I said, afraid to tell her the good news in case she accused me of being selfish, too.

"Good," she said. "Wouldn't want to see my favorite girl be sad."

Scott complained about the music the driver was playing, something old by the Mamas & the Papas.

Darlene said, "I think Mama Cass was far out."

"She died choking on a ham sandwich," Scott said. "You know that?"

"She did *not*," Darlene corrected.

We all bickered about it, laughing with every word, until we arrived and laughed some more. No more sadness for me that night. Just joy so intense it began to terrify. Smiles so big they stung, so big they had to be strained for.

I fell into glasses of wine until I was giggling enough to beg someone to kiss me on the lips. Floyd wasn't there but I needed affection. No one indulged me, and I tried to play off my pleas as a joke.

"I love Holiday Sun!" I screamed, loud enough that everyone listened and everyone cheered. "Burning Love" played loud and I spun, dancing with every person I could see under the flashing red lights.

The music crackled in my ears so loudly I couldn't hear the lyrics. I wished the deejay would turn it up. Crank it so high the roof of the building cracked.

The song began to end and the strings turned chaotic, overlapping and looping, growing so raucous I thought they were lifting me off the floor. I was floating right through outer space, past the rockets and the moon and all the stars.

Not floating—hurling.

Two Photos

Scott, eyes bloodshot, fingers blistered, flipping me off in the studio. Darlene's behind him, trying to convince him to smile.

The girls walking down the carpeted studio hall, arms linked, drifting, full of hope.

8.

THE NEXT DAY, I MARCHED INTO FOTO FANTASY AND AN-
nounced I was quitting. Enzio was unsurprised. He didn't even ask
me to return my uniform. I didn't know what to do with it, but Josie
suggested we destroy it as a symbol of my emancipation.

We lit the uniform on fire with twin matches. When its polyester
caught aflame too fast, we threw it into the bathtub and soaked it,
laughing madly, until the whole apartment smelled like burned plastic
and freedom.

MY COLLEGE ROOMMATE, Beulah, wrote to ask if I'd come home for
Christmas. She offered me a place on her plastic-covered couch and
all the gingerbread I could eat. I turned her down. Beulah's house had
the same floor plan as my childhood home.

It was the first holiday season without my mother and if I spent it
in a place identical to the one I'd shared with her, I'd imagine her behind every closed door. I'd spook myself into thinking she was about
to come around the corner toting a plate of honeyed pineapple rings,
moaning about something Aunt Lissy had done, telling me she heard
a rapist was loose in our neighborhood, and accusing me (rightly) of
sneaking out to kiss boys.

RIDLEY DAGG'S INTERVIEW came out in the December issue of *Asking*. I brought it to lunch with Floyd in the park, where we flicked
stray ants off our picnic blanket. Floyd said he was cold, but a winter
temp of sixty-six degrees was warm enough to me that I laid on the
ground and watched the clouds.

"It might rain," Floyd said. He pulled his hand-painted jacket tight, the yellow floral swirls wrinkling with the pressure.

I said if it rained, I'd open my mouth and swallow down the drops.

"Sweet girl," he said. "You talk like you're living in a fantasy."

I *was*. Nights painted with neon lights left me in a perfect, helpless daze. I daydreamed about myself.

Floyd touched my hair and popped a strawberry into his mouth. "Read me the article?" he asked, pointing at the magazine.

I obliged. The article filled an entire page, with a splash photo collage accompanying it. Nikolai's pictures were crystal clear and manufactured. They were great PR and nothing like my Polaroids. My photographs were too personal to fit in a music magazine like this. I studied the details of the 35-millimeter shots. The photos were arranged in a perfectly measured formation, featuring the band either smiling arm in arm or looking attractively pensive, except for two. Near the bottom of the page, there was a photo of Josie and Cal, captioned HOLIDAY WITH HIS STONE FOX GIRLFRIEND, JOSIE. Had they left out her last name on purpose or not bothered to ask for its spelling? Next to it, uncaptioned, was the goofy photo of Kitty and Kent that Kitty so insisted on. It was blurry but clear enough to make out the stars in Kitty's eyes.

I read:

They're older. They're wiser. They're wilder. Holiday Sun are back in their home state this winter after a nationwide tour, and they're glad.

"We've missed the sunshine," Howie Guerrero says to me, glancing out the window. "We work best in California. Lots of sun. Lots of inspiration." Whether he means the beautiful vistas of the San Fernando Valley or the beautiful women surrounding Holiday Sun, he does not say.

Cal Holiday nods, clutching the hand of his breasty girlfriend, and chimes in that, as a native Brit, California is sunnier than seems possible. He's happy to be a new U.S. citizen, he says, although he sometimes misses the U.K.'s food (his favorite meals were chip butties and Sunday roasts). Kent Pearce tries to tell a joke about England but struggles when it comes to the punch line. I can't fault him—he's too boyishly likable to mock.

Holiday Sun still have a youthful charm, even as they navigate their thirties. Their age is not a burden on their career, Scott Sutherland says, but a benefit. "We figured out what we're doing," he says, then turns to Darlene Dear, his wife, and asks if they have a babysitter booked for the evening. Don't be fooled—despite his paternal status, Sutherland's still cool. He and the rest of Holiday Sun are just as popular as ever.

The article continued, touching on their current recording sessions and recounting anecdotes from their last tour. It never said they were *good*, but certainly insisted they were popular, which some people thought was the same thing. People liked them and that was all that mattered. *I* liked them.

The wind was picking up. Maybe it was too cold for a picnic after all. I pestered Floyd to tell me how his work for Harry Carling was going, with the benefit concert only a few weeks away.

Floyd lent me his jacket, talked about light bulbs, and pointed out shapes in the clouds.

"Do you have Christmas plans?" I asked. I had none of my own.

He nodded. "Sort of. Goody Plenty invited me to her Christmas party."

"*Who* is having a party?" I asked.

"Goody Plenty."

"Her *name* is Goody?" I asked. "She couldn't think of anything better?"

"Oh, it's not that bad," he said. "She's this . . . legendary groupie—woman, I mean. Her parties are good. They're hard to get invited to. I don't know why she invited me. They're more of a schmoozing thing than anything else. She didn't invite you?"

"No," I said.

"But Josie can bring you along, right?"

When I said Josie hadn't gotten an invite either, his face fell; he was seemingly embarrassed to have mentioned it at all. He mercifully changed the topic, but my mind was stuck on Josie.

I couldn't believe anyone would turn down the chance to spend time with her, but Goody Plenty wasn't the only one. Josie's mother had told her not to come home for the holidays, because there was no space in the spare rooms at home, which was either a lie or a forced inconvenience. Josie said it didn't bother her, which she said every time there was a rift between her and her mother. I'd hugged Josie enough times while she cried over these slights to know she was lying. I said nothing. I knew things would repair themselves when Josie called with good news or sent an expensive gift.

Josie and I had busied ourselves baking sugar cookies in those weeks before Christmas. We fed them to the band, thinking we could bind the men to us before they set off on their grand adventure of the week: a trip to New York City to perform on *Laugh Riot,* promoting the first single off the upcoming album. *Outfield Flowers* was supposed to be released in April, but trouble organizing how I'd shoot the album cover and arguments over which songs to cut from an overstuffed demo made that date ambitious at best.

After Floyd dropped me off, I found Josie on the couch, her hair up in a ponytail, a silk robe draped over her body. Her fingers were hooked into her blanket, fiddling with its knit pattern, eyes trailing the characters on TV. "Hello, darling," she called from the sofa. "I'm waiting for *Three's Company* to start."

A bottle of wine sat half empty on the coffee table. Cal had only been gone for three days, but it seemed Josie had already forgotten how to exist without him. Fair enough—I didn't know how to exist without Josie. We all needed someone to look at as we moved. Ducklings in a row.

I plopped beside Josie and she dropped her feet onto my lap. The theme song to *Three's Company* began to play and Josie sang along in that breathy way of hers.

I asked, "Do you know a woman named Goody? Floyd said she's having a party on Saturday."

"Oh," Josie groaned, "not goddamn Goody Plenty." She affected a royal British accent when she said her name. "She's *ancient*. Every time I've seen her, she's told me about three hundred times about how she used to go out with Cal."

"We're not doing anything else for Christmas," I said. "Unless you're going home after all."

"This is my home," she said. Josie's face twisted into painful focus. "Goody's been having parties for centuries, and they *are* pretty fun. Rumor has it last month, Bowie himself came and brought pasta salad."

"No way," I said. I *had* to go now.

Josie fiddled with the blanket some more and finally said, "I'll call her and tell her we're going. I am only doing this because you asked and I know Floyd is too chicken to bring you himself."

"Well, he probably can't," I said, defensive. "Isn't this an exclusive thing?"

"Girlfriends are acceptable plus ones."

"I don't think I'm—we haven't discussed—I'm sure he has a good reason."

She added, "You know, since Saturday's Cal's *Laugh Riot* day, we could watch it there." Josie loved to show off, and what a chance this would be. We sometimes watched *Laugh Riot* from the comfort of our living room, eating bowls of ice cream and debating whether or not it was funny. But home was too regular a place from which to watch Holiday Sun perform. We weren't regular, Josie always insisted, and I finally believed it.

Josie made her call to Goody, and I leaned in toward the speaker.

"My love," Josie said into the receiver, her voice dripping with honey, "I simply *have* to come. You know how sad I was to miss the Christmas party last year."

The scratchy voice at the other end said, "I don't recall you being invited last year."

"Cal was invited," Josie said, "so of course that means I was invited, too. Since he's in New York this week, though——"

"Fine, why not?" Goody said. "Wear something red. Don't bring anyone."

Josie hung up and I looked at her, mourning. "She said not to bring anyone," I said.

Josie shrugged. "I didn't hear her say that. Did you?"

I shook my head no, smiling. I called Floyd as soon as Josie left to search through her closet for something festive and flirty. He barely had time to say hello before I started gushing excitement about being invited to Goody's party. How simple it was to fill me with joy—tell me I was wanted, and I'd fall at your feet, lips pressed in a kiss. Belonging swelled me up like breaths into a balloon.

I was so utterly delighted that when Josie asked me to order some Chinese food, I obliged, only realizing afterward I had a measly $20 left in my possession. Enzio told me my last paycheck was coming in the mail, but the U.S. Postal Service didn't feel the same urgency I did. Once I got that check, I'd budget a bit until I didn't need to budget anymore. I was going to shoot Holiday Sun's album cover, after all. I collected my spare bills into a pile, holding them down with a painted rock from a jaunt to Venice Beach. Everything I saved had to go toward my future—toward film.

JOSIE AND I put on Santa hats and skimpy red dresses and hailed a cab to Goody's beach house. Josie downed a whole bottle of wine before we left while I sipped from a single glass, not wanting to drink anything else she'd purchased. She said it was fine that she paid for most of our expenses, but I still felt guilty. I was supposed to be self-sufficient, too. Not a desperate, begging tagalong.

She sucked her fingers and I flipped through my purse, making small talk with the cab driver. I'd packed a handful of favorite photos again. I was proud to tote a portfolio. It made me feel brave. A few minutes from our destination, Josie advised, "Just play along at Goody's."

"What do you mean?" I asked, my heart suddenly pounding.

"Do as I do. As the dreamy Steven Tyler said, 'Walk this way.'" There was something admirable about Josie turning every sentiment into pure drama.

I walked her way indeed, keeping pace with her steady strut up the ornamental garden path that led to Goody's front door. The ocean crashed behind the house, waves sputtering and echoing. Josie begged we take a quick picture, so I turned the Polaroid backward and snapped blindly, hoping we'd both end up in the frame.

Josie knocked on the front door and Goody Plenty opened up, a rosary around her neck and a spatula in her hand. "Who is this?" she asked Josie, pointing to me with the spatula.

"Faun Novak," Josie said. She offered no further explanation, which implied importance.

Goody considered. The smell of good pot and fish casserole wafted out the front door. Goody adjusted her clear-frame glasses and stepped back, letting us into the foyer. We threw our coats onto a pile of other outerwear and Goody disappeared into the house. A delighted shriek rose from the kitchen. We waited. Two white cats brushed past my exposed ankles. "Oh, wow," I said.

"You see why I wanted to get drunk for this?" Josie asked.

"You get drunk for everything," I said.

"Don't say that. That's not funny, Faun." She looked away.

"Jeez, I'm sorry," I said. She kept frowning. I couldn't bear it—she was my dependable one, my true-blue pal, and to upset her was unthinkable. I searched her face for what she wanted me to say and tried, "I love you. You know I do." No one wants their friend to point out that they get too drunk. That sometimes their rakish charm gives way to excessive indulgence. That sometimes, they keep drinking and snorting hours after the party's ended, after they've gone home and the sun's settled back in the sky. I didn't know why I'd said it at all. "Sorry," I said again.

For a second, she stayed stoic. Then the wine got the best of her and she melted. "Yeah, I do."

I'd do anything to placate her without ever thinking about what made her upset. Josie wintered me through every nervous laugh and hesitant move and if I didn't do the same for her, I'd feel selfish.

Josie pointed out a delicately embroidered tapestry. Her eyes reflected the lights in the room. They weren't so much looking as they were gobbling up every sparkle and glint of glitter. Black holes hungry for glamour or light or love. As much as Cal thought she was his, and Josie thought she belonged to rock and roll, I thought she was mine. We were all wrong. She was no one's and everyone's. A true groupie for the people, who'd pretend to like anything as long as you gave her five seconds to privately disapprove first.

Goody returned, taking her time, running her fingers along every surface. Her bare feet sank into the shag carpet. "I've pulled an extra chair to the table. It'll be a tight squeeze," she said, her face funeral somber. "Dinner is in an hour, and if you're starving, there's appetizers in the living room."

"Thank you," I said brightly.

She pointed to my Polaroid camera and said, "No photos."

"You don't understand," I said, "I'm a professional. This is what I do. This is why people invite me places."

"Oh, I understand," Goody said. "But if I recall correctly, you two invited yourselves. No photos, *please*." She smiled, facetious and saccharine.

I took the strap off my neck. Goody plucked the camera out of my hands and put it on the entryway table. She let me keep my purse and the already taken photos inside it, which I fiddled with incessantly. "You want a cigarette?" Goody asked.

I looked to Josie. "Sure," I said, playing along.

"Ask around, I'm sure someone has one." Goody disappeared, her gauzy dress billowing.

Off-key jazz echoed from the living room, which Josie and I stepped into slowly. Josie explained my goal: even though no one knew who I was, everything I did should serve to convince them they did.

I waved to Floyd and brushed my freshly curled hair with my hand. I swerved through the haze, leaving Josie behind. She fluttered beside a young actress, Dana Copeland, whom I recognized as the teen daughter from a first-season sitcom. Josie's mention in Holiday Sun's *Asking* article had raised her status. Recognition flickered in the actress's eyes.

On my way to Floyd, I passed a disco starlet, Louisa Hayes, smoking cigarettes in front of the fireplace and poking at the flames with the heel of her platform shoe. A third cat bounced off a television set, hopping through one of Louisa Hayes's smoke rings like a lion through a circus hoop.

Three gilded bowls sat unassumingly on the coffee table, filled with heaping mounds I quickly realized were cocaine. Finger paintings decorated the walls and thick candles draped in macramé (a definite fire hazard) lit up the baseboards in thin, dancing rows. Clusters of recognizable faces chattered in swirling quarters, all impressed with themselves and ignoring the sweaty, perfumed couple engaged in almost full intercourse on a beanbag chair in the corner.

Floyd pulled me close as I leaned on the edge of his armchair. The bearded man beside him sang the praises of two-girl blow jobs and spat sunflower seeds into a glass of brandy.

"Have you ever gotten one of those?" I asked Floyd, teasing.

He laughed. "Sounds a bit too wild and crazy. I'm not into that shit anymore."

"Wait," I said, my face suddenly hot, "I'm not wild and crazy?"

Floyd didn't answer, just shrugged and laughed, like he was trying to convince me to laugh, too.

The man beside Floyd dropped his bag of seeds and when I leaned down to pick it up for him, he pinched my ass.

"Don't touch me like that," I said, practically spitting. "Who *are* you, anyways?"

"Faun," Floyd said. He said nothing to the man, which said enough.

Across the small room, Josie snapped, "Faun! Don't be silly! You know Clifford Agnew."

The name rang a bell, but the distractions of the room left me blank. I searched my brain for any remembrances of liner notes he might have appeared in. *Walk Josie's way. Put up with it.* "Right! Of course," I said, gently rubbing his knee. "You're a . . ." I struggled to remember again. "A producer. You're a legend."

"Indeed. And, for a very, very brief period of time, I was in the Manson Family. They had weird vibes, babe, let me tell you that. Pussy was good, though." He rambled more about his late-sixties misadventures as Floyd twirled my hair into his fingers. I sat up straight, resisting my usual slouch, and waited for my turn to talk.

"Oh, come *on*." There was Stanley in the kitchen archway, squinting at me with the same expression you'd use to search for bedbugs. "Here to blind everyone with more Polaroid flashes?" He was growing sick of me, long over my novelty. He was too professional—too put-together and put-upon—to tolerate someone snapping photos left and right of things he hated to have his clients photographed doing. Sickened, too, by my stunt at the recording studio.

All I said, cool and light, was "Hi, Stanley."

"Good grief," he muttered and returned to the kitchen, his KISS THE COOK apron flapping against his thighs. I itched to take pictures but understood why I couldn't.

I alternated between kissing Floyd and gasping at gossip as we waited for dinner. Someone said they heard Clementine had shown up topless to a Led Zeppelin concert and stormed away when Jimmy Page refused to look her way even though she'd painted his initials above her nipples. Someone told the same story, but about Yvonne at an Allman Brothers show. I ignored the similarities, letting myself marvel at false, wondrous scandal.

"Speaking of Yvonne," Floyd asked as I shoved my face into his neck, "does anyone know where she ran off to last year?"

Goody, drifting through the room, offered, "She went home to Seattle. She has VD."

"No, she *had* VD. They can cure gonorrhea," Josie corrected, revealing too much.

"I knew it was gonorrhea!" Clifford cried.

Josie clapped her hand across her mouth, then laughed along with the room.

Floyd chuckled but I didn't think he meant it. "Must have been . . . painful." All he could contribute was neutrality, fearful of leaning any wrong way and therefore leaning nowhere at all. A pendulum that couldn't swing.

This cycle continued until we grew bored and decided to create some gossip-worthy moments of our own. The bowls of cocaine were put to good use, and I, in favor of feeling in place, was soon vacuuming it up my nose. Oh, if my mother could see me now, I thought. My brain swirled with ideas that all seemed very good and very fun, but my skin and face turned numb.

"Ooh, Faun likes it," Josie teased.

"Huh?" I asked, unbearably high and rubbing my palms against Floyd's legs to the rhythm playing from the stereo.

Dana Copeland fell against the tinseled fake tree, nearly knocking it over and spooking two of the three cats. She laid on the floor, laughed, then asked, "Who's got Quaaludes?"

I JUMPED WHEN Goody rang a miniature gong to signal dinnertime. We hustled into the dining room, gathering around the oversize table, and waited for Goody to allow us to begin the feast. None of her dishes matched. Even the pieces of silverware had different patterns embossed on them. The table was round, covered in flower petals and bits of hay. A magpie nest. Incense burned, letting off signals I tried to read.

My seat was a stool, a few inches lower than all the other chairs, wedged into a corner beside Josie. "I had to make do," Goody said. "There's only so much space."

"I'm just happy to be here," I said. I meant it.

Dinner was served to the confused delight of the room. Slices of this-or-that in Jell-O and ambrosia salad landed on our plates. Goody passed around bowls of penny candy and Tootsie Rolls. No turkey. No potatoes. Only sugar and fluff. We were all so high that no one was hungry. Josie poured me a full glass of red wine. Goody gave a small prayer of thanks to "the sun and the earth," then we dug in, unwrapping our sweets and poking at our Jell-O.

Dana Copeland hummed "Joy to the World" as the woman beside her licked nearly all the gloss off her own lips. Floyd lit a cigarette and tapped the ash quickly into Clifford Agnew's glass, winking at me as he did it. He was too far away, and the drugs put me on edge. I tried to reach for his hand but there were about a thousand silver knickknacks blocking my path. Oh, well, I thought, and reached for Josie's hand instead. She held it under the table and popped a petit four into her mouth.

"Stuart," Goody said, catching the attention of the oldest man at the table, whose snowflake-patterned sweater was pilled and stretched, "when's the movie coming out, and *what* should I wear when you bring me to the premiere?"

Stuart laughed and gave a nonanswer. He expressed discontent toward some actress named Janine and the table erupted in groans. I groaned along, not knowing who Janine was, but feeling that she couldn't be as awful as he was making her out to be. Stuart didn't seem like a blast of a guy either.

Goody changed the conversation to something I understood. She asked, "So, Josie, you and Cal have been together for how long?"

"Oh, ages," Josie said. "It's really great. He's really great."

"I remember when he and I had our tryst. He was always getting into bar fights," Goody said, light nostalgia trickling out, "but that's over for him now? He's settled down?" She was withholding something, but I couldn't figure out what. Women sometimes speak without talking. She squinted, suddenly appearing half worried, before dropping into pleasantry again.

"Of course he has," Josie said. "He's wonderful and everything is going absolutely wonderfully." Josie was stewing beneath her smile, something strange brewing below her soft insistence life was peachy. Her expression confused me, too.

"I think Josie's his girl of girls," Floyd suggested kindly. "Maybe a wedding's coming up?"

"Oh," Josie said, blushing, "I love him. I do. But I don't know if we'll be together forever. That's a long time, and we've both got a lot of years left, you know?"

"Mmhm," Goody said.

"She wants to keep her options open," said the woman, laughing, who had been having sex in the corner. "Didn't you say earlier, Josie, that you'd kill to spend a night with Chevy Chase?"

Goody sighed. "You young girls are something else. One man's never enough for you."

Josie poked her fork through the air and said, "No, it's not that. Not at all. I love Cal very much and I'm happy with him. But if I could—in a perfect world—I'd shrink him down. I'd shrink all the boys I want down and carry them around on a little string. I'd keep them in my pocket. I'd collect them." She laughed, then poured herself more wine.

I'd been raised to fend off excess, to take only what I sorely needed, but Josie didn't, and she was thriving. She wanted everything. Now I did, too.

Josie kept laughing, but when she stopped, the room was still waiting on her to speak more.

I tried to help. "Cal and the whole band are on *Laugh Riot* tonight. We could all watch it."

There was a murmured agreement and Josie squeezed my hand.

"How do you know Holiday Sun? What do you do?" Goody asked, pointing at me.

"I'm a photographer," I said automatically, annoyed that she'd forgotten. "I'm shooting their new album cover. It's coming out next year. It'll be called . . ." I forgot.

Josie helped. "*Outfield Flowers*. What a nice title, right?"

Stanley concealed a laugh across the table.

Floyd shot a look his way. "I'm sure Faun will shoot a killer cover."

"Thanks," I said, picking at my food.

"You're brand-new," Goody said. "I can tell."

That hurt. What would it take for me to stop feeling pitiful? Success. That had to be it. Professional success. Existing independently without needing two people to vouch for me before I could step through a door. The album cover idea was good, but it still hung unrealized in the air. It still had the potential to be bad.

Clifford toasted to the holiday season. We sang "Jingle Bells," then "Dreidel, Dreidel, Dreidel," then "Hare Krishna."

DINNER FINISHED AND the party returned to the living room in time to catch the start of *Laugh Riot*. Josie sat cross-legged inches from the TV screen, suckling a bottle of wine. Floyd whispered interesting things to me about the partygoers coming in and out of the house like shuffling cards. Louisa Hayes disappeared and now in her place was a beady-eyed punker who kept lighting his eyebrows aflame.

"You're gorgeous," Floyd said, his words backed by a comedian screaming something about hamburgers on the television.

"What?" I asked, then said, "Thank you. You, too." My feelings for him had stiffened, suddenly. His forced neutrality dug at me.

Finally, the long-awaited moment arrived. Everyone turned their full attention to the television screen. The host of the show stood in the corner of the screen, glanced at the cue cards, and said, "Ladies and gentlemen, Holiday Sun!"

The studio audience applauded and the camera shifted to the band. Seeing them on TV was having them within me. These men I knew—these *friends* of mine—were being broadcast to the entire nation and I was grateful and grinning and kept forgetting they were real. They looked so tiny but were so big. I wanted to reach into the screen and pluck them out—keep them on a chain like the one Josie spoke of.

How special it was to see your friends sing to you from three thousand miles away.

The band started the set with "Sheila." They hated that song, but it made them millions so they played it whenever they were asked. Then, they played what was set to be the lead single off the new album: "Bee Sting." They were dressed modestly, Kent in a beat-up graphic T-shirt and the other members in button-ups of various patterns. Cal's shirt was half undone, and he played with the other buttons as he wailed out the chorus:

She's high along the highway, screaming my name
These girls with their earthly pleasures—all the same
Little bright nightbird, up in the sky
Backwards and forwards, asking me why
I tell her everything
Baby, she's a bee sting.

Scott swerved to the front of the stage for a guitar solo, the studio lights flashing in pinks and purples across his skin. I watched with my mouth half open, wholly entranced in the ecstasy of the entertainment. Josie's eyes never left the screen.

The song ended, and the studio audience began to applaud. The ending of the *Laugh Riot* musical act was always the same—for the ten seconds after every performance, the artist filled time while the cameras captured the pre-commercial applause. Often they'd bow, or gesture to their bandmates and clap for themselves. Howie leaned into his backup microphone and called, "*Outfield Flowers* comes out April seventy-eight!"

The crowd roared. I'm sure the broadcast was about to cut to a Charmin or Alka-Seltzer commercial, but Cal leaned into his microphone, too, affecting the same casual pose as Howie. He waved down the crowd, hushing their clamor to say, "Quiet down. I've got an announcement, too—I'm getting married in May! Thank you, I love you all! Josie, at home—I love you most!"

The crowd *screamed*. We all did, too. The broadcast cut to a commercial. Every face in Goody's living room turned to Josie. Her face, blue in the light of the television set, stayed transfixed on something invisible.

She didn't smile.

She didn't cry. She just turned and listened to the room.

The commercials played on. *Don't squeeze the Charmin*.

"So much for collecting them all, huh?" Goody said, cigarette smoke spilling out of her mouth.

Josie stood up from her floor seat, brushed off her dress, and said, quite carefully, "I do hope you can all make it to the wedding."

We all clapped, hands damp. After the applause died and the sketches resumed, Josie pulled me into the dining room. We leaned against the table and pretended to look for something in her purse while she whispered nonsense. I couldn't process the news—Josie never seemed like she'd settle down. Especially not with Cal—sure, he was famous, rich, and bold, but my mind flew back to the bruises on Josie's face and sides. No—they were accidental, not from him. No way. I wouldn't let them be. I pictured her with a wedding ring on and almost laughed. I stared at her and asked, "Why didn't you tell me? Do you have a ring?"

Josie perched at the head of the table, her back facing the rest of the party. "You'll come to the wedding, won't you?" she whispered.

"Of course I will," I said, still bewildered. "Of course."

Josie pulled a mirrored compact out of her bag and flipped it open. "Guess I should call my mother and invite her," she said.

"She doesn't know yet?"

Josie laughed so loudly a few people turned to look. "You know, *I* didn't know until about five minutes ago." A couple seconds later, she added, "It's so exciting, isn't it?"

We toasted three times to the upcoming wedding, each toast turning Josie drunker. I was drunk, too. We all were. Always. We were partying, weren't we?

That night drained Josie like no other. Around one, she asked Goody if she could take a quick snooze upstairs. Goody pointed her to the bedroom, reminding her Cal and Goody had slept on that very bed together. She asked Josie if she wanted guidance, but didn't specify if she meant up the stairs or something else. Josie ascended the stairs alone and slept. I checked on her after spending half an hour worrying. I hopped over a pile of worn lingerie and mothballs, stepping into the dark bedroom. Her thin frame was a snoring heap on the bed, her fingers clasped around a fuzzy throw pillow.

"Hey, Josie," I said, inching closer. I sat on the mattress and touched her bare arm. "Are you sleeping?" Dumb question.

She rolled over and opened her eyes. "Are we leaving?"

"Do you want to?"

In one swift motion, she rolled back into her old position and cradled the pillow under her head. "It's all right," she said, her voice muffled. "Just wake me up when you want to go."

"Are you sure?" I asked. "Are you really-truly-absolutely sure?"

"I'm not going to spoil the party," she said. "Go have fun." A good-time girl through and through, Josie would never dare kill the buzz.

I went back downstairs. Famous faces entered the house in droves, some of them offering gifts to Goody as their gracious Christmas host. Whispers ran amok about who would be popping in next. My hands itched for my camera. There was so much to see.

Everyone in the room became distracted and perky, even Goody. Screw it. I dashed to the hallway and retrieved my Polaroid. I snapped a handful of quick photos of easy poses—things that were guaranteed to look good. Stuart holding a candle like a Christmastime ghost. Dana Copeland splayed upside down over the arm of a wicker chair, her curls spilling like water onto the ground. Clifford Agnew sipping a drink as two women look at him, rapt.

"Hey, no!" Goody said, dead serious. I stared at her until she broke her severity. "Bad, bad, bad girl." She laughed, her cheeks round and red.

Stanley loosened his tie, joining in the festivities, and Floyd pointed out how when he drank, he sweat enough to soak his hair. I asked Floyd again when I'd get to meet Harry Carling. "Soon," he said, hesitant. "I know he's your favorite singer. But be patient." The concert was soon, but not soon enough.

"Patient," I said, my lips brushing his ear, then kissing his neck. "Why do I always have to be *patient*?"

"You're drunk." He laughed.

"Yeah." I sighed brightly.

Floyd left me on the chair while he offered a greeting to the Goodnews Brothers, who had rolled in while I was upstairs with Josie. I squinted at broad-armed Floyd with them, my face in my hands, and was lonely again. I made funny comments to an imaginary friend. I had done this since I was small. My mother once said before I spoke to her, it seemed like I was talking to myself. She would hear me babble alone in my crib, but as soon as she'd open the door, I'd be silent again.

Someone said Darlene might be dropping by. I prayed it was true. A familiar face was all I wanted. I leaned over and tapped Dana Copeland's shoulder, starved for attention. She turned and I tried to introduce myself.

"I hear you're Holiday Sun's photographer? For their album?" she asked, head tilted like a cocker spaniel's.

"Yes," I said. "I'm their personal photographer, too. I'm . . . essential." She and her friend seemed to be impressed but returned their attention to the Goodnews Brothers. "Well," I said, "do you want to see some photos? I have gobs of 'em."

"Yeah, sure," Dana said.

I got to work, peeling open my purse and picking out the perfect pictures to display. At first, only Dana and her friend looked, but slowly I garnered the attention of half the party. People leaned over each other's shoulders to see the pictures, and I held them proudly, tilting them so everyone could see.

Clifford grabbed a photo out of my hand and asked, "Who's this?"

"That's Kitty. Kitty Krause," I said.

"Shit, I've fucked her!" Clifford shouted, much to the delight of the room.

"You have *not*," I said, laughing and hoping I was right. "Kitty Krause is Kent Pearce's girl now anyways." I didn't add that she was sixteen. I didn't feel like I was allowed to.

Paul Goodnews turned at the sound of Kitty's name.

Dana nodded quickly and said, "She is *such* a whore."

I couldn't stand them talking about Kitty that way. Gossip was only good when you didn't care for the people it was about, so I shoved my hand into my purse and fished out more photos to shift the conversation. The Polaroids transferred from hand to hand. They made their way back to me, and my crowd waited for something more. Floyd came through the huddle and sat on the armrest of my chair.

I passed around more photos than I could count. All the money I'd spent on film was worth it. The room ogled beautiful shots of Josie in silks and Yvonne in pearls and the band—of course—in suits and leather and bare skin.

"Oh, Faun," someone cooed, "you are so cool."

Floyd corrected them. "She's talented. Isn't she?"

Everyone mumbled, agreeing, encouraging, smiling.

Everything was so perfect, so ethereal and exquisite. I woke Josie up to tell her everyone thought I was fabulous. She said congratulations, then threw up out the taxi window on our way home. I patted her shoulder, smiling at my own reflection in the other window's glass.

One Photo

Josie and me outside Goody Plenty's worn-out Malibu beach house. Josie's face is clear, in focus, and mine is barely in the frame.

9.

ON NEW YEAR'S DAY, I TOOK SAMPLE PHOTOS FOR JOSIE, TEST shots for a "titillatingly secret" casting call. She wore a black slip, posing against a sheet pinned to the wall after debating for an hour whether to wear her engagement ring in the pictures. The ring was a chunky gold thing, with a cluster of diamonds surrounding a massive opal. I thought it looked like a gilded tumor, but called it lovely when Cal slipped it onto Josie's hand at the first get-together following the band's return from New York. We decided to take half the photos with the ring and the other without. When Josie picked her favorites, she only selected ones with her fingers bare.

Josie started lamenting the jewelry again as I dashed to the ringing telephone.

I picked up the call, telling Josie to stay in the good lighting we'd found. "Josie and Faun," I said into the receiver, hoping to sound busy enough to incite brevity.

"Oh, God, Faun," Kitty groaned across the line, "I need you and Josie to come pick me up right now."

"Why? From where?" I asked.

"From *home*," she said. "My mom saw the picture of me with Kent in *Asking* and is going ape. Please, can you come get me? Please? Please, will you?"

Josie called over, "Who is it?"

I moved the receiver from my mouth. "Kitty. She wants us to pick her up."

"She lives in Inglewood. Too far. Tell her to call a cab!"

Kitty, having heard Josie, yelled in my ear, "It is *not* far! My mom won't give me my wallet so I don't have any cash for a cab. I'm only, like, half an hour from Fairfax. I've got my things packed. Just come get me and bring me to Kent's place, *please*."

What else was there to do? Wasn't taking care of Kitty taking care of the band? I agreed, telling Josie we'd have to delay the rest of the shoot. She pulled a pair of jeans over her legs and tucked the slip into them. I tossed her the car keys and we left for our rescue mission.

JOSIE SORT OF knew Kitty's address, so after looping the block a few times until she was positive, she parked at the end of the driveway and honked. Josie glanced at herself in the mirror, adjusting a silk scarf around her head. I turned up the radio because ABBA was playing and they were Kitty's favorite. Josie slammed the horn three more times.

The front door of the beige bungalow flew open and Kitty ran out, clutching two leopard-print suitcases. She made it halfway down the lawn before her mother, who looked like Kitty's gray-haired, exhausted twin, propped herself up in the doorway. "Katherine, you come back here right now!" Kitty's mother said, fiery.

Kitty continued her hustle, ignoring her mother. She pulled open the trunk of Josie's two-door Gremlin and threw her bags inside. I opened the passenger door. Josie muttered an ill-timed hello as Kitty turned to face her mother.

"I am *never* coming back!" Kitty said. "You don't understand anything at all!"

Her mother threw up her hands. "I should have known! I should have known you were whoring yourself out like this! And now, what? You're leaving your family to go be some rock star's plaything?"

"We are in *love*," Kitty muttered. She puffed up her chest and flipped her mother off. She ducked down, picked up a rock from the street, and chucked it toward her mother, who barely dodged it.

"Katherine, cut the crap!" her mother yelled. "You're a little girl!"

Kitty screamed at her tiny mother, her freckled face reddening like she was about to explode, "Fuck you!"

She dove inside the car, wiggling over my lap in the front to get to the back seat. I shut the door as Kitty made faces at her mother through the window. Kitty instructed Josie to drive. Kitty burst into angry tears, and we let her cry. I turned up "Honey, Honey." She sang along, blubbering.

This was what Kitty wanted, so it must have been right.

"Well," I said, "Happy New Year. Which way to Kent's place?"

Kitty gave shoddy directions to Josie, who struggled to drive as Kitty leaned over her shoulder, admiring the engagement ring on her finger. We dropped Kitty off at Kent's apartment, making sure she got in the door. I thought about her mother's desperate face and the way she had screamed. I didn't know whom to pity.

Josie insisted Kitty would be happier with Kent. She said Kent would take care of Kitty better than her mother ever did. I believed her. I had to try to see the best in Kent—in everyone. Life would flicker out into grimness unless I forced light into it.

THE NEXT DAY, Josie called Cal, telling him the legendary tale of Kitty's violent coming-of-age moment while I tried to prepare for Harry Carling's benefit concert. When I slid past Josie on the way to the bathroom, searching for a curling iron I could have sworn I'd bought, I could hear Cal laughing through the phone.

I was shaking so hard all morning that I could barely do my makeup. I wasn't starstruck by Holiday Sun anymore, but Harry Carling remained such a faraway fantasy that the prospect of seeing him made me feel like I was about to die.

By the time I got my hair how I wanted—not flawless, but as close as I could get with my nervous hands—Josie was done with the telephone. Floyd was due to pick me up in fifteen minutes and I still didn't know what to wear or what to do or what to think or how to breathe.

"My darling," Josie said gently, touching my arm, "relax. You'll have a good time."

"I think I'm gonna puke," I said.

She shook her head and pulled me down onto the worn-out futon, playing with my hair, and put on a serious face. "Listen," Josie said, "I know how crazy you are for Harry. You've always been crazy for him. So if you have the chance to get with him, do it. You'll regret it forever if you don't."

"What about Floyd?"

"Floyd wouldn't care," she insisted. "You're not his goddamn girlfriend. Plus he's *Floyd*. You're not . . ." She trailed off, then laughed. "Engaged."

Was she right? Floyd was sweet, but oh, how I'd wanted Harry forever. I practiced my greeting to him in my mind and imagined pressing my lips to his. Josie picked my clothes for me, like a mother on the first day of school. She spiffed me up in time for us to hear Floyd honk from the street. Josie wished me luck as I headed out on my first L.A. adventure without her.

I lasted all the way until Franklin Ave, when I got too jittery to function again.

"Relax," Floyd said, fiddling with the rental car's radio. "What are you nervous about?"

"I'm just a big fan. I don't want it to be bad. I don't want to, I don't know, fall on my face in front of him."

"You won't." He laughed, then sarcastically teased, "You got a little crush?"

"No!" I said, nearly swallowing my gum. I laughed, too high pitched. "Don't be—don't be—oh, get real." I calmed down enough to reapply my lipstick. *Don't twitch.*

"I've got a backstage pass for you," Floyd said. "It's in the glove compartment."

I started shaking again. Floyd didn't notice. He didn't mention it, at least.

I wore the pass like a gold medal from the moment I stepped out of Floyd's car until I found myself in the wings of the theater. Floyd said Harry was too busy to meet anyone before the show, but that after it ended he'd make his backstage rounds. Floyd set off to test lights.

I wanted the concert to start so I could hear Harry sing, and wanted it to end, too, so I could hear him talk. I snapped photos of assistants and directors, who were all happy to see me as soon as they saw my backstage pass.

Rattling anticipation shuddered through me as the house lights of the Hollywood Bowl dimmed. Radio chatter buzzed and suddenly Harry Carling stepped onstage.

The crowd was cheering too loudly for him to start singing. He seemed desperate to keep his composure. A smile played at his lips when he said, "Thank you all for coming," but he tried to wipe it away. He attempted to be serious, but I *saw* how happy the crowd made him. The Bowl became enveloped in earthy witchcraft with the slow, deep roll of Harry's voice. He was better in person than on his albums. He was so real and so good. Cal was smooth-moved and oil-slick, with a professional grin. But Harry was raggedy, spur-of-the-moment, and sparking. Holiday Sun had started to shift away from authenticity, too assured in their determined image, but Harry didn't try to be anything. He just *was*.

The way his white button-down poked out from below his cable-knit sweater—that twinge of something hidden, of layers being ready to be peeled back—was identical to the outfit on the triumphant revelation that was his '69 album *Saints in Rainboots*. That record was his breakthrough, when he'd stopped dealing in nothing but anti-war ditties and standards like "500 Miles" and started singing in his own voice.

My mother hadn't minded him until then, but when she found out *Saints in Rainboots* featured titles like "Whiskey Hours" and "Puritan Orgy," she announced that he had been corrupted. I scrounged all the dimes I could, laying them on the record store counter in the hopes they'd add up to enough to buy the double LP. I clutched the plastic-wrapped album to my chest the whole walk home, tracing the contours of Harry's photographed face. I slipped the records themselves into blank sleeves and stuck double-sided tape to the back of the original sleeve. I pinned it above my freshly made bed.

I'd look at it every so often, imagining what would happen if one day we had a chance meeting. In an expensive coffee shop, where my photos hung for sale on the wall, he might be dressed down and humble, seeking good art. He'd see me and say, "Hey, honey," and I'd melt into the golden, transparent mess he'd called me. At the beach, he might be picking seashells or strumming guitar and see me in my bikini (which I would have felt beautiful in) and ask where I was from. At a concert, like this one here—I imagined him seeing me backstage and telling the whole crowd I was the most gorgeous girl he'd ever set eyes on. I imagined him coming up to me, begging to know my name.

One late night, in a moment of true adolescent infatuation, I'd stood on my pillows and pressed my lips to the picture. Back then he'd tasted like paper and ink—would he taste the same now?

These childish fantasies were easy to fall back into. I spent the next hour so busy imagining that I barely realized when the concert ended.

A final cheer rose from the audience. A crashing wave. Harry didn't let it bowl him over, instead raising his guitar above his head and basking. I cheered, too, pressing my hands together like praying. With a final bow to his adoring audience, Harry started toward the wings.

He came my way but before any of my fantasies could come true, he was whisked away by his entourage. I fiddled with my skirt and turned to the tour manager, who was also heading to Harry.

I couldn't keep him inside my head. I needed to prove he was real. I spotted Floyd and waved, gesturing desperately toward Harry, who moved farther away every second I waited. Floyd, still mostly engrossed in coiling up a cable, pointed toward Harry with his free hand, inviting me to approach him.

Any hint of hesitation vanished.

I dashed toward Harry's group, my ankles buckling. The stage lights were off now. Harry and his flawless friends stood laughing in the darkness. Every face was hazy but his.

I affected Josie's sweetness and Yvonne's confidence as I pressed my way between two women, solidifying my space in the huddle.

"Hello," Harry said, his voice careful. He scanned me, face to feet. "Who are you?"

"Faun," I said.

Someone whispered to Harry and he nodded, understanding. "Ah, you're with Floyd," he said.

I said, "Yes. I'm his friend," punctuating the last word. "I'm also a photographer. I'm shooting the cover for Holiday Sun's new album."

Harry's entourage began dissipating, noting how much money was raised and how well Harry had commanded the crowd. Roadies with wet foreheads peeled up the tape marking the stage floor. A member of the backup band snapped a guitar string and cursed.

Harry stepped closer to me, bidding the clipboard-toting assistant at his side a temporary goodbye. "Are you any good?" he asked. When I nodded, he said, "How about you take some photos of me?"

I said yes.

My Polaroid nearly fell to the floor as I followed him. I couldn't hear him over the pounding in my ears, so I told him he was "far out," which he seemed to like.

Invited to take a seat, I propped myself up on his dressing room table and wished he'd kiss me. A garland pinned to the wall swayed. He shut the door and glanced at his reflection in the mirror.

I touched my hair, nervous it was too flat, and said, "You're so cool."

He grinned, leaning against the same counter I sat on. He looked so serene, so inviting, and I couldn't help but brush my hand across his shoulder. He moved a careful inch closer.

Harry began to change out of his sweat-soaked sweater and shirt. His skin glistened, gold-tanned and supple. If it sounds like I'm gushing, *good*—he was worth gushing over. He pulled on a new white button-down and started rolling a joint. I watched, eyes darting, as he licked the paper with his pink tongue. The end of the joint flickered in firefly bursts as he lit it.

My breaths came fast and shallow as I stood, pulling my body toward his.

"Open your mouth," he whispered.

I did. He sucked on the joint, inhaling deeply, then planted his open lips onto mine. He exhaled into my lungs, and I struggled not to cough—both from the smoke and the shock. It wasn't a kiss, but it was close enough. He didn't taste papery. Harry's mouth was wet, stinging with cognac and cannabis.

"Wow," I said, despite myself.

We smoked, sitting cross-legged, as I floated five inches above the floor. I dared to touch his knee and he let me. I told him all about my exciting, famous friends and he listened. Eventually, after my brain was jumbled enough so I could be brave, I asked, "Do you have a girlfriend?"

He cocked his head. "Do you have a boyfriend?"

I rolled my eyes and leaned closer to his damp face. "Does it matter?"

"Does it?" he said.

"Why won't you answer my questions?" I asked, laughing.

"Why won't you tell me what you want?" he countered, leaning back on his hands.

I stood up, blinking hazily from the pot, and said, "You *know* what I want. Don't you?"

"You want to take photos of me," he said. There was nothing to read on his face.

After a second, I said yes. Maybe he was right.

He let me pose him and I threw a blanket over one of the floor lamps to give the room a warmer glow. He made eyes at the camera. I resisted the urge to melt. Mostly. I was grateful for my Polaroid's swiftness, because every so often I could pick up a photo from the pile on the floor and lean against Harry, showing him how handsome he was.

In twenty years, Harry would be half forgotten, making self-deprecating appearances on local morning shows, talking about omelets and his comeback tour, but that night, he was celestial.

I coaxed him to unbutton his shirt, and he did, laughing.

Then a knock came at the door. It opened before either of us had a chance to reply. The white hallway light bled into Harry's dressing room, hardening the shadows. Floyd poked his head in. "Sorry to interrupt." He glanced at half-undressed Harry and said again, slower, "Sorry."

I fell to the floor and gathered my shots. Harry began to rebutton his shirt and I said, "Say, Harry, I'll get you copies of the photos, if you'll let me give you a call."

"Sure," Harry said lightly.

I left with Floyd and only realized halfway out of the building that Harry hadn't given me his phone number. Maybe he didn't want me to call him, I considered . . . or maybe he forgot. Yes, that must have been it.

Floyd didn't say anything about Harry, just wrapped his arm around my shoulder and recounted all the things I'd missed while taking photos.

"That's interesting," I said to each story. We weaved slowly to the stage door as people I didn't know waved or shouted greetings our way. I told Floyd, "You must be popular around here." Strange for a light-stringing roadie to be so well-known, but Floyd had a humble charm that endeared me and surely others.

"Faun, they're talking to you."

He was *right*.

I began to wave back, riveted by these strangers' recognition. Famous, I was not, but known? Absolutely. I guess I'd met some of them before, at blacked-out parties, but their faces blurred into a collective. They were all vying for my attention, so why was I crushed Harry hadn't taken to me like I'd wanted?

Floyd and I drove back from the Hollywood Bowl in his rental car.

He didn't mind my rhapsodizing about Harry's concert, even turning on his latest album. When we made it to Floyd's unheated apartment, I blew smoke into his mouth the same way Harry had done with me. We fell asleep under the blanket together. By morning, I'd wrapped myself in it, leaving nothing for Floyd.

I TOLD JOSIE how popular I'd been at the concert late the next night, as we were wandering the Strip like we did when there was nothing else to do. There was always someone to see there. Someone to be seen by.

"Lucky you," she said. "And you were so worried about fitting in."

I nearly kicked up my scraped heels at the idea of belonging. "Am I really part of it now?"

"Oh, my love," she said. "Of course." Then, giggling, she prodded me in the side. "Now you can't escape!"

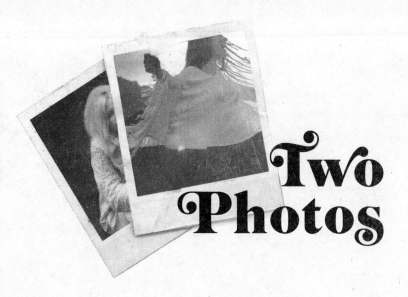

Two Photos

Harry Carling in his dressing room, half undressed, a joint in his hand and heaven-clouds of smoke around his head.

Floyd in his kitchen, burning toast.

10.

THE ALBUM COVER PHOTOSHOOT STARTED WITH BITTEN NAILS and countless cups of coffee. I spilled creamer on my pants at the craft services table and walked with wet legs as Stanley gave me a half-hearted tour of the studio. He showed me the set and explained the concept, both designed by someone I had never met and never would. The band would pose in retro baseball uniforms against a suburban backdrop. The painted pastel houses sat in neat rows. It was pristine and manufactured, a carefully constructed place for the band to perform their visual act.

Stanley wiggled his finger at various props he said we could use if I "really needed them" for a photo. "You know," he said, "I went through a lot of trouble hiring people to do these things. If you were a real photographer, you'd have designed this. You'd have picked out the costumes. We had to do it all for you."

"Well, I'm sorry," I said. It wasn't as if he'd asked for ideas—all I'd gotten was a date and time to show up. The minutiae of the job were unknown to me, and Stanley knew it. It didn't matter—once the album came out, my name would be on it. The pictures would be mine, even if the backdrop wasn't. I'd be behind the image each fan held as they memorized the new lyrics.

It was hard to not feel entirely incompetent as Stanley asked, "You're shooting on the Polaroid?"

"Yes. It's my niche."

"Still?"

"Yeah," I said, wracking my brain for justification. "Can't they just blow up the picture once it's taken? It'll look like a family photo. It'll look . . . authentic." I still couldn't afford my own SLR, but wouldn't admit it.

"Good grief," he said. "Yeah, I suppose."

I poked at the Astroturf spanning the length of the backdrop with my shoe, trying to see if there were bugs in it before I realized it was plastic. Too bad. I set up my Polaroid on a stand, Stanley reminding me every few minutes this was my *first* photoshoot. I was too embarrassed to correct him—I'd have to bring up the jobs I'd had in Massachusetts in all their nonglory.

Holiday Sun rolled in late, around one, yakking with each other as Patty-Ann, the young, bespectacled costumer, urged them into their outfits. Kent complained he had to wear a helmet and no one else did, then almost burst into tears when Cal said it was to cover his bald spot. Scott broke a spotlight with a baseball bat, which almost made Floyd, who I had no trouble insisting run the lights, also cry. All the girls but Yvonne arrived. When Darlene came in with Wendy, all work paused so everyone could pat the baby's head and try to get her to say "motherfucker."

I got a few solid solo shots of the individual men (Howie by far the easiest to capture), but when it came time for the cover shot, it was a game of who could fluster me more. I lined the band up, each on an angle behind the others, and counted down to what I envisioned as the perfect shot. As soon as I said "one" and triggered the flash, Scott faked a cartoonish sneeze, sending the rest of the band into hysterics.

"Guys, come on," I said. "One serious one. Please." I was running out of film. I should have packed more, but if I told Stanley I hadn't thought ahead, he'd have another reason to think I was useless.

The band posed and Scott fake-sneezed again.

"Are you five years old? Can you focus?" I said, exasperated.

Cal muttered something that sounded like "What a bitch," and Josie leapt toward him.

She churned her fists, shouting at Cal, then to the band as a whole,

"Don't you dare call her that! What is wrong with you? Can you all behave yourselves for—"

"Sit down," Cal said, his voice flat.

"Cal."

"Sit."

She did, sitting near Kitty and Wendy, both asleep on the studio floor.

Kent spat on the fake grass, and I hoped his phlegm wouldn't show in the next shot. I considered another test shot, wanting to fiddle with the exposure, but was too afraid to waste any more film.

We were getting nowhere, and Stanley loved it—he sat on a folding chair in the corner, laughing and flipping through a *TV Guide*. Scott wanted a break and Cal agreed, hustling out of the room with a cigarette in his mouth.

We broke for lunch. I picked through the Polaroids, all awful in different ways. What a disaster. How stupid I was to think I could make this work—that I could pretend to be something I wasn't. I almost broke down when Darlene dragged me aside, far out of Stanley's earshot, and pulled me to her clove-scented chest. I jolted, but she held me harder, cooing.

"Hush up, baby," Darlene said, petting my hair. I hadn't realized how much I missed my mother until Darlene held me. For all my mother's faults, she had always known when to hug me. "Do you remember when you came to Howie's house? Do you remember what Yvonne told you?" When I didn't reply, she helped me out. "Your job—our job—is to give the band lots and lots of love. Not scream at 'em. Not go nuts telling 'em what to do."

"It's my *job* to tell them what to do right now," I insisted. "I have to be professional."

Darlene let go. She took a deep breath, bounced on her toes, then exhaled. "Don't let them think you're ungrateful. All right, baby? You love them, don't you?"

"Yes," I said. "Of course." I was starting to doubt I still did. If I ever did. But they'd given me so much—too much, maybe, too quickly—and I was in their debt.

"That's what I like to hear." She pinched my cheek, then kissed it, leaving a faint red lipstick mark.

Lunch carried on, everyone munching on soggy catered sandwiches until Yvonne appeared. When she walked in, her stride unmistakable, Howie chucked away his ham sandwich so he could stand and look at her.

He didn't move. She had to come to him. Howie was playing cool, but so was Yvonne. Neither wanted the other to notice they were trying to be noticed, a combination that did not work.

"Are you mad at me, Miss Yvonne?" Howie asked so everyone could hear. Kent, beside him, looked up from the soup he kept spilling on his costume.

Yvonne turned to Howie and blinked. "No."

"You coming to dinner after this?"

Yvonne shrugged.

"Fine," Howie said, then pointed to me. He smiled. "Faun, you're doing great. You'll come to dinner, won't you? We can sit together."

I looked to Darlene, pleading silently for advice. Beside her, Yvonne fumed, arms crossed and eyes darting. Darlene gestured a smile. "I'd love to come to dinner," I said.

Howie rubbed my shoulder, goose bumps running down my back. Floyd didn't see. I didn't want him to.

Yvonne left wordlessly, leaving only the faint smell of strawberry lotion behind. Playing hard to get didn't work with Howie. Maybe it once had, when he was wet behind the ears, intoxicated by any offer of interest. He was spoiled now, and Yvonne the enigma was too complex compared with the easy adoration given by so many other girls. By me.

Poor Yvonne, running out of tricks.

WHEN THE PHOTOSHOOT resumed, I let the band organize themselves. I'd lead with a compliment to try to adjust them ("Scott, your hair looks so good from the left—how about you turn more that way?") but I resigned myself to never prodding. We didn't get the shots I wanted, but we got ones Stanley said would suffice. In the Polaroid I liked best, the band was barely holding it together. That wasn't a detriment—their almost-laughter left sparkles in their eyes. I liked it. It had the authenticity I worried other photos of the band lacked.

Stanley, overcaffeinated like me, squirmed as I showed him my choice photo.

"This one's good," I said to Stanley.

"It's good enough," he scoffed.

I looked at the bin of props, mostly silk scarves and magician-trick pieces toted over from a storage room. "Can we try a few shots with the band in day clothes? For the insert?" I asked. I pushed my luck and added, "And can we give them flowers to hold?"

Stanley said we didn't have time.

"Maybe we ought to use some *other* photos I've taken, then."

"For fuck's sake," Stanley said, then told the prop master to find some bouquets.

Patty-Ann directed her assistant to guide the band to the dressing room.

I returned to my friends, who, despite their best efforts, were bored out of their minds. Wendy yanked out the braids Darlene twisted into her hair, and Josie fixed them, muttering about a haircut. Josie told Kitty and Darlene I'd had an "intimate encounter" (her exaggeration doing wonders for my ego) with Harry Carling, then called for an on-set assistant to grab her a beer.

"About time you got over Floyd," Kitty said to me. "Yvonne says it was getting ridiculous."

"What?" I asked. "I'm not over Floyd."

"Oh," Darlene said, genuinely surprised. "Well, you don't seem to mind Patty-Ann flirting with him."

"Well, yeah," I said quickly. "We aren't steadies or anything."

Darlene and Josie laughed at my juvenile language. I blushed.

Josie said they were being mean. "Floyd is sweet to Faun. She deserves sweet."

"He's *boring*," Kitty said. "Faun needs to get herself a musician." Kitty turned to me and wiggled her finger wisely. "You need to, like, curate the guys you pick. Like me, for example—a guy from school named Brad asked me to the winter formal, but I said no, because Kent is way more interesting."

While the props team coaxed a bouquet into Cal's hands, I went to Floyd. Were the girls right? Even Darlene with her doe eyes thought Floyd was a bore, and I was beginning to believe it. Floyd *was* a little short, and when he was tired, his eyes glazed over in a way that was dim instead of dreamy. Sometimes a bit of drool would dribble from his lip when he got too excited. He snored. He never turned any heads. He'd never signed an autograph. He lacked the glow the band had, even if he still had the warmth.

I hoped there'd be a pimple on his forehead or a glob of spit on his lips when I got close, but there wasn't. Still, sticking to my newfound guns, I said, "Isn't Patty-Ann such a bunny?"

Floyd knelt on the floor, unscrewing a bulb from a lighting fixture. I hopped down beside him as he answered, "She's all right."

Damn it. "Well," I said, faux bashful, "I overheard her talking about you." He didn't ask what she said, but I volunteered anyway. "She told Josie that you're a stone fox."

He looked up. "Really?"

"Mmhm," I said.

All he asked was "Why are *you* telling me this?"

"So you can . . ." I trailed off. "So you can make a move on her. So you can get yourself a cute Coke-bottle-glasses lady."

Floyd made a laughing noise, but his face stayed still. I laughed, too, which made him stop altogether. "Maybe I'll talk to her," he said quietly. "If you think I should."

"Sure you should!" I waved to Darlene, who was staring. Wendy was yanking her hair. "Also," I said to Floyd, taking my chances, "could you write down Harry Carling's phone number for me?"

"For what?" He plucked a new light bulb out of its case and began screwing it in. He fumbled for a second, almost letting it shatter on the black studio floor.

"Does it matter?" I asked, meaner than I meant to be.

"Guess not."

"Thanks."

"Should I call you tonight?"

I swallowed. I looked away, down at his hands still clutching the clear bulb. His thumb left streaks across its surface. "If you want."

He rolled his eyes. "How about I call Patty-Ann?"

"Do whatever you want."

"I will. Congratulations on getting this photoshoot. Must make you feel real important." His voice was acrid.

He made me wait a minute while he finished adjusting the lights, but he gave me Harry's phone number. I left him with a curt thank-you. I looked back to see him approaching Patty-Ann and my heart hurt, suddenly jealous. He smiled at her and she giggled. Was that how I'd looked when he talked to me, all googly and gawking? I wanted to take it back, apologize for dropping him, but if I did, I could never call the phone number in my hand.

So, jealousy still coursing, I chose Harry over Floyd. Shame bubbled but dissipated every time I ran my finger across the outline of the folded-up phone number in my jeans pocket.

Dinner with Holiday Sun's bassist tonight, and a potential phone call with Harry Carling tomorrow. Life kept getting better. Broader. My world was expanding so quickly that I couldn't stop it, nor did I want to. I didn't look at Floyd for the rest of the shoot. There was no point.

THE PHOTOSHOOT WRAPPED around seven, four hours later than we'd hoped. Josie followed Cal to the band's dressing room while everyone else sipped expensive champagne. I had begun to learn the difference between good and bad champagne by the look of the bottles alone—on my tongue, every bubble felt the same.

Howie suggested we all head out to a Mexican place for dinner and drinks to celebrate the day's success, reminding me I just *had to* come. I leaned against the craft services table, popping grapes into my mouth.

Kitty sighed. "I wish he'd mentioned it earlier. I'm already having dinner."

I looked at the paper dish she was poking her fingers into. "That's just a bowl of Ruffles."

Her voice raised in defense. "Well, I put chili flakes on them."

Scott, Howie, and Kent decided they wanted to leave soon, so I marched down the hallway to search for Cal and Josie to let them know.

I may have been the photographer, but I was still a groupie first, and thus ran all the band's social errands. I was scared to invade Josie and Cal's privacy. I'd already caught them in too many compromising positions and would prefer never seeing either of them naked again.

They didn't see me as I peeked around the doorway. They were too deep into the dressing room and too deep into their argument. A second of staring, I thought, then I'd ask if they were ready to go. Maybe by the time I'd worked up the courage, they'd have stopped spitting cruelty at each other.

Josie stood with her arms crossed, whisper-shouting, "You were all so unprofessional. It was pathetic. What an awful, terrible way to treat—"

"Oh," Cal said, rolling his eyes until they looked ready to fall out of his skull, "because you're the bloody peak of professionalism. Nice tits, Jo, I'm sure the whole studio loves seeing them."

"I'm sure they do," she said, blowing a kiss.

"Little fucking smart-ass," he muttered.

"Oh, and by the way," she said, rearing back now, "good thing you didn't *ask* me before pulling that stunt on *Laugh Riot,* because I never would have said yes to you."

"You're so ungrateful," he said. "You're no one, love. You're a slut. That's your job. You should be grateful for me."

"I'm *not*!" she shouted. "You are pathetic."

"Don't say that," he said quietly.

"You *knew* I wouldn't say yes," she said. "You knew because you know you're pathetic, and *old*, and *awful*—"

Cal struck her open-handed across the face. She tilted and nearly wobbled over. She clutched her cheek, her manicured nails pressing against her skin.

He looked at her.

She said, "Sorry."

I remembered the first L.A. photo I ever took of Josie—that pretty one in the bus station with the hidden bruise. Those other bruises, too, so quickly excused and forgotten about. Had I been blind? Had I been dumb? Why did I ignore something so obvious, and why, even now, did I ease toward telling myself I had misunderstood? Maybe there was something I didn't get. Maybe it was a trick of the light, or an illusion. Maybe I'd fallen asleep for a second and dreamed it.

Anything was easier than reflecting on the stinging red mark erupting on Josie's face. I rapped on the door, my breath curdling in my throat. "Uh, hey, lovebirds," I said, my voice so soft I could barely hear it. "We were all going to head to dinner."

I shuffled my feet in the doorway as Josie slathered cover-up over her cheek and Cal talked aimlessly to me about New Year's resolutions. He talked like I hadn't just seen him hit my best friend. Like my world hadn't just tilted.

Josie and Cal followed me down the hall. I couldn't bear to look at either of them. If I didn't look, I could pretend they were holding hands and smiling. If I didn't look, I couldn't know if Josie's face was bruising again.

FLOYD AND HIS crew were still cleaning up when the girls and the band hopped into two cars and drove off to drink margaritas at El Carmen.

Kitty stole a bouquet from the set, swearing it smelled real. I stuck my face close to the plastic and tried to detect the sweet perfume of roses. I couldn't. Josie asked to hold the flowers. I gave them to her, her face bursting into a grin so tight it yanked her skin.

I had Harry Carling's phone number in my pants pocket and Howie Guerrero's hand in mine as we strolled into El Carmen. I didn't care if I'd ever touch him again. Sometimes it was enough to feel someone else's skin just once.

The red paper lanterns made us look sunburned, and the constant chime of glasses made it hard to hear any conversations. Darlene made a fuss about getting a baby seat for Wendy, and the kid ended up at the head of the table, waving her arms at a hand-painted portrait of a *luchador* on the wall.

Cal groaned. "Now we'll all hear it when she cries."

"Hey, that's my kid you're talking about," Scott said, pretend anger in his voice.

Cal laughed. Josie laughed, too, fingers brushing Cal's sleeve.

Stanley made a show of presenting me with my check—all nine hundred incredible dollars of it—and I could have burst. I fanned myself with it, entertaining Kitty with my affected wealth.

The talk at the table turned sloppy as Stanley ordered us a near-endless stream of margaritas. We dug into tacos. Howie kissed my cheek. I took a handful of fun photos, not bothering to pose them, hoping to capture something genuine.

Two teen girls, still buttoned into their starchy school uniforms, approached the table, both nudging the other to speak. Eventually, the one on the left, who had a *CliffsNotes* for *Romeo and Juliet* tucked under her arm, took a sharp breath and asked, "Hi, are you, um, Holiday Sun?"

The other girl chimed in, with awkward excitement, "We knew it! We saw you ten minutes ago and wrote you this letter. We love you." She pulled a piece of paper out of her pocket and thrust it toward Scott, who was closest. "Here!"

They fluttered away, practically chirping with excitement. Girls in groups always act like birds. Scott passed the note around the table, letting everyone skim it. It was a desperate fan letter, with hearts over the *i*'s and gratuitous wishes to be able to "spend a whole night" with anyone in the band. Ten minutes later, the teens left, passing the table and shouting, "Congratulations on the wedding!"

Kitty shrieked with remembered elation, and made the engaged couple divulge all the details.

"Well, we were looking at late May—after the album comes out," Josie said, the words seeming rehearsed.

"Josie wants the beach, but I want a hotel or somewhere really classy," Cal said.

We took an informal vote that decided nothing. Darlene begged, "Say Wendy can be the flower girl!"

Josie looked to Cal, smiling, and they both said, "Sure."

We toasted to true love and true fans.

I wondered if Josie's family would come to the wedding. Her little sister, Pamela, had always been a try-too-hard priss, but I knew she'd want an excuse to dress up. A couple nights ago Josie's mother called to wish her congratulations, and Josie apologized for an hour and a half because she had neglected to tell her the news herself.

Her mother didn't keep up with rock-and-roll news, she'd said, and she found out a week after the proposal/announcement/demand aired on *Laugh Riot*. Josie's mother had debated for weeks about calling. Josie said, cynically, that she was sure her mother was reconnecting so she could have a free trip to California and feel famous. That if this had been some barefoot wedding, her mother would have forgotten she existed at all.

Howie ran his callused fingers along my spine, tickling me and laughing as I squirmed. He thought this was *hilarious,* so he continued until I flailed, nearly knocking over the communal bowl of salsa. I fixed it as it wobbled, glancing up at Josie.

As soon as she caught my eye, she announced, "I need some fresh air. Faun, my true love, come outside with me, will you?"

As a good friend, I said yes, and followed her out the front door onto the streetlight-lit sidewalk. Faint strains of mariachi music underscored Josie's cursing attempts to light a cigarette, her hands fumbling with a stolen Zippo. I lit it for her. She flicked a flake of dandruff off my head.

"So," I said, afraid to speak in specifics, "the thing that happened earlier. With Cal. Was that—"

Josie said, "Don't worry about him and me arguing." She paced back and forth past a parking meter.

"It's more than arguing. It's . . . bad."

Josie looked at the cars whizzing along the street and sucked her cheeks in so her face looked hollow. "I know what's best. I don't want—I don't need—you don't have to do anything. I can handle myself."

"Josie, he hit you," I whispered. I came closer to her, trying to make sense of what she was saying, trying to get her to listen. "He can't do that. It's not right. He shouldn't—he shouldn't do that."

"It's fine," Josie snapped. I didn't think she meant it. "He's a good man. He really is."

I folded my arms, sliding my hands under my open corduroy jacket. "Are you sure?"

"Yes," she said, taking sharp, joyless drags from the cigarette. "It's nothing. We like each other. I promise." Liking wasn't loving. I liked tequila and red licorice and songs by Joan Baez. Josie laughed and rolled her eyes. It stung to watch her try to look indifferent. She deserved to smile every second of her life. "Tell me you'll ignore it," she said.

I did.

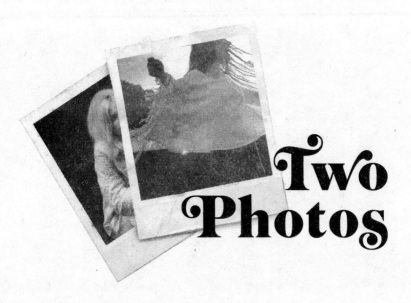

Two Photos

Holiday Sun lined up diagonally in the studio in their costumes, pretending to be serious, pretending to be sporty, pretending to listen to me.

Kitty, in the restaurant, throwing up two middle fingers to the camera. If you look very closely, hiding in a shadow is someone else flipping her off right back.

11.

THE BAND SCHEDULED A PRESS CONFERENCE FOR FEBRUARY 14.
Josie spent the whole week leading up to it grieving her and Cal's
overdramatic Valentine's Day plans. I'd spent the last week chick-
ening out every time I was about to call Harry Carling while Josie
moaned that she ought to be more important than some blah-blah
press conference. I'd console her, patting her shoulder. Apparently
Floyd was taking Patty-Ann to a ritzy Japanese restaurant, planning
to anoint her with silver bracelets and hand-carved soaps. I told myself not to be jealous, that it was my own fault for dumping him. I had
much better things to look forward to . . . as soon as I managed to
dial that daunting string of numbers standing between me and Harry.

Josie and I both needed a change of pace.

In high school I would have bought tickets to whatever Robert
Redford movie was playing and gotten a popcorn for us to share. But
by 1978, I struggled to understand anything that wasn't a party. I
consulted a tourist brochure before deciding today was as good a day
as any to visit the Santa Monica Pier.

JOSIE WORE A sweatshirt with a wild Palomino horse on the front, its
coat the same color as the boardwalk below our feet. We walked arm
in arm, ignoring all the lovers who'd chosen the pier as their place of
celebration.

"Do you want to go on the Ferris wheel?" I asked, chewing on a
corn dog. "Or we could get cotton candy. Wouldn't that be cute?"

"We can do whatever," Josie said.

We sat on a bench overlooking the beach, admiring the etched
graffiti on its surface. The smell of hot spun sugar drifted down the

boardwalk. It felt like the sun had been up forever in the cloudless sky. It was a beautiful day, a clear and mild wonderment, so why were we so solemn? Sometimes the sun's too bright. I preferred the world when it was shrouded in slight shadow. My Polaroids were like that—a bit underlit, with sides and seams a touch invisible.

Josie sucked the ocean air, saying the beach was prettiest when there was no one on it. When it was barren and free to mind its own business. "I want to get married here," she said. "You'll be my maid of honor, won't you?"

"Of course I will," I said. "I'd be honored."

We laughed at the redundancy as Josie grabbed my hand and jogged us toward the shoreline. The blue sky met the water, turning everything before us into a robin's-egg infinity. Josie, suddenly bright-eyed again, recounted the time her little sister tried to dig a hole to China. Pamela had been six, slamming all her weight onto a garden shovel. She was so small then, dirty and spry like all children are. Josie had been eight, egging her on when she should have been keeping Pamela out of the filth. "She really thought she could do it. She was practicing her *ni hao* while she dug. She got five feet deep. And when my father saw," Josie said, "he'd just died laughing. He hollered for my mom." Her face fell. "Well, she didn't think it was as funny." She bit her cheek.

Every word we said echoed for ages across the water.

Like a snake shedding its skin, Josie peeled off her sweatshirt, kicked off her shoes, and stood shirtless, her wash-faded white bra blinding against her tanned skin. No bruises on her ribs today. I breathed deep. She took off her jeans, too, their bell-bottoms catching the sand when she dropped them. She waded into the frigid water, splashing me.

She begged me to join her, but I didn't want to get cold. Josie walked in up to her waist until she was just a torso bobbing on the waves.

I took her photo. I took another one later, after she'd started shivering and wrapped herself in an abandoned Aztec-print towel. That second photo was so close to her face you could count her freckles. So close she could kiss you through it.

WE TOOK THE bus home from the beach, Josie with her shoes off, picking sand off her painted toenails. She narrowly missed stepping on a fractured beer bottle with her bare foot. The brown-tinted glass seemed to remind her she wanted to be drunk, so we hopped off the bus and popped into a liquor store.

We were in a loud mood, and I made a terrible show of paying for our purchase with the wads of bills from my just-cashed check. The change in my pocket rattled like marbles.

On our walk home, Josie said, "Let's pretend we're lovely roommates preparing a sorority dinner." I could tell it really had been ages since her days studying psychology at UCLA, because who else would *play* at being in school?

I wished Josie had been my roommate at Mount Holyoke, but this was almost the same. No, it was better. We could end the fantasy whenever we wanted.

We dipped into a convenience store, stocking up on enough pasta to make a casserole that would make any suburban mother proud. Josie cracked open a pull-tab beer in the aisle and her batting eyes froze the clerk from kicking her out.

Once home, we made up names for the sorority sisters we hated and loved. The pot of water on the gas stove nearly boiled over. Josie opened another beer and we split it as she hand-addressed a stack of wedding invitations.

Post-dinner and post-cleanup, Josie took our game a step further. "Faun," she said, "don't you wish our sorority sisters were *here?*"

I was having a perfect time with her, but Josie thrived on excess. I shrugged and said I'd dial up some of the groupies.

"Don't let Darlene bring the baby," Josie said after a moment of deep thought. "If she doesn't bring the baby, then she'll definitely bring the coke."

Oh, so we were *that* kind of sorority.

Darlene agreed to come quite easily. Kitty considered for a minute or two, then agreed, saying Kent's apartment was too big with him out of it all night. Yvonne was initially a hard no but called back five minutes later, saying she could rearrange her plans.

The sun had set by the time the girls rolled in. Kitty brought a plastic bag full of cinnamon hearts and spilled them all over the floor. No one swept them up, and every so often, one of us would crush a candy heart under our heel, letting its sugar turn sticky on the floor. Yvonne said there was something poetic about that. I avoided them.

When we realized there was no one to impress or take care of but each other, we curled up on the floor and humored Kitty by playing some party games. Yvonne poured raspberry wine into mugs.

Josie nudged Darlene. Darlene pointed, her long nail glinting in the yellow light, to her oversize purse sitting below the coatrack. Josie rifled through it as Kitty prepared to play Two Truths and a Lie.

"Okey dokey," Kitty said, breaking open an almost rotten apple with her hands. "Here are my two truths—"

"Nah, nah, honey," Darlene said delicately. "You can't tell us which ones are the truths. That's the point."

"Oh, right," Kitty said, nodding. She gave us her three facts and we struggled to determine if the lie was that she had a third nipple, knew how to embroider, or had accidentally killed her third-grade pet hamster by tying a ribbon around his fuzzy neck. Innocent facts that seemed so much younger than the false-maturity Kitty presented.

When we grew tired of games, Josie cut us lines of Darlene's coke. We turned chatty and truthless, exchanging groupie lore, our social currency. The nightly news interjected that the Hillside Strangler still hadn't been captured and that food coloring was going to poison us all, but we weren't listening. We excited each other, saturating each other's minds with visions of celebrity encounters. But I didn't miss the band. It was so easy to talk without them around. There was no proof of anything we said. We trusted the invisibleness of it. If a sliver of it—if the feeling it gave you—was true, then the whole thing was as good as.

Darlene told us how once, when she was a road wife instead of a legal one, Scott shoved a (corked, thankfully) champagne bottle up inside some overexcited local girl.

Yvonne nodded. "You know what? I heard about that. Was that seventy-two?"

"Or the year before," Darlene said. "I was still blond then, and fresh from Georgia. I wonder where that damn girl went. She looked like you, Faun, with the same ol' googly eyes." She sniffled and wiped her nose.

Their stories continued, and I listened, spellbound. I pictured the girls in the situations they described, the images bursting across my mind in streams and stark flashes. Lips against lips, bodies inside bodies, bones writhing against bones—mouths gaping and eyes lolling. How gruesome and delicate it seemed—how tempting. I wanted good stories, too. I wanted that reckless, heart-stopping love. It's so easy to want love, and so hard to get the kind you want. I considered sharing stories about Floyd, but none of our moments were as jaw-dropping as what the others shared.

Yvonne lit cigarette after cigarette, ashing them onto a Chinese takeout flyer. I asked why she'd stormed out of the band's photoshoot.

"That's my personal business," she said. She softened. "I've got to sneak away sometimes. It makes them want you to come back."

Josie said, "Howie's over your disappearing act, you know. He brought Faun to dinner. He didn't think about you."

"He *will*," Yvonne said. She insisted that if he didn't want her, a million others would. It was a big world. "Anyway," she said, "I'm going to make it big. I've been busy booking acting jobs for my clients."

Josie prodded, "Who? I heard Howie doesn't want you managing him anymore."

"I have two clients," Yvonne said. I couldn't tell if she was telling the truth. "And yes, Howie and I have parted ways professionally. Our visions for his career didn't coincide."

"I know you'll make it big as a manager," Kitty said, giggling. "You're so bossy."

"Shut up." Yvonne laughed, pushing against Kitty's shoulder. Pink glitter, applied liberally, rubbed off onto her hand.

"I think you'll all make it big," Kitty said dreamily.

We divulged our professional exploits, exaggerating when we had to and brushing past our sensitivities. We were doubted so often that indicating fear would be too close to admitting defeat in a world that expected us to fail. I talked about my impromptu photoshoot with Harry Carling, to get all the girls swooning. The conversation shifted to kisses and sex and heart-fluttering things until we were spilling over the brim with love to give. Lacking our usual targets, we wracked our brains for an option. Josie cried out, after a minute of making eyes at the mustached TV reporter, "Faun! Call Harry Carling!"

"Oh, God, please!" Kitty said.

Maybe our sorority game was still going, because we giggled as I shakily dialed the number on the slip.

We laughed as we waited and laughed when he picked up, then I hushed the room. "Hello." I sighed into the blue plastic receiver.

Josie gave me a thumbs-up, her pupils big enough to swim inside.

"Who's this?" Harry asked, his voice as lovely as I'd remembered.

"It's Faun, from the benefit concert," I said. "I took photos of you, remember?"

"Right," he said, then called something I couldn't hear to someone I didn't know.

I steadied myself. "I was wondering if you'd like to maybe see me."

"Faun-from-the-benefit-concert," he said, "I don't know."

I couldn't fail —I couldn't —and suddenly, I was struck with a perfect idea. "Oh"—I sighed—"my *girlfriends* will be so disappointed. We were really hoping you could drop by."

The line was silent. I thought he'd hung up, but then he said, "What's the address? Are you in the Valley?"

After giving all the necessary information, I hung up and prepared for Harry's arrival. My stomach churned. We watched the stars come out above the city, and Josie beckoned me to do another line. I couldn't say no to her, so I did, but it made me feel worse. Soon I was bent over the toilet, violently heaving, praying Harry was stuck in traffic and wouldn't arrive while I was clutching the porcelain bowl.

"No more for Faun for a while," Yvonne said from the living room.

Josie patted my head.

I puked again. I thought ejecting my insides would clean me out somehow, empty my body so I'd have the chance to be fresh, but puking my guts out did nothing but hollow me. A Halloween pumpkin. I hardly felt renewed. All I wanted was to poke around in the vomit in search of some missing part of myself.

Eventually the tide of nausea passed and after flushing the evidence away, I hurried to the sink and sloshed Listerine in my mouth. I flossed. I repainted my face with a thick sludge of cover-up until I looked good as new.

A sharp knock came at the door. My knees buckled. Josie dashed toward me in the bathroom, then gestured wildly at the door. It was a thin cedar thing, and any sound carried easily into the hallway. I touched my cheeks, then my neck, unsure what I was checking for. Then, with little steps, I made my way to the door and pulled it open.

No one had ever looked prettier in an apartment hallway than Harry Carling did. I forced myself to be casual, so instead of proposing marriage right there and then, I said, a cool smile playing at my lips, "You made it."

"Barely," Harry said.

Was he joking? I laughed either way.

Josie slipped beside me, batting her eyes. "What did you bring to the party?" Her voice dripped with suggestion.

Harry shrugged slyly. "What were you expecting?"

"Let's make some introductions!" I said.

Harry followed me on a small loop around the apartment. The girls waved and made clever comments. They were so good at it. They could turn on these cooing selves in a second flat. I still struggled.

Harry sat on the couch and asked what was on TV.

I gave a nonanswer and stared at his perfect, glowing face. Josie turned on the radio and swayed her body to "I'm In You."

I scooched closer to Harry on the couch and asked, "Do you want . . . coke? We have lots." As an explanation, I pointed to Darlene. "She's here."

Harry shook his head no and mimed smoking a joint. He was having such fun with me and I took him so seriously.

"Oh, we've got pot, too," I said, unsure that we did. "Right, Josie?"

"Huh?" she asked, twirling in place. "Oh, yeah, in my panty drawer."

"Don't say 'panties,' say 'lingerie,' that's classier," Darlene corrected.

We got Harry the pot he wanted and after he smoked half a joint, I managed to curl up beside him without him shrinking away. I had a hummingbird heart.

Yvonne pointed to Harry and said, "So. We hear you kissed Faun after your save-the-trees concert."

Harry looked at me and said, "It wasn't really—"

Josie, trying to save me, interjected, "We hear you're a *great* kisser. Care to prove it?"

"Me first, 'cause I'm, like, the cutest," Kitty said, raising her hand.

We sat in a circle as Harry kissed each of us (except Darlene, who said she could never be unfaithful to Scott). I hated to watch his lips touch Kitty's and Yvonne's, but consoled myself by knowing he didn't mean it. When it was my turn, I thanked God for mouthwash and cocaine. Harry leaned into me without any feeling, and when our lips touched, it was a thoughtless act, not a fireworks explosion. Maybe I shouldn't have pulled away so willingly; maybe I should have grabbed him and gobbled him up—but I didn't, so we parted a second later with me still holding my breath.

It was Josie's turn. She hopped on his lap and wiggled. He didn't move as she begged, "Won't you give me a kiss?"

"Josie," I said. I didn't want her to make it such a big deal—besides, the purpose of the kissing chain was to get Harry to me. Couldn't she be like faithful Darlene?

Harry obliged and dove onto her. Soon they were sucking face so feverishly you'd think it was going to be illegal the next day. I could have vomited again. I wish I *had*, because maybe that would have stopped them. I slid off the couch to avoid intersecting their tongues.

I was stupid for thinking Josie wouldn't want to kiss him, too, but I still didn't understand it. She didn't like his music. She didn't care for him. Why couldn't I have him for myself? Why did Josie always end up better than I was?

I reached for my truest friend, my Polaroid, and made sure it was loaded with film. With a pained smile, I said, "Let me take a photo!"

Josie posed for the first one, which I let drop to the floor, and in the second one went right back to kissing Harry. I didn't know what to do with the pictures, but needed them to prove my anger to myself. I prided myself on unfiltered, raw, beautiful documentation, didn't I? The act wasn't beautiful but the people doing it were. And God knew this was unfiltered and raw.

"Faun's jealous!" Kitty laughed, tactless but truthful. She braided the tassels of a throw pillow.

"Am not," I said, forcing a smile onto my face. I was furious but if I played along, the moment would pass.

"Faun, you're jealous?" Josie asked. She hopped off the couch and kneeled in front of me. Sympathy flickered briefly behind her eyes, then she reverted to brightness. Kitty was still cooing about my apparent green-eyed rage, so Josie (maybe) tried to fix it. She redirected it, purposefully misunderstanding. "If you're jealous of Harry, I can kiss you, too."

"Oh," I said.

Our knees touched. She kissed me, her lips closed and sugary, in something beyond a peck but before romance. Her mouth tasted like cigarettes and candy.

Everyone laughed and we all moved on. Distraction successful. I kept glancing at Josie, then to Harry, thinking about jealousy and lips and sugar.

The night wore on. Josie showed no further interest in Harry. My anger fizzled. I stopped feeling like the ground was about to open up. I added the Polaroids to the pile I'd made in my dresser, taping them together so only the backs showed.

Harry left and I managed to kiss him goodbye. I did it better then, but it wasn't perfect. Not like making out with him, forcing all my friends to watch.

Kitty and Darlene left together. Josie called a cab, saying she was going to visit Cal. I was left alone with Yvonne, who was packing up her things, too. We stood in the front hallway, unsure whether we liked each other. Yvonne laced her black boots. I watched and picked dirt out from under my bitten nails.

"Little birdy told me you got nine hundred dollars for the album cover," Yvonne said. She unzipped her purse, rearranging its contents.

At least I had that to be proud of. I swelled. "Yeah, I did."

"Sucks," Yvonne said, pulling on her overcoat. "The guy for the last album got about three thousand."

"What?"

"You got fucked over, babe," she said.

"That's Stanley's fault," I said. I threw all my anger toward him, not daring to blame myself for accepting whatever I was given. It felt illegal to blame the band. They gave, and Stanley was the one who took.

"They'll all fuck you over."

"That's not true."

"I've been here awhile."

"Why are you still here, then?" I asked. "If you hate everybody so much. If you hate the band. If they fuck you over."

Yvonne shrugged. "I can handle it." She was so good at making you mad about anything. "What? Still fuming over Josie smacking lips with Harry?"

"I'm jealous of her," I said, too honest for comfort.

"Why? 'Cause she's prettier than you?"

I knew Josie's all-American apple cheeks and thick lips were nice to look at. I knew she was prettier than me. But no one had ever said it before. Not in front of me. I hated to hear it, because it made me aware of the confused resentment I felt toward her—tonight, and maybe always. I hated everyone I loved. It was a balancing act, a seesaw, and the love was usually heavier, but sometimes resentment would creep out and remind me of all the things I wasn't. "I'm not pretty?"

Yvonne didn't answer. "Don't be jealous. She's stuck. She's getting fucked over, too. We all are. But we get fucked along the way. Isn't that fun?" She meant it and she didn't.

Fucked over was a good way to put it. Whatever, I thought. Whatever.

Nine hundred dollars was still more money than I'd ever had at once. Yvonne talked about my situation like it was the end, but I knew it wasn't. It was a beginning. Once the album came out, with my name stuck within the liner notes as the photographer, people would take notice. I'd carry on. I'd shoot another album, then another, and another.

I'd meet more wonderful people and be able to say "fuck you" to Stanley and anyone who thought less of me. Things would carry on. They had to.

I went to bed and dreamed about flying over mountains and falling off cliffs, which I guess were close to the same thing.

Three Photos

Josie, a blip in the ocean water, a tuft of blond drifting within deep blue.

Josie, too close to the camera, smiling with her eyes, so beautiful she looks pretend.

Josie, kissing Harry Carling, not looking at the camera, not looking at me.

12.

I COULD SEE JOSIE'S PERFECT VENEER LOSING ITS GLOSS, BUT the rest of the world still adored her. She got a phone call from America's favorite porno mag, *Foxy* magazine, asking her to come for a test shoot. I asked if she was going to share the good news with our friends, but she replied, "Oh, I can't jinx it." I wondered if that was the whole truth, or the truth at all. I was leery of trusting her after learning she didn't say a word to Cal about her kiss with Harry (and the fact it happened at all). Still, she had good reason to not trust Cal. I knew that now, even if I wasn't allowed to say it.

The test shoot was booked for two weeks later, in mid-March, and that's how she treated it—as a test. She pored over back issues of the magazine, studying bare breasts and thighs with the same fervency an SAT prepper used for mathematical formulas. When Kitty chopped her hair into a shaggy Linda Ronstadt bob, Josie pined for a haircut of her own. She booked an appointment with a beauty school, hoping the trainee girls could offer a lower rate, but canceled it at the last minute. She reasoned the magazine was expecting to shoot the Josie they knew and loved—not some unrecognizable girl with crooked bangs.

IN THE MEANTIME, we flew to parties and concerts, dividing our time between days spent getting drunk at two P.M. and nights spent forgetting to go to sleep. One late night, after shuffling home from Howie's house, the telephone rang over the snoring. Josie didn't stir, so I peeled away my blanket and picked up the call. I muttered, "Hello," yawning.

Across the line, a voice said, "Faun?"

"Harry?" I said too loudly, then lowered my voice. "How . . . how are you?"

"I'm great," he said, "but I believe I left my sunglasses at your place."

I searched through piles of crinkled soda cans and discarded lace socks, wondering who Harry had hoped would pick up when he called. No luck. I picked up the receiver again and said, "Can't seem to find them." He was about to hang up, but I said, "Say, don't you want to talk for a while?"

He did. We spoke for two hours about heartburn and pet birds and if we believed in ghosts. He told me about his rustic hometown house in Paducah, and I told him about the Snow White cottages I'd seen on a walk in Los Feliz, cartoonishly beautiful. We both liked when real life looked like a fairy tale. I was breaking through. I could feel it. He was so difficult to crack, so impossible to steal, that I refused to give up. I took notes as we talked, hanging on to every sacred word. He was up in San Francisco writing placid songs with other plaid-shirted folk music heroes. I pictured his fingers dancing across guitar strings and wondered when they'd dance across me.

He said he'd call again so I spent the rest of the month waiting patiently, plaintively, for that call to arrive.

HOLIDAY SUN PLANNED a promotional concert for *Outfield Flowers* to remind people they still existed. They couldn't afford to coast through this promotional cycle. The band had reached that dangerous musical age where they'd become a memory, a novelty, or an icon. Newer bands, with flashy names like Venomous and Northern and Eastcoast, were encroaching on Holiday Sun's rich radio-rock niche. Loyal, Josie and I counted down the days, watched all the band's TV appearances, and made sure every local record store would be carrying the new album.

I was half dressed and fully ready for the promotional concert when the telephone rang again. Josie was at the post office, sending last-minute wedding invitations to people she didn't want to invite, hoping they'd get lost in the mail. She said the wedding planner Cal chose could never do anything right, so she snatched all the chances she could to take over and fulfill her girlhood dreams. She said that in middle school she'd put magazine cutouts of Chantilly veils and baby's breath arrangements in her hope chest. Now someone else was doing the hoping for her. The wedding was less than two months away, and I still couldn't believe it was happening. I almost hoped it wouldn't, but I couldn't tell Josie that.

I picked up the telephone, preparing to greet Harry, but he wasn't on the other end. Floyd was. His calls had become disappointing. The other girls were right about him. I wasn't going to lower myself back down to dating a roadie; roadies were starting points, not end goals. But hearing his voice was comforting, a tinge of familiar tranquility in an otherwise antsy day.

He apologized for calling and asked if I had an extra ticket for the concert tonight. He wasn't working it, had moved on to some other contract.

I said no (the truth).

"Well, are you free to catch up tomorrow?" he asked.

I said no again (a lie).

Any night could be the night Harry called. I would have rather spent the night with someone famous I didn't really know than someone insignificant whom I did. Was it too late for a key-chain collection, like the kind Josie had joked about at Goody's party? Maybe I could keep Floyd an arm's length away, close enough to go back to. I said, "I'm sure I'll see you around. That's the same as going out."

"I shouldn't have asked."

"What do you mean?"

He didn't say anything.

"Hey," I said.

"Yeah, sure," he said, souring, "I'll see you around."

"And, I mean," I said, "we could get dinner if I'm not busy, or—"

He hung up.

Taking a page from Josie's book, I downed half a bottle of wine and layered on more blue eyeshadow.

Josie and I met up with Darlene an hour before the Troubadour was set to open. We knocked on the stage door. Josie's backstage pass sat cufflike around her wrist, while Darlene used hers to tie up her frizzing hair. An affected gesture of coolness—not only were we let backstage without having to ask, we were so important we didn't even care. I held my pass, still surprised to have one. My Polaroid bag sat snug against my shoulder. I held it close.

Darlene said she missed the struggle of trying to get backstage. How it used to be a prize.

We found the band in the greenroom watching Scott light pieces of paper on fire and douse them in water. Darlene slid next to him. He waved a lit match past her hair and caught a strand on fire. She didn't move, even as she noticed her own body smoldering. She waited, stone-faced, for Scott to extinguish her. He did, just in time.

Stanley burst into the room, overexcited to share that the show was sold out, and that there were reporters from *Asking*, *Rolling Stone*, and *Creem* already at the concert hall bar.

Howie brought up doing a cover of "Little Wing" on tour. I dangled off an armchair, twisting around its back so I could see Howie better. He waved to me, and I snapped his photo. "You like Hendrix, Faun?" he asked. "Yvonne does. She's not coming, is she?"

I said, "Probably not," and suggested, "If she doesn't come, maybe you can make do with me." I felt slimy but said it anyway.

Then Yvonne appeared in the greenroom like a wish being granted.

"Thought you were done here, Miss Yvonne," Howie said, cool as ever.

Yvonne laughed half-heartedly. "I always come back." Lightly, she added, "I got bored of walking around waiting for something to happen."

Roaming the streets alone didn't scare her—it bored her. It bored all of us. Sure, socially I sometimes felt anxious enough to puke, but when I was out walking, I was never afraid. The world seemed bright and open-armed, not deadly. My mother had been wrong about everything.

We were at the very end of the golden era of fearless girls. Soon, women would learn distrust, pumped full of fear by serial-killer news-reels and common sense. But those things weren't in our reality yet. They existed but seemed impossible. Faraway. False. Sure, soon, every girl would look over her shoulder at every turn and lock her car as soon as she hopped into it—but not quite yet. We were still lawless and mindless. Gaggles of bright-eyed girls would prod at each other on the bus, sharing lipstick by kissing, leaving home with only a five-dollar bill and, if they were cautious, a house key. It wasn't true, but we thought everyone loved everyone else. We'd kiss anyone and touch anyone and go anywhere with anyone, as long as the person smiled.

That night, too, we'd do anything anyone told us to. Kent poured sloshing glasses of tequila and we downed them, forgoing the salt and lime for just the shot. I took pretty photos and ugly photos, liking them both. I nodded along to Kent and Kitty's discussions about blow jobs and barbiturates, not noticing how drunk Josie had become. Cal was drunk, too, but he held it better. I looked at him, trying to see the goodness Josie had insisted existed in him.

Darlene slipped off to the bathroom, complaining of nausea and holding her bobbling head. No one blinked at her leaving, but when she didn't come back after fifteen minutes I worried. I weaved through the backstage halls, familiar with their twists. I found an oc-cupied bathroom and knocked. "Darlene?" I asked. "Everything co-pacetic?"

"You can come in," she said.

I opened the door to see her face smudged with mostly dried blood. A few fresh drips fell from her nose, and her lips were streaked with the cold glint of red, too. It left marks on her face like trails splitting from a forest path. Fjords breaking off into the sea.

I grabbed a towel and wet it, leaving the tap running to fill the silence. Flakes of white powder were spread here and there on the countertop. Not snowdrifts—sprinkles. There, on Darlene's face, too, were the same smatterings. The coke queen, indeed.

I started dabbing at her face. Darlene wiped a solitary tear and announced, "I went a little too nuts, I guess, but I'm fine."

"You aren't," I said. "You're all bloody."

"I'm peachy keen, Faun, I'm fine." Darlene picked a dry flake of blood off her cheek and muttered, "Why'd I have to smudge it all over like that? Does anyone know I'm here?"

"No," I lied.

"Good. Stop your worryin'. You don't have to do anything," she said, taking the wet paper towel from my hand and wiping most of the blood off her own face. "I always pick myself up and put all my little pieces back together."

"Are you ready for the show?" I asked because I couldn't think of anything else to ask or anywhere else to go.

"Yeah. Jesus, I need a fuckin' beer." She licked her lips, smiled at herself in the mirror, and clucked her tongue. She wet a finger and ran it across the counter. She sucked her finger, rubbing her gums, and grabbed my hand. I asked if she wanted a photo, and she said yes. I took one and let the few remaining bloodstains show.

We walked back to the band together.

They rallied to do their traditional warm-ups, basking in superstition, but Cal sat out. The rest of the band grumbled for a while, but they still went Cal-less into the hall to hum. Yvonne, Darlene, and Kitty linked arms *Wizard of Oz* style and skipped down the venue's hallway to position themselves backstage.

I stayed behind, watching the bubbles in a glass of champagne swim to the surface. I didn't listen to what Josie and Cal were talking about until Cal said, "I wouldn't like it."

Josie mocked, "Oh, no, you wouldn't *like* it?"

Stanley rapped on the door, took one look at the unfolding argument, and scrambled away again, head down. He was no help. I wasn't any either, because I was too invested in the soap opera that was transpiring to worry about stopping it. That was how I saw it: as pretend and as easy to escape from as a bad daytime show.

Josie announced, "I'm going to cut my hair."

"Josie," I said, thinking I was helping, "what about *Foxy*? I thought they wanted your hair like this."

Josie started slurring, gesturing violently, saying to Cal, "I got a phone call from *Foxy* magazine and they want me inside—in it, because they *like* me! They like—they love me!"

I could have said *stop*. It would have been an easy syllable to choke out. But I didn't.

"How do you think they know who you are?" Cal asked, his tone cutting and precise.

"Not 'cause of you," Josie said.

"How else, princess?"

"You're both being so ridiculous," I said. "Cal, Stanley said it's time to go."

"Shush, Faun," Josie said. With untrained hands, she plucked a pair of nail scissors—those shiny metal ones—from a cosmetics case, stared herself dead in the mirror, and lopped off a chunk of blond hair. It fell to the floor, mingling with the dust.

Josie went to cut the other side, to even it out, but Cal grabbed her arm. I tried to interject but someone called my name from the calm of the hallway, and I turned around. When I turned back, Josie and Cal both fought for the scissors. They grappled, trying to pry the scissors away from the other, until Josie thrust her body to the left.

Her arm slipped from Cal's grasp, and the nail scissors stuck in the fleshy part of his left upper arm. Josie smiled and groaned at the same time. It was her last resort—her bee sting.

Cal turned to me, steely calm as blood bloomed onto his denim shirt. "Faun. Get someone."

Josie burst into tears and shrieked apologies, drawing the attention of the entire backstage population. I dashed into the hall and called for someone—*anyone*—who could apply a bandage and fix him. The scissors stayed in his arm, like a pin in a cushion, until a security guard with nurse's hands extracted them.

"We'll cancel the gig," Stanley said, as we all gawked. "We'll reschedule. We'll call a car to take Josephine home. We'll take you to the hospital."

Cal shrugged. He spoke to Stanley but looked at Josie, his eyes clear despite the obvious pain. "Nah, Josie's staying. We'll go on."

Josie sighed, either out of relief or strange disappointment. It was a flesh wound, Cal explained later. It didn't cut him to his core. Nothing could. He tore off his denim shirt and borrowed Howie's leather jacket to wear bare-chested. He had nothing underneath except a mighty mound of gauze bandages that ended the night soaked with blood and sweat.

Josie cried so hard she hiccupped as the band went onstage, and nothing consoled her until we hopped onto a road case and held each other's hands as the band played "Sheila."

Cal smiled onstage, and all the wet-faced teenagers in the crowd sat silent for him.

Josie screamed from the wings, "I love you!," loud enough for the microphones to pick her up.

I hate to think she meant it.

The crowd joined in on the declarations of love. Cal responded, shouting out to the crowd but pointing one finger at Josie's hidden spot backstage, "Love you, too!"

Nothing was fully true, but I didn't expect things to be anymore.

I liked things that were pretty, not true. Truth was for photos. When there wasn't a lens between me and the world, all I wanted was niceness.

Afterward, Darlene chain-smoked and fixed Josie's hair. Josie and Cal kissed but seemed ready to spit in the other's face. We went out and we partied and forgot about Josie's red-faced bawling and Cal's stab wound and everything else. We danced close-bodied and voraciously. We drank and forgot and laughed until our bodies ached.

Every night we started over, and there was infinite comfort in that. *Infinite* maybe isn't the best word—while the comfort itself was impossibly potent, the *quantity* of it felt dwindling. When you get down to the last bit of orange juice in the carton and pour it out sip by sip instead of glass by glass.

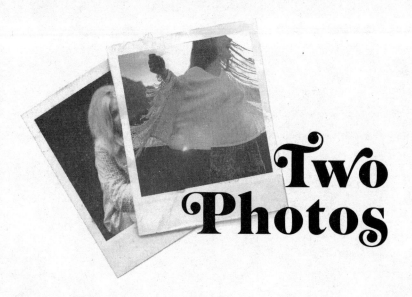

Two
Photos

The band and the groupies spread out backstage, sitting on chairs, glimmering, talking, waiting for something to happen.

Darlene looking over the camera, at my face, the dried blood on her lips as bright as lipstick.

13.

THE NAIL-SCISSORS INCIDENT WAS ALL ANYONE ON THE SUNSET Strip could talk about for a week but soon fell into the grand mythos of groupie lore. It was a party story, and despite the three stitches Cal got and Josie's snot-bubble tears, most of us started to laugh about it.

Josie, who drowned in big jackets and drank everyone under the table, was not a threat. It bothered her how quickly everyone dismissed her. She'd grumble when someone mentioned it, grumbling further when everyone got confused and made the story about Clementine and Jed Tooley from Antelope Valley.

I went with Josie to get her wedding dress fitted. The bridesmaids (her sister, Pamela, and Darlene, Yvonne, Kitty, and me) were told to pick any dress we wanted as long as it was pastel green. Josie pretended she was respecting everyone's busy schedules, but I suspected she just didn't want to see Pamela until she absolutely had to. Her family wasn't even set to arrive until the morning of the wedding, when they'd fly into LAX and promptly be taxied off to St. Eustace Church downtown. Josie and Cal both spent hours waxing on about how God wasn't real, but the church made for good photos, so they booked it.

Josie was trying to do less coke in preparation for the wedding ("I'm too sniffly these days," she said, "I'm starting to sound like goddamn Darlene"), so she began drinking a cup of coffee every half hour.

On the evening of the album release, Josie winced through three cups of black coffee as she painted her toenails. She did mine, too, saying that the band's photographer ought to be perfect from top to bottom. We put on knee-length cocktail dresses and listened to Olivia Newton-John, elevating our speech and practicing the long, elegant steps we'd take into the record-label-run album release party. It was set to be a suit-and-tie, champagne-pouring function, with a tasteful six P.M. start at a hotel in West Hollywood.

We took a taxi there, sober and straitlaced. I carried my Polaroid in a new white leather case, brushing stray hairs off its milky surface. Josie couldn't wait to get home from the stuffiness awaiting us; she'd allegedly been "begged" by Cal to attend to keep up the appearance of their being a happy, respectable celebrity couple. She approached the night imbued with a grim sense of purpose, but I faced it with quiet hope. Not hope—assuredness. Resolved anxiety over never "making it." Tonight was when everyone would know I'd made it, a real-true professional at last.

The taxi pulled up to the curb of a high-rise hotel. Josie shook her head. "This looks so plain. What is this? They couldn't book something at Tower Records?"

I said, "Well, you know how the label is." I didn't really know how they were—my only knowledge of record execs came from secondhand complaints. We stepped out of the car, and I stretched my shoulders, trying to grow taller. I took a deep breath, and brushed my hair out with my clean, nervous fingers.

Throngs of fans littered the entrance to the hotel, with hand-painted T-shirts and just-popped zits, hoping to catch a glimpse of the band who were surely already inside, snuck through a back door. They shrieked, expelling excitement at the very idea of being on the same block as Holiday Sun. I wondered when my own thrill for the band had slipped away, and how I could get it back. A girl in white coveralls pointed to Josie, whispering something to her friend. A murmur passed through the crowd.

She smiled to the fans but whispered to me, "This is going to be lame. Guess we'll have to make our own fun." She lit a cigarette. I didn't. Any indulgences could mar my newfound professional image. We stepped through the lobby doors and gave our names to the man toting the guest list. Josie blew smoke in his face, maybe accidentally, and I smiled to apologize.

The security man ran his finger down his clipboard and found Josie's name, labeled a "special guest." He couldn't find mine. I implored him to look again.

Josie leaned close to the security guard and added, "I called Cal—my fiancé, Cal Holiday?—to make sure she was on the list."

I chimed in, smiling like a dumb, proud kid. "I took the cover photo. It's my photo." I pointed to a large laminate print of the cover near the ballroom. Men in gray suits milled past it, no doubt commenting good things (they had to be good things) about its composition and coloring. "That's the photo. On the cover. That's the cover, I mean."

"Right," the security man said. He flipped one of the pages over and found my name, scribbled onto the end of the list in blue ink. "Ah, there you are."

He gestured for us to continue to the ballroom. Josie waved left and right at people she didn't know, waiting to see someone of clear significance or an open bar. The band weren't in the room yet, probably preparing for a suited-up short performance to center the celebration.

A bright voice called from across the room, "Josie! Faun! Over here!" Kitty waved to us, standing on her tiptoes in a too-big gown. She was alone, tapping her foot, pretending not to be lost. Josie and I moved across the floor past hordes of music professionals who glanced at us but made no introductions. These men loved shaking each other's hands while looking past our heads.

"Where's Darlene?" Josie asked.

Kitty rummaged in her purse, a bag unnecessarily huge for the occasion, and said, "Home with Wendy. They've got pink eye. Yucky."

"Scott's in the clear?" I asked.

"He hasn't been home for a while," Kitty said, then paused, catching herself before saying anything unpleasant. "For safety, obviously."

"Obviously," I repeated, a bit too darkly.

Josie poked me with her elbow.

"Are you two as bored as me?" Kitty asked. Before we answered, she pulled a bottle of vodka out of her purse. "I've been putting it in my punch."

Kitty and Josie took giggling swigs from the bottle like teenagers hiding under the bleachers at homecoming. I didn't, purposefully square. I took a step away from them, trying to catch the eyes of any half-significant figure in the room. I took a few photos of men who didn't notice. Flash Holtz, a cool-guy manager with big aviators, didn't look my way. Neither did Morty Blackenmueller or J. J. Simmonds, two label executives who were busy complimenting each other's identical cravats. That was fair, that made sense—how would they know I'd taken the cover when no one had a copy of the album yet? The only man who looked my way was Clifford Agnew, familiar from Goody's holiday party. He threw up a hand and said, "Hey, you again! Looking cute."

The low music trickling out of the ballroom speakers ("Bridge Over Troubled Water") cut off, replaced by the studio version of "Bee Sting." The room turned their attention to the tidy, small stage at the front of the room, clapping politely. Kitty jumped up and down, hooting shrill hurrahs. Josie cheered, too. Kitty threw the now-empty vodka bottle to the ground, and I stepped farther away. A cluster of people looked, startled by the clatter.

Stanley stepped out and tapped on the live mic. I crept closer to the stage, brushing the wall of the room, and took his photo. "Ladies and gentlemen," he said, straightening his suit jacket, "I am excited to be able to introduce one of the biggest and best bands playing music today, and proud to be here to celebrate the release of their fourth album, *Outfield Flowers*. They will be playing an intimate set today for you, and after they finish—"

Josie cleared her throat and shouted across the crowd, "Hey, Stanley, looking sexy in that bolo tie!"

He turned beet red. Some members of the crowd tittered, others murmured in worldly disapproval. "After they finish, I invite you to receive an autographed copy of the album from one of the gracious girls working at our gifts table." He gestured to the side of the hall. Two women in up-dos and shopgirl uniforms waved.

Kitty, liking how everyone laughed when Josie shouted, yelled, "Stanley the man-ly, I'm your biggest fan-ly!"

The crowd laughed again, a bit louder. I wasn't sure if it was at Kitty or Stanley. Stanley kept his composure and said, "Without further ado, Holiday Sun!"

I snapped Polaroid photos, catching them and placing them by my feet, as the band emerged from behind a red curtain. The lights dimmed. The crowd applauded and Holiday Sun walked slowly toward the cheers of their equals. Cal stepped up to the mic, dropping his denim jacket off his shoulders. He wore a T-shirt with the sleeves cut off, despite the bandages around his bicep. He looked to Josie. Josie smiled and he didn't. He'd shifted his look, just a bit—part Springsteen, part James Dean, all look-at-me-I'm-fresh-again. The rest of the band was feigning formality better, in sport coats and slacks.

I took Polaroids until I ran out of film. Howie looked my way for a few, making photogenic faces that I made up my mind to thank him for later. I finished the set by whirling through the crowd, overeager to get my copy of the album. My copy of my own photo. I name-dropped along the way, emboldened by urgency. Holiday Sun finished their final song, Scott wailing out a last triumphant riff, as I reached the gifts table. I asked the girls behind it for a copy of the album, and they handed it to me. I held the record to my chest as the crowd began to applaud, feeling, for just a second, that the celebration was for me.

I slipped into the hall to examine the album. Chatter blared from the ballroom, but the hallway was still, with a rotary fan above providing coolness and a slight clangor. I bounced my copy of the album up and down, imagining I could tell something about it by its weight. I ran my fingers over the embossed cover, tracing the nearly perfect picture I'd taken. I wished I'd gotten Kent to smile less or Scott to fix his hair—but who cared? It was my cover, really, truly *mine*.

I flipped the record over and pulled out the liner notes. My eyes scanned past producers and songwriting credits in search of my own name. I couldn't spot it, so I looked again, thinking I was so excited I'd overlooked it.

Patty-Ann was there. Josie was thanked. Floyd was there. I skimmed lighting designers and session musicians and backup vocalists and seamstresses and found absolutely nothing.

I wasn't there. I laughed, then almost burst into tears.

I flipped the album back over, the smiling photo of the band looking up at me. *Hi, Faun,* they seemed to say. *You didn't really think we'd let you have this, did you?*

Fine. Stanley hadn't wanted me to sell my pictures, so he'd given me the album cover. Or so I'd thought—it wasn't mine. What was the point of having something if no one knew it was yours? How was I supposed to establish myself as a photographer when my first and only work was cruelly anonymous?

I tucked the album under my arm and marched back into the ballroom, seeking Josie or Kitty or anyone to validate my anger. Seeking someone to fix it for me. Someone to explain why I was always an afterthought. No—I wasn't even a thought at all. I found Josie, who by now had her own copy of the album. She smiled, reaching for my hand. I didn't take it.

Josie asked if I wanted to say hi to the guys, but I couldn't bear to. Seeing Holiday Sun—seeing Stanley—would be the cherry on top of my shame. Josie asked what was wrong, so I told her. She dismissed me, saying, "Well, all you did was take the photo. No offense. But isn't it enough they let you do it at all?"

It wasn't.

Josie's name was on the album, thanked for just existing. She didn't know what it was like to be ignored.

Josie went to see the band, and I followed. I didn't want to, but I did. We met them at the room's center table. I couldn't look any of them in the eye. Kent played with the hors d'oeuvres, feeding the bits he didn't like to Kitty. Josie curled up under Cal's arm. I glowered at the smiling room, catching Stanley's attention with my scowl. I picked at the corner of the record sleeve, tempted to rip the cardboard apart.

Stanley grabbed my arm, gently, and pulled me aside. He asked, "Happy with the photo, Faun?"

"Yeah, who took it?" I asked. "They're not credited."

"I guess we forgot you," he said, shrugging lightly before returning to a conversation with a bespectacled somebody. He smiled, and the band smiled, and the crowd smiled. Everyone was conspiring against me. Against wannabe Faun. Wasn't it funny to make me feel like I mattered? To make me think I might be valuable? I was a bled-out doll in a room of shark-toothed men and their moonfaced cronies.

Stanley said it wasn't on purpose, but the idea that not a single person remembered to credit me was absurd. This was intentional. Underpaid and uncredited I might have been, but stupid I wasn't. Stanley had essentially broken his promise, so I resolved to break mine, too. I tore the sleeve in two and let the record smack onto the ballroom floor.

I stomped back home along Fairfax, my Mary Janes clacking against the pavement.

I EMPTIED MY Polaroid drawer, bringing upward of two hundred pictures to Garter Photo Hut, figuring Otis would know best which ones were saleable. I told myself I was going to him out of necessity, not spite. After all, I needed more money. The little I had wouldn't last forever. I only thought about the future when it was convenient.

The store wasn't stuffy anymore—after a winter of stagnant air, it was absolutely stifling. I didn't recognize the woman at the counter, so I asked, shifting my bag on my shoulder, "Hey, does Otis still work here?"

She snapped her gum and said, "Yeah. He's in the back." Then, looking over her shoulder, she shouted, "Otis! Customer for you."

When Otis saw me, he laughed.

"You want to sell some pictures for me?" I asked, sliding to a corner of the counter crowded with empty canisters and open envelopes.

"Of what?"

I pulled the bag off my shoulder and placed it gingerly before him. "Whatever you want," I said. Then, reaching around in the dark of the bag, "I have some great ones in this stack." I handed him twenty beautifully composed pictures tied together with a rubber band. Those were pictures I'd be honored to have anyone see, ones where ceiling lights cast halos over the band's heads and smiles twinkled like stars. I loved those photos. Otis shrugged after shuffling through them.

"These are snoozers," he said. My heart sank. He rifled through the bag and pulled out more Polaroids. He glanced at the one of Scott lifting the naked girl and nodded. "Now this," he said, "is good shit. No one buys pretty shots. They want grit. They want shit they don't even realize they want to see."

"So you think you could sell this one?"

"Yeah," he said. He pulled out a few more, only liking ones with tits or blood. Bonus points for both. After a minute of selection, he pulled out the two photos of Josie and Harry I'd taped together, peeled them apart, and asked, "Damn, is this—?"

"Yeah, it's Harry Carling," I said, then added regrettably, "and Josie Norfolk. Cal Holiday's fiancée."

"This is a go. This is a thousand bucks right here," he said.

"No," I said, my guilt getting the best of me. I couldn't sell a photo of Josie smacking lips with Harry. It wouldn't hurt Stanley, only Josie.

"It would sell. I guarantee you that. It's good."

I took back the two photos and stared at them, wondering why I'd taken them when all they did was make me angry. The camera caught the pink of Josie's tongue poking into Harry's mouth. His hands on her waist. Her hands on his lap. They were smiling through the kisses, and I was scowling, staring down at them.

"Come on," he said.

I hesitated for a moment. Josie didn't care that the band had tossed me aside when it came time to give credit. She got credit for show-ing up. She got Harry. I got *nothing*. I was starving for attention and money, and Stanley had denied me my fair share of both. Hunger breeds desperation.

"Okay," I said, and handed them over. I stuck my hands into my pockets. My fingers felt dirty.

Otis collected all the pictures he wanted in a haphazard pile, tying them together, and asked, "This an anonymous thing?"

"No name," I said. "Please." I'd gone from being bitter over not getting credit to desperate to avoid it. "And I want you to make cop-ies," I said quickly, "I want the originals back. I'll give you my phone number, and I expect you to call me as soon as they're sold. You can leave a message, but just with your name. No information. All right?"

"All right. I'll shop 'em around and call you when there's a taker."

I grew suspicious, not knowing why, and said, evoking the most intensity I could, "Steal them and I'll rip your nuts off."

"Whoa!" He laughed. "Cool down."

"I'm not joking," I said, unable to take myself seriously.

He nodded, smirking in that awful way people do when they think you're an idiot. "We'll discuss terms and my cut of the money over drinks. I'll get my things. Wait here."

He retreated to the back room to fetch his keys and wallet, and I imagined the smell of sulfur lingering in his place. Stop feeling so dirty, I told myself. Stop feeling evil. If Stanley honored only the bar-est semblance of our deal, then I was free to do the same. Besides, I wasn't even *really* the one who'd be selling the pictures. Otis was. I had just . . . given them to him.

We set off into the evening, staying a yardstick's length from each other. We went to his favorite bar, an "authentic" place, where the tables were sticky and the bathrooms were caked in a layer of sludge. Otis claimed Fatso's Taphouse was the "only place in California that still sold cheap beer and played real music."

There I was at ten P.M. in a half-empty dive bar, pressed in a corner.

Otis was practically sitting on me. Droplets of beer caught on his curly muttonchops. "You're almost hot, in a no-tits kind of way," he said.

Instead of retorting that his facial hair made him look like a young, alcoholic Martin Van Buren, I remembered what was at stake and said, "Thanks, Otis."

I kept trying to turn the conversation to the photos, but Otis only wanted to share his almighty thoughts on everything from Pink Floyd to breast implants.

He ordered a plate of miniature pretzels to share, and I shoved them into my mouth as he said, "You must be obsessed with Holiday Sun to have all those photos. I know you're their friend, or whatever, but to go to all their parties . . . that's a lot, girl. I mean, *I*'d love to go to one. Wouldn't that be something?"

I got nowhere by being resistant. "You'd have a blast. If you're nice enough, maybe I'll take you to one." A major lie, but I didn't care.

Our exchange became this: Otis would spew nonsense music philosophy, and after ten minutes, I'd question him about our financial arrangement. He'd answer, we'd argue for a few seconds, then he'd return to sermonizing. Rinse and repeat. Otis was dead set on giving me a flat rate and keeping whatever excess he procured for the Polaroids. I bartered until the rate was higher than what I'd gotten for *Outfield Flowers*. The actual amount wasn't too important—only the validation that someone could want my pictures was. Otis wrote me a check for $950 (with instructions to not cash it until next Friday) and I tucked it into my purse.

By eleven, the bar was filling up and I was trying to get out. He tried to kiss me twice before I stood up and started toward the door.

"Faun," he said, "don't spoil it."

"There is nothing to spoil," I said.

He followed me out and we faced each other on the dark street. I clutched my tote bag, filled with the rejected photos, and asked Otis to ensure he had the choice shots. He did.

"Let me walk you home?" he asked.

I shook my head. "This isn't like that."

"People know who you are," he said quietly. A fly buzzed past his face. "At least a little bit. At least a few people."

"Oh," I said.

"Are you sure I can't walk you home?" he asked. He meant more.

"Yes, I'm sure." Also meaning more than I said, I asked, "Please don't tell people you did."

He did, but it didn't matter. Gossip a nobody tells only spreads within nobody circles. And I, of course, thought I was above any circles muttonchops Otis ran in. Superiority is an easy feeling. We went our separate ways, guilt growing tumorous within me.

WHEN I GOT home, Josie was spinning an old record by Holiday Sun and trying to paint her nails while reading her new "spooky little obsession," *Salem's Lot*. She kept spilling droplets of paint over the pages, but she smudged them away with her pinkie, obscuring the words with faint red marks. Blood-colored.

I hummed to avoid having to listen to the music. Josie turned it up, not realizing the triple-clapping chorus of "Sheila" was about the last thing I wanted to hear. Not realizing after being thrown aside like trash by the band and their manager, I wouldn't want to jam to their music. Not realizing anything.

I threw my tote bag to the floor beside the couch and yanked off my shoes, massaging my tired feet and pouting at everything. I was all anger and guilt and bitter, bitter disappointment.

Josie spilled more nail polish as I went to take a shower, feeling like the queen of melodrama as I cried. Tears and water droplets mingled on my face until my skin stung with salt and heat. I turned off the water and wrapped a wash-faded towel around my body.

The blow dryer made it hard to hear the knock at the bathroom door. Josie pushed the door open. She asked, gingerly, "I know you're awfully mad right now, but I called Cal and he says the guys want you to come to a party tomorrow. It'll be the last good one before the wedding. Please, won't you?"

I didn't respond.

"Faun," she said, "they want you there."

That was all she had to say. If I said no, they might never want me again. Giving that up, despite everything that had transpired, would be foolish.

After I dried off, Josie tossed over a sparkly dress and told me to try it on because she wanted to go dancing. It fit, so I took a self-portrait Polaroid in the bathroom mirror.

As we waited for our taxi, I was pre-dancing drunk enough to ask Josie about something that still sat in my mind. "Is Cal behaving himself?"

"Of course," she said. She laughed, drunk, too. "Does it even matter?"

"What's that mean?"

"Oh," Josie said, "the wedding's all booked. The whole world's waiting. Of course I'm excited. Of course I'm going through with it."

We set out on the town. Soon I'd be helping pack Josie's clothes and knickknacks into boxes, shuttling them to Cal's house. Soon I'd be just Faun, not half of Faun-and-Josie. But that night, we were a superb pair. She brightened me up, and I forgot, every so often, that I was an awful friend.

Everything would get better. It had to. But the perfect fantasy we lived in was so close to collapse.

Josie told me she loved me.

She told me the band loved me.

And I wanted so desperately to love everything back.

One
Photo

Me in the bathroom mirror, in a borrowed slip dress, faceless
behind my camera, obscured by condensation.

14.

ON THE DAY OF JOSIE'S WEDDING, DARLENE NEARLY STEPPED ON a hypodermic needle hidden in the shag carpet of Kent's apartment. She made a fuss until Kitty bent down and chucked it into the wastebasket.

We were grateful Kent let the bridal party get ready in his apartment because he lived only five minutes by car from the church. Josie and I lived too far, and Josie had declared all the available nearby hotels too "unsuitable" to accommodate us. Kitty had talked up the view from Kent's pad, convincing Josie it was the ideal setting. So much for wanting somewhere nice—although Kent's place was gorgeously built, with floor-to-ceiling windows and ornate metal decor, it was ruined by discarded trash and half-empty bottles.

What a funny party we were—Kitty, Yvonne, Darlene, and I, hastily cleaning the apartment in bridesmaid dresses and flower-crowned hair before Josie and her sister, Pamela, arrived. I'd spent the morning feeling out others' opinions on the wedding, but no one wanted to be open. "We shouldn't be speculating," Darlene had said. "We shouldn't be in Josie and Cal's business." Everyone else reacted the same way. No one denied that she was in trouble. No one was able to do that.

Kitty flipped the never-marked calendar on the wall to May and added a few flattering activities like "volunteer at dog pound" and "read to dying children." Yvonne wasn't doing much cleaning but did an excellent job at bossing us around. Wendy sat on Yvonne's lap, asking her to sing "Disco Duck."

Darlene kicked a stack of papers underneath the TV stand. "Wendy loves 'Disco Duck,' doesn't she?" she said.

"I don't know it," Yvonne said, looking too seriously at Wendy.

I began to scrub at the dishes, but Kitty said, "No, let's do all the obvious garbage first."

Yvonne laughed. "That means Faun's out."

"Mean," Darlene muttered.

Our mad dash of cleaning continued. Kitty marveled at how much space there was when every surface wasn't clogged with dirty plates and white-powdered mirrors. She twirled in her bell-sleeve minidress (a reject from her high school homecoming), saying she couldn't wait to meet Pamela.

I told her not to get her hopes up. "Pamela is, um, a little stiff." I twisted my hands and stood in front of the girls. "I don't mean to suggest we don't know how to handle ourselves, but Josie's been a bit worried. So here's a few ground rules: no one does blow, no one gets so drunk they puke, no one gets naked, no one talks about their breasts. In general, don't do or say anything Josie's Irish Catholic family wouldn't like."

"So we're all supposed to be June fuckin' Cleaver?" Yvonne asked, disregarding the impressionable toddler on the cushion next to her.

"Pretty much," I said.

"What about the after-party?" Kitty asked, voice eager.

"It's called a reception," Yvonne corrected.

I laughed. Darlene picked up Wendy and danced with her, telling her to stop picking at the embroidery on her dress.

"I won't be at most of the reception, so I won't be there to watch you," I said. Not like it would matter. Yvonne would do anything I asked her not to, looking me in the eyes the whole time.

Harry Carling had called in the early morning. His hello had sounded like wind, and I'd imagined him standing alone against the great glass eye of a hotel window or at a street-side pay phone, his hands sticky with the remnants of all the other calls dialed there. He asked if I was free to drive up to San Francisco and see him today, and I was sad (was I sad?) to reply I couldn't, due to my obligations as Josie's maid of honor.

"Come after the ceremony," he said. "I want to see you."

Josie hadn't seemed to mind when I told her (but she never *seemed* to mind anything), agreeing to lend me her Gremlin as long as I promised to stay for half the reception. "You'll make it into the wedding video, won't you?" she asked.

I would, but the only parts of that video anyone would remember were how Darlene spent the entire reception barefoot, how Cal kissed Josie every second he could, and how Brooke, drunk, spoke directly to the camera, making a joking fuss about not being a bridesmaid.

We kept cleaning the apartment, Darlene pretending to be Cinderella, until the buzzer rang. Kitty answered it, and I scoured the living room for any remaining trash. There was another needle under the couch. I wrapped it in a tissue and chucked it into the bin.

Yvonne asked, "Since when is Kent shooting up?"

"Does it matter? Whatever, Darlene's on coke all the time," Kitty snapped, done chatting with Josie across the intercom. "That's basically the same thing."

Josie's signature triple knock came at the door. I opened it to greet her and her sister. We all cooed that Josie was a vision—an angel— with her big curls and flowing prairie dress. We threw a token compliment to Pamela, who was unreceptive and unbelieving. She rolled her un-mascaraed eyes when Darlene said she looked nice. Pamela looked a lot like Josie, with her elfish smile and almond eyes, but her slouch and ruddy cheeks made it harder to believe they shared the same blood.

Pamela and Josie had been on good sisterly terms when they were little enough to not realize their mother was the only person who liked Pamela better than Josie. Their relationship grew tense, competitive over every facet of teenhood. When Pamela regrettably confessed a crush on Skipper Bronson, our school's basketball captain, Josie asked him out to a movie. Pamela countered by telling the rest of the basketball team that Josie had the urban-legend-slash-curse of a vagina full of sharp teeth. "Why do you think she never keeps a boyfriend?" Pamela had asked. Skipper broke it off with Josie, fearing accidental castration or worse. Josie countered by throwing Pamela's pristine Archie Comics collection into the family's firepit. Josie moved on and up, finding a different captain to pine for, and Pamela got nothing.

I wondered what it was like to be Josephine Norfolk, soon-to-be *Foxy* model and soon-to-be celebrity's wife, with her white teeth and toned stomach. With her skin that tanned and never burned. With her way of going anywhere she wanted and never being questioned. A dream life for a dream girl. Then I looked at Josie's face and wondered why she wasn't smiling.

As Pamela was about to slip off her sensible flats, Darlene said, "Honey, I'd keep your shoes on."

Pamela looked Darlene up and down, unimpressed, and said, "*You're* barefoot. Is that a baby? Josie, where did you meet these people?"

"They're my friends," Josie said, evoking unbelievable lightness. "Play nice, Pamela."

We helped Josie get ready, even though there wasn't much to do other than mentally prepare her. Kitty tried fruitlessly to make friends with Pamela. Yvonne called the limousine company to make sure they'd arrive on time. With Josie's makeup already done and her hair already curled, all we had left to do was wait.

We were close to leaving when Josie asked, for the fifth time that hour, "Does the dress look all right?"

We all said yes except for Pamela. She squinted at the slit running down the bust and said, "Do you want me to stitch that up? It's a little tacky."

Josie immediately burst into tears. Wendy started crying, too, innately empathetic, and I grabbed Josie's hand and pulled her into the apartment's uncleaned bedroom. I hopped onto the rumpled bed, ignoring the soiled boxer shorts and bras tangled into its sheets, and patted the space beside me. Josie sat, her back straight and severe. She wiped her tears with her pinkie fingers. Dainty.

"She didn't mean it," I said. "You look beautiful. You're a perfect bride."

That made her cry harder. Josie tugged on her dress, not to adjust or smooth it but—seemingly—to tear it off. I ran my hands through my hair, frizzing my fake perm but too stressed to care. Josie's tears sounded strange, like gargling. I knew I shouldn't have said what I said next, but I did anyway. I thought she needed to hear it. "You don't have to get married," I said. "If you don't really want to."

Josie shrieked. "What a disgusting thing to say," she said. "There's no reason for you to suggest that—to say that—"

She was seething, but I, dismissed along with my genuine concern, was angry, too. I whispered harshly, "He's awful to you. I've seen it, Josie, and I think he's just awful—"

"No!" she yelled. The murmur of conversation in the living room fell. Might as well listen for gossip. Might as well hear what the perfect bride and her impossible maid of honor were squabbling about. Josie continued, "Don't say that! Don't you ever say that! On my wedding day, of all days, you've decided to be, what—my little savior? Guess what? You only want me to stop crying. Nobody fucking cares about anything."

"You don't make any sense," I said. "You don't make any sense at all." She did. And she didn't.

Josie stood up, tugging at the slit in the front of her dress. She said, "Cal likes the dress. I like the dress. I love it. I love him." Again, she said, "I love him." On and on she went, repeating it as she paced Kent and Kitty's musky bedroom. She stopped crying. Her face dried. And soon she turned back to me, took a meditative breath, and said, "Is your dress new? Is it Gunne Sax?"

JOSIE AND CAL got hitched without a hitch. The wedding was tacky enough to satisfy the bedazzled California crowd, but traditional enough to appease both Josie's no-money Boston-born mother, holding a framed photo of Josie's dead army-captain father, and Cal's stodgy parents. The ceremony was short. The only interruption was Kent's delirious attempt to drum along to "Here Comes the Bride" on the pew ahead of him. Josie stood still as she gave the standard vows promising she would be true and beautiful forever. Her bouquet spread from her clutched arms like front wings. Cal's vows had half-funny jokes, not ribald but ribbing, about Josie having chosen a "boring old bloke" like him over her "thousand magazine-reading admirers."

Josie and Cal kissed when they were supposed to and smiled at all the right times, too. Josie's pale hair gleamed under the church candles, and Cal, tucked into his best velvet suit, was clean-shaven and fully awake for the first time in months. There was a freshness to them, a brightness. Josie shoved her bouquet against Cal's nose to make him smell it, and he laughed. Everything was bound to be better.

Forget the debauched nights of bloody noses, torn knuckles, bruises, and numb gums. Soon they were to share quiet evenings together, right? I didn't realize a marriage certificate is nothing compared to the heat of tour bus antics and the itch you get when all your friends are drinking tequila without you.

I *felt* things were going to change for Josie and Cal. I felt like he wouldn't hit her, when he was mad or bored or whatever sparked it. (I suspected nothing sparked it, that it was random, like lightning strikes that electrocute the same tree too many times.) No—I felt like they'd be the perfect couple I'd always wanted them to be. A last-chance shift was crawling into the frame. But feeling isn't knowing, despite what my eager heart wanted to believe. Half of feelings are faked, and the other half are ill-advised. To feel happy is not to *be* happy. Was Josie happy? Was I?

THE WEDDING MADE a mass taxi-shuttled exodus to a reception hall decked in hundreds of rose bouquets, all smelling sweet, and all with the thorns still on.

Josie's mother was more interested in the floral arrangements than all the fame surrounding her. She didn't notice Donna Summer's backup singers standing behind her in line for the restroom. Pamela, however, drank her first glass of champagne and gushed to me about every face she recognized. At dinner, the girls and I sat with Cal and Josie. We hadn't had much time to get to know Cal's two brothers, who were the non–Holiday Sun groomsmen, but they seemed nice enough.

We ate sickly sweet white cake and took stiff-shouldered photos. I noted to Yvonne that Floyd would have hated the cake—icing made his teeth ache—and she said that he would have been grateful for having cake at all. He wasn't there.

Everything was bizarre in its normalcy. Josie's little cousins knocked over a table playing tag in too-big dress shoes. After dessert, Cal's older brother, Winslow, gave a heartfelt speech that barely mentioned his brother, going on about the hills in the countryside and the freedom of fresh air. The four-hundred-strong wedding guests clapped and turned their attention to me. Right. I was the maid of honor, so I stood up to give a speech I hadn't prepared.

My manicured hands twitched around my champagne glass, and I wanted to down the whole thing in one gulp. Darlene handed me my fork, and I beat it against the glass.

"Well, everybody," I said, unsure where I was going. Was I speaking loud enough? Why hadn't I prepared this? Why hadn't I realized this wedding was real until right now? "Josie and Cal are . . . married now." Everyone laughed, and I quickly said, "I'm so happy for them. And I know they're happy together. They act like they can take over the world when they're together. Who knows, maybe they will. I'm so glad—so happy. Josie, I remember when I found out you two were getting married, and I remember how you were so happy to . . . to get to tell me. You deserve to be happy. You both do. I'm happy about this day. Congratulations!"

Happy, happy, happy.

When it was time to dance, Josie and Cal started the night off with a waltz. Scott and Kent almost pissed themselves laughing at how serious it was, but I didn't. Neither did Kitty, or even Yvonne. Goody

Plenty held her man-of-the-week and stared at Josie and Cal swaying in heaven-light on the dance floor. Days and nights of desperate adoration were worth the chance to revel in the delicate hope that groupie love could someday become real love. *Was* it real love? I wasn't convinced. Not anymore. But everyone else seemed so adamant, so assured, that Josie and Cal were perfect that I thought I was wrong for believing otherwise. Maybe everyone had the same fears as me, but, like me, no one said so. All fooling each other.

After the waltz, the hired deejay started requests, so Wendy got to hear all the disco novelty songs she wanted. Josie picked Wendy up and spun her, then handed her off to Cal, who spun her, too, before letting her run to Darlene. Josie and Cal flapped their arms to the music, flamboyant and careless, getting down to the beat.

Josie kissed him hard. He said, "You're the prettiest girl in the whole world."

"Will you take the prettiest girl in the whole world on a honeymoon?" Josie asked, kissing his cheek.

I danced past them, flapping my arms with Cal's brother Winslow, not so much a disco duck as a headless chicken.

"I'll take her on *tour*," Cal said. "We can call it the Honeymoon Tour. We're even going to Europe, you know."

"It's not the same," Josie said, and laughed, "and it's ever so *far* away."

"It's soon," he said. "It's barely a month away, love! We'll go! You'll come."

THE NIGHT WORE on, and we dipped and delighted in the purity of a good old-fashioned wedding. I danced with everyone and forgot I was bad at it, then stood at the back of the hall with Scott and Darlene, watching life transpire. Darlene entertained my critiques of the poor form of the hired photographers and videographers. She agreed I could have done better, but wasn't it better to be able to relax at my own best friend's wedding?

"Give this to Uncle Cal," Scott said to Wendy, handing her a bow-wrapped package. "Go on, go."

Wendy toddled away, making a haphazard beeline to the happy couple reseated at the table, greeting guests who approached them like their royal subjects.

"What's the gift?" I asked, aching to volunteer I'd bought them an electric skillet and a nice Brie from the farmers' market.

"Coke," Darlene said. "Eight ounces."

"Oh," I said. "That's . . . a *lot.*"

"Spare no expense," Scott muttered.

We turned to watch Wendy chuck the present onto the table, nearly knocking over Josie's wineglass. Wendy clapped for herself, and as she waddled back, the three of us clapped, too.

IT WAS GETTING late, and I knew I had to leave. Driving to San Francisco would take about six hours, and I didn't want to fall asleep at the wheel. I glanced out the reception hall's oversize windows and remarked to Josie, whom I had managed to steal away for a moment of privacy, that the deep gray clouds looked like rain.

"It doesn't rain here. This is California, you know," she said, half serious. Her lipstick had all but rubbed off, and she bit her lips, tearing off any final flakes. She gave me a hug, breathing slowly, and said, "The Gremlin's outside Kent's place. Drive safe. Have fun. See you soon."

It poured all night as I drove in the dark to San Francisco in my bridesmaid dress, the highway glistening.

One
Photo

The wedding party standing shoulder to shoulder on the steps of the church, stiff and almost laughing from how unfamiliar it feels to be there.

15.

THE FRONT DESK GIRL AT HARRY'S HOTEL WAS ASLEEP ON HER overnight shift.

I was glad, because as I stepped through the blue-carpeted lobby, watching my reflection on the gold-mirrored walls, I realized my makeup had run. A rained-on watercolor painting. I'd been rubbing my eyes on the drive up without realizing. I leaned close to one of the walls, searching for a smudgeless section of the gilded surface, and used the sleeve of my gown to wipe my face clean.

Harry was running a fever when I found him in the hotel room he'd given me over the phone. His milky skin shone wet, reflecting the moonlight dripping in through his curtainless window. My heart strummed in my chest. Tonight was redemption. Tonight was all I had been waiting for and wanting. Tonight I wasn't a background girl; I was the sole object of Harry's desire. How beautiful I felt.

"What an outfit," he said, clicking his tongue. I shrugged, tugging at the sleeves of my bridesmaid dress. Then, he said, "You made it."

"Of course." I sat at the foot of his bed and said softly, "I'd make it anywhere for you."

Sweating and sipping from a hotel room cup full of either coffee or brandy, he paced the red low-pile carpet and pointed at silver pens and guitar cases, telling me nothing facts about them as I nodded patiently.

"I really like you," I said.

Here's a teen magazine question for you: *If my number one dream crush brings me into his hotel room, how long before I can ask him to ravish me and how long until it feels real?*

He kissed me and, for a splendid second, it was everything I had dreamed of. Better than that spin-the-bottle-style smooch we'd shared in my living room. We were alone and intentional now. Then, I worried I'd catch whatever bug he had from the sickly breath he exhaled onto my neck. Who cared? If Harry Carling wanted me to get sick, it would be for the best.

He hitched his legs onto the bed around mine and we fell onto the comforter together. He kissed my neck and asked if I wanted something to drink. He opened his bedside drawer and pulled a bottle of whiskey onto the bed. We passed it back and forth, talking in poems about the state of the universe.

Eventually we ended up on the carpet as Harry plucked out a brand-new song for me. He turned all the *baby*s in the lyrics to *Faun*s and I could have collapsed. How could a person be so good at making you fall in love with him? Especially when he didn't even want you to?

I took photos of him on my Polaroid, each with him sticking his tongue out or in a different stage of undress. Those were pictures I'd never do anything with. I'd tuck them away, and every so often I'd pluck one out and stare at it, trying to remember the moment I'd wanted forever. I told him he was handsome, and he laughed, saying I was too cute for rock and roll—that I should come be a little hippie with him instead.

"No, no." I laughed. "I'm big and scary. I'll bite you." I pretended to snap at him.

"You're so tiny," he said. "Not starving-tiny like your friend Yvonne, though."

"That's mean," I said. He rolled his eyes, so instead I said, "Thank you." Then, without realizing I was speaking aloud, "Fuck me, please."

He tossed his guitar to the floor. It clanged out a chord of its own and Harry nearly tore my dress searching for its zipper. His fever-skin was hot and rough, but it felt like the sun on my face instead of coals. I melted to imagine Yvonne or Floyd or anyone seeing me now.

I imagined everyone I'd ever seen peeking in through the twentieth-floor window of the hotel room, pointing and murmuring about how lucky I was.

Harry emanated the stale, clammy smell of illness, but I didn't care. He was the one running a fever, but I might as well have been, too. I felt as hot and reckless as anyone burning up.

"I worship you," I said, kissing each of his fingers. "I'd die for you, and I mean it."

"You're good at this," he said, and I didn't know if he was talking about how I was touching him or what I said.

I sprawled, writhing on the hotel bed as he moved inside me, and prepared myself for lightning strikes. He kissed me. I said kind things about everything he did, even if it felt like nothing. Was I too drunk? Was I expecting too much? Why did his hands turn me numb and why, oh why, was I so afraid he'd stop touching me? He finished, sweatier than he'd ever been, and came all over my thigh.

For a moment, we both laid still, then I stood naked and watched him light a cigarette with his eyes shut.

I was expecting resurrection, but all I got was semen dripping down my leg and a mouth-shaped bruise on my neck. Was that it, then? Why was I still myself?

I was expecting the sky to open up.

In the bathroom, I washed up, trying to tell myself I was excited. My neck burned from the hickey he gave me. Then I reminded myself it was a Harry Carling hickey, born from his perfect-pretty mouth. Why didn't that make me feel better?

He was asleep when I came back from the washroom. His T-shirt, a ratty thing with an old anti-war graphic (VENUS DE MILO DID IT—DISARM), was crumpled on the floor. I picked it up and put it on. I poked his shoulder to wake him, and he muttered, "You can sleep here, if you want."

"Thank you," I said, not realizing his offer was hardly generous.

We slept back-to-back. As I fell asleep, I imagined clipping him onto my collectible key chain and wondered how Josie was doing on her wedding night.

HARRY BID ME off in the morning with a shot of whiskey and a blown kiss. I asked if I could keep the shirt I'd stolen from the floor, and he said sure. I tucked it into my purse, because I had no change of clothes and was back in my bridesmaid dress.

"Call me up when you get back to L.A.," I said. "We could do another photoshoot."

"I'll be busy," he said. "But I'll try—you live in Redondo, right?"

"I live off Fairfax," I said, laughing. I stopped when he didn't think it was funny. "Do you want to show me San Francisco for a little while?"

"I need to get breakfast, Faun," he said.

"Well, me, too."

"I'll call you," he said, with painful finality. Then, tossing me a shard of hope, he said, "I'm glad you came. I think my fever's breaking."

THE HIGHWAY WAS lonelier in the daytime. Harry had said I was tiny, and now I knew it. In Josie's Gremlin on the forever-stretching paleness of the freeway, I was as miniature as the bugs burst open dead on the windshield.

I got home after two stops at gas stations, where I bought egg sandwiches and chocolate bars to tide myself over. Josie had spent all day moving out, and without all her trinkets and baubles, the apartment was empty enough to echo my voice. I fitted the bed with the sheets from the futon couch and tried to sleep, but my mind hummed with the new song Harry had played me. That was special, wasn't it?

I slept for three hours, then rose at midnight to call Kitty, then Darlene, then Josie to see where the party was. When I couldn't find one, I tried my small collected list of half-famous musicians. Zilch. Of course. The one night I needed bright lights, I got nothing.

Who else? Who was left? I called Otis to check on my photos and he said I could come pick up my original prints. He'd found a buyer. There was no time for regret. At least I'd have money for rent.

I pulled Harry's protest T-shirt out of my purse. Smoothing it out, I stuck it on a hanger and pinned it to a bare nail sticking out of the wall.

I went back to sleep, arms wrapped around myself.

Two Photos

Harry, guitar in his hands, smiling just for me, putting my name in a song, his fingers red.

My hand and Harry's foot on the garnet swirl of the hotel carpet, the only proof we were together, captured by accident as he played with my Polaroid.

16.

THE BAND WERE SO COOL.

I'd forget it for a second, then Howie would sling his arm around my shoulder or I'd get to stand beside Kent as he waved to a crowd of fans, and I'd fall back into the precious joy of orbiting importance. I wasn't the sun and I'd never be, but being a planet was fine, too. It was still in the sky. I wasn't really the band's fan anymore, but I was still a groupie. Those things intersect, and can overlap, but can exist independently—they're a Venn diagram. I was the band's friend. Still loyal, still proud, but past adoration. Past obsession. Still deep in debt.

Holiday Sun would rehearse all day, then get bored, turning self-conscious and catty. The girls and I would comfort them, assuring them of their godly status. We'd all go party and wonder if we were dying and tell each other how good our faces looked. The upcoming tour put pressure on the band to behave, giving them an outlandish need to refuse. They needed to rebel—although against what I never quite figured out.

There was nothing like a party in your own home, so the band threw them on a rotating schedule. Their time in L.A. was soon to give way to midnight drives through middle America and breakfasts of gas-station coffee, but I didn't want the band to leave me. Sure, I could follow them, but then I'd have to find the magic all over again in an unfamiliar place.

I didn't want it to end. I would have rather ended with it.

JOSIE'S *FOXY* PHOTOSHOOT came and went. Despite my intentions, I didn't accompany her. She went alone, with Cal's denim jacket on her shoulders for luck. Over the telephone, she gushed for hours before swinging by the apartment to show off some proofs. We sat at the kitchen table, drinking cold coffee and preparing to admire Josie's seductive image in ink.

"You've got to promise not to scream when I show you," she said, fiddling with the facedown stack of photos, "because they're racy, but it's a fair trade-off because . . ." She did a small drumroll on the table. "I am officially June's cover girl!"

I gawked, confused by how quickly it had all happened. "Does your mother know?" I asked.

"I haven't told anybody." She cackled. "I want it to be a surprise, but I can't keep anything from you." She added, "And Cal knows, of course. Here's the photo they're putting on the cover." She slid over a glossy print. You could tell she was nude, her tanned skin glowing under the yellow studio lights, but her nakedness was covered by Cal's denim jacket, which she clutched over her chest. The jacket was paramount with its signature pins and patches. It was recognizable. It reminded anyone who looked at the photo who she was—and how this random blonde had worked her way onto the cover of America's favorite nudie mag. When she pulled out the photograph set to be the centerfold, she said, dead serious, "My cooch is in this one. Can you handle it?"

I nodded diligently, then admired Josie's stature and smile, making a point of looking everywhere but her "cooch."

Waiting for the photoshoot had taken forever, but Josie said the magazine would be out in a week. Funny how things glide faster than you can handle once they finally start to move.

Josie collected her pictures into a doodled-over manila folder and gave me the address of the hotel she and Cal were staying in. They should have been already settled into his Laurel Canyon home, but a late-night kitchen fire had turned the house unusable for the next month. They took this near-tragedy as serendipity—a reason to redo the kitchen and a reason to book a penthouse and spend every pre-tour night having a high-rise blast.

There was a thrilling intimacy to those parties. With only twenty or so invitees, each person was distinctly aware of their own importance. This intimacy bred intensity, and night by night, things turned more outrageous.

AT THE FIRST of the nightly parties, Josie pulled me to the balcony, the bones in her hand churning under her skin. The party turned muffled as she slid the glass door shut. We clutched the railing with steely hands and held ourselves too close to the edge, gazing at the world spread out below. The hot summer wind tangled our hair, blurring our vision, but the city lights sparkled brightly through any obstruction.

"That's the whole wide world out there," Josie said with a hint of self-aware glibness.

"It's just L.A.," I said.

"Nowhere else matters," she said. "Nowhere else is real like this."

For once, she was the naive one. Too pure. Too sincere. And there I was beside her, still hiding the fact I'd gotten Otis to sell those unbearable photos of her. I had to tell her before she found out on her own. If she wanted to throw me off the balcony, I'd have let her. I'd rather have splattered on L.A. concrete than anywhere else.

"Josie," I said. "Listen, a couple weeks ago I—"

"Oh, shit!" she said, catching view of something happening in the penthouse. She grabbed my arm. "Clementine's bare-ass naked!"

So I didn't tell her about the Polaroids that night. I told myself I'd do it the night after, but I didn't do it then either.

Each night split into fractured, unplaceable moments. I forgot I cared about telling Josie about the pictures—I forgot about everything that mattered. Josie spent half a party asleep, and only waking when someone uttered the name Steven Tyler. Once, Kitty sat cross-legged on the couch, eating pretzels as Darlene tried to teach her astral projection and Clementine did cartwheels. The night after, I left the room for a moment and came back to see that Kent had brought a miniature pony into the room. An hour later, the horse was gone.

One night, I wore the T-shirt I'd proudly pried from Harry Carling and waited impatiently for someone to ask where I'd gotten it. When Kitty finally did, I answered, "Oh, this? It was a gift."

She and I went on a cigarette run for the band, feeling important to be sent out but annoyed to *be* out. We were in the midst of a contest to see who could walk fastest backward in our platforms when she said, the neon lights reflecting off her clean teeth, "I don't ever wanna go home."

I didn't want to go home either. Why sit on my own and think about myself when I could dance and laugh forever?

"You mean back to Kent's?" I asked. "Or back to your mom's?"

She shrugged a little. "Does Howie smoke Kools? Kent says they're for pussies. Kent smokes Winstons because that's what *The Flintstones* smoke."

"Since when am I the Howie expert?" I asked, secretly flattered.

Kitty pushed open the convenience store's door. She grooved to the song playing over the store radio, picked up a jumbo bottle of ginger ale, and said, "Howie wants you. Like, he wants you bad."

Cigarettes and snacks in hand, we burst back into the penthouse to be told that apparently Elton John had popped by and we'd *just* missed him. Kitty burst into tears, hiccupping so hard her face turned red. Yvonne rubbed her back like she was kneading dough while Darlene cooed relaxing sentiments. Once Kitty calmed down, Yvonne bid us farewell, leaving alone.

She was a solitary creature.

Not like me, who shot so quickly toward Howie you'd have thought he was a magnet and I was a pin.

Howie welcomed me onto his lap. "Hey, there," he said. "Where's your camera?"

"It's somewhere," I said, then considered calling Josie over to spill my guts about the photos I'd sold.

Before I could decide, Howie twirled a piece of my hair and said, "You'd look so cute if you braided this."

"Yeah," Scott said, chiming in, picking at his teeth. "The way you part your hair now makes you look like Robert Plant."

"Tell him to fuck himself, Faun," Howie said.

I did, and they both laughed.

I didn't sleep with Howie that night, but decided I would soon. A groupie's determination is akin to wildfire. That violent desire is so rich and heavy it makes your heart burn. How easy it can seem, to turn determination into reality, and how difficult it really is to get the one you want to want you back.

THE NEXT NIGHT, Yvonne occupied all of Howie's attention. I watched, camera in hand, from the corner, waiting for her to get fed up with his dismissal of her, waiting for my turn to give him what he needed. I'd arrived that night and every other one in earnest, just like all the other girls, but Yvonne only had to pop by sometimes and play it ever-so-cool. She was growing bored of the California scene—something I couldn't fathom. She said she was planning on a grand journey out to New York. She had a cousin there who sang punk songs in dive bars and wanted a new manager. There were broader things out there where the "real artists" were. California was too commercial. Yvonne romanticized her hypothetical disappearance, waiting for someone to talk her into staying. No one did.

One night, close to the end of things, Yvonne lifted herself up onto the thick balcony railing. It creaked below her and she beamed as the wind hit her face. Her drapey dress sputtered in motion, her fingers dancing on the pole she clutched.

Josie, who was chain-smoking and had been on the balcony for half an hour, said, "Girl, get down."

"I'm feeling the wind," Yvonne murmured, her voice nearly lost in it.

I grabbed at her arm, then realized what an awful idea that was, because it only made her flinch. Some people steer away from touch, fearing skin on skin. Yvonne wobbled, tightening her grasp on the pole. With a slight turn, she looked right in my face and laughed.

Yvonne started to lift her fingers off the rail, one by one, counting aloud. She had only two left when with a fell swoop, Josie grabbed Yvonne's stomach, her arm brushing across her ribs, and pulled her back onto the cold concrete balcony.

"I wasn't going to do it," Yvonne said.

Josie rolled her eyes and lit another cigarette. "You're welcome."

Yvonne looked out at the sky and started to cry. She went home again, saying she wasn't coming to the party Darlene and Scott were hosting Sunday in their ranch-style home.

Holiday Sun were set to fly out to Dallas next Tuesday to kick off the tour, which left Saturday to recuperate and relax, next Monday to pack and prepare, and Sunday to go hog wild.

Darlene photocopied hand-lettered invitations on Monday, tossing stacks of them to Josie, Kitty, and me with strict instructions to distribute them as widely as possible. Darlene said, giving me my stack of yellow paper, "You'll bring Floyd?"

"I don't talk to him much anymore," I said, biting into a room service pâté-topped cracker.

"Well, you're the only gal with his phone number." Darlene laughed.

An hour later, Kent talked Kitty into snorting heroin. She nodded off in a crumpled mess of fliers. She'd made a snow angel in them. Cal assigned me to poke her every fifteen minutes to ensure she was still alive. Her shaggy bangs fell across her eyes, and we all whispered about how stupid she was to have let Kent talk her into it, knowing we would have done the same if we were the one he'd asked.

JOSIE'S EDITION OF *Foxy* hit the stands the next day. Cal, chuffed with his wife's "worldwide recognition" for her beauty and breasts, bought three hundred copies to give to anyone who cared to have one. Josie made Cal answer the phone every time it rang in case it was her mother calling with Christian outrage on her mind, but it never was.

That Tuesday night, at yet another penthouse party, Cal coaxed Josie into standing up on the table as we all clapped for her. He distributed the magazines. Clifford Agnew made a point of pulling out the centerfold, sticking his hand under his sweater, and miming his heart pounding.

Josie said she was thrilled and Cal said he was, too. But when Josie looked at the cover, she paused. Above her head, in yellow block letters, was the text: ANGEL OF THE SUNSET STRIP—MEET JOSIE HOLIDAY.

She laughed to Yvonne they'd gotten her name wrong. Yvonne suggested that no one would know who she was if the magazine didn't remind its readers of Cal, which offended Josie so deeply that she snatched Yvonne's copy out of her hands and refused to give it back.

"Oh, no," Yvonne said, "what will I do if I can't look at your tan lines?"

"Shut up," Josie said.

Cal chimed in, "Yeah, Yvonne—don't be jealous."

"I'm not jealous," she said. "*Foxy* is hardly helping women's lib. Ever heard of Gloria Steinem? Audre Lorde?"

Kitty laughed. "Oh, like you're some big feminist?" She looked to Josie, stars in her eyes. "I'd love to be in *Foxy*." We'd all had our moments of curiosity about the movement, but admitting to seeing the allure of feminist arguments would be admitting to the men who wove us into their world that we didn't really need them. And thinking we were their dependents, their social baby birds, was why the band liked us. Maybe Kitty, thrown from total dependency on her mother into total dependency on Kent, without any moments of lonely self-sufficiency to learn from, thought she *did* need him. Yvonne seemed to only play at needing the band lately, letting them think she'd die for them just to grab their offerings and gifts. Other women wouldn't have even done that. Other women would never pledge allegiance to some too-loud band just to be told they were pretty.

I couldn't decide on an opinion. A fence-sitter forever. That's how I kept my place. That's how I was comfortable. Still, I mulled it over, wondering how I weaseled into this world—wondering when my dependency on the band stopped being pretend and became unfortunately, overarchingly authentic.

I wanted freedom. Real, on-the-road, nobody-but-me independence. But the voices around me and the voice in my head insisted that women's lib was a pipe dream. That I'd be indebted, somehow, to men until I died.

I sat on Howie's lap and took photos but couldn't force my way into going home with him by the time the sun began to rise. Flattened and lonely, I scoured the emptying room for anyone of interest. When I found no one, I lowered my standards and considered Lorne the roadie (who was balding and hardly my type) and Clifford Agnew (who wasn't half-bad looking, but had called me "shrill" three times that night). Maybe fate could decide for me, I thought, not understanding why I didn't care who it picked. I asked, "Who's taking me home?"

Lorne and Clifford both looked at me. Clifford said, "Do you live far?"

I asked, "Do you live close?"

He did. I went home with him, slept with him, and went back to my own apartment. I felt nothing but a low rumble of either pride or hunger. Clifford made me want Howie more. I was insatiable, unstoppable.

JOSIE'S PICTURE PEERED out from every corner, promising unnamable things to anyone who shelled out the $2 for a copy.

Thursday night, after we were all a bit partied out, Josie fell onto the glass table and shattered it into huge, glinting pieces. She was left with a scratch on her arm and guilt on her face as everyone whispered she was too wobbly to still be drinking, and that she was bound to have broken something eventually.

No one whispered about how Cal pushed her. We all pretended we didn't notice, so loyal to Cal that we betrayed Josie.

She fell asleep in the hotel bed and slept until the lights came on. I asked if she wanted help taking her makeup off.

"Can I go home?" she asked.

"Cal said the house is still under construction," I said. I knew she meant home to the apartment we used to share. I wouldn't admit it.

I scrubbed her face clean, running the shower so she would stop whispering and talk in a normal tone. Josie was once obsessed with openness, wanting everyone to know her business, but now only spilled her secrets to me.

"You shouldn't get this drunk," I said.

"Whatever," she said. "It's my party. I'll barf if I want to."

I hummed Lesley Gore's "You Don't Own Me" as I unraveled her French braid. "You've got glass in your hair."

"Pick it out, would you?" she asked.

I did. The shards glinted, reflecting the golden shade of her hair so the glass itself looked like glitter. It was beautiful, technically, until I realized spots of blood and scabs spread across her scalp, too. Cal had pushed her. Cal pushed her right in front of us. I repeated the thought as I grabbed little shards with my fingers, until I said aloud without meaning to, "He pushed you."

"Huh?" Josie said. "Did he?" Her tone was expressionless, as if she were unable to keep up the facade after long nights of saying all was well.

"Yeah," I said. "And that's—that's fucked."

"I'm staying here."

Fine. I didn't have the words—the means, the gall—to push further. I kept picking glass out of her hair and threw bits into the wastebasket. I cut my own finger and sucked the blood off, the taste rancid and dark.

"I met Debbie Harry the other night," she said. "And Trixie Childs, too. They're so pretty. So blond and so nice. I want a bath."

"Wow, that's cool," I said, wondering why I sounded so bored. "I'll run you a bath."

She pulled her clothes off and stood naked in the center of the bathroom as I put in the drain plug. There was a chunk of vomit on the toilet bowl, which Josie reacted to with vivid disgust before throwing up herself. Her upper arm had grab marks, four grape-size blue bruises. Above them were deeper marks shaped sort of—no, exactly—like the rings Cal wore. I touched her arm, my fingers skimming the bruises, hoping they'd rub off. I bit my tongue so hard it almost bled. "Do you remember," I asked, steadying her as she stood and moved toward the bath, "how in high school they voted you most popular?"

She laughed, sliding into the steaming bathwater. "Do you think I'd still win that now?"

"Mmhm," I said.

She asked me to take her photo and I said no, afraid she'd regret it. I was still guilty over the Polaroids I'd sold, suddenly realizing I *still* hadn't told her about them. I resolved not to admit to them until I had to—if I ever had to.

"I wouldn't win," she said. "Not if the whole world voted. Cal and I were at dinner and I heard some fan—some ugly schlub of a girl—say to her sister or whoever that she'd bet a million bucks I'd trapped Cal. That I must be pregnant. She said that's what Darlene did to Scott."

"I don't think—"

"It doesn't matter that it's not true," she said, splashing her reflection in the water. "People think it is. Take my photo, please."

I took her picture, pure and untouchable in the tub, then helped her into a bathrobe and to bed. Josie went back to sleep. I forgot all about her, too hung up on wanting Howie to want me. I followed love where I thought I saw it, not understanding Josie wanted love from *me*. A different kind than the type I chased every night, but love nonetheless.

Two Photos

Josie clutching her *Foxy* cover, her tiny hands peeking out from the sleeves of her white fur coat and her eyes welling with happy tears. There's a blue balloon above her head.

Josie with her head on her knees, wet in the boiling water of the hotel bathtub, staring straight through the lens of the camera.

17.

DARLENE CALLED ON THE SUNDAY OF THE SUTHERLANDS'
party, asking if I'd watch Wendy while she prepared hors d'oeuvres. I
took the bus with the weekend commuters, my Polaroid swaying with
the frequent stops and my body aching. It was a dull pain, and while
I blamed it on a summer flu, I suspected weeks of near-blackouts had
begun to disagree with me.

I was hardly eating, because my money was better spent on things
more exciting than chicken breasts (and besides, no one else ever
seemed to eat). I only wanted to sleep when I was in someone else's
bed—when there was another breathing body next to me making the
covers too warm.

The Sutherlands' home hid behind trees in Bel Air, with white
gable windows and a dark gray roof. The floors were pristine hard-
wood, but the bottom two feet of the walls were covered in crayon
smudges from Wendy.

Darlene hated the house—she said it looked too much like the
home Sharon Tate was murdered in, full of dark corners. It was nearly
ten years since the Manson murders, but only three since Squeaky
Fromme's attempted assassination of Gerald Ford. The Manson girls
were jokes by then. Punch lines at parties. Their destructive devotion
now rang immature and passé. But I understood them—if Charlie
Manson had happened upon me when I was young and crying, I probably would have believed him, too.

I threw my shoes off when I arrived, walking barefoot behind
Darlene as she gave me a house tour. A few minutes later, I smelled
something burning and told Darlene (her own olfactory senses were
hardly keen). We dashed off to the kitchen where swirls of smoke

emerged from the oven door as she opened it. "Damn," she said. "My pigs in blankets are scorched."

Wendy, invigorated by her midmorning nap, scampered around Darlene's feet and begged, "Piggie, please, Mama! Piggie!"

"Piggies are burnt, baby," Darlene said. "Can I offer you a cucumber sandwich?"

"Yucky," she said, then pointed to me. "Photo please!"

Darlene pulled premade puff pastry out of the fridge and began to roll it out, hands sticky with flour and butter. I took her daughter's photo, not having to tell her to smile. She already knew.

The doorbell rang. Darlene ran to answer the door, nearly knocking her rolling pin off the marble counter. I scooped up Wendy, bouncing her as Darlene yelled about personal business. Wendy looked across the house to her mother's voice, her eyes sharp and clear. People always said I looked at things like Wendy did—innocently. Wide-eyed. Like everything was new and grand.

I sang to Wendy as Darlene made a well-practiced drug deal. She shut the front door, then jogged up and down the stairs, her silver housecoat billowing like steam. She opened the front door again, exchanged her lipstick-kissed envelopes of coke for a stack of green bills, and waved her visitor goodbye. Dancing with independence, she tucked the bills into the pocket of a fur coat hanging on the garage door. She noticed me staring. "Well, my mama sold Mary Kay. Every gal's got to have something giving her a purpose. And money. Ain't that what Betty Friedan was talking about? I might read her book. Yvonne said I should." I supposed her music career, while maybe creatively fulfilling, wasn't raking in the big bucks.

Darlene turned on the television for Wendy, who jumped out of my grasp to plop onto the couch. Darlene's mothering was the unrestrictive, wildflower kind that sprung up in the wake of Woodstock. She went back to the hors d'oeuvres, telling stories about when she first met Scott, back when they were just starting to become real people.

Scott was soft back then, she said—a hippie in a cloud of patchouli.

That was before Holiday Sun, and before Scott had started to laugh about third eyes and chakras. Sixty-nine in San Francisco. Darlene was working as a nanny, trying to escape her Southern hometown. Scott was penniless, cutting guitar strings for a living. He took her to see Jefferson Airplane, gave her herpes, and said goodbye. Darlene considered that summer the most romantic one of her whole life. She learned to play piano. She learned to sing with a trilling twang. In '71 she spotted Scott and Holiday Sun on *Carson*. Darlene took it as a cosmic sign that she should pursue her musical aspirations, too— that she should find Scott and become big by his side. She left for L.A., spending months searching, lionhearted, for another connection to him. Darlene skimmed over the difficult details of working her way into Holiday Sun's inner circle, just saying she was proud of her "nerve." She said her own musical career was still just starting to pick up. That she'd had to support his first, and now that he'd been stable for long enough, she could devote herself to herself again.

She put a tray of spinach puffs in the oven and sat on a kitchen stool. Wendy giggled at Dynomutt from the living room.

I bit into an undercooked coconut shrimp. Darlene leaned close and said, "So, now I've told you all *my* little secrets." She pulled open the top drawer of the kitchen island and took out a dog-eared copy of *Weekly Examiner*, a supermarket tabloid. She slid the magazine to me and said, "Wanna tell me some of yours?"

Shit.

I flipped the magazine open to a folded-over page and was met with a blown-up, high-contrast version of the Polaroid I'd taken of Josie and Harry Carling.

Double shit.

I could have lied, saying someone must have stolen it at a party. I could have told the truth—that I was greedy and more spiteful than I wanted to admit. But I just stared at the page, then looked back to Darlene.

All she said was "Whoever sold this picture isn't very nice."

It was obvious the "anonymous source" the photo credited was me. Darlene didn't say it, but she knew it. It was as kind as she could have been without being complicit. The photo took up the entire page, with only a small square at the bottom devoted to a reprint of Josie's *Foxy* cover and a wedding shot. I was stuck staring at the glossy shame of Josie's unfaithful tongue in Harry's mouth, given context by the caption:

> Free love prevails as blushing bride JOSIE HOLIDAY locks lips
> with HARRY CARLING at a house party. Shh—don't anyone tell
> CAL HOLIDAY! With Holiday Sun off on another tour, Josie will
> have plenty of time for more personal endeavors like this.

Darlene pushed a plate of creamed corn in front of me. "I don't know who else has seen it," she said. "I don't know if Josie has."

I had to stop being such a coward and show Josie the magazine. All my whimpering and wimping out needed to stop. Tonight.

I went to work on the food without being asked. It felt good to help create something, especially with Darlene. I liked that she was someone's mother. It gave her a warmth. A worriedness I had forgotten existed in people.

Darlene checked the California-shaped wall clock compulsively. When the band and some "volunteer" roadies were due to arrive and set up a makeshift stage in the yard, Darlene tidied, wiping the counters. She asked if I wanted to borrow an outfit for the party. I knew her asking meant I was underdressed, so I hopped up the spiral staircase to the upstairs roost.

The hallway was lined with ferns in hand-painted Peruvian planters. One of Wendy's pacifiers was on the floor outside her bedroom, which I peeked into, watching the ponies on her mobile twirl. I thought of Josie and the Palomino horse. Across from Wendy's room was a back staircase leading outside that I doubted anyone ever used. Past that was an empty bedroom Scott used as a storage area for guitars, awards, and jeans he meant to mend. Across was the master bedroom. At the end of the hall sat a tiled bathroom, with the door half ajar and the lights shut off.

I slid into the red-walled master bedroom. My camera was downstairs, sitting patiently on the couch, so I tried my best to commit to memory everything I wanted to document. The dirty socks on the carpet. The lipstick stains on the mirror. The folded note on the dresser I didn't read, and above it, pinned to the mirror's wood frame, a photo of young Darlene and Scott with flowers behind their ears. I turned the photograph over and read the inscription on the back: *my darling Darlene.*

I almost laughed at Scott's unfamiliar expression of mush.

Darlene's closet was a disaster of velvet and lace. I pored through it, finally choosing a black dress. Halloween-store Stevie Nicks. I smeared on Darlene's dark pink lipstick and waited a heavy moment before going, trying to decipher the newly arrived voices downstairs.

The beginnings of the party had moved outside into the setting sun.

I stepped barefoot onto the lawn toward the band, Darlene, and Josie, who went everywhere with Cal now. Past them, near the back fence, were three roadies fiddling with the planks and amps that formed a semi-stage in the yard. Floyd was there, sweat pooling behind his ears and staining his T-shirt. I called, "Hey, Floyd!"

He didn't look back at me.

But Howie, who was closer, looked up and winked. I inched toward him, winking back. He pulled me tight to his side, asking if I was excited.

"Very," I said. "But I'm sad you'll be off on tour so soon."

"Why don't you tag along?" Kent asked. He laid on the grass, squinting at the clouds in the sky and pointing out which ones looked like animals. He added, "You know Howie needs a road wife or he'll go ape."

"And that should be me?" I asked, teasing. "I'll have to check my schedule."

Josie laid her head on Cal's bare shoulder and asked Howie in a playful whine, "What about Miss Yvonne?"

"Yvonne's being—Yvonne's always been—impossible," Howie said. "She's going to New York. She says there's more 'opportunity.'"

"I don't buy that shit," Scott said, lighting a cigarette. "Her little management career? Yeah, that was a clever ruse."

"Good riddance." Cal laughed. "She was a bitch." How quickly they all turned.

"She was not," Josie said, pulling bits of grass out of the lawn.

We shot the shit for half an hour, bathing in a cloud of clove cigarettes and pot smoke. The sun kept shifting toward the horizon and Darlene grew antsy, worried no one would come to the party. Scott whispered that people would show. They always did. She bit her nails as we grew high and light-footed. Darlene danced while the band practiced a gentle cover of "Lay Lady Lay." She reached to me and Josie and swept us into the clouds. We twirled for a forever minute as the band crooned, to us and despite us.

Once the band finished, Darlene tapped my shoulder. "Didn't you want to show Josie something?"

I didn't *want* to, but Darlene wasn't giving me a choice. Josie skipped behind me into the kitchen, muttering excitement for whatever surprise I had planned. Wendy was asleep on the couch, so Josie stayed quiet as she pulled open the fridge for a can of Heineken. She cracked it, drank half, then opened the fridge again and pulled out an orange. She peeled the fruit as I paced without meaning to.

"Well, what is it?" Josie asked, her mouth full, her eyes expectant. She popped another slice of orange between her teeth while I considered the best way to break her heart. I picked up the tabloid that still laid on the kitchen island and pushed it toward her. She peeled back the cover to the table of contents. "What?"

"The dog-eared page—flip to it."

She laughed, rolling her big eyes, and stopped laughing as soon as she followed my instructions. Josie blinked at the full-page spread of her tongue in Harry Carling's mouth.

I didn't say anything.

"Faun," she said quietly. Maybe she didn't want to wake Wendy, who was still stuck in a dreamland better than any we knew. She didn't cry, or scream, but I wish she'd done both. All she said was "Oh, Faun" over and over, like I was some disobedient child who had broken a prize vase. Like I was a puppy who'd wet the carpet.

I still didn't speak—all I did was stand there, openmouthed.

Josie, after a long moment, said, "For all the fuss you made about not being credited on *Outfield Flowers*, it sure is shocking you don't have your name plastered all over this page."

"That's mean," I said in a half whisper.

Josie raised her voice enough to make me shiver. "That's mean? This," she said, pointing to the magazine, "is mean. You're mean." Josie flipped the magazine shut, and stepped toward me, her feet light and decided.

I could have apologized—I should have—but I convinced myself that if I didn't, maybe I wouldn't be wrong at all. Maybe it was Josie's fault, I rationalized. Before I meant to, I said, "Well, if you hadn't kissed him in the first place—"

"No," Josie said, "don't you dare. If Cal sees this—"

"If you weren't being such a *slut*," I said, "then you wouldn't have had to worry about this."

She balled her hands into fists and slammed them down onto her tanned legs. "I might be a slut," she said, smiling with pageant-queen softness, "but at least people like me." Going for the final blow, she stuck her nose in the air and said, "Your 'photography career' is a real flop if you're stuck selling shitty party shots. So much for professionalism. Not like you ever had any. Not like you were ever anything but a groupie."

"Josie."

"*No.* I did so much for you. You know they thought you were boring. They thought you were a narc, for God's sake."

"That's not true," I said. "You're a bitch. You're a stupid bitch." It was her fault for kissing Harry. It was her fault for not caring I photographed it.

"Me? No, I'm nice. This whole time, I've been dragging you along. I've been giving you chances. I've been annoying everybody trying to make you a part of everything and *this* is how you repay me?"

The doorbell rang. I dashed to open it, eager to get away from Josie. She went back to the yard to announce guests were arriving. Darlene tucked Wendy into bed for the night. Once the lights turned off, the night fell hazily. The party ebbed and flowed with a reckless familiarity. I tucked a slice of delivery pizza into my mouth, trying to murmur something nice to Josie, who leaned steadfast against Cal's denim-jacketed side. Josie brushed me off but let me sit with her while we both ate, silently watching the house fill with guests, pretending we weren't fuming at each other.

Kitty lit up when she saw us, and pointed at the two girls beside her, introducing them. Her "best friend from high school," who blew gum bubbles big enough to stick to her nose, was named LaTonya. LaTonya's little sister, Tess, had a speech-and-debate sweatshirt and shiny silver braces. They smoked cigarettes like it was their job, but coughed on each one.

Kitty toured them past Kent, to whom she blew a tiny kiss. He nodded off, high and babbling. He waved to Tess.

Cal said the band was set to play in a couple minutes, just as soon as Floyd and the other roadies finished setting up.

Let it be soon, I prayed. Let it be right now.

One Photo

Wendy in Bert and Ernie pajamas, smiling with her hands under her chin, exquisitely practiced and posed, drooling.

18.

THE PARTY CROWD HUSTLED OUT FOR THE BACKYARD SHOW. WE curled our bare toes into the grass and told each other how lucky we were to be there. Darlene was the first one outside. She looked up to the moon and raised her arms to it, basking in its reflected glow. "The moon is a lady," she said, for anyone listening. "And she loves everybody."

"*I* love everybody." Josie laughed.

Goody Plenty, who was five feet off the ground, in a bridal carry in Clifford Agnew's arms, called, "We know! *Weekly Examiner* told us!"

"What's she on about?" Cal asked.

Before Josie could answer, I said, "Nothing. Goody's nutso. You'd better hurry. Your band's waiting."

Cal kissed Josie on the top of her head and jogged to the makeshift stage. Josie stopped smiling as soon as she was out of his sight and flipped me off as she sat down on the grass. She was right to be angry, but I didn't apologize. My pride told me I didn't have to. Nobody apologized to *me* for anything. Nobody apologized to *anyone*. We carried on and pretended life was normal, which meant no one stopped hurting. You'd fuck up, drink a bit, then forget it all and go back to dancing. It was easy and unsustainable. "Can I sit?" I asked, ignoring Josie's sneer.

Josie rolled her eyes. I sat anyway, running my nails over the silky strap of my Polaroid. I didn't offer to take her photo—it would have been in poor taste. I wish I had taken one more while I still had the chance. I wish I'd taken a million. She looked so pretty that night. Impossibly hopeful, even as she scowled. Josie would have looked pretty in any form, even with scum on her teeth or her eyebrows shaved off.

She picked something glinting off the grass. A little red pocket-knife, for whittling, dropped from someone's grasp. "Better put this away," she muttered, "Wendy could get hurt." She folded it shut and tucked it into the side of her boot.

Darlene scuttled toward the porch light. Moths fluttered around it, bopping against the brightness. Floyd signaled for her to shut it off, and she did, ceremoniously preparing for the band to begin.

I split from Josie and scoured the crowd for anyone to stand beside. I took a couple photos but couldn't find anyone satisfying. I was bored by the regular orbitals. I was bored, a bit, by Holiday Sun. They were all so small, and I was dreaming of bigger things. Josie's comments about me never being a real photographer rang across my brain. Was it true they'd thought I was annoying? That they hadn't ever wanted me around? Whatever. It was time to move into the murky terror of a social world outside of my own. How funny that a year ago I'd worshiped at Holiday Sun's feet. Now they were just men I knew. Important men, yes. Men I needed and held on to. But still men, not superhumans.

Maybe that wasn't right—sure, I knew them, but when they were onstage, they became something else, transforming into grand, glorious visions. They were falser up there, and they were better, thanks to their unattainability. No longer were they Cal, Scott, Howie, and Kent. They were "oh-my-God-it's Holiday Sun" when the stage lights came on, surrounded by tangled extension cables that curled, snake-like, around their feet.

When he stood beside you, Howie was short, but onstage, he was taller than God. Scott's frowning face wasn't unappealing when he was playing music—it was moody and delicious. The Cal who sat on couches with his arm motionless around Josie was sour. That Cal was violent and bitter, but the Cal we watched onstage was breezy and bloodless. He would never break anything, except for maybe a few teenage fans' hearts.

Sometimes the panel dividing the looking-glass world from the real one slipped. That night, Kent cracked it, because he couldn't keep the beat. The band began with a slowed-down version of "Bee Sting," but even a slower tempo couldn't stop Kent's opiated hands from missing cues.

Scott turned around to face him for a second, mouthing, *Focus up, man.*

Kent slugged offstage. Kitty jolted toward him, then yelled "Woo!" at the stage. Overcompensation.

Scott swung the song into a guitar solo, and the rest of the set was played half acoustically because Kent couldn't handle coming back. Cal sang, smiling, twirling the rings on his hands. An earnest fidget.

It ended. The band melted into the crowd. The night really began.

Josie got up without a second look at me, dashing to giggle with acquaintances and point, swooning, to Cal. Whatever. I didn't need her to boost me up anymore—I could be my own person. She wasn't special. People liked *me*, too. They did. They wouldn't have let me hang around this long if they didn't.

A joint illuminated Howie's face in flickers. He rested, cool and easy, on a wooden chair. Josie laughed from across the yard, and I decided to be brave and desperate. Howie played with a lighter as I said, "Hey, there." He liked brashness, so I added, "How is it fair you're *that* good all the time?

"Babydoll," he said, calling to me and naming me at once.

Darlene took to the stage for a performance of her own, tying a blue ribbon to the mic stand. Scott hollered for everyone to pay good attention, but only her closer friends and those craving the cool night air stayed to watch. She sang with sincerity but not total success, garbling phrases. Maybe she wasn't perfect but at least she meant what she sang. At least she was creating something unprecedented. No one could call Holiday Sun original.

I slid onto the arm of Howie's chair. He grabbed my waist and pulled me onto his lap. He pretended he was Santa Claus, bouncing me on his knee.

Howie jumped as Clementine tapped his shoulder. She shouted into his face, "I'm taking birth control pills now!" Howie didn't reply, so she added, "I'm leaving tomorrow with Northern for a little while. Lester Bangs says they're 'violently new.'"

"Aw," Howie said. "Ain't that so cute." He turned back to me, passing me his joint.

I sucked it, its burning paper saccharine with sugary saliva and sweet smoke.

Darlene pointed to every person in the crowd while saying colors, shaking a maraca. Some sort of aura thing. Howie was sliding his fingers up and down my back. I smiled when Darlene pointed toward us and said, "Double pink!," before she began a cowbell-backed Dolly Parton cover.

"Where are you going after this?" Howie asked. My groupie heart skipped a beat. I *knew* what that meant. He wanted me. Suddenly I was ready to grovel and plead to him again. I cared so much it tore holes in me, but I couldn't let it show.

"Holmby Hills?" I said, remembering where Howie lived.

"Yes," he said, "that seems right." He rubbed the back of my neck as Darlene wailed. Howie drummed the music's offbeats onto me. "So," he said, tapping his fingers across my shoulders, "you're from Massachusetts." He pulled a strand of my hair into his hands. "You like Holiday Sun." He pressed his lips to my cheek. "You like me."

"Yes," I said, answering all three questions at once. He wanted more, but he liked Yvonne, so he liked coy.

"Are you bored?" he asked. "Are you excited?"

"No," I said, swatting at a bug.

"What are you, then?"

I laughed and plucked the joint from between his fingers. I took a hit and forced myself not to cough. "I'm me."

Darlene finished the song, Scott leading the applause.

Howie asked, "Faun, do you know if Yvonne's coming?"

Wasn't I enough? Why couldn't he have been crazy about me? He liked me enough to take me home with him—but I was still his second choice. And I still threw myself onto him on the backyard chair.

I said, "She's in the Chelsea Hotel or the Plaza or somewhere. But I'm here."

Darlene sang about moonlight and placentas as Howie and I chased each other's tongues. He tasted like tobacco onions. I kissed him until my lips went numb, until my stolen/borrowed lipstick wore off and left a pinkish rim around his mouth. "Double pink," I muttered.

It felt good but also like nothing at all—like kissing the crook of my elbow. The best part was when we'd briefly break away from each other and I'd get to open my smoky eyes and peek at his face.

WE SPLIT FOR a while and I wound up back inside with Kitty, watching as she told everyone how honored she was to accompany the band on their tour.

Goody tapped her on the shoulder and told her to check out the basement. I followed Kitty, hoping to latch onto her, curious what Goody wanted her to see so badly.

There in the basement was Kent, pants-less and panting, on top of Kitty's friend's little sister, Tess.

"Oh, fuck you!" Kitty cried. She had nothing to throw but gestured chucking something at him anyway. Kitty yanked at Kent's T-shirt and pulled him to the floor. He laid breathless on the brown carpet as Tess pulled her plaid skirt back over her thighs.

"Kitty, I'm sorry," Tess said quickly, her voice teary.

Kitty ignored her apology and instead pointed at Kent, emphasizing, "Fuck *you*!" Kent blinked, confused, and Kitty continued. "I did everything for you. You said we were *real*," she said, slapping a wooden cabinet, rattling the china. Her own personal earthquake. "I am *never* going to see you again!"

"What about your things? You gonna—you gotta come pick up your things!" Kent was desperate, clawing at his body in search of a reason for Kitty to stay.

"My things?" Kitty asked. "Yeah, I've got a bottle of scotch and a fistful of Quaaludes. You can keep it all. You can go right ahead and take them. Take them all and go die, for all I care!"

Kent didn't understand. He looked back at his fourteen-year-old victim. Tess put up her hands, looking straight at Kitty. She expected a fight, but Kitty didn't want one. Tess picked a piece of food out of her braces, rolled up her sweatshirt sleeves, and wordlessly wandered back to the party.

I followed Kitty up to the dining room, where the lights were dimmed and most conversations were quiet. She didn't cry, but kept tearing out strands of her own hair. "Good riddance," she said. "It doesn't matter. He's, like, stupid. He's no one, anyway. I should have known this shit would happen." She shouldn't have known. She *couldn't* have. Kent plucked her up when she was young and unaware—probably *because* she was young and unaware. Maybe she still was. Maybe we all were babes in the woods waiting for someone to tell us what to do. Kitty sighed. "Yvonne was right. He doesn't care at all. Holiday Sun doesn't care."

She'd had the grand revelation I was too timid to have myself. Shocked, I asked, "Are you going home?"

"Where's that?" she said, laughing. "No. I'm going to the Riot House on Sunset, I guess. I'm sure I know somebody there. There's a lot of nice guys who stay there. Musicians. *Real* ones."

I gave her money for a cab and asked what name she'd be under at the Riot House.

"My name. I'm not special enough for a fake one. If you can't find me, check the Zeppelin floor!"

I couldn't bring myself to go check on Tess.

THE PARTY SWIRLED into pools of decadence, our Darlene-seen auras all mashing together. Would all the colors in the world make a rainbow or mud?

I drank too much that night. For so long I had been afraid to drink at all. I didn't know what I was rebelling against now. My dead mother? My disappeared father? Nothing and everything. Darlene and I shared a bag of pork rinds until she started to sniffle, moaning that people kept laughing about her performance. "Was it bad?" she asked, snot dripping from her upturned nose.

I tried my best to be comforting while preparing to shotgun a beer. I considered what I really thought of her music. I didn't understand it. But did that mean it was bad? The band and their cronies (myself, sometimes, included) called her Yoko behind her back. But our tastes—my tastes, by then—were tainted by the desire to devote ourselves to whatever would grant us the greatest popularity. "No, it wasn't. People don't understand art," I said. Maybe she was an artist, or maybe she was deluded. Maybe she was experimental, or maybe she just listened to too much Zappa. Same with me—I thought I was a photographer, but most would argue I was just a groupie with a camera. A try-too-hard groupie, at that. Not especially pretty or charming or young or old. Just one providing a self-indulgent service. My professional efforts were effectively fruitless—ruinous, even—so why bother? Tonight I'd party. At least everyone agreed I was passable at that.

But Darlene perked up when Scott picked her up and spun her, laughing. He set her on the kitchen island beside the *Weekly Examiner* I'd never put away. It had been flipped through a couple times by aimless partygoers, but no one paid attention because the best gossip was playing out in front of them.

Darlene and Scott argued about whether to bring Wendy on tour. Kent licked icing off a cinnamon roll. I strolled around, reading fridge magnets and teetering. Josie shrieked with joy from the living room, where she spun from arms to arms. I did a shot of tequila. Cal, who had come to the kitchen "starving" for food, looked over to Josie.

"Let's turn this swill music off," he said, glancing across the countertops. I put my hand over the cover of the *Weekly Examiner*. Just because I'd been cruel and gotten those photos published didn't mean

Cal ever had to see them. But I was too obvious about it. He asked, dripping with docility, "What's that, love?"

I didn't move my hand. "What?"

Darlene asked if she could kiss me. I didn't answer. Josie waved to our group and smiled. Scott said he heard Wendy crying. Darlene did a handstand. Somewhere within all this, Cal cracked a beer and Kent slipped the magazine out from under my hand and flipped through it. Ash dropped off his cigarette and smoldered on one of the pages. I wish it had caught fire. My fingers twitched to pull the pages away.

Josie laughed loud as she spun to the music, her giggle carrying across all the noise. I wanted to join her but when she saw me, she rolled her eyes.

Darlene grabbed my hand and pulled me forward. "Let's dance, baby, let's dance!"

I hesitated but joined her on the makeshift floor, our foreheads pressed together in laughter and meditation. When I became dizzy, I swayed and turned back to the kitchen just in time to see Kent show Cal a page of the magazine. Darlene slipped away, out of my grasp.

Cal laughed at the page, so loudly the crowd around him quieted. He smiled until Kent looked away, then his face fell into a dark bitterness. Sour. Rot. The smell of bad coffee.

Oh, fuck. My mouth ran with the coppery taste of—blood? vomit?—and I collapsed straight onto a pair of white loafers. I looked up to meet the face they belonged to, and said, trying to be lovely despite the stars above my head, "Oh, hi, Floyd."

"Hi," he said.

Josie saw me and slid through the dance floor bodies until she was above me, too. "You oughta sit down." She bent down to help, but the guilt of what Cal now knew was too much to bear. I swatted her manicured hand and the way she flinched broke my heart.

I wobbled back to my feet, Bambi on the ice again. Josie's face was so soft. So kind. So unfairly kind to me, who had possibly just ruined everything for her.

"Easy, easy," Floyd said. "I'll take you to sit down."

"I'll take her, too," Josie said. "You barely even know her."

I said, "Let's sit."

I teetered my way off the dance floor, trailed by Josie and Floyd. Halfway to the staircase, where I had set my sights, Cal called Josie's name.

Her head turned sharply, her face tilted in a gentle greeting. "Yeah?"

"Can I steal you for a second, love?" he asked. She nodded, then smoothed her white dress. He considered for a second. "You look so good tonight."

Josie winked. They stood together, ribs beside ribs, looking like strangers. I dashed for my camera, asking them to wait so I could take their photo, trying to capture how happy I hoped they were. All I got was a washed-out documentation of Cal gripping Josie's bare shoulder, her hair falling in loose waves over the rings on his hand. I gave Josie the photo and she handed it to Cal, who tucked it into his pants pocket.

Josie leaned close, pushing my hair behind my ear. "Be right back." She hooked her fingers under my camera strap, pulling it off and slinging it around her own neck. "Look, I'm you, Faun!" she said, then snapped a picture of me before I was ready.

I laughed.

Cal tickled Josie's back, trying too hard.

I stopped laughing. Cal smiled but it didn't reach his eyes. I knew what he knew. We were all keeping the same secret from each other. "Josie, do you want to go outside with me?" I asked. "I need air."

Cal shook his head at me, then turned to Josie. "Baby, I need to talk to you. Upstairs?"

Josie looked back and forth between me and Cal. Her two options, neither ideal. One safer. She chose. "Okay, Cal."

"Josie," I said. "I really need some air."

"I'll be right back," she said.

They chased each other cat-and-mouse style up to the empty second floor, the camera nearly flying off Josie's neck. I slid onto the second step of the staircase. I stood guard, against what I didn't know. Floyd sat next to me, making sure I hadn't fainted again.

"Hi," I said. "So who are you working for these days? Anyone cool?"

"Is that all you care about?" he asked. I didn't understand his disdain. We used to spend hours recounting stories to each other, and he'd always loved telling them. "I'm trying to help you," he said. "You nearly passed out. You look like you don't eat anymore. You look like a mess."

"What's got you so pissed?" I asked, standing up. "I don't need to talk to you. I'm with Howie tonight, anyway."

"You and everyone else."

I rolled my eyes. "Not my fault all you get is the band's leftovers."

Floyd stood, too, taller than I remembered. My eyes hit the bottom of his chin instead of his eyes. Hadn't I kissed him once? Hadn't he made me happy? Hadn't I thought we were the same? It all blurred. Floyd poked at my shoulder, testing if I was solid matter, and said, "Better than being the band's leftovers."

"You're an asshole," I said. "I liked you. I still do. Don't you know that?"

"Bit late for that," he said. I thought his eyes welled up, but he could have blamed it on the smoke circling off his cigarette. He wiped his left eye with tense hands. I reached to pat his shoulder, but he just shrugged away and laughed, so close to my face that his hot breath blew onto me. I didn't need to reconcile with him. I stormed through the party and tracked down Howie. Ten minutes later, I was blowing him in the downstairs bathroom, out of a twinge of desire and a mountain of spite. My knees stung where they pressed on the bathroom tiles, but I didn't care. I moved diligently, bobbing with praying hands. I kept checking Howie for approval, but his closed eyes told me nothing. I moved faster, not enjoying it but making sure he was.

"Come home with me," he said. "Let's go now."

He came in my mouth. I swallowed it. Before I realized it, I was sitting, thrilled and terrified and lifeless, beside him in the back seat of a taxi.

I'd done it—I was en route to Howie's house, doing a perfect job at telling him he was perfect. Magic burgeoned thick around us. "You're lovely," I said, blinking hard. Was he real?

He pulled a vial of coke out from under his shirt, where it hung on a gold chain, and tipped a bit onto his finger. He snorted it, then offered some to me. I took it as he said, "Tonight's beautiful."

I snorted his coke and wondered why we could never look at each other without something blurring our vision or clouding the air. He pointed out constellations as I said, "Josie thinks L.A.'s the whole world. Isn't that funny?"

Two raindrops hit the front window. The cab driver put on the wipers and glanced back, once, at Howie. "That *is* funny," Howie said. "I think she's a nice girl."

No one called her that. No one, ever. I realized that in eleventh grade. We'd been at a spirit rally for our win-nothing football team, shaking pom-poms like our lives depended on it. When the game ended, we filed onto the football field and mingled. Battle stripes painted on our cheeks and school-color ribbons (navy and silver, for the Knights) in our hair, Josie and I joined the horde. I was jealous of her then. I was jealous of her now.

Brian, Josie's pockmarked beau, waved her over and I followed behind. He had a friend beside him, named Richard or Randall. Brian's friend grabbed my ass under my cheer skirt, letting go as soon as I looked at him. I didn't say a word.

He reached over to Josie, too, as she talked to Brian. His hand cupped her backside and Josie spun around, slapping him across the face.

"You ain't nice," he said. "You're not a nice girl. Faun's a nice girl."

Nice girls were afraid to hit back. I was nice. Josie wasn't. That brashness, that bold motivation without any worry for the future, was her gift. Her curse, too. But it was better to hit back. It was better to try.

It hadn't rained that night at the football field, but it was raining now. I could count the times it had poured while I'd lived in L.A. on one shaky hand, so I watched each fat drop as it fell against the taxi window.

The drive was quick. When we parked at Howie's place, the taxi driver asked him for an autograph. He signed a receipt from a Pay-Less drugstore, and we made our merry way up the winding path to his front door.

The rain soaked us, so we threw off our clothes and threw our-selves at each other. He was impossibly soft, so gentle I sometimes forgot he was touching me at all. When we finished on the bed, we kissed like we'd known each other for years, pulled on our under-things, and waltzed into the kitchen.

I sat on the kitchen counter, the same place I'd lingered at that first house party at Howie's. Now there was no sign of Brooke even pre-tending to live there. Howie spread Miracle Whip onto white bread and made himself a ham sandwich. College-boy food. He could have any-thing he wanted, but he still wanted this. The same principle applied to his desire for me. He fed me a bite and I tried my best to look sensual.

He came close to my face. "Miss Faun, you are the loveliest."

He'd said that to Yvonne once. I was the girl he wanted me to be—not myself. I didn't mind as much as I should have. I remembered Yvonne's word when Howie looked at her the way he looked at me now: *Flatterer.*

Howie shook his head and slipped off one of his three necklaces, placing it around my neck. The silver medallion was cool on my chest, unforgettable and stinging sweetly. "I've given you the moon."

Any girl would fall at his slippered feet. "Thank you," I whispered.

"Let me take your photo." My only offering.

"Where's your camera?"

I'd left it at Scott and Darlene's. "I have to go get it," I said, but Howie didn't want me to leave. He put on some old Sam Cooke, and we danced to "Chain Gang." I asked if he had any Carpenters. He didn't, but he had a bottle of bourbon, which he poured me generous glasses from as he warbled love lyrics. I wasn't his forever love—not even his nightlong one—but nothing like that mattered. Howie was special to me *now*. I was special to him. Maybe when he went on tour, he'd think about me in passing and tell other bands who to call when it was time to take the photos for their next albums. In exchange, every chance I got, I'd tell gorgeous stories about how he glowed when I had kissed him.

Side A of the record finished. Drunker than I'd been at the party, I pulled Darlene's dress back on. Howie helped me zip it, complaining about me leaving.

"Stay," he said, "I'll be lonely."

"I'll come back," I said, laughing about everything. He wanted me around so badly. "I'll get my camera and be right back." He kissed me, cupping my face, and I repeated twice, in between kisses, "Right back. Right back!"

He offered to call me a taxi, but the walk wasn't too long. Something about the rain was irresistible. Intoxicated decisions from a girl who wanted to pretend the world was magic. Howie shook his head, saying it wasn't safe.

I spun in the rain for thirty-five minutes and came to find a hollowed-out version of the party I'd left.

It was maybe four by then. Past witching hour and into the almost morning. The casual crowd had vanished, leaving small strings of remainders. At a certain point, people have seen what they came to see. That's when most people go home. They burn out on one scene and move on to another. Anyone who stays after everyone else has left—those little leftovers—were never going to go home. Not if they could help it. It's the four A.M. crowd who really love it. It's the four A.M. crowd who have nowhere else to go.

Maybe that's why I was back.

Stanley, half asleep on the oak floor, opened his eyes. I hadn't noticed him at the party. I only noticed shiny things.

"Have you seen Josie?" I asked. "She's got my camera."

Darlene, bare-breasted with a feather duster in her hand, popped around the corner and whispered, "She's not down here. Haven't seen her. I reckon she left a while ago. Her and Cal both."

I drifted from room to room, picking up Polaroids I'd forgotten I'd taken. I paid no attention to anyone because no one was Josie. She might have left my camera upstairs. As I climbed the stairs, Darlene told me to be quiet lest I wake Wendy.

Floyd's painted jacket laid on the banister. Guess he was a four A.M. person, too.

Downstairs was quiet, but upstairs was impossibly silent. Drunk, and reeling from where Howie had touched me, I ran my hands across the wallpaper. I traced its floral patterns with my fingers and knocked a sculpture from against the wall. It fell on my feet, and only then did I realize I'd forgotten to put my shoes on.

I peeked into the master bedroom. The sheets were rumpled but there was no sign of my camera there. I borrowed Darlene's lipstick again, reapplying without turning on the lights.

Wendy's door was shut, but I pushed it open and peered inside. No camera there either. Just a sleeping baby. I checked the spare room, but there was nothing there but dust.

This left the bathroom, which had a closed door, too. I knocked on it but didn't hear anything. I mumbled, "Anybody home?," then laughed silently at my own good humor.

No answer.

I pushed the door of the shadowy room, but it would only open halfway, hitting some mass on the floor. I slid sideways into the bathroom, curving my body against the wall, and realized my feet were wet. It was too dark to see. I slid my hand across the wall, feeling for the switch. I found it and flicked it up.

My camera was lying shattered on the white tiles.

Beside it, leaned against the claw-foot tub, was Josie, covered in blood as bright red and sticky as the gloss on her lips.

At her feet was Cal, pale and knifed open. Dead.

One
Photo

Josie and Cal on the stairs, unreadable darkness above their heads and glitter glinting around their feet. Josie's smiling widely. In Cal's pocket, rolled up, is the copy of *Weekly Examiner* from the kitchen.

19.

JOSIE AND I GASPED, BOTH STUPEFIED BY THE SIGHT OF THE other. She stood up and dropped the red pocketknife, lifting her hands. The metal clattered on the tiles like an alarm bell. I stepped forward and shut the door behind me, holding my breath.

Her eyes, blank and wild, looked downward. I looked down, too, unblinking and mind blank, at Cal. At his body, rather—he wasn't there anymore. Any life had leaked out the same holes in his stomach that his intestines had.

"He was going to kill me, Faun," Josie said. Her voice cracked, but she didn't cry. In her hands were Cal's rings, pulled off his fingers, their metal and jewels cloudy with sweat.

My heartbeat thrummed in my ears. I touched my chest, suddenly suffocating, surprised at its solidity.

Josie stepped toward me and almost sobbed before covering her own mouth. Her face was swollen and purpling, radiating bruise-heat and shiny with dried tears. "He was going to. Really. Really." She licked her split lip.

I believed her. I looked at Cal's body, wet and gooey and suddenly cavernous, and to his face, not cast with fear but with rage, and I believed her. She began to explain, stunned and spitting words, but I told her it was fine. "I don't want to know anything," I said. She'd go to prison. She'd go for life. I'd never see her again, except through a glass panel. I lifted my foot, realizing it was resting in a puddle of blood.

"You've gotta help me," she said, pleading. But I couldn't. She knew that—at least I thought she did—because she modified her plea. "Please don't tell anybody. Don't tell them it was me."

I swallowed, hard. "I won't."

"Promise."

"I promise."

Josie leaned close, her skin burning hot, and kissed me on the cheek. She bent and picked up her pocketknife. Her lips moved like she was speaking but I couldn't hear any words.

I couldn't hear anything.

I realized there was vomit on the floor. I realized, a second after, that it had come from my mouth. I poked at Cal's limp foot and Josie kicked my hand away. Her index finger moved, begrudgingly making the sign of the cross, before she opened the bathroom door. She was still gore covered, completely conspicuous, but neither of us was in a state to begin washing up. She stepped into the hall.

"Take the back stairs," I said, gulping. I pointed to the alternate exit. "It goes to the yard."

"It'll be all right, won't it?" she asked.

I didn't answer. "What are you doing with those?" I asked, pointing to the rings in her hands.

She looked at them, then at me, then shrugged. "Maybe—maybe I'll pawn them. Run away across the border. Or . . . I don't know. Throw them out. I don't know."

"Josie," I said. I didn't know what I was going to follow it up with. I didn't say anything else.

She turned and made her way down the stairs, her blond hair swaying in matted chunks behind her. A stumbling ghost. She disappeared.

I held my tongue for as long as I could, swallowing bile until my throat stung. I looked over my shoulder to the bathroom door, ajar with its terrible secret inside, and couldn't take it anymore.

I screamed, begging for Darlene like she was my own mother. Wendy cried from her crib and I wished I was in one, too, all swaddled and small, as I slid down against the hallway wall. Darlene hollered as she came up the stairs that I needed to shut up because I'd woken the baby, but stopped yelling when she looked where I was pointing, straight into the bathroom. "Oh, God," she said. "Oh, God. Oh, God," she repeated. She wasn't speaking in vain—she was pleading.

She lifted Wendy from her crib and held her face to her chest, shielding her. Scott came up the stairs, too, reeling sideways from drink. Darlene pointed him to the bathroom, which he peered into for a second before reeling some more.

"What's—what's that?" Scott asked.

Darlene looked to Wendy in her arms, who was still wailing, and said, "Can you call the cops?"

Scott looked at me. "Faun, did you—" He shuddered, then reconsidered. "Did you see it happen?" When I shook my head no, which wasn't lying, he said, "Maybe he fell. That's possible, I mean—"

I vomited again onto the hall carpet. The metallic smell of blood leaked into the hall. Scott looked at me, then to Darlene. This was never supposed to happen. We were never supposed to see Cal dead like that. He was never supposed to die at all. It was all wrong, like somewhere along the way a train shifted onto the wrong track.

"Where's Josie?" Scott asked.

Scott was about to say something else—his lips reached toward it—but he didn't. Wendy said, "Sleepy. Sleep."

Darlene repeated, her voice wavering in a way I'd never heard it do, "Scott, call the cops. I'll get everyone to leave." She said something more, but I couldn't understand. "Faun? D'ya hear me?"

I shook my head.

"Stay here for now," she said. I thought she was being kind, but now, I think she just didn't want everyone downstairs to see my hands and feet covered in blood. Darlene and Scott left to shoo the crowd away. I pictured Josie sprinting across the city to nowhere, her skin still scratched red as she sped along the concrete world. I pictured Cal's body behind the bathroom door, stiff and starkly human. I split into countless tiny, elegant pieces, unsure who or what I was mourning.

The police—two long-legged men with fresh-shined boots and unhappy faces—arrived while Darlene was chucking the guests out of the house. Stanley was still snoring on the floor, the clunk of the officers' boots failing to stir him from his oblivious dreams. I was downstairs by then, pacing mindlessly, exhausted but unable to sit down. It felt like hours since Darlene told me to stay upstairs, and hours more since I hadn't, returning step by step to the ground floor. It had only been twenty minutes or so.

Scott shook the officers' hands. The bigger one, with a mustache scraping his thin lips, said, "Say, aren't you from that band—my daughter likes them—"

The second officer, shorter and scratching the mole on his nose, interrupted. "We've got a dead body here? Is that right?"

Scott said, "Yes, Officer."

The second officer glanced around the room, his eyes trailing wine-stained glasses and loose flecks of marijuana, then rolled his eyes. "I need a bit of information before we scope it out. Do you know the deceased's name? It's fine, sir, if you don't." He tried to pal up to Scott, leaning closer. "Between you and I, we get a lot of dead-party-girl calls this time of year. Overdoses and all that."

Scott cleared his throat. "It's Cal Holiday."

The officers shifted, suddenly somber and apologetic for ever thinking the corpse upstairs could be someone unimportant. They started up the stairs, hands practically over their hearts, preparing to inspect a king in repose. Bullshit. If it had been Josie who'd bled out—if Cal had done what Josie was scared he'd do—they'd still be smiling. Still cracking jokes while looking at a cracked skull or gored face or cold body. They only cared when someone told them they were supposed to. The officers' voices echoed down the long hall, their words indecipherable but plangent.

The shorter one came downstairs and pulled Scott aside. Darlene slid over beside him, rocking a now-sleeping Wendy. I didn't understand how anyone could sleep now. I thought I never would again. Darlene pointed over her shoulder to me. Despite the blood on my feet, the cop lacked suspicion. Darlene must have explained my arrival and noninvolvement, marking me a harmless and pathetic creature.

The officer came toward me. I looked at my feet until he cleared his throat to get my attention. The tears on my cheeks had dried, leaving my face tense and shiny. I had a look of slept-in insanity, with eyes that felt burst, but I didn't cry again.

"Hi, miss," the officer said. He wasn't sympathetic, but he played at it. His eye twitched. "Could I grab your name?"

"Faun," I said, my voice low and crackling. Campfire tinder the wind stops from burning. I gave my age, occupation, and residence. My lips were numb. Everything was.

"Can you tell me what happened to the man upstairs?"

"To Cal?" I asked dumbly.

"Yes."

I knew, but I couldn't tell him—not all of it. Not the parts he couldn't figure out himself. "I don't really know. I just found him like that. Dead." I gulped, swallowing thick spit. Floating in space, I continued, "I didn't see anything happen." That was true. My heart began a nervous pound as I thought back to my recent, impossible promise of silence to Josie. Where was she now? I shook the thought.

The officer clicked his pen a couple times and scribbled onto his notepad. Darlene gave me a cigarette. I didn't light it and picked at its paper until bits fell to the floor like the first snow. Fiddling killed some time, but when I looked up, the officer was staring, his patience waning. "Don't play around with me," he said.

I almost insisted that I wasn't, but I was scared to lie. He saw right through my skull into my nervous, secretive thoughts. I let the rumpled remnants of the cigarette fall.

"Miss. I understand that you are very frightened, but I want to help. And I think you want to help, too." He glanced behind him at his partner, who'd come downstairs by then. "You seem smart. Smart enough to know what happens to people who refuse to help investigations like these."

"Oh," I said. Why'd he call me smart when I was trying to play stupid?

He leaned close to my face. "Miss. It's a crime to lie to the police. It's a crime. It's a dangerous thing, and I don't want to have to take you in just because you can't remember what happened." He looked into my eyes and neither of us blinked.

My eyes welled. He was right. Of course he was right—he had all the power. He could do anything to me. His suspicions were too correct and my attempts at evasion were too transparent. "Got it," I said. "I can try to help."

"Can you think back again to when you found the body, and tell me if there are details that you may have forgotten initially?"

"Um."

"This is very important."

"Right, I know that, let me see—"

"Was anyone else in the bathroom when you found the body?"

I couldn't lie. Visions of being thrown into a cell for conspiratorial no good—ness swam around me. There was no way to shimmy out of this, but once I said something, it would be over for Josie. Oh, Josie.

I was sorry.

I was ashamed.

I was a bad fucking friend.

I said, "Josie. His wife. Cal's wife. Josie."

"I see." He nodded and wrote something else.

I jumped forward, trying to fix what was already done. "I . . . I didn't see anything happen." Fuck. Fuck, fuck, fuck. I tried to explain, to retwist the situation, to blurt out something useful, but it didn't work.

"And where is this Josie now?"

"I don't know! I told you I didn't see anything."

I thought I was clear—crystal—but he muttered I was slurring and said, turning up his nose, "Someone take this girl home."

Howie had arrived while I was talking to the cop, standing patiently against the front door, so quietly I didn't notice him until he took my arm and walked me out. He told me later he'd wandered over, worried I'd fallen into a puddle and drowned because I was "so small." I couldn't laugh at the idea of dying, but I liked that he worried. He said he regretted letting me walk alone. He wore a T-shirt with his own band on it. I stumbled over my feet. I tried to link his arm in mine but he didn't let me, instead holding his hand against the small of my back, guiding me forward like I couldn't see.

When we reached a puddle, dark and shiny under the streetlamps, I stepped into it. I let the filth of the road linger on my feet, the rainfall water brushing off Cal's blood. There was nothing inside me—no feelings, no thoughts. Maybe this was a dream. Maybe tomorrow I'd wake up and it would be September again. Josie would be never-bled-on and never-hit and never-a-killer and full of hope again. I'd be full of hope again, too. Howie watched me slosh around in the puddle until I fell down and sat, soaking in the water. He carried me, fireman style, back to his home.

He made us coffee. We sat on his couch saying nothing worthwhile. The numb lull of tragedy rolled through both of us, our veins still pumping with adrenaline that did nothing but make it impossible to think. I tried to shower but kept hopping out of its stream, on the lookout for nothing in particular. We didn't talk about Josie, and we didn't talk about Cal. I put on Howie's satin pajamas. How quickly things slither into nothing, I thought, running my hands across the fabric. Howie told stories about Tampa and monsoons. He gave me a down pillow and a blanket and set me up to sleep on the living room couch. He went back to his bedroom. I watched the static on TV.

After a while I grew antsy all alone, so I tried the door to Howie's room, hoping for a meaningless hug. He'd locked the door. I thought he must have been scared of me, suddenly considering the danger of women. Sliced by the realization a woman had killed, he began to fear us all, unsure of our differences. That was how they always thought, though, wasn't it? These musicians swapped one woman for another, barely learning their names before picking an identical, unsoiled replacement. Like cigarettes out of a pack, burned up, then tossed below their feet.

I wanted to find Josie and tell her everything would be okay, but I knew I would only make things worse for her.

No sleep for me. I stepped into the yard, breathing pollen and walking in circles. I told myself I'd stay outside until the sun came up, waiting for everything to go back to normal. Waiting for it to be a big joke. But nothing could be normal again. Holiday Sun's world had been gleaming and impossible. We had sat around waiting for the balloon to pop, knowing any breath could inflate it beyond capacity, but blowing anyway. I hated it for whom it had made me and what it had done to Josie. I mourned it, too—its reckless joy and the way it had made me feel righteous and genius and important. I walked aimlessly, smudging the makeup on my face with my hands, wiping it onto my legs, leaving streaks of color on my skin.

The TV light reflected onto the damp grass through the living room window. I stepped into it every thirty seconds in my loop. A little glow.

I thought the band glowed, but they didn't.

They didn't radiate light.

They absorbed it.

I STAYED UP until the morning programming started, sitting down on the couch to watch. I flipped to cartoons. The Road Runner was always a few steps ahead of Wile E. Coyote. Yosemite Sam was always burned and screaming. Bugs Bunny never got hit with the bullets Elmer Fudd shot.

Howie woke up, saying *Good Morning* should be on by now. He walked to the television like he'd rehearsed it. His face was flat. My adrenaline had worn off. All I wanted was to sleep, but the promise of the news giving clarity was too good to miss. Josie hated *Good Morning* because the host, with his short white hair and beady eyes, looked like her uncle Willard.

Howie flipped to *Good Morning*. "Do you want cereal?" he asked.

I shook my head no, my eyes trained on the TV screen.

"Right on," he said. He turned away quickly, bustling into the kitchen and away from me. Whatever he was feeling, he didn't want me to know. The sad pride of a man who was scared to mourn. To show his heart.

First was the weather. It was set to be sunny today. I shifted in Howie's pajamas, thinking I could feel my bones breaking.

Howie shouted from the kitchen that he was going to call Stanley so I shouldn't interrupt.

The weather report ended. I leaned toward the television, hypnotized by the electric dream that they hadn't caught Josie. That they'd decided it was somebody else or an unbelievable accident after all, pinning the crime on a tuxedoed mob boss or a spree-killing maniac rather than on my best friend.

The anchor began, "Out of Los Angeles today, a rock-and-roll fairy tale has come to an end. Singer Cal Holiday of the popular rock group Holiday Sun was found dead in the Bel Air home of his bandmate Scott Sutherland. Holiday's wife, Josephine Norfolk-Haslegrave, more commonly known as Josie Holiday, has been arrested and charged with his murder. She is a twenty-four-year-old nude model, most recently seen in *Foxy*. The pair married just earlier this year. Holiday Sun was set to embark on their 'Honeymoon Tour' this week. We here at *Good Morning* offer our deepest condolences to Holiday's family."

The program cut between clips of a bedraggled Josie being tossed into the back of a cop car and clips of Cal smiling and waving to an adoring stadium crowd a few years back. The footage looped, mocking me. Cal was going to be forever handsome and forever pure, and just like that, Josie was shredded. Not unjustifiably either—she'd knifed one of young America's favorite men. It didn't matter right now if it was self-defense. On *Good Morning*, all that mattered was that Cal was dead and Josie was to blame. I watched her tense, weeping face on the screen and shut my eyes. I sobbed, hiccupping until my stomach grew sore. I was so goddamn lonely. I'd never link Josie's pinkie again.

I stood, disgusted at my self-pity, and slid to the kitchen. Howie jumped when I walked in, spilling his glass of water all over his bare chest. His eyes were red and glassy. His cheeks were damp with hot tears. His lip quivered, swollen and bitten. He stood straight, ashamed at his own agony.

"I'm sorry," I said. He could take it however he liked. "I should go."

"Stay," he pleaded. "I'll make you breakfast. Pancakes. Anything." Hours ago he'd locked himself away from me. Now, in the daylight, he wanted me again. Did I look different now, or had he just gotten desperate enough to trust me?

"It's just not right. It doesn't feel right."

He considered, weighing his options. I yawned, exhausted. "Coffee?" he asked.

I accepted, sitting on the same side of the kitchen table as Howie, sipping from my oversweetened mug and pretending I didn't notice him crying. He didn't bad-mouth Josie like I thought he would. He'd seen the bruises on her arms as often as I had. We watched the birds in the backyard until the phone rang. He picked up, said hello to Kent, and I knew it was time to go.

I left Darlene's dress in a heap in the living room. I borrowed a pair of Howie's shorts, belting them so tight I thought my organs would burst, then pulled tighter. I combed my hair with my fingers, ripping out tangles. I slathered my face with a slightly too dark shade of cover-up Brooke had left in the bathroom. Like wearing someone else's face. Howie lent me a ratty T-shirt, and I picked at its Iggy Pop graphic (LUST FOR LIFE) until he told me to stop. I was barefoot.

"Where are you off to, Miss Faun?" Howie asked.

"Kitty's at the Riot House," I said. "I want to see if she's all right."

"I'll catch you soon," he said. "I'll catch you around."

We both knew that wasn't true. On my index finger was a fleck of dried, dark blood.

I SKULKED DOWN Benedict Canyon along the curb, putting each foot ahead of the other like I was working a circus act. Streets like these weren't made for walking, but I walked them anyway, the sickly perfume of snapdragons drifting around me in a haze. When I hit Sunset, I tried to ignore the Monday papers and TV store windows blaring the same story. Everything was dark in the sunshine.

Every radio station deejay thought they were the cleverest, playing "Killer Queen" and "Evil Woman," dedicated to you-know-who.

In a few days, every paper would be plastered with dreamy photos of dearly departed Cal. His face would look down from each newsstand. To its side, Josie's body would be pictured in the trashier tabloids in the lewdest positions. Her *Foxy* cover was pulled from the stands. Years later, pristine copies would go for thousands at morbid auctions.

I arrived at the Riot House—the Hyatt—one of the only daytime sanctuaries for a misplaced party girl. I basked in the air-conditioning, pulling its cool deep into my lungs. I expected levity, a mild escape from my distress, but I should have known better. Two girls in black slips sat on either arm of a wingback chair. A portable radio was on the cushion, tuned to a marathon of Holiday Sun songs. Across the lobby, another woman slung a sheet over a gilded mirror, preparing to sit shiva. The opening chords of "Sheila" bled over a low, banshee wail echoing through the lobby.

I walked to the front desk. Two men I recognized from Goody's party (roadies or musicians, maybe—no, former cast members on *Laugh Riot* who'd left the show for movie careers a few years prior) snapped and swatted to get my attention. The taller one asked, "Are you the coke girl?"

"Afraid not," I said.

"Well, I recognize you," he said. "Where do I recognize you from?"

I shrugged. The old urge to make everyone adore me didn't emerge. Now all I wanted was a friend. Someone to reassure me that I wasn't evil for not being torn to shreds over Cal. For worrying for Josie. I leaned over the counter and got the attention of the clerk. "Is there a Kitty Krause staying here?"

"Probably," the clerk said, gliding on his office chair to the roster of guests.

I picked a complimentary mint out of a bowl and unwrapped it, trying to smooth its covering until it was perfect. "Any luck?"

"No Kitty Krause."

"Try Katherine?"

He couldn't find her. I should have known Kitty wouldn't have a room of her own. She survived off charm, not money. I could charm my way into the Riot House, too. I popped the mint into my mouth, crushed it between my molars, and swallowed. The comedians were still there, discussing the latest sexual conquest of their producer. I tapped the taller man—James, I recalled—on his pudgy shoulder and said, "You know what? We *do* know each other! Goody Plenty's Christmas party, right? Wasn't it a blast?"

James's eyes lit up, then flickered. He glanced quickly to his friend (Dave, I thought), who chuckled nervously. James said, "Oh, right."

Dave chimed in, still emanating a half-surprised chest laugh. "Ha, are you gonna kill us? You're gal pals with that crazy Josie chick, aren't you?"

I nearly choked on my own spit. That was what they thought of her, wasn't it? There was no sympathy. No question of why or how or who made her that way. Just an easy, cruel adjective and an antsy little laugh about a crazy groupie. A *groupie*—a title dripping with filth. Yes, let's all gather over photos of a just-arrested woman's tits and shake our heads. Let's all murmur to ourselves that even though we didn't know her, we just *knew* she was trouble all along. Only using Cal for his fame or his money or his cock.

Barely anyone other than those who knew her—other than just me, maybe—could understand why Josie had done what she did. Josie hit back. Not cruelly, not spitefully, but defensively. That's what I thought, but the street whispers made me question it. Had I known her at all? Had she lied when she claimed self-defense?

Everyone had loved her when they thought her life was one they wanted. Glamorous and glittery. Golden-hued. She'd been adored backstage. She'd been miraculous and darling and bright. But in the daylight, Josie had been nothing compared to Cal, and still was nothing. The daylight was what mattered. The daylight was the real world.

That goddamn real world—the world with station wagons and office jobs, with college diplomas and pussy-bow blouses, with promise rings and iced peach tea—was a world where Josie was a slut. I was, too. We were probably herpes-laden hell fiends with senseless actions and selfish ideals. We were cruel and impatient and vain and never as beautiful as we thought.

We were living the dream.

We were disgusting.

We were told to need love, then spat on once we dared to ask for it. Once we tried to defend our right to it.

I wanted to scream all of this to the comedians, but I couldn't. I couldn't say it to anyone, not unless I wanted to give up my celebrity-satellite status forever. It wasn't like my photography could get me inside the Riot House, or anywhere at all now. All I could get I had to gain by groveling.

My mouth felt dirty as I nodded to James and Dave. I grabbed a handful of mints to avoid looking at their faces and fake-laughed. "I *was* friends with Josie. But not anymore. She's . . . nuts. Everyone knows that."

After ten minutes of flattery and a visit from the real "coke girl,"

I linked arms with both of them and joined them in the elevator to the fourth floor. I imagined I was above my own head, watching myself emulating all my friends. Mimicking what I was supposed to be.

They asked me to get ice and I used it as an excuse to leave. I wandered the hallway and crept into the frosty ice room. The lights were off, with the only illumination coming from the icebox's "on" light. Within that electric gleam was Kitty, sleeping sitting up against the wall, wearing a bathrobe and nothing else.

I rattled the ice in the box with the plastic scoop. She awoke, her round eyes fluttering open and shut a few times. "Jesus," she said, slurring, "do you have any tact? Like, at all?" She pulled a Valium out of her beaded purse and swallowed it dry.

"Those aren't very good for you," I said, stupidly overprotective.

"Thanks, Mom," she said. "I'll have you know that I am in *mourning*." She massaged her throat, seemingly pushing the pill down into her stomach, where it could dissolve and make her float. Her facade broke and she rushed toward me, pulling me into a hug. She pressed her face to my breast, soaking the photo of Iggy Pop on the front of my shirt until his face was covered in tears, too. "Faun," she said, "I can't take it. I just can't take it. I feel like my heart is going to break. I feel like I'm going to die. It's not right!"

"You're right," I said, struck with the idea that she felt the same way about Josie that I did. That she pitied her, too. I brushed Kitty's hair, twirling its soft strands between my fingers. "It isn't fair to her at all."

Kitty let go and stepped back. *"Her?"* she asked. "Fuck Josie. Cal's dead!"

I understood what I should do. "I'm so tired that my words slipped. I meant him. I did. It's terrible what happened . . . to him."

Kitty offered me a Valium. I put it in my pocket. She yawned, stretched, and led me into the hallway. She was headed back to Kent's apartment today to collect her things. She didn't care about patch-ing things up with him, saying he was too smacked up for any honest conversation. "I'm staying with Tommy Burnaby and the other guys from Three Lungs now. They were supposed to have a show at Whisky a Go Go but they're considering postponing. You know, to be respectful to Cal."

I rolled my eyes. She didn't notice. She pulled me into room 418, picking up a Styrofoam cup of rum and a handful of french fries off a discarded room service tray. Tommy Burnaby reached up and mussed her pixie cut. She offered me a sip of rum, but I turned her down.

"I don't feel like partying," I said.

Kitty's jaw dropped. "I am not partying. I am coping."

She pulled me back into the hall and stood up straight, swaying slightly on her heels, blistered from her shoes. "Why are you acting so mad? I'm sad Cal's dead, too, you know, but my life can't, like, end because of it. Holiday Sun might dissolve forever or whatever, but I'll still be around." She seemed to be convincing herself as much as me.

I couldn't take lying anymore. I lowered my voice. "What if I'm not as sad as I'm supposed to be?"

Kitty's cheeks blushed red with rage. "You're a fake fan. You always were. You're just Josie's tagalong and I bet you hated Cal as much as she clearly did. She ruined the band and I hate her and maybe I hate you, too!"

"Why don't you go home?" I asked, nearly begging. "Why do you want to be around people who don't care about you?"

"You think you're better than me. You think you know everything. You don't know anything at all." Kitty stepped back into the room. "Why don't *you* go home?"

One of Kitty's newfound band boys started to roll a joint with a page from a Gideon Bible. I left, not sure where I was going.

I wandered the city until I was sweating and sore, seeking solacing addresses but finding nobody at their doors. Before I knew it, I found myself on a Koreatown side street, knocking pitifully at Floyd's front door. He opened up, looked me up and down in my too-big clothes, and said, "Nice outfit."

His Mr. Bill pajamas proclaimed wash-faded anxiety at the prospect of being squashed. "Same to you." Then, "Can I come in?"

He stepped aside and I succumbed to his place's stuffy air of relaxation. It was the same it had been when I used to sleep on its sheetless mattress, empty and gentle. Floyd touched my back and flinched away, like I'd burned him. Maybe I had—he'd always been so cool. Sometimes he simmered, but I was always at a full boil.

"What are you doing here?" he asked.

"Well, I missed you, and, you know," I said, stuttering, "I'm, uh, running out of friends." I tried to be flippant, turning away and pointing my attention to a bunch of bananas on the dining table. I peeled off their rainbow stickers and held in a sniffle.

He leaned against the stove, his palms skimming the unlit, charred burner. "Are we friends?"

"I think we'd be good as friends." I meant it. Maybe we weren't meant to be one-true-loves. We didn't fascinate each other so much as we were fascinated with what the other could *tell* us. He liked spilling road stories and I liked doing the same with backstage party tales.

"We had a lot of laughs," he said, nodding side to side, weighing options.

I smiled, despite myself. "I need laughs." I crossed my arms and leaned back, mirroring Floyd's position. We looked at each other for a long time. I didn't need to tell him I had nowhere else to go. I'm sure he knew. I had no one left to see who I thought could understand me. Maybe he didn't either. "Today's the worst day."

He laughed. "Yeah, yeah, you're right about that." He began to form a word, then bit it back in. He poured two cups of stale coffee from a grody percolator. He handed one to me and said, very slowly, "Do you feel bad for Josie?"

If anyone else had asked that, I'd swear up and down that I didn't. I'd opened up to Kitty and been blacklisted, but there was something remaining in Floyd that I could trust. "Yeah." I sipped my coffee. "She's my best friend. And Cal . . . you saw how he treated her. How they were."

"He was mean," Floyd said, wincing at his poorly brewed cup. "He was cool and he could *be* nice, but he was mean when it mattered."

I nodded so hard I thought my head would fall off and bounce like a ball on the wood floor. I nodded and nodded and suddenly, again, I was crying. Floyd wrapped his arms around me, and I tucked my head into the crook of his neck.

"Can I stay with you? For a bit?" I asked once my tears cleared.

"You don't have any things here," he said.

"I'll go get them. I'll bring some clothes and my toothbrush. Just let me stay for a few days. A week."

"Faun, we're not getting back together."

"I don't want to!" I said, angrier than I meant to be. I calmed myself, picking at my thumbnail. He was the only person I felt like I could talk to, and I needed someone to talk to *so* desperately. I could find party-time company easily enough (Clementine's kin would surely welcome me into their fold), but it was TV-rerun and leftovers-for-breakfast company that I needed. But that was selfish, wasn't it? That same selfish girl whom Floyd probably regretted ever associating with. I'd have to give him something in return, and I barely had the cash to offer to cover part of the rent. I'd already spent half my blood money on useless clothes and trinkets. "I thought it could be nice for both of us to have a roommate. Someone to talk to when the day is over. I can run errands for you. I bet you're busy. I can get groceries and cigarettes and take laundry to the cleaners."

Floyd looked at me for a long time. A bird flew past his window and sun glinted in, dancing across the dirty floorboards. He said, "Go get your things," and I did, gladly. Desperately.

I WALKED THE hour back to Fairfax wearing Floyd's sneakers, now fully decked in garments that weren't my own. Good. An alternate skin. I dreaded each step I took because it meant I was closer to the apartment. It had never felt like my home. It was Josie's. Every coffee stain and nail hole in the wall were her doing. Even after she moved out to live in Cal's big, fancy mansion, I hadn't shifted the apartment to my possession. She'd taken most of the knickknacks and special bits—novelty mugs and piles of fine soaps. She left a shell that I crawled into to inhabit like a hermit crab.

I came back to rotten apples I'd been ignoring for days, buzzing fruit flies, a sink full of dishes, and a ringing phone. I picked up and the voice at the other end was shocked to have an answer. It was Pamela, calling long-distance, hoping I'd bad-mouth her bad sister with her.

"I'm not in the mood to talk," I said. "I have a lot to take care of."

"You aren't going to visit her, are you?" Pamela asked. She breathed heavily, engaged in hatred. Pamela had never liked Josie. But to hear schoolyard jealousy turn to vitriol stung.

"I might." That was an idea, but I didn't know if Josie would be able to stand the sight of me.

"Don't," Pamela said. "My mother says nobody should. Josie's a dirty murderer. She's rotten. She doesn't deserve your sympathy, and you know it."

If I didn't give her sympathy, who would? I was the only one Josie had left. I hung up, not caring to hear from Josie's mother, who was apparently waiting to get on the line.

I repacked my suitcases, stuffing them full with rumpled fabric and the horror paperbacks Josie'd left behind and stacks upon stacks of Polaroids stuck together with paper clips and rubber bands. Was I running away? Just across town. Just far enough to pretend the stars looked different. To pretend I had a different life, where there was nothing but quiet and calm. I changed into the shorts Josie cut for me before that first Troubadour show.

I did the dishes and took out the garbage, drowning the counters in Clorox and scrubbing the crown molding until the paint chipped.

It didn't matter how clean I made it. All I could think of was the smell of rot. This wasn't a good place anymore—just a somber reminder of times that could have gone so much better. Wasted potential. Missteps. I looked to the window ledge, remembering how Josie's bare feet would dangle from it as she ate snacks and consumed the sights of the city.

I shut the door. I slipped a sheepish note under my landlord's door with notice I was vacating. I couldn't stay. I couldn't be alone. The next week, I took out newspaper ads and sold the furniture, staying full-time with Floyd.

The Strip halted, tripping over its unguided feet in a dirge for Cal. In its pause, Floyd and I made lasagna for dinner and drank warm milk before bed. We weren't shacking up. Our promises to each other to be nothing but strange, bed-sharing roommates stuck. We watched *All in the Family* reruns. Archie Bunker wailed at his wife and every time his voice raised, I thought he was going to hit her.

One morning, Floyd, knowing I needed something to keep my brain busy, sent me to the grocery store with $20 and a list of non-essentials. I left at eight in the morning, hoping to hit the streets while the sun was fresh and the pavement still cool. The supermarket was quiet and bright, with scrubbed white tiles and ready-stocked shelves.

With a jar of Tang rolling around in my shopping basket, I took a shortcut through the floral section of the store, landing next to the magazines. A clerk loaded up the stands with new editions of everything from *Weekly Examiner* to *Rolling Stone*. The pages were glossy and freshly inked, and more than half of them had Josie's or Cal's face and name plastered on them. I'd tried to pretend I'd dreamed the events of that awful night, but it hadn't worked. I hadn't talked about it at all, but it was the only thing on the nation's collective tongue. I pored over the magazines and the tabloids, scouring the headlines for things I didn't know and things to make me fume.

On one: Josie's teary-eyed mug shot and a declaration that

America's favorite "villainous vixen" had her bail set at an impossible $25,000. Another: a Vaseline-lens photo of Cal holding a rose onstage, promising in enormous letters THE COMPREHENSIVE CAL HOLIDAY TRIBUTE within. Another: a pouty outtake from Josie's *Foxy* shoot with a nervous-looking photo of Cal superimposed in the corner. Another: an anonymous source, who upon inspection was Clementine, divulging all the dirty secrets and rumors she'd heard, including the scissors-stabbing incident. Still another: on *Weekly Examiner,* a smiling photo of Josie and Cal I had taken, sold by Otis, captioned SEX, DEATH, AND ROCK AND ROLL.

A young teen shopping with her mother bit her thumbnail and said, pointing to a gossip rag with Josie on the front, "Ma, look. That's who killed him. That girl."

Her mother squinted at the censored shot of Josie topless, shaking her head.

My face was on one of the covers. Well, it was three-quarters of my face, with the photo semi-darkened anywhere that wasn't Josie. Without thinking, I picked up a copy of each magazine and laid them into the basket. I wanted to cut out all the photos of Josie to keep them. Slice off all the false captions. Collage her face into something truer and throw all the pictures of Cal into the trash. Burn them in the sink, if I had to.

I finished my shopping, picking out bread and kielbasa and Fudge Stripes. I used all of Floyd's $20 and then some.

The cashier flipped through the magazines to count them, then paused. She snapped her gum and slowly looked up to meet my eyes. She glanced back and forth, and asked, pointing to a cover, "This you beside that killer girl?"

"No," I lied. "You think I look like her? Like the girl with Josie?"

The cashier considered for a moment, then said, "Nah." She clicked her tongue, gazing down at glossy Cal, and sighed. "What a waste, huh?"

THE MAGAZINES WERE just the start of the ensuing media circus. There'd be slimy jokes and deep thoughts broadcast on every late-night show. There would be pun T-shirts and close readings of lyrics for hints as to whether or not Cal suspected Josie was out to get him. I started to get recognized by die-hard followers of the case when I'd walk downtown. I took to wearing sunglasses, even indoors. There would be reporters outside Scott's house, shown on television, and flashing lights, and it would all be too much.

Floyd started getting calls about working shows at the Rainbow and the Roxy. I stopped myself from begging him to stay and be an indoor cat with me forever.

The rock-and-roll lull began to shift, its eleventh hour arriving with the TV broadcast of Cal's funeral. His memorial, rather—the funeral itself was reserved for close friends and flown-in family, held in a clapboard chapel. Darlene called from a hotel, where she was staying with Scott and Wendy, and caught me up on the funeral. She said it had been "so quiet, like everyone was afraid to speak." They laid soft lilies over his grave in a prime plot at Forest Lawn. I watched the memorial alone, Floyd busy stringing lights for a touring band at the Bowl.

The memorial was a star-studded, overproduced affair. Friendly singers and other celebrities Cal had never even met arrived in black limousines before slinking into a mighty, century-old church. The news condensed the event into swallowable clips. Scott, Howie, and Kent spoke a few short words. "Ave Maria" played. Cal's mother cried. And outside the church, screaming their heads off, were hordes of fans clutching funeral flowers and framed photos. They were just as fervent as when he'd been alive, but now they were weeping instead of cheering. Cal was martyred on the evening news.

I shut off the television. I drafted a letter to Josie about it, then wondered if she'd want to know at all.

I wrote a different draft, catching her up on all my nonhappenings, but considered that it might make her jealous.

On a third try, I wrote out my well-wishes and apologies, but doubted she'd believe me.

I threw every version into the wastebasket.

Each day, Floyd came home to see me curled under blankets, saying Norman Lear had outdone himself with every episode of *All in the Family* I watched. I smoked all Floyd's pot and wondered where the summer was going.

One Photo

A low-resolution shot cut out from a magazine cover, a vignette partially darkening anything that wasn't Josie's smiling, unknowing, unprepared face.

20.

I WAS NURSING A TENSION HEADACHE WITH DOUBLE-BREWED tea when Julio Serrano, the head prosecutor in the trial against Josie, called. It was a month after the murder. Darlene had told him where to reach me. "It was hard to find you," he said, croaky voice obscured by a chewed pen or cigar. "You should list yourself in the phone book."

"I'll keep that in mind," I said. What did he want? "Right now, my residence isn't necessarily . . . permanent."

"It had better stay permanent for a while, young lady," he said. "I want you to come in to see me tomorrow at noon. We'd like to ask you some questions about events we believe you may have information about."

I answered with a hitch in my voice, embarrassed to ask, "I'm not in trouble, am I?"

He laughed. I didn't. He said that since I was an "amateur photographer," I should bring any photos I took on the night in question. He gave me directions and hung up. I went to bed, mulling over how I'd be able to save Josie. If I could.

I took the city bus to meet Serrano, Polaroid photos in my purse. The bus stank with summer sweat, wet bodies, and hot metal. The bus driver noted a "bit of a breeze" when I got on, but I didn't feel it. I clutched the pole until my hand turned slick. I switched hands and leaned against the window. I mouthed the possible answers to possible questions I'd rehearsed after a sleepless night of debating how to paint Josie in the best light. I'd sold her out (necessarily, maybe, but the guilt remained) already, but there was time to redeem her.

The bus was too hot, but the room Mr. Serrano led me into was clinically cold. The hallway outside was nearly silent. All I heard was the gurgle of watercoolers and the clack of kitten-heel steps. I shifted on the couch's plastic covering, eyeing Mr. Serrano's tin of chewed-up pencils. There was a photo of twin baby boys on his desk. I wondered what their names were. I crossed my legs.

Mr. Serrano looked like a bird, all sharp angles and beady, black eyes. He lit a cigarette and the smoke spilled out of his mouth like he was an amusement park dragon. "I don't want you to be tense, Ms. Novak," he said.

I nodded. We talked passively about the weather and current events. He didn't offer any water so my throat grew dry. We moved on to preliminary questions about the night in question. I answered emotionlessly. I'd gone through the events so often that voicing them was simple. The questions turned from pure fact to something shakier.

"Were you drunk?" he asked.

"What does that have to do with anything?" I rasped. My face flushed. "Yes."

"It's important," he said, playing with a number two pencil, sliding it between his fingers. "We need all the details we can get and the truth will out, as they say. You need to answer honestly. Was Josephine drunk?"

"Yes," I said.

"And Mr. Haslegrave?"

"Not sure."

"Was there cocaine at the party?"

I squinted at him. A spider climbed across his oak desk, and I watched it teeter away. "Yes."

"Heroin?"

"Yeah."

He traced his thumb down a list. "Quaaludes, animal tranquilizers, marijuana, Dexedrine, DMT, speed, LSD, and/or shoe polish?"

I shrugged. "Probably."

"To which one?"

"All of them."

He looked at me with the droopiest puppy eyes. Gross. He said, his voice dripping with insincere sympathy, "How did a girl like you get mixed up with all this?"

I shifted on the plastic, and it squeaked. I asked something I thought I never would: "Can we talk about Josie, please?"

It took three hours for Mr. Serrano to drain me of almost all the information he wanted. He asked about everything—what kind of ring Josie wore, her reaction when Cal proposed, and whether Cal had ever given her expensive shoes as a gift. I avoided the way he led me toward admitting my knowledge of her technical guilt. So far, he'd only gestured at it, and I just gestured ambiguity back. It was a back-and-forth game. He asked so many questions in such rapid succession that my guard wore down. By the time he got to the meat of the questioning, I was exhausted, my body aching from the tension.

He cleared his throat and asked, "Ms. Novak, did she kill him? Really?"

"Oh," I said. If I lied, that would be a crime. That would be prosecutable in itself, and as much as I pitied Josie, I didn't want to be in her place. But I'd promised. I'd gone so long without saying the true thing, the thing everyone knew I withheld. But I couldn't anymore. I shut my eyes and answered quick, like ripping off a bandage. "Yes. From what I know . . . yes."

I broke the only part of the promise I had managed to maintain. Mr. Serrano offered me a glass of water and I glugged it down. I'd just dug Josie's grave. Paved her path to the electric chair—did they have those? My mouth still wet, I burst into speech at once, saying anything—everything—to try to unhook Josie from the proxy bait I'd swallowed. "Here's the thing, sir," I said. "Cal was a very bad person. He was mean. He'd hit her and yell and control her. He was terrible to her. He was cruel." I gave him details, recounting every little instance I could muster. Sour looks, offhand comments, backhanded slaps, sideways shoves—I shared them all.

But Mr. Serrano didn't seem fazed. He asked, "And did, uh, Josie ever retaliate?"

"Well," I said. Trapped again. "Yeah." I gave examples as he asked. I withheld all I could without being a criminal, but it wasn't enough. One last try. "She doesn't deserve to be locked up. She was defending herself. That's what I believe."

"Ms. Novak," he said, shaking his head like I was a silly little girl. "Belief is well and good but what I need from you are facts. Facts are what the court cares about. You've given me plenty of those. I can tell you're getting frazzled, so how about we call it a day?" He smiled, gloating in his power to pick how people's lives would proceed. He didn't care about Josie's mistreatment. The world had no sympathy for her. I didn't know the specifics, but I started to worry the laws didn't either. To men in wide-collared suits like Mr. Serrano, a battered wife was supposed to put up with it and put her own fists down. Mr. Serrano thanked me for my time.

I said nothing, storming out of the building. I rode the bus back to Floyd's apartment, pinching the skin on my legs until it darkened in tiny bruises. It was evening by the time I got back to Koreatown. Floyd asked if I wanted to talk about what the lawyer had said, or about Josie, or about anything at all.

I said, "No. I'd like to dance, though. Let's dance. Let's go to the Roxy."

He didn't want to, so I went alone. I drank a whole bottle of wine before seeing a band I can't remember the name of. I wanted to be happy as an oblivious clam again. Floyd had said I should get back to my old self again, so I did. Violently. I got back to the parts that were easy and made me forget. I went out the next night, too, and the one after that. I didn't care who was playing or who I was with. I didn't care what I drank or what I snorted. Party girls party. Good-time girls have a good time. Fuck the guilt. Fuck the feelings. Fuck my stupid little photographs. Fuck it all. Have a good fucking time.

When I'd walk the Strip, people would call my name, asking questions I wasn't sure I was legally or morally allowed to answer. I wasn't a celebrity, but recognition began to follow my nervous footsteps. I didn't know if I liked it or loathed it, but it got me free drinks, so I let it continue.

I couldn't stop thinking about those hordes of mourners on the TV funeral extravaganza. They'd been so close and so *tight*, huddled together with their limp arms around each other's tense shoulders. I was torn into lonely shreds, even with my nightly jaunts to clubs. Everyone on TV had been united in their devastation over Cal, and I was isolated by my lack of it. So, spinelessly, I tried to learn how to mourn him, too, and called up Clementine.

She'd returned to L.A. following a four-week West Coast tour with Northern (whom Howie hated because they filled "the same niche Holiday Sun did—do"). I dug out her phone number. She didn't seem to be mourning, not anymore, but she was certainly having fun with apparently true-blue pals. I sweet-talked her into becoming my Sunset Strip sister for a reckless span of weeks. We spent long strings of nights jutting from celebrity party to forest party to beach party to concert to celebrity party again, telling everyone we were having the very best time.

One night, when I came over to get ready, Clementine's roommates warned me she wasn't the kind of girl most would associate with. One, a nursing student in loafers, said Clementine had gotten the clap twice last year.

I shrugged. "Her and everyone else."

I did my makeup in Clementine's closet-size bedroom, sitting in front of a fingerprinted mirror, swirling my eyes in lines of black and gold and singing along to sad Paul Simon songs. I searched for what it was like when a vinyl record with soft guitar was enough for me. If it ever was.

Clementine said Paul Simon was a "boring little man" and turned on the Buzzcocks instead.

She took me to a party at the Goodnews Brothers' house and I remembered Kitty's story about the quilted upstairs bed. Clementine whined about every pebble and puddle in her way, but Josie had kicked the rocks away and splashed in the ocean. Nothing was ever as good without her, but I pretended it was. I wondered, pulling mascara globs out of my eyelashes, if Josie had made friends in prison. If she liked them as much as she liked me. If she still liked me, too.

No slow burn. As soon as Clementine burst through the door and I followed her (why did I always follow?), we had anything we wanted thrust into our hands. This house was cherry-tinted wood, off Mulholland Drive.

"You'll give me half the taxi fare, right?" Clementine asked.

I said yes and never did.

I wanted to make friends. All anyone asked was what I knew about the case (I said, "Nothing at all"), and if I missed Cal (I said, "Who doesn't?"), and if I missed Josie (I said, "I guess sometimes"). A record exec named Larry told me he was heading to Nevada tomorrow with his boyfriend to drop acid until he knew the secret to Elton John's success. I told him that was exciting. He gave me a baby-blue envelope of shitty coke I snorted immediately.

Clementine dared me to jump into the pool so I did, soaking my thin blush-colored dress so it looked the color of my skin. Hordes of people jumped in after me, and we bobbed around, brushing wet shoulders. I floated on my back and wondered where the stars had gone. I couldn't see them in the sky.

Dana Copeland, from Goody's Christmas party, tapped my shoulder with a manicured fingernail. "Do you still have your camera? Could you take photos of us?"

"I don't do that anymore, but I'm still lots of fun to have around," I said.

A guy in little leather shorts laughed from a pool chair. "So who's the new object of your affections, Faun?"

Clementine, still dry on the pool deck, narrowed her eyes.

"Faun didn't even *like* Holiday Sun that much," she said. "Don't you all know scary Josie just brought her along because she didn't have any other friends?"

"No," I said. "That's wrong." No good lies came to mind. I was dried up.

"Kitty says you were a fake fan," Clementine said, harsher. "She says you were barely even *sad* when Cal passed." She crossed herself, eyes cast in the wrong direction, to heaven.

I let her be cruel to me, unfocusing my eyes and imbibing her insults. I took it all inside me and let it stew. I thought I was learning resilience, but I was just trying to hurt myself. I just didn't want her to leave me alone. I laughed, the internal motion wounding, and said, "Clementine, you are too much! Quit teasing!" I smiled, showing my good-natured ability to take a joke.

I dove to the bottom of the pool, over and over, waiting for my body to stop floating back up, but it never did. I always came up for air.

I left the pool and sat in the kitchen, eating popcorn balls and watching Clementine juggle wineglasses. The clock struck four A.M. I got up, unstuck a kernel from my molar, and tracked down someone who'd tell me I temporarily mattered. I bent over and had sex with the Goodnews Brothers' manager in the basement bathroom, all the while imagining hot blood on the tiles. I went home and reset in preparation for the same night to happen again the next day. This continued for weeks. My skin grew pallid, so I smothered it in bronzer. My hair fell stringy, so I teased it. My eyes grew glazed, so I chugged coffee until I looked chipper.

Every so often, Mr. Serrano would call me in to ask more questions. I never said no. I never asked for a lawyer of my own. I didn't even think to. Mr. Serrano knew my inexperience and ran with it, the same way so many other men in this city had.

Floyd pointed out, after I came home at noon after a two-day crosstown bender, that the trial was soon. Although my trips to see Mr. Serrano had prepared me for the prosecution, the defense would probably want to talk to me, too. They hadn't left me any messages, which I didn't understand. Sure, I couldn't help acquit Josie, but I had plenty of knowledge that proved she acted in self-defense. I tabbed through back issues of newspapers until I tracked down Josie's defender. I called and called, but they kept insisting they didn't need me. Want me, even. I told them I could show them photos that might help, but when I consulted the main one, the one of Josie in the bathtub, I realized it didn't really show any of her bruises. The lighting was off, the focus blurry. Eventually they started hanging up when they heard it was me. Was that on Josie's orders? Whatever. I tore some pages out of an old notebook and wrote my own notes for the defense, reading over them in my spare time, trying to remember each delicately chosen phrase.

The trial crept closer.

I kept going out with Clementine for a while but quit when she started giving pleading, sympathetic interviews on any television station that would have her. A HOLIDAY SUN SUPERFAN AND INSIDER, the captions always called her. *Good Morning* aired a clip of her moaning, "I just know that the jury will make the right choice and lock Josie up. I just know it. Poor Cal Holiday deserves to have his death avenged, and I firmly believe the fine people of California will do just that." Avenged, my ass. "He was a good man. The best man I've ever known!"

Like *she* knew him, I thought, then realized I didn't know him either. No one had. Maybe Josie had gotten a glimpse, and what did it say about him that once she did, she'd struck him dead?

I pestered Floyd into scoring me tickets to a concert, hoping to recapture joy. I watched from beside the bar, admiring the twinkle of the lights and trying to find magic in them. Everyone shook my hand and said hello. I slept beside Floyd when I wasn't in a stranger's bed. I sold old photos to Otis and made money. I made friends. I cried every single night.

I was lonely—Darlene and Scott were both witnesses so we weren't allowed to communicate anymore. I read in *Asking*, though, that Scott was writing a solo record, Darlene still not included. Rumors swirled that Kent checked into rehab, but he'd really just gone on a spiritual journey to see the Joshua trees. Howie found a new acting manager and started booking bigger parts in B movies. Howie's trysts moved in circles through the house. Kitty was freshly back from Oregon, where she'd worked for two weeks mending buttons for a jazz band. Yvonne was in New York City.

Summer disappeared, making way for the slow wheel of September to roll in again. I was less green than my last September in California, but just as unsure. Josie's trial began but I shut my eyes from it, lest the news taint my memory. My subpoena arrived in the mail, and I read it like a prayer book five times a day, memorizing the harshness of it COMMANDING my arrival. My meetings with Mr. Serrano had clued me in to exactly what questions he'd ask about Josie. He advised me to answer before the judge the way I had when it was just us in his chilly office, but I didn't *have* to. I couldn't lie, of course, but I could alter my answers like an ill-fitting dress. Make them mold to my truth of Josie more than the prosecutor's.

I TOLD MYSELF I'd be daring, but when my day in court arrived, I was as tiny and sightless as a worm. I had reporters screaming in my face as soon as I stepped out of Floyd's car. He'd helped me get dressed, basing my outfit on the way his "office-lady cousin Laverna" dressed. He gave me cold water and bubblegum to calm my nerves, reassuring me that he'd be in the "audience" so I could look to him.

I swore to tell the whole truth and sat up straight in the witness stand, wishing the sparkling water in my glass was something stronger. I toyed with the collar of my blouse.

Josie was seated with her lawyer, her arms crossed across her chest and her eyebrows furrowed. Her hair was clean and pulled into a tight bun, straining the skin on her forehead. Her pursed lips were smattered with scabbed bite marks. A nervous tic. She didn't look at me even as I recited my name for the jury. I stared as she bit her cheek, the skin pulled into her mouth. There was no way to tell her I was on her side. Was I, even? She looked at me and I mouthed, *I'm sorry*.

Josie was pleading self-defense. I knew she was telling the truth. But the burden of convincing all twelve jurors, on their stiff oak chairs, felt like it all fell on my slumping shoulders. They scanned back and forth between Josie and me, inspecting our faces for some lovely flicker of believability. Fuck that—fuck loveliness.

Mr. Serrano stood, moseying before me and the jury. I looked past Floyd, a swarm of court reporters with clean notebooks, and Stanley. At the back of the room were Clementine, Kitty, and other clusters of Cal's remaining faithful (mostly girls I'd met at parties or snorting coke at the Roxy). His postmortem Manson girls. Josie had no supporters, not openly. Just girls who stared daggers at the back of her head, wishing they could kill her and crush her and, maybe, become her. Kitty glanced at me. I resisted the urge to wave.

Mr. Serrano nodded gently. I nodded back. "Ms. Novak," he said, "how are you feeling today?"

"I'm well, thank you."

"You're acquainted with the defendant here, aren't you?"

I nodded. "Yes. We're best friends."

"Could you tell us about your history together?"

"Sure. We went to the same high school. King Philip Regional. In, um, Wrentham, Massachusetts. Then we split up for college. She moved to California, and I stayed in Massachusetts. Then last year I decided to move to Los Angeles, and she let me stay with her."

"This must be a difficult situation for you to cope with." He was vague, hoping the jury would make assumptions about what he meant.

I pushed back, just a bit. "It's difficult to see Josie being prosecuted."

He squinted. "Why is that?"

"Even though she's pleading self-defense," I said, reminding myself and the court that no one here feigned innocence, "it makes me sad it came to this." Was that good or bad? "She's a wonderful person. She's a—a beautiful, wonderful person. She's kind. She's—"

The judge banged his gavel, making me jump. "Only answer the question, please, Ms. Novak." He turned to me, offering advice I'd been given (and ignored) from Mr. Serrano a month back. From the judge it was serious. Believable. "Be specific with your answers. Be precise, and don't overstep. You seem like a smart enough girl. You should be able to follow along."

"Sorry," I said.

Mr. Serrano continued, "Best friends tend to talk a lot. Confide in each other. Did the defendant ever confide in you?"

"Sure. Yes. Of course."

"About what?"

I shrugged and took a gulp of water. "Everything. About Cal, a lot. She would always . . . sometimes she'd complain. You know how girls talk. It wasn't *all* complaining. But she complained a lot." I considered pushing further but was scared to overstep again. I held it in, gurgling with frustration. The bang of the gavel still rang. The sun streamed into the courtroom, casting white panels across the floor and my face. I squinted.

"What did she complain about?"

Specificity. Nothing more. "About Cal being very mean to her."

"All right," he said. "Do you personally recall any instances of observing his 'mean' behavior?"

I thought back to the past year—more, now. I thought of all the strange ways Cal would grab Josie, how he'd kiss her too hard like he was proving something, and I thought, most of all, about the violence. About how he'd slapped her clean across the face after the album photoshoot. "I saw him hit her—he hit her once," I said. "Once that I *saw*. And there was once that she fell onto a glass table, but I think I saw him push her."

"You think or you know?"

I held in a sigh. "Well, I guess I can't confirm he definitely pushed her, but that's what it looked like. Also, she would have odd bruises. Those I saw clearly. She'd never want to explain them. Last September Cal, um, beat up a man named Rajiv Patel at a party at Howie Guerrero's house. It was really bad."

"And Josie," Mr. Serrano said, "was she ever violent towards Cal?"

I held my breath, waiting for the right thing to say to pop into my head. "Um," I said, "I'm not sure if I remember."

His eyes narrowed. We'd been over the scissors incident once in his office, but I thought I could play the forgetful, fretful friend and get away without mentioning it in front of the jury. He didn't seem to agree. "Are you positive?" He gestured a cutting motion with his fingers.

I looked to Josie, who was looking at her lap. I shut my eyes and said, "I think she might have poked him, or stuck him, with some nail scissors once. I thought it was an accident."

Mr. Serrano pointed the jury to medical records showing the stitches Cal had apparently gotten that night. Mr. Serrano made me repeat myself over and over until I was sick of talking.

"Josie is pleading self-defense," he said, "I'll remind you. So she asserts that she did, in fact, take Cal's life. Did you see Josie around the time the murder allegedly occurred?"

"I saw her at the party."

Mr. Serrano sighed and shot daggers at me. "Did you see her with the body?"

I held my breath. If I said yes, he'd shoot me a million questions about the blood and gore and make Josie out to be a jolly black widow. More, I'd be opening myself to charges—aiding and abetting, and probably other big words I didn't want to face the consequences of. If I said no, I'd be perjuring.

"I don't remember," I said.

"Did she say anything to you in regard to the murder?"

"I don't remember."

"Can you think hard? Do you remember?"

"I don't really remember." I took a sip of my water and said, smiling, just a bit, "I'm very sorry I'm not of more help." I looked to Josie. She didn't smile but she looked, for the first time all day, into my eyes. Hers had become sad, her cheeks turned hollow.

Mr. Serrano turned steaming and spiteful, barely holding back his obvious rage that his star witness wasn't cooperating. I thought, for a second, that I'd won it for Josie. Then Mr. Serrano calmed. He breathed deep. His pupils dilated as he stepped toward me, smiling a salesman's smirk. Suddenly I was his secondary prey. "Ms. Novak," he asked, speaking as if each syllable was essential to his point, "do you ever drink alcohol or take illegal drugs?"

The defense tried to object, citing irrelevancy, but the judge overruled.

"Sometimes," I said.

"Had you imbibed alcohol on the night of June twenty-fifth, 1978?"

"Yes."

"Had you taken any drugs on the night of June twenty-fifth, 1978?"

The defense objected again, but the judge overruled again. Why did it matter? I answered slowly, blushing with each word, "Uh, yes."

"Which ones, can I ask?"

The defense objected again. The judge sustained this time. That was almost worse—now the jury was free to speculate in soft focus about all the unnamed things I might have smoked or snorted.

Mr. Serrano turned to the jury, nodding with a pitying smile. Condescending asshole. They were all condescending. Of course, his point was this: "Ms. Novak, is it possible the drugs and alcohol may have affected your recollections of the night? Or, rather, your inability to recollect the night?"

"Maybe," I said. "I guess." My clever little plan had backfired. I could claim I didn't remember, but Mr. Serrano could throw it back at me like chewed-up food and make it worse. Slimier and unappealing. I was a fool to think I could beat Southern California's top prosecutor at his own game, but for once I had been brave enough to try.

Mr. Serrano ran through more questions. If he couldn't use me for his mission of conviction, he was going to ensure I couldn't be trusted for anything else. He questioned the accuracy of all my memories—rerunning through episodes of my life with an insincere, false-pitying glint in his eyes. Did I *really* remember Cal's cruelty correctly? Josie's half confessions? When I arrived in L.A.? Who my friends were? What my name was? I was a deluded burnout, twirling her Linda Kasabian pigtails on the stand and staring with dead-doe eyes. Exposing my drug-addled dream-look into Cal Holiday's dark cult of personality. I thought about my bed and my pillow at home. At my real home, with my mother. But there was no going back now.

Then Mr. Serrano dug even further, starting to question me about why I'd been smeared with Cal's blood. How it was strange that Josie's best friend had raised the alarm about Cal's death. How it was strange, too, that I'd had a rift with her earlier that night, yet still was here on the stand trying to attest to her goodness. Things weren't adding up, he said, and I knew that. It was all so complicated, in that messy, awful way all parts of life are, but Mr. Serrano didn't seem to understand that. He wanted black-and-white clarity. All I could offer was gray.

All I did was stutter, blush, and sweat through my white blouse. Jesus Christ. You could, when the sun shone through the courthouse windows correctly, see my nipples. I crossed my arms over my chest and tried not to scream.

I was excused to use the washroom before the cross-examination started because I'd been sitting for two hours. I spent all my time there staring at the mirror, trying to remember what I looked like, pulling out my eyelashes just to wish on them.

Josie's lawyer—whose name I was told and immediately forgot—had that salt-of-the-earth, thrift-store-suit, smiling energy of a defender who wants everyone to think he's on their side. Mr. Serrano was cool as metal, but Josie's lawyer was earthy like tree bark and unrefined. Mr. Serrano had turned on me so I laid all my hope—

little as it was—in Josie's lawyer. He seemed to have empathy for me, but everything in the courtroom was so false, so rehearsed, that I struggled to trust it. Was that the point? Josie's lawyer waved at me, his smile warm like butter just beginning to soften. "Ms. Novak," he said, "we'll take this slowly. It's normal to be nervous. I'm sure you care a lot about your friend Josie, here."

"Thank you," I said. "I do."

"I want to give you a break from talking about Josie." Thank God. He was on my side. Mr. Serrano had never been—he'd strung me along on my assumption that I had to give him everything. Josie's lawyer said, "I want to talk about you for a while." He picked up a pencil-marked page. "It says here you are a photographer. Is that accurate?"

"Yes," I said. "It is."

"What subjects do you photograph?"

"Just people," I said, pulling my arms tight across my body in a hug. I met Floyd's eyes in the courthouse crowd and continued, "I take Polaroids. Or I did."

"Any pictures I've seen?" He laughed, gently. The jury did, too. Was that good or bad?

"Um," I said, laughing, too, and not knowing why, "maybe. I took the photo on the cover of Holiday Sun's album *Outfield Flowers*. That was at a studio but more—most—of my photos are just taken out and about. In the moment. Candid stuff, you know?"

"Do you still have your camera?"

"No," I said. "It was found broken on the night of the party at the Sutherlands' house."

He turned to the jury. "We remind the jury that it was Ms. Novak's camera found next to the deceased's body, with both Novak's and Norfolk's fingerprints. Ms. Novak, did you take any photos on the night of June twenty-fifth, 1978?"

"Yes," I said. "I took a few."

He picked up an enlarged print of the smiling picture I'd taken of

Cal and Josie on the stairs of the house. Josie was throwing up a peace sign and Cal had his hand wrapped tightly around Josie's shoulder, his four rings sitting in their usual place. "Is this a photo you took of Calvin Haslegrave and Josephine Norfolk-Haslegrave on the night of June twenty-fifth?"

"Yes, it is," I said.

I took another sip of my water as Josie's lawyer pointed the jury to look at Cal's hand in the picture, emphasizing his rings. Cal wore them every day of his life. Josie said once, when they were both asleep, they scratched her and she woke up bleeding. The lawyer went on, pulling up a print, this one blown so big that you could see the ink dots. Red speckles across a snowy background. Blood on the snow. Josie's lawyer brushed his hand across the photo, his fingers tracing Josie's neck. He pointed out the rings' patterns, slammed into her skin. I gulped to see the bruises blown up. They were so obvious—red darts skewering Josie's sad, just-arrested face. They had always been obvious. I'd just been pretending they weren't. If I hadn't—no, no time for should-haves and could-haves.

"I'm sorry if this question makes you upset, Ms. Novak," the lawyer said, "but we have a photo here we'd like you to tell us about. You mentioned Cal was shown a copy of *Weekly Examiner* that contained images of Josie. Is this right?"

I answered slowly. "Yes. Kent Pearce showed it to him around maybe midnight, or one A.M."

"Can you describe the image of Josephine that was contained inside?"

"Um, yes," I said, hating to picture it. "It had her and Harry Carling, who's a singer, sitting on a couch. And they were kissing."

"Do you know who took this photo? Sounds very . . . scandalous."

Oh, no. I cleared my throat and said, "Uh, I did, actually."

"So how did it end up in a gossip magazine?"

I looked down at the grainy wood of the witness stand. I ran my pinkie finger over its patterns as I said, trying not to feel anything at all, trying not to cry, "I sold it. I gave it to an acquaintance of mine who knew people who bought photos or whatever."

"Why did you sell it?"

"I don't know. I needed money."

"Do you have a job?"

"No. Not in the traditional sense."

"Why did you take the photo?"

"I don't know. I take photos of everything," I said, shame burning.

"And it didn't concern you that Cal might see it?"

Why was *I* on trial? Mr. Serrano finally stood, scowling, objecting so loudly his glass of water shook. He said these questions weren't relevant and the judge agreed. The defense had to move on, but the damage was done. *Let's turn the star witness into a desperate whore, your honor. Let's show everyone what a shitty friend she is. What a vapid, unreliable nobody.* I forgot that I might have helped prove Josie's self-defense claim, instead focusing entirely on the social destruction I'd just stepped into. The airing of the dirtiest of laundry. Shameless, apparently, but so ashamed. In Josie's lawyer's attempt to establish the world of violence that loomed over that night at the Sutherlands', he also established my heavy hand in bringing it to life.

"More so, Ms. Novak," Josie's lawyer said, "I am interested in reaffirming that you are the only person whom the defendant allegedly confessed to. Is that accurate?"

"To my knowledge, yes." What was his strategy now?

"Again, just for posterity, I do want to reaffirm that you and the defendant had also fought on the night of the alleged murder. Is that accurate?"

"Yes," I said, "that is accurate. But that didn't matter to me."

"What do you mean by that?"

I spoke very slowly. "I mean that I don't think it was relevant to what happened afterwards. Specifically, I don't think that the argument affected my actions when I saw Josie with . . . in . . . in the washroom."

Josie's lawyer shrugged and glanced to the jury. "How can we be certain that your anger wasn't a factor here? How can we be sure you're telling the truth?"

I'd ruined both sides. I was on no one's side anymore. It was everyone against me, turning me into the ultimate unreliable witness. Mr. Serrano objected again, but it didn't matter. Josie's lawyer kept picking and prodding. My hands became shaky and numb.

After two more hours of holding back tears, I was finally dismissed.

21.

I WENT TO THE BATHROOM AND BREATHED DEEP UNTIL THE crowd noise in the hallways settled. Floyd and Stanley were waiting for me outside the washroom. "Nice to see you, Faun," Stanley said, seeming to mean it. He fiddled with his bolo tie, flapping the ends together so the beads clicked.

"What are you doing here?" I asked. "Come to gloat about Josie getting caught? Come to mourn your poor little rock star?"

"Faun, come on," Stanley said. "I'm offering you some support. Take it."

"I don't need it. Go back to crying about Cal."

Stanley rolled his eyes and said, "We're both having bad days. You lost two friends. I lost two, too."

We called it square, not digging deep enough into our feelings to find the differences in our distress. All we needed was a person to say we were sorry to. All the anger we'd harbored toward each other before seemed so juvenile. Life seemed grimmer now.

Floyd rubbed my shoulder and said, "Stanley'll take you home, all right? I've got to go to work."

I didn't ask where he was working or whom he was working for. Floyd ducked out, giving me a lukewarm, unreciprocated kiss on the cheek.

Stanley said, "Nice and cool in here, isn't it?"

"I guess," I said. Then I asked the question I asked everyone, to feel out their allegiances. "Do you miss Cal?" I modified it, softening the investigation: "Do you miss him a lot?"

"Oh," Stanley said, taken aback. He leaned down and took a sip from the water fountain, the cold stream crackling on the metal surface. "I do. But the way you miss a friend versus a client, I guess, is different." He pulled his long jacket off and slung it over my shoulders, adjusting it before popping a pair of Wayfarer sunglasses onto his own head.

That wasn't good enough. Hiding how I felt was so rotten, it was festering within my chest. I leaned down for a sip of water, too. I came back up, brushed near Stanley's ear, and said, "I say fuck him. I say he would have killed her if he had the chance."

Stanley's eyes widened. He looked left and right, the setting sun's light from outside catching on his shades. He nodded side to side, weighing possible responses and deciding on nothing. "Let's go." He didn't deny it. Good enough. I let him pull the jacket over my head, leading me headfirst into the media circus waiting outside the courthouse doors.

All the reporters were standing in the weeds for me, the star witness, to make my exit. Not the kind of star I'd hoped to ever be. Instead of being told I was bold and talented and lovely, I had seven different people ask if I was "in on it" and a handful more tell me I was a squealing shrew. I was a fame whore, a bitch, an idiot.

The exact words varied, but most agreed on one thing—I was a groupie.

Even with Cal dead, I was still a groupie.

I yelped, tripping as I made my way down the first step of the long stone staircase to the sidewalk. Stanley slung his arm around my back and steadied me. "Is she drunk?" one reporter called. "Tell us! How was your testimony? Did you speak to Josie?"

Another called, "What do you know? Did she do it?"

"Tell us!" another cried.

A microphone was shoved in front of my sweaty face. Stanley was pulling me fast toward his car. Before he opened up the back door for me, I said into the microphone, "You all know what happened—" I cleared my throat. "You've made up your minds already. You think you know everything, but you don't—"

"Faun!" Stanley interrupted, beseeching me to shut up, but I didn't want to. No one ever let me talk. I grumbled in acrid indignation as I slid inside the car and Stanley shut the door behind me. Cameras flashed in every direction. Unflattering and uncomfortable. Stanley revved his Chevy's engine and we zipped away, his jacket still on my shoulders and the mob turning tinier behind us. I caught a camera flash again, suddenly understanding the song on the radio about being blinded by the light.

I pleaded for Stanley to come into Floyd's place and have a glass of wine with me. He agreed.

I ASKED HIM quiet questions about what his job would be now, and he said he didn't want to talk about it. He said the band was taking a break. Re-forming, shifting, like how a caterpillar has to turn to goo before it can flutter. I thanked him for letting me shoot the album cover, and he laughed, saying that was a nice way to describe bribery. Bribery that didn't get the right results. He'd only taken one sip from the glass I'd overfilled for him when he announced he had to head home. "This isn't appropriate," he said.

I propelled myself forward, balancing on my elbows on the couch. "I don't want to be alone."

"You can't have someone with you all the time."

He was right and I hated it. That was my problem—I needed someone to love me every second or I'd drown. Stanley left and I listened, eyes shut, to the low rumble of his car pulsing farther down the street, into the night I didn't dare navigate on my own anymore.

I turned on a record and tried to dance by myself. I couldn't, so I picked up Stanley's abandoned glass of chardonnay and swallowed its contents down in one heaving glug. This used to be fun, I told myself, and it still can be. Once Floyd comes home, you can have a two-person party. It'll be perfect. I thought about Cal's rotting body in Forest Lawn. I thought about Josie rotting in a cell, then thought about her running free, barefoot on the beach. A Palomino horse. I drank from the bottle and twirled to "Take It Easy."

Then I turned the TV on and saw my own face, squinting at the flash of cameras, on the evening news. I looked like a child, half formed and half awake. Ready to glow in the gloaming but not sure how to start. Josie was the bee sting the band had sung about, but I wasn't even a firefly. I was a gnat. Just buzzing. Buzzing but not buzzed enough, I laughed to myself, pouring the remaining wine from the bottle into Stanley's glass.

Soon the record stopped spinning, so I tossed it to the floor, feeling light as a moonwalker, and scoured Floyd's crates for something violent. What would Josie listen to? I blasted *Led Zeppelin IV*.

In twelfth grade, Josie's beau Brian had stolen a copy of an earlier Zeppelin album from his older brother. He, Josie, and I spent hours admiring it. Josie said it was "transcendent." I tried to transcend now. I wished I believed in astral projection, like Darlene did, so I could zip through the stars and hold Josie's hand in her cell. I wished I believed in anything.

When would Floyd be home? The sky went fully dark and starless. I finished a second bottle of wine. No friends to call. No parties to scream at. Just me, Led Zep, and Floyd's sparse liquor cabinet. I wasn't much for gin, but I tried a few glasses of it anyway, drinking it like nectar until I couldn't stand up right. I slid across the wood floor, laughing all the way and feeling my stomach bile churn, to flip the record.

I tried to dance but kept falling, so I swayed and spun until the whole world turned blurry. I was supposed to enjoy this. I drank more, determined to have fun.

My arms shook and I realized I was shivering. I pulled a crocheted blanket around my shoulders like an old woman's shawl, then listened, eyes bleary, to the record player. The song said something about a woman drinking all the wine. About a woman with star eyes. About a woman who I would never be as much as I wanted to be—so what was the point? I wasn't the type to have a song written about me. I wasn't the type to do anything but whine and cry and drink all the goddamn wine.

The record ended and I put it on again. I wanted to play it over and over and over until it sounded different. I suckled the bottle of gin, forgoing the glass, counting the dots on the ceiling. I threw up on my own chest. I tried to keep counting but kept forgetting what came after twenty-four.

When Floyd came home, he threw his coat to the floor and charged toward me, his eyes bulging like he'd spotted a ghost.

"Hi, Floyd," I said—or tried to. The words made sense in my head but out loud, they sounded wrong and mumbled. I cursed my mouth, commanding it to behave. "Do you want to kiss me? I drank all your wine, like Led Zep said to."

"Faun?" he said, bending down over me. He winced as he got closer to my puddle of vomit. "Faun, do you understand what I'm saying?"

Why was he asking that? Of course I did. I said, "Yes, stupid, yes, of course."

Floyd yanked me up and leaned me against the wall, the top of my head skimming the bottom of his framed Willie Nelson poster. He shook me by the shoulders the way you'd wake someone from a nightmare and asked again, "Faun? Faun?"

I mumbled something. God, was I ever tired.

I drifted off and woke up, wailing like a newborn baby, to bathroom ceiling tiles and a group of paramedics. The backs of my arms stuck to the porcelain of the tub I laid in and I realized, right then, there was a tube stuck down my throat. I gagged.

I'd already spilled my metaphorical guts during the trial. Here came the real ones.

"Keep it down, Faun," one paramedic said. She sounded like my mother. "Keep the tube down."

I tried to pull it out and the paramedic with my mother's voice pulled both my arms behind my back. Time-out.

This wasn't glamorous anymore—when Darlene bled in bathrooms or Yvonne hacked up a lung, there'd been some kind of mystique. Some gorgeous inexplicability making every moment lovely. I never had that skill. That charisma. All I had was the dire feeling that the world was about to implode.

They pumped my stomach and I cried the whole time, equal parts embarrassed and bitter they had done it at all.

The paramedics left, giving Floyd stupid instructions on caring for stupid little me. I was tucked into bed, wearing a clean pair of pajamas and a heartless frown.

Floyd scrubbed the tub, sighing to himself.

When he came back, he stared me down with such intensity I burst into laughter. He didn't laugh at all. He looked so old. I remembered how Yvonne had thought he was embarrassing—well, how everyone had, myself included. I still didn't understand why. Floyd loved things like I loved things, which, I think, is why he put up with me. Besides, I couldn't think of any musician who would have tidied me up like he did. None would have cared that much. When I cried in front of Howie, he'd gone to bed.

"How was your day at work?" I asked, playing at normalcy. "Where are you working now?"

Floyd sat on the edge of the mattress, letting it sink under him and cushion his body. "Linda Lessinger, the girl who sings 'Love Me Nightly,' is putting together a tour. She's pretty good. Lots of lighting design ideas of her own but none of them are very good. It's just spotlights and strobes, strobes and spotlights."

"That's fun," I said, yawning.

"I'm going on the tour," he said, quickly, like it hurt. "Next month. I'll be flying out to Sweden. It's starting there."

He was leaving me. Fine. If he was leaving L.A., I could, too— once the verdict of the trial came out and I was free from the public eye, I'd spend all my money on a bus ticket and head anywhere I wanted. I said, "Good. I'm going to New York once the trial's over."

"You gonna live with Yvonne?" he asked, laughing. I had forgotten she was there. I shrugged. "So Faun's running away."

"I'm not running away," I said. "I'm an adult. I can go wherever I want."

"So why are you going somewhere that's not the Valley? Thought you loved California."

"I want to go somewhere else." I meant it. Everything was too much in L.A. It was too heavy and too thick with smog and people. New York wasn't a reprieve from either of those things, I considered, but they had snow. They had cold. I could shiver in the air and see my breath ahead of me. I could have visual proof I was alive. Maybe things would be better in New York. Yvonne must have had a reason to go there. She must have known something the rest of us didn't.

I was sick of letting everyone down. Sick of letting myself down, too—making impossible promises to myself and failing, time after time, to maintain them. To sustain any semblance of follow-through. Josie's trial was the nail in the coffin of my California dream. Sure, the Beach Boys said all girls should be California girls, but I couldn't do it anymore. If I could get away, get far fucking away from L.A. and everything within it, then I could be better. Be good. Maybe that dream, too, was just another promise that couldn't be fulfilled.

My stomach turned and I said, "I feel awful."

Floyd slid closer. There were bags under his eyes. I didn't deserve his kindness. "Why do you treat yourself like this?" he asked.

"I don't know," I said, pitching my voice up too high to sound believable. "I treat myself fine."

"You could have died."

"Thanks." I rolled my eyes. I *knew* I was being immature. I knew I was being infantile and rude and eternally ungrateful. But I couldn't bear to admit he was right. It hurts too much to realize you don't love yourself.

Floyd turned away from me, fluffing his pillow. He said, quietly, turning to the floral-shade lamp on the dirty floor, "I always thought you were a different breed, Faun, but I don't know anymore. You're just like all the other girls."

"Maybe I am," I said, thinking of Darlene's fearlessness and Kitty's brashness and Yvonne's confidence and Josie's shine, and continued, "And if I'm not, I want to be. I know you think that's a crime."

"Stop blaming yourself for all this bullshit," he said.

"I don't."

"You do."

"Nuh-uh."

"Jesus. Shit. You realize you're pathetic, right? You realize you're exhausting to be around?" His lips snapped shut, his face contorting in immediate regret. "I just meant—I meant—"

"It's fine." He was right. The words stung like vinegar but were as clear as it, too. I couldn't argue. "Turn off the light, I'm tired."

One Photo

A magazine cutout of me, shielding my eyes, running to Stanley's car, hating to be looked at.

22.

I'D WATCH THE TRIAL UPDATES ON TELEVISION, TAKING NOTES in a bargain-store notebook, doodling in the margins and feeling guilty each time. I'd watch until the newscaster mentioned my name, then I'd change the channel, unwilling to see my own face. My own mistakes. I wrote a letter to Josie on stolen Hyatt letterhead, thinking that the Riot House address stamped in the top left corner might give her a giggle. I kept busy, trying to prove to Floyd that I wasn't pathetic. My chest was chasmic, echoing, but I pretended it wasn't. If I was occupied with useless puttering, I wouldn't have time for useless whimpering. I baked bread. I went on long walks to nowhere, sometimes barefoot, just to feel the sting of the sidewalk. I tried new foods and trimmed my bangs and revised the letter to Josie.

I'd switch words back and forth, trying to be sympathetic and sorry without being sugary. I left out most of the mush. I settled on:

Dear Josie,

I'm so sorry. I hope I was some help to you. I wanted to help you. I think you know that. Or I hope you do. I'm still very sorry. I kept all our promises, but that doesn't mean a lot I guess.

I haven't been up to much. Watched Death on the Nile, *which was a slog. They put the Pope's funeral on TV, which was also a slog. Things are boring without you. I know we'll get to be together again soon and everything will be back to normal.*

Tell me if you want anything from me. I can send you books. There's a new one by Stephen King about the end of the world (how spooky!).

> *Hope to hear back soon. I included some extra postage in case you don't have any.*

> All my love,
> Faun

I PULLED ON a cardigan and walked to the post office, using my backstage wiles to convince the clerk to help me decode the prison mailing system. I sent the letter off with a lipstick kiss on the seal, hoping Josie would appreciate the glamour. I went down to Redondo and walked along the beach. My feet turned filthy, but I stayed shoeless, watching as the waves washed pebbles into the shoals. Maybe I stepped too heavily, but as I was leaving, I swore my footprints were still there in the sand, sharp as ever.

There was nothing for half a mile down the beach but sand. I loved the emptiness. I craved it. It wasn't loneliness I wanted, but fortified solitude. Instead of reaching for any willing hand, I swatted them all away. I found a Polaroid of me, Josie, and Cal in one of my jacket pockets and cried for ten minutes.

On the bus home, a pair of old women, knitting, were discussing the "linchpin" of Josie's self-defense so I covered my ears and hummed. Just a little break. Then I'd turn the TV on and take more of my notes. I only trusted the trial through my eyes.

The coverage stung. Usually the newscaster delivered cold facts, listing the day's witnesses, name-dropping when appropriate to keep the listener engaged. Everything sounded so heartless reported back-to-back with movie reviews. Once, after a vital day of Josie's testimony, they cut to a female courthouse reporter. Her soft brown hair curled inward, like halves of cartoon hearts, across her turtleneck collar. She stood close to the exterior courthouse walls, tendrils of wilting geranium leaves spilling out of their planters and over her feet. When she recounted Josie's testimony of Cal's abuse, her voice wavered. The secondhand news of screams and slaps sank her eyes back. Her mouth stumbled over the words, suddenly caught in a nervous twitch, a flash of fear. Maybe she knew what it was like for Josie. Maybe she, too, cursed the world that required a battered woman to point to all her bruises for public inspection.

A few days later, Josie would say one thing—only one thing—to the courthouse reporters. The clip made it to every channel. One reporter, from a trashier network, goaded her, asking over and over if she missed Cal. Josie, hustled along by security guards, leaned close to the white microphone nearest her face. She said, "I do. I never hated him. I loved him." It was true, I think. True in that inexplicable way that ruins all the easy ways of seeing things.

FLOYD LET ME watch him do the prep work for Linda Lessinger's lights. Sitting on a crate and complimenting him as he ran cables felt like old, better times. I fell into a blissful nostalgia until another roadie, whom I didn't recognize, waved me down.

He said hello and asked how I felt about "screwing over my friend." I didn't know if he was talking about Cal or Josie. Turns out it was both. "Girl," he said, shaking his head, "you played some dirty tricks."

"I don't think so," I said. He didn't know anything.

"Why'd you sell that photo of Josie kissing what's-his-face, then? If you knew Cal liked whacking his ladies?"

"You're a pig."

"Hey, am I wrong?"

"Oh, please," I said, crossing my arms, sniveling. "Who are *you* to tell me anything?"

"I'm everyone." He laughed. "It's what everyone's thinking."

I stared at Floyd, who said nothing except, "We need to replace this bulb. Light's about to die."

I WAITED A week for Josie to write back. The letter only had to travel a couple miles to the women's jail where Josie was. It was called the

Sybil Brand Institute, a name so hoity-toity you would've thought it was a finishing school. A women's college, maybe. I didn't get an answer, so I wrote again:

Dear Josie,

I miss you very terribly. I miss when we lived together and had fun. I miss when we were little and in school and laughing at stupid stuff. I miss whispering to you and having dinner together. I live with Floyd now, temporarily, but it's not the same. We are not back together but do share a bed. Scandalous, I know.

I am sorry for everything. Please let me know if I can help you.

Love,
Faun

A WEEK LATER, I'd gotten no answer to either message. I double-checked the addresses, made running tallies of all the mistakes the postal service sorters could have made, considered ways the letters could have disappeared or blown off into the sky. I didn't want to consider the obvious reason I never got an answer: Josie didn't want to give one.

I wrote three more times, throwing in useless facts about my daily routine, aiming to elicit anything from her. It didn't work. I told her I was going to New York. Radio silence. I told her I could visit. Nothing. I told her I missed her over and over and over. No reply.

I TURNED ON the news one day before Josie's verdict was expected. It was nearing Halloween. I pulled my trial notebook onto my lap, playacting at understanding what was about to be said. All my wishy-washy feelings and drunken stories were about as useful as Darlene discussing Josie and Cal's incompatible auras in detail on the stand. I hoped, helplessly, that somehow I'd done something good.

Everything I'd loved I'd lost, and every time I'd lost it, I said it was my own fault. A lot of the time it was. But not always. Self-pity is so simple. So is self-blame. Easier than having to understand the world doesn't revolve around you, that it doesn't always love you back.

Floyd was in the kitchen scrubbing a pan. Our domestic arrangement remained out of convenience, not love. Usually we sat in silence, fiddling with the radio and waiting for the smell of cactus flowers and crocuses to drift around us through the window. We got along better with both of our departures looming. An end always prompts endearment. That's the reason limited-edition snack flavors sell out, the reason TV specials get better ratings than regular episodes.

Wasn't this trial talk the best TV special yet? The news intro's globe spun under the tube's static. A bearded news anchor said good evening.

I bit my nails on one hand, fiddling with my pencil eraser with the other, as the anchor said, "After an announcement this evening, we have word that tomorrow the jury for Josie Holiday's much-publicized murder trial is to give their verdict. The twenty-four-year-old California model was accused in June in the stabbing death of her husband, famed rock singer Cal Holiday of the band Holiday Sun. Her team is arguing self-defense. Many are suggesting that a linchpin photograph taken by Faun Novak, a photographer, may be the key to convincing the jury Josie's life was in danger—sources reported the defense focused on a particular arrangement of rings worn by Cal Holiday that matched cuts documented on Josie Holiday's face and neck after her arrest."

The rings. The rings that Josie had ripped off Cal's hands and run away with in some inexplicable act of resistance or foolishness. They weren't on his body when the police found him, but it didn't matter that Josie had made a mistake in removing them, because I'd managed to accidentally document them anyway.

The news continued. "The prosecution argues that this is nothing more than a cold-blooded passion killing." Contradictory, but the reporter didn't flinch. The camera cut to a photo from Josie's *Foxy* shoot, zooming slowly toward her censored bare chest. "If Josie Holiday is convicted of murder, she could face up to twenty-five years in federal prison."

Twenty-five years. Twenty-five long, reeling years on the line. Twenty-five years, longer than Josie had lived so far, threatening to be spent shuffling from cafeteria to cold cell to exercise yard to cold cell again. She'd be nearly fifty by the time she emerged, squinting like a mole, grayed and grizzled and unloved. I swallowed, belatedly comprehending that the news anchor had said my name—said I'd done something useful. My photograph, useful? Valuable? Had he said I was the linchpin in Josie's *favor*?

The thought flickered as I went to bed.

I flipped on *Good Morning* when I woke up, watching the cackling assistant anchors drone on about the dangers of teen drinking and the importance of booking your ski vacations early. I watched, holding my breath in my throat, until the lead anchor announced the breaking news. I crossed my fingers and my toes.

There was the anchor, wearing a black suit. Was he mourning, or was it the only thing clean?

There was the familiar favorite photo of Josie, pouting under paparazzi flashes.

There was the verdict.

Guilty.

Josie was guilty, guilty, guilty.

The air choked me as I tried to breathe. Everything gagged me. Everything was too real and eternal. My cup of rooibos tea spilled all over my lap. I was soaked and livid and breathless. She was gone. She was alive but she might as well have been dead, disappeared behind concrete walls.

I did nothing in the days leading up to her sentence. I ate untoasted bread. I drank water that Floyd poured for me. I slept and tried to read but couldn't focus on the words in my books.

When it was time for the sentencing, I barely wanted to turn on the television. I bit my nails so short they bled, then listened to the report.

The judge had announced that Josie was given a barely sympathetic, lower-than-maximum sentence of twenty-two years.

But that little erasure of the maximum time—that little reprieve—must have meant some part of Josie's fight had been won. Maybe it was my photo, proof those bruises came from Cal's hands, that had helped. I didn't care that all the enraptured girls insisted Cal was too handsome to hurt. The obsessive documentation that tired my friends (and ruined Josie) had brought miniature redemption. I had to tell myself this or I'd break. I'd split right down the middle, peeling until all my guts were splayed.

I burst out the door. Two boys with bowl haircuts pedaled past me on wobbling two-wheelers. I bought a bottle of peaches-and-cream soda from a Korean grocer and sipped it as I wandered off to nowhere. The streets didn't curve enough for me so I weaved up and down, like thread through fabric, until I was lost. The world smelled like tar and daisies as I passed gravediggers in the Hollywood Cemetery and blue-capped street sweepers at a farmers' market. There were wild dogs outside a country club and house cats with bells on their collars outside punk shops. Eventually I found myself at the door of a Goodwill, still unsure where I was but sweaty enough to ask for directions.

I approached the cashier but stopped, caught by a glint of light across the room. A Polaroid—with a cherry body and scuff marks. I slipped past the women's pajamas and men's shoes to pick up the Polaroid, looping its polka-dotted strap through my fingers. A ladybug. Those were good luck.

I bought it. I kept walking, slower this time. A strange stillness filled me, and I liked it, savoring the lull. For the first time in months—who knew how many—I wasn't worried. My heart didn't thrum like it was about to stop, my fingers didn't ache from twitching, my stomach didn't twist into impossible knots. There was nothing to fret over, all the aches decided one way or another.

I wasn't happy, but I was fresh. I looked up at a street sign and realized I was in Miracle Mile.

I kept walking until I was on Santa Monica, trying to catch the strains of music drifting out of the Troubadour. I leaned against the posters, squinting through cigarette smoke and entranced by neon lights.

I was so lost in the beauty of finally doing nothing that I didn't notice Clementine until she spat in my face. Her saliva landed, wet and thick, in my left eye. "How could you say what you said about Cal?" she asked.

"Take it easy," I said, wiping my face.

"How could you?" Clementine screamed.

Beside her was Kitty, who shoved her and said, "Clementine, quit it!"

"Faun Novak is a band-betrayer! Faun Novak is a liar!" Clementine shrieked, loud enough for the whole street to hear. "Faun Novak is a bitch! Lying goddamn *bitch*! Scum!"

Kitty grabbed my hand for a second and squeezed. I rubbed Clementine's mint-scented spit out of my stinging eye. Kitty let go of me when Clementine dragged her down the street, their platform boots slamming the pavement in perfect unison.

It was time to leave L.A.

I MADE A final trip to see Otis with a stack of photos in hand. None of them were personal or precious—mostly old snaps of random celebrities I'd weaseled into waving at the camera. People I didn't know. Who I could pretend were fake and painted faces.

Otis said he saw me on TV, that I looked like the girl who played Laura Ingalls Wilder on *Little House*. He was in the same Zeppelin T-shirt as when I'd first met him. When I left, having struck a deal that he'd give me $400 flat for the lot and keep any excess profits, I wondered if he'd stay there forever, collecting dust.

I needed him so I could eat, yet hated him. He didn't change me—he showed me who I was.

I came back to Floyd's after dark, my legs cramping, still calm. He got home even later. We looked at each other with expectancy but were unable to express anything but hunger. We made meatballs. I smoked a menthol cigarette. I told Floyd about my walk to nowhere and he screwed his face up, confused.

"I don't know anybody that walks like that," he said. "What's the old adage?" He laughed, pushing a meatball around his plate with a broken fork. "Nobody walks in L.A."

"Well, I do," I said. "I always go for walks." Even if I'd had a car, I'd still walk. I liked the slowness of it, the rhythm. The way the buildings grew or shrank block by block. The smells pouring out of every restaurant. The dropped receipts and personal garbage fluttering across the sidewalk cracks. Alone in the world, alone with others around me.

I WROTE JOSIE a letter saying I was sorry about the verdict. Being positive felt impossible but I tried anyway, offering craft supplies or a phone call. I didn't get a letter back, but figured her mail days were probably inundated with official documents and requests for comment. Things would quiet down, and then she'd get back to me with her full attention.

Floyd left early the next Tuesday for Scandinavia, kissing me a polite goodbye with a closed mouth. He gave me a parting gift—two packs of Polaroid film, for my replacement camera. He wasn't sure if it was the right type of film. I popped it into the camera and snapped a photo of him. It came out bright and clear, the quick click of the shutter filling me with sentimentality.

"See?" I said. "Perfect."

"I'll miss you."

"I'll miss you, too." I would. In a realm of grudges and spat-in eyes, he'd forgiven me.

He took a deep breath, eyeing his suitcases. "I'm sure I'll be hearing lots about you. Don't go too crazy, you dig?"

"We'll see." I laughed. "Look me up if you're ever in New York. If I'm still there by then."

He nodded, leaning to kiss me again but backing away. He waved. He left lugging all his worldly possessions, Willie Nelson poster included, behind him.

I made myself jam and toast and riffled through my address book until I found Yvonne's New York phone number. I'd gotten it from Darlene months ago without the intention of ever calling. The food was dry and tasteless as I waited for Yvonne to pick up, imagining the operator giving her my name and Yvonne sighing over and over until her breaths formed an abyss.

She picked up. "Calling collect? Really?"

"Hi, Yvonne," I said. "It's Faun, from California."

"I know. The operator told me." She paused for a second, then laughed. "Oh, Faun, what do you want?"

"How's New York City?" I asked, pushing my plate away.

"Empty," she said slowly. "Probably better than where you are. Cold. That trial was something, huh?"

"Yeah, really something," I said. "Do you have an extra bed?"

"I live in a Travelodge."

"I heard you were in the Chelsea Hotel."

"That, too. I'm all over."

I cleared my throat and announced, "I'm leaving tomorrow. Can I stay with you?"

She paused for a long time, then seemed to laugh again and gave me the address.

I confessed, despite myself, "I didn't think you liked me."

"We're sisters," she said. "We look out for each other. Bring me some records and we'll be even. I want the new Springsteen."

I WROTE JOSIE one more letter before I left:

Josie,
I'm moving to New York. I'll write you when I get there so you can
have my new address. Yvonne is letting me stay with her until I get my
bearings. Who'd have thought?
I can't wait to hear back from you. I really can't.

Love,
Faun

AT THE GREYHOUND station, I called Yvonne and gave an estimated time of arrival. I could practically hear her rolling her eyes, so I prepared to navigate my own way to her Travelodge room when I got there.

There's some metaphor I could make about my three days incubating in a cross-country bus, something that would make me sound biblical, but I was no Jesus. I was the common repentant no one.

In Nevada, I wondered if I'd ever get married, and in Utah, I slept through the bus-window sights. Colorado was pretty enough to stare at and, when I went out to stretch my legs, it smelled like smokeless fire. Kansas was gray. Missouri, too, but wetter. By Indiana and Ohio I started to see familiarity, but spent most of those states rereading Josie's copy of *Salem's Lot* for the second time and eating peanuts from a gas-station bag.

I was surprised I remembered how to walk once I arrived in New York, and more surprised that Yvonne was there waiting for me, reading *Creem* on a bench inside the station. David Bowie, in high-fashion gentlemen's attire, bowed at me from the cover. Yvonne didn't notice me until I hooked my finger over the spine of the magazine.

"Your tits got smaller," she said.

"Thanks, yours, too," I said, glancing sideways at anything *but* her breasts.

My T-shirt clung to my stomach. I'd had it on for three days be-cause I didn't want to be a pest and ask for my luggage. Yvonne came with me to the restroom so I could change, despite my insistence I could go alone. I was glad she did—the grime made me want to gag, and I feared the eclectic, reeling drifters near the restrooms. Port Authority was not the mecca I'd envisioned. A fluorescent lamp burned out with one final buzz. The only light came from a tiny open window.

"Everyone in this city wants to get killed or kill you. It's fun. Don't be scared. Come on," Yvonne said from outside my stall. I shoved my old shirt into my bag as she said, "Hurry it up."

I said nothing, still changing. Half a minute later, when Yvonne rapped on the door and jiggled it, I shouted, "I am changing my under-wear! Can you wait two seconds? Do you want to see my bare ass?"

Someone laughed from another stall and I blushed. Yvonne didn't apologize but she stopped knocking. I emerged feeling like I was in different skin. I'd worn my jeans in anticipation of the wet, cool East Coast weather, that same weather I'd started to miss after perpetual sunshine. There was something magical about dimness. About the half dark, and those moments after sunset when the pavement's still warm.

Yvonne wasn't a terror, like I'd thought. She took everything too seriously, but God, didn't I, too?

We walked down West Forty-first Street. The streets were warmed by density, bustling with foot traffic. Strangers with beige briefcases and straw hats and bell-bottoms and spray-paint cans and sky-high Afros slipped past my shoulders. No one said hello, and no one said excuse me, but I didn't mind. We moved together, all on separate journeys along the same path. Street crowds had terrified my mother, so we'd never visited the city. We'd gone to middles-of-nowhere—lighthouses in Maine, dusty museums in colonial towns. Never some-where as layered and swirling as this. Manhattan was so crowded and shifting I was shocked the island didn't sink. Yvonne told me to pick up the pace and I did, my head turning side to side to take in every hand-painted sign and square-bodied honking car.

Yvonne asked if I wanted dinner. I said yes, so she told me to buy us both hot dogs. I did, passing change to the vendor before finding a bench near the fountain. I beamed up at the clouds as Yvonne stared at her relish-slathered dog, picking off bits of the bun and chucking them at pigeons until she ran out of bread.

"I saw Cher at Studio 54," she said.

An autumn leaf floated down from an oak tree and landed in my hair, which was so dirty the foliage stuck. "Far out," I said.

Our conversation was plain and full of emotionless name-dropping, but it was better than how everyone had spoken to me in L.A. Yvonne was surprisingly avoidant. She didn't want to talk about the trial—all she asked me was how I had been.

I said, "It's been too much."

"So you ran away?" she asked, finished with the bun and now picking at bits of her sausage. "I don't blame you. I need to move around, too. I start to suffocate." She absentmindedly ran a finger across the long, fading scar on her forearm.

"A change of pace never killed anybody," I said. "It's easy to leave L.A."

I wasn't running away from the city, but maybe I'd tried to run from myself. That was no use. You can't abandon your own body. Your constant companion. I could go to Coney Island—I could go to Maui, Tripoli, South Africa, the moon—and I'd still be Faun. From a shop window, I could hear "Hotel California" playing.

"Take my photo," Yvonne said. "Like the old days."

She wanted shiny California back. I did, too, but we didn't have it. We wanted to be forever-muses who never muttered a complaint—who never *had* one to mutter. But we'd never really been that. I took her photo and noted all the familiar parts. She took me to her Travelodge haven, dragging me past burlesque clubs, pointing out one she'd worked at for "two shitty weeks" before she got her first paycheck from the band she was managing. The band—Baby Stout—featured her cousin Cora rasping and two "okay guys" on guitar and drums. They played tiny venues with vulgar names that Yvonne showed me along the way. The neon lights flickered across her, turning her every color block by block.

I dropped my luggage off in Yvonne's motel room and she presented all the places she'd seen a cockroach. One spotting seemed the freshest because there was a tiny brown stain squished onto the yellow carpet.

Yvonne hastily explained she was rarely here. "Consider it a storage locker," she said. "Now, come on. Did you bring me my music?"

"Mmhm," I said, and unzipped my bigger suitcase. I handed her *Darkness on the Edge of Town*, still in its plastic, just like an altar boy passes along the Bible.

We drank sparkling water on the balcony, towels under us so we wouldn't get dirty, and I told Yvonne I was thankful for her. Three kids sketched out a hopscotch court on the sidewalk and tossed pebbles at each other, playing superheroes.

"I almost died a couple weeks ago," I said quietly.

"Oh, you and me both," Yvonne said.

"I mean it," I said. I popped the bubbles in my water with my pinkie.

"Don't be dramatic."

"I'm not. I mean it," I repeated, staring at her. Yvonne crossed her arms, thinking about something I couldn't place. Maybe she meant it, too. "They pumped my stomach and it felt like being hollowed out." I dug the dirt out from under my thumbnail. "I—I kind of feel dead. And Josie is—"

"Josie's not dead."

"I know." What was her game?

"She's alive."

"In prison."

"Alive, either way," Yvonne said, very slowly. "It's no crime to be alive. Springsteen said something like that. He's a fucking poet."

There was no point in imagining you were a dead girl, because once you were, you wouldn't know it. None of us was dead. Paul Simon was the only living boy in New York, and here I was, a newly living girl.

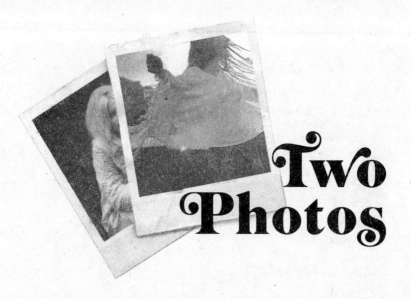

Two Photos

Floyd in his kitchen, ready to leave for somewhere new, looking older than he'd been before.

Yvonne on a Bryant Park bench, dark shades pushed down the bridge of her nose, forever glamorous, forever trying to be.

23.

WE LOVED PAINTING EACH OTHER'S FACES AND BRAIDING EACH other's hair and cheating the bill at restaurants and yelling back at catcallers and kissing strangers and chewing stolen breath mints and telling everyone we were important—all the bright, free pleasures of a discount-driven life lived out of motel rooms and strangers' beds. I wrote letters to Josie about my day, drafting beautiful sentences for hours to paint as clear of a picture as I could. The trees in Central Park didn't have branches, they had "dangling frozen boughs." The subway performers weren't singing, they were "preaching music." I wasn't grifting, I was "discovering secrets and living off kindness." I didn't get a response. I started to lose heart, writing less often. Was the address wrong? Was it really that far to the other coast? What did I have to do for her to remember me?

Yvonne and I had no money except for what we borrowed from half-important men we'd meet at clubs. Yvonne would show me all the spots she hung around. I felt like I knew the city even though I couldn't find Queens on a map. We waxed poetic about the culture we saw in Greenwich Village and Bed-Stuy. All the folk-singing Ginsberg-wannabes I attached myself to were just draft dodgers with berets and unwashed beards. Yvonne and I did acid with a James Taylor type and ruminated on buying bus tickets to see the Dead play somewhere upstate. I lived dreams and did nothing, counting every dollar I spent and didn't earn back. Yvonne worked for two weeks at a Jewish deli to pay off half the motel bill. Life was rainbows and muck.

Yvonne hadn't been back to the motel room for two days when she called me, telling me to come see her in the Chelsea Hotel. She was messing around with Antelope Valley, a group I'd never cared much for, and wanted me to come to a party they were having. I took the subway from Hell's Kitchen to Chelsea, keeping my head low and deciphering graffiti.

Yvonne was on the sixth floor of the hotel, reading poetry on the bed. Across in a chair was Antelope Valley's Roman-nosed singer, Jed Tooley, sticking out his tongue and running a lighter under a spoon. His two bandmates were on the floor, playing Old Maid. Three tired, pink-lipped women sat cross-legged around them, the carpet's thick floral pattern leaving imprints on their skin. Hardly a party but I was still glad to be invited.

It was a foggy night, but that was fine—instead of stark moonlight or lamplight, all the light was misty and cool, making me feel like a pixie in a rock-and-roll forest. My skin was pale again, my California tan finally faded.

I sat beside Yvonne on the bed. She kept reading, tracing the printed letters in her book with her index finger. My eyes trailed the slow flicker of Jed Tooley's Zippo flame. Yvonne tried to read me part of "Ozymandias." I didn't pay attention—all I could see was the slick way Jed Tooley's blood slid into the pooled heroin in his needle, how the red dispersed and turned everything dark pink.

He asked me to take a photo of him with the needle in his arm and I did.

One for the album.

He slumped over. Yvonne carefully helped him take the needle out of his arm, her face painted with the strangest maternal glee as he muttered, "Thank you."

Too much blood. I got up, saying I needed air, taking a peek out the open window and stepping into the hallway. The hotel wasn't all gore. Most of it was wonderful and wild. That was why the viscerality of Jed Tooley's needle shocked me—I thought I'd escaped things that prong, that prick, that stab. But shiny sharpness dwells every-where. Usually the softness is enough to hide it.

I explored, running my hands against wood-grain walls and won-

dering how everyone was in L.A. Wondering if Kent had been en-
lightened on his spiritual journey. Wondering if Wendy knew full
sentences yet. Wondering if Howie had settled. I supposed I could
call Darlene and ask but long-distance was expensive and I liked her
too much to call collect.

Yvonne continued her mother-wife fantasy with Jed Tooley, and I
occupied myself, taking Polaroids and overhearing just-written songs.
A woman in a newsboy cap dropped sugar cubes on my tongue, and
when I asked if they were acid, she said, "No, they're just sweet to
taste." A dachshund nipped at my ankle as I drifted through the lobby
in quiet pursuit of a man I thought might have been Warhol with a new
Brillo pad piece, but was really a deliveryman. A punk rocker with a
Mohawk asked for help painting it blue, handing me acrylic paint and
horsehair brushes.

Was I alive, I asked myself, or was this a living dream?

So much was lovely. So much was strange. I was enjoying myself,
truly and bravely, thinking all the while of poor Josie, who wouldn't
get to see any of this new life.

No moping, I told myself. Take some photos and get better at what
you're good at.

So, camera around my neck, I sat on a lobby bench, sipped a glass
of white wine from the bar, and tried to find something to photograph. But I'd already documented everything exceptional tonight
twice over. Tomorrow there'd be new glories.

Instead, something—someone—found me.

A woman in a pinafore dress with a Virginia Slim behind her left
ear gawked for a moment when she came into the lobby. She was
alone, but looked like she knew how to find company wherever she
went. "Sorry," she said before anything else, her running shoes sliding quickly across the lobby tiles. "We've met. Uh, at Wall-Mount
Recordings? You were with Holiday Sun. Right? Sometime last year.
Faun, right?"

"Oh, right," I said, trying to place her. Too gentle to be a groupie.

Too mild to be a singer. Too comfortable to be a no one. It clicked. "You were with Ridley Dagg!"

"Yes," she said, coming closer. She had little pimple scabs all over her face. "My name's Rhoda Weaver. I don't mean to be a creep or anything, but I've been kind of following you. Not physically! In the press, I mean. Through the trial. I like your photos."

"Thank you," I said, then sipped my wine and asked, "Should I take one of you?"

"Sure! That would be amazing. I know a lot about you. I *love* your Polaroids," she said, then added, trying to brag after gushing too much about me, "I've been bumped up from Mr. Dagg's note girl."

"Really?" I asked. "That's . . . that's great. I haven't moved up much. Or at all." She was easy to be open with.

"*Asking* is looking for a photographer," she said slowly. Her eyes darted with thought. "I know you took Holiday Sun's last album cover, and, well, you carry a bit of notoriety that is *perfect* for a rock mag."

"You think I'm dangerous?" I laughed.

"Aren't you?" she asked. God, she meant it. "Say you'll do it. Say I can give your number to my editor. Oh, please! I saw your photos in some . . . other magazines. I liked them. They're authentic."

Cal had hated the photographers who hung around the band in California. He said they were worthy of being spat on. That they had no care for music, only for self-promotion.

I had been different, because I'd tell them they were miraculous before I'd take their photo. The pictures I'd taken of Holiday Sun—and Harry Carling and everyone else—weren't magazine shots. They were love letters to people who didn't realize I was sending them. That was wide-eyed, green stuff, but Rhoda offered me sincere professionalism, something I'd never known but wanted all the while. The thing that had been dangled over my gullible head, like a carrot before a donkey.

Cal had hated professional photographers, but, fuck it, I hated Cal, so I said, "Bitchin'. I don't have a real phone number, but I can take your editor's." I toughened up, curling my lip in a way that was either Elvis or a wasp sting.

"Far out," Rhoda said, beaming, "Far out, far out, far out! Oh, she'll flip. You're perfect. This will be perfect."

"Would I get paid?" I asked, then corrected myself. "How much?"

"Not sure," she said, with a soft laugh. "You can discuss it with Tzipporah. That's my editor. I'm really just a scout but," she continued, emanating the faux importance I recognized from myself, "I'm here to do an interview with Don Undergrove. It was supposed to be Alice Cooper, but he flaked." She grabbed a CVS receipt lying lonely on the floor and scribbled a phone number and a smiley face onto it. "Here," she said, handing it to me. "Call her. She'll give you a sweet deal."

Rhoda took me up to the seventh floor to watch her interview Don Undergrove and I stopped myself from laughing every time her voice cracked from nervousness. Poor girl, stuck awake at three A.M. interviewing a second choice. Better than sleeping, I guess.

I'd never heard of Don Undergrove, but from what he told Rhoda as he sat backward on a metal chair, crunching candies and dropping their wrappers onto the grayed carpet, he thought he was the "bad girl's Peter Frampton." What a shitty self-compliment. He'd had two radio hits, and when he hummed them, I realized I'd heard them. My thumb wasn't quite on the musical pulse anymore, but I could readjust. I took a few photos of him after adjusting the table lamp so it cast harsher shadows. For the "bad" image, of course. I liked him. He was earnest. Real. Kind, although he was pretending not to be. When he'd get famous a few months after this, I'd shake my head at the self-aware fear he'd held in that hotel room and hope he still had it.

I said goodbye to Rhoda, who went home to whatever East Side bachelor apartment her parents were probably putting her up in. I stayed in the takeout-box-laden room Don Undergrove resided in, taking a few more Polaroids. I finished up, collecting my things and zipping my purse tight like New York had taught me to. Don Undergrove asked me to stay, but I was too tired to amuse him.

I slipped away into the liminal space of the hotel halls. I went downstairs and fell asleep in the room next to Jed Tooley's.

THE NEXT MORNING, Yvonne woke me, moaning that Jed Tooley was driving her crazy. We drifted out of the hotel, eating bagels and lox on a park bench and pooling our change so I could call Rhoda's editor, Tzipporah. Birds chirped and church bells chimed.

Yvonne stood beside me as I twisted the pay phone cord around my arm until my hand went red. I prepared to dial the number.

Yvonne stuck her finger up, issuing a warning. "These magazine people try to run anyone they can into the ground," she said. "They're not like us."

"She's gonna give me money," I said. "It's a perfect job."

"Not enough," Yvonne said, considering. "Fight for more than they want to give you. Go. Call." She huffed impatiently before I'd even begun speaking to the voice on the other end.

When Tzipporah picked up, she asked who I was and I tried to answer in a way that would make her like me. Every sentence I spoke flipped up like it was a question. "I was given your number by Rhoda Weaver. My name is Faun Novak—uh, I was told you're looking for a photographer and Rhoda thinks I might fit the bill."

"Faun Novak from the Holiday trial?" she asked. A pen clicked.

"Yeah," I said. "The same."

"Ooh," she said. Tzipporah Weyes spoke breezily, like she was floating on a lazy river, and took too long to reply to any of the hurried answers I gave about experience and expectations.

I told her I had lots of photos ready to be looked at, dropping names until my mouth turned sticky with them. That turned her attention to full. She asked me to come to the New York *Asking* offices tomorrow to meet with her. It started to flurry. The snow turned to light rain, and I stayed dry in the glass shelter of the phone booth. My bare legs prickled with goose bumps, from either cold or tension, but my arms, swathed in the stolen fabric of a plaid hunting jacket I found in the seventh-floor hallway, were warm under wool. The sky above was cotton white and pristine.

We hung up at the same time and I told Yvonne the good news—that I had almost cinched the job.

"People are gonna call you scum," Yvonne said, holding a newspaper over her hair to keep it dry.

I thought about Clementine in front of the Troubadour, her thick spit stuck to my skin. Then I thought about the foul looks shot my way by the pin-straight men and women I passed on the street. "Some people already do."

I HATED OFFICES, even ones like Tzipporah's that were admittedly very cool. She had three beaded necklaces hanging over her desk lamp and a pop-art portrait of herself on the wall. Tzipporah looked like Mama Cass in a business suit. An orchid on the windowsill bent toward the light. I was five minutes late for the appointment we booked, because I missed my subway stop and had to run two city blocks from the next one over.

Tzipporah offered me sparkling water and I drank it, hoping she couldn't see the beads of sweat sticking to my forehead.

"Are you hungry?" she asked, and I said no, even though I could smell cinnamon and toast wafting from the hallway. Yvonne said Tzipporah was the antithesis of everything good about rock and roll, so I stayed hungry in silent protest. Sure, I'd take her money, but her food? Too far and too friendly.

I'd packed a fine selection of my best Polaroids. I kept the assortment to musicians who would be familiar and marketable to Tzipporah. I brought photos of Josie, too, but tucked them into the hidden pocket in my purse, behind ChapStick and deodorant. Good luck charms.

I laid the photos onto the mahogany desk like showing my hand in poker, and waited, holding my breath, as Tzipporah picked each one up and examined it through a pair of horn-rimmed glasses. Sometimes she'd say, "Good," or mouth the name of the person she was looking at. She smiled at a photo of Harry Carling backstage at the Bowl. She squinted at one of Cal, unsure what face to make. She blew air out of her nose. He was tainted now, either a martyr or someone who got what he deserved, depending on who you asked. He was rare, too. An unseen photo of Cal revived people's already flickering memories. Tzipporah muttered, "Like trading cards."

"What do you think?" I asked, impatient.

Tzipporah collected all the photos into a neat stack, aligning their corners, and said, "These are good. I want a few. We'll buy a couple right now, then hire you to do a photoshoot or two. You like taking backstage photos?"

"That's the only thing I really ever do," I said.

"Well, you're good at it. Who were you with before?"

"What do you mean?"

"How did you get backstage for all these photos? How did you meet all these people?" Her eyes narrowed.

I shrugged. "I find ways." Stay mysterious, I told myself. Stay aloof. Don't seem too googly.

She nodded, her pin-straight hair falling in front of her eyes. "We'll buy the Holiday Sun shots. Harry Carling and Don Undergrove, too. Undergrove's our cover story next month since everyone loves an up-and-comer, and this one"—she pointed to a photo of him wearing three pairs of sunglasses—"is a good cover. Jesus Christ, where have you been?"

I reached into my purse for ChapStick, my lips dry from the unfamiliar New York cold. My fingers brushed the stack of Josie Polaroids and I paused.

Tzipporah, long practiced at reading slight shifts, asked, "What's wrong? You're not happy?"

"I just have other photos, too," I said. I put the ChapStick on my lips as an excuse to think. "You just—well, I don't think you'd want them." I toyed with the sharp edges of the Polaroids. If Tzipporah wanted to hire me, she had to want to hire all of me. Enough tucking away parts of myself that weren't "right." Enough carving out new selves like I was soap. Time to be myself. My whole, self-loathing self. I couldn't sell photos of Cal without the world knowing I stood by Josie. It would be just as dirty as all my other tricks. "They're of Josie. Josie Holiday."

Josie's name sucked the air out of the room.

There were two copies of *Ms.* magazine on Tzipporah's desk next to a statuette of a blue horse. That was a feminist mag, wasn't it? Yvonne once had a copy that she'd flipped through, pretending to know the name of every article's author already. And if Tzipporah was a feminist, maybe she'd have some sympathy for Josie. For a woman defending herself, no matter what the court said. But—fuck—there was also an Andrea Dworkin book with a cracked spine lying beside them. And I knew enough from chats with Yvonne's proto-feminist friends that Dworkin probably wouldn't like Josie's nude-modeling career. Who would Josie be to Tzipporah? A villain? An antihero? A nightmare? A cautionary tale?

A fascination. Tzipporah took a sip from her coffee mug and said, "Let's see them. They could be interesting."

I laid the photos out for her. The one with the party balloons. The one at the beach. The one in the tub. The ones where she was alone, in love with no one but herself. I gulped down spit and said, strategizing, "She's no hero, I know, but she's my friend. She got dealt a bad hand in court. She deserves—I don't know—"

"Redemption?" Tzipporah picked up a Polaroid of Josie on our rooftop. It was someone else's rooftop now.

"Validation. She's an amazing model. She's *talented*." My brain clicked into movement. All or nothing. Tzipporah would take all of me or nothing at all. "If you want to hire me, I want two things: I want to get paid the same as you'd pay any other photographer, and I want an article, a section, a *something*, about Josie. An interview, maybe. I could give an interview and you could include all these photos and she could be something more than . . . whatever she is now. I want a—"

"A special feature?"

"Yeah." I refused to bristle.

Tzipporah leaned back in her chair, and I prayed to every god I knew she'd agree.

She said, "We can't throw out special features left and right. Besides, we don't have the budget to pay you for all the pictures of her."

"It doesn't matter. I don't want money for the photos of her. Listen," I said, begging, "I can get concert photos. I can get backstage. I can get anything you want, as long as *I* get the one thing *I* want." I'd been too forceful. Too ungrateful and assuming. Here was a wonderful opportunity, and I might have just thrown it away in the name of selfishness. No, not selfishness—consideration for Josie. Josie, who deserved redemption. There was so much I wanted to say—that Josie deserved a print revitalization to prove she was a whole person. To show all the stiff collars she wasn't just a common whore. That even if she were a "common whore," she'd still deserve decency. That it had been him or her. That she was a person no matter what. That she shone like the goddamn sun. All I managed to say was "People don't like her very much. Anymore. But she's my best friend."

"Right."

A different approach. "It's controversial. It's provocative. People will buy it."

Tzipporah didn't throw me out. She seemed to understand, in the way most women do when they've been around enough powerful men, that *wanting* can be a hard thing to express. She paused for a long time, then said, "If you don't mind not getting paid for the special feature, then . . . sure. You have enough photos of her to fill a whole article?"

"More than enough," I said, beaming. "Pleasure doing business with you."

"You got parents?" she asked.

"I'm twenty-four," I said stiffly. I might have looked like a baby, like a farm animal thrown into a motherless pen, but I wasn't.

She repeated, "You got parents? I could send them a free copy or five of your special feature."

I breathed in, embarrassed at my assumptions of condescension. "Oh. No. I don't."

I could have asked her to send a copy to cat-faced Aunt Lissy, whose Christmas card had wished me luck finding a beauty school that'd take me, or to Great-Uncle Tippy, whose hardened hands had held my waist too tight at every rare family function. I could have sent them to my Texas cousins, whom I'd never met, but I didn't know them. Not well enough. I asked Tzipporah to send a copy of the special edition to Darlene and Scott. Not family, but close.

And of course, I would send a copy to Josie. If I were in her shoes, I would have wanted to stay out of the spotlight for good, but Josie was different. She *had* to reply to seeing herself in print again. My apologies wouldn't be hollow anymore. I'd show the whole world I was sorry just to show *her.*

I also asked for a handful of copies to laminate and bury in a storage box, worrying I'd lose them before I ever had a box to store them in. Worth a shot.

I left with warm cheeks and a check in my jeans pocket for the non-Josie Polaroids. Sun streamed through the spaces between skyscrapers like water spilling over countertops. Impossible to catch.

I bought a bag of stale discount Halloween chocolates at a bodega and ate them for dinner outside the Central Park Zoo, melting the candy in my mouth and listening as chimpanzees shrieked conversations inside. Candy for dinner. Child eyes on a woman. Despite all I'd seen, I still wanted to see more. I finished the whole bag and wished I'd bought another.

I took the subway back to the motel room, where I found Yvonne writing in a diary I didn't know she had. I told her the good news about the special edition and the job, and all she said was "Baby's growing up."

Yvonne and I moved into a different motel because the owner of the last one "complained too much" every time Yvonne would talk on the lobby pay phone for hours on end in the middle of the night. Our new place was a Howard Johnson's honeymoon suite. The bed frame was shaped like a turquoise shell. I took twenty Polaroids of Yvonne on the bed posing like *The Birth of Venus*. She looked through them every morning, smitten with the evidence of her beauty. We considered trying to stay with people we knew at the Chelsea Hotel, but hopping through other people's rooms was starting to lose its charm.

I went to the *Asking* office every week or so, discussing the special feature with Tzipporah. I sent letters to Darlene and Kitty asking for anything they might want to submit. After a while, I sent one to Pamela, too, who responded with an envelope stuffed so full of childhood photos that the glue had begun to lift. The appearance of sweetness was ruined by the note she attached: *Mom was going to toss these anyways.*

I almost sent a letter to Josie asking if she wanted to contribute, but Tzipporah told me not to. To have Josie speak to the nation would be too much. We could provoke, but never too far. Fine.

I gave all the pictures to Tzipporah and her team and let them do what they would. Sometimes I gave context (especially to party shots). Tzipporah would often complain about how "apple pie" Josie could look. She *was* apple pie, I said. She was ice cream and canned peaches. Peaches-and-cream. Faun-and-Josie.

I gave my interview to Rhoda, telling all the good parts and some of the bad.

New York became home.

Yvonne and I met girls who talked and looked exactly like us with funny names like Aphrodite and Jellie-Bellie-Jean, and went to parties, exclaiming how good it felt to be alive. Sometimes it felt like gloating, but only sometimes.

Three Photos

Jed Tooley, looking half dead and high, in the hotel. Yvonne's beside him, impishly smiling, waiting for him to want her help.

Don Undergrove, posing too hard, letting me tell him how to look appealing.

An old high school photo of Josie and me, wearing fresh-pressed cheerleading uniforms and wide smiles.

24.

IN MID-DECEMBER, SALVATION ARMY BELLS RANG EVERYWHERE I went.

I liked the motel Yvonne and I stayed in, because it had a roof we could creep up onto. On cold nights without a party, we bundled into every jacket we owned and went up, looking at the stars. I told Yvonne I wished there was no money and no world below us. Just stars and cold, cold air that made your face sting.

When I realized I had no permanent address for my copies of the *Asking* magazine special edition to be sent to, I wondered if it was time to settle. Roots are hard to plant in concrete, so I never got around to it, despite continuously promising myself I would.

It was nice to think of settling, but it wasn't *that* hard to drop into the *Asking* offices to get the magazines. There was something definitive about carrying out five copies in my hands, the pages pristine and without an address sticker stuck over half the cover. The cover was one of the Polaroids I'd taken of Josie in front of a bedsheet backdrop. She'd never sent this one anywhere, because her eyes were too crinkly and her smile was too wide for anyone to take it seriously as sexy. A strange vision for who the nation had dubbed a murderous wife, strange enough that Tzipporah spent long hours wondering if it would endear or deter potential readers. She liked the photo for its controversial spin, its wholesome unwholesomeness. I liked it because Josie was smiling. She wasn't redeemed, but she was human.

People said she was self-obsessed and conniving, only interested in Cal and his kin for the fame. People said the same of any groupie. We all want things. Desire's not deviant. It's human nature.

The magazine's header read: STILL THE ANGEL OF THE SUNSET STRIP? INSIDE JOSIE HOLIDAY'S WORLD.

Some of Josie's friends gave quotes. Tzipporah procured a copy of our school yearbook from which to xerox Josie-focused pages. I gave my interview and my photos, trying to avoid the controversy that would come from a blatant defense of her. I reminisced about the past and refused to speculate on the future. Yvonne contributed a few lines about how Josie was another victim of the justice system's failure.

It was uncomfortable to read the seamless blend of nostalgia and sleaze. Smiles and scandal intersecting, interweaving. Maybe that made sense. Josie *was* the girl who'd striptease on a coffee table. She *was* the girl who'd scream her delighted head off at every concert and beg to go backstage. She was a girl at ease in life and sex, uneasy with wave-making unless those waves were going to make everyone like her. Or if not like her, look at her. I read through it all, unsure if I really understood my best friend after all. Unsure if the woman written about on those pages was Josie at all, or some mythologized version. Unsure if it mattered.

She was a flame too bright to be snuffed out, so she burned and burned until she melted herself down. Different visions of her materialized in the pages, like silk scarves pulled from a magician's sleeve. Critics called the feature dangerous, the magazine trying too hard to get the public's reaction. Concerned mothers called into the *Asking* offices in pearl-clutching, voice-shaking rages, cursing the magazine for its "normalization of illicit, evil acts." Very few people called record stores to protest the Cal Holiday tribute box set of Holiday Sun deep cuts that was coming out for the Christmas season.

It was a study in groupiedom. In pain. In joy. In good. In evil. In life.

I wrapped one of the magazines in plastic, tying it with a bow before slipping it into a manila envelope. I paid for shipping insurance and first-class service to send the copy to Josie. I tucked a letter inside, short and to the point:

Josie,

I made it sort of big with your help, as always. I hope you like this magazine. You're still a cover girl and I still love you.

Faun

A WEEK PASSED.

In that time, I dreamed once about Cal. We were in the backstage hallway of the Troubadour, but the floor was wet soil. He shook my hand and said it was good to meet me, good to really meet me. I couldn't say anything, my voice falling back into my throat before it could come out. He shook my hand harder, squeezing until the bones in my fingers shattered and splintered, poking out of my skin like spikes. His stomach split open, bleeding down his Levi's and onto the dirt.

I dreamed about Josie, too. We were back in her green Gremlin, speeding down the streets we haunted in high school. I was driving. We laughed about old teachers and old jokes, but when I turned to look at her, I couldn't see her. She shifted to my peripheral. I turned around and around, twisting on the car seat, confused until the car began to career. Josie laughed from behind me and said, "What's wrong?," and I woke up.

Thoughts of Josie and Cal rose every so often while I was off living life, but not as often as I'd anticipated. The constant occupation they'd once held in my mind gave way to passing visits. This was a blessing, I supposed, but it felt like a betrayal, too. I tried not to dwell on how to think the correct way. I tried to just be.

Tzipporah sent me out weekly to shows in Brooklyn and the Bowery with a preapproved backstage pass and company money in my pocket. Yvonne and I walked long loops around Manhattan, through the smells of Christmas balsams and the Hudson's salt water. She talked for hours on end about her big plans for her cousin's band—how she'd book the tours, who'd be their openers, how she'd market them. For so long we'd lived moment to moment, unsure of our place and too full of present concerns to consider what was to come. Now, we were steadier. Better fed. Warmly clothed. Making plans for the future is a privilege, I thought. Josie in prison couldn't make plans. They were made for her.

Don't linger, I reminded myself. Keep moving.

I shot photos of Yvonne's cousin's band. The members of Baby Stout were too demure and decent for the shoot they wanted. They wore jeans too clean to fit their grimy ideal. Yvonne's cousin Cora wore a sailor dress better fit for a church girl. Fine—I made it work. We took the subway to Coney Island in the middle of a snowstorm, the trains empty and cold. I told Cora to slip off her coat. She shivered but hopped up onto the top of the seats, her two bandmates leaning toward her knees. "Be like a doll," I said, shooting Polaroids every time the sun streamed through the subway windows. The flash was too hard to depend on here—I needed daylight's natural glow. She batted her big eyes, surrounded by filth and graffiti. Snow shimmied outside the subway car, soft as a lamb's back.

I dropped the shots off at the *Asking* office, trading them for a letter the secretary said had come for me. She popped one of her own complimentary mints and took a call that came through the canary-yellow telephone. The envelope's corners were crushed from being transferred bag to bag. I read the return address: *Sybil Brand Institute.* Josie.

I clutched the envelope and ran out the door, blasting through Manhattan with hope in my hands. I couldn't open it in public. This was a private moment, an unobservable joy. I barged through the door of the motel. Yvonne was asleep in the shell bed. I slipped into the bathroom and filled the heart-shaped tub with hot, stinging water. Steam coated the mirror so I cracked the window open. I glided into the water, propping my elbows on the pink tiles and faded grout. The envelope fell to the floor, and I unfolded the letter, holding it high above my head, unsure if I should prepare for glory or destruction.

I read, in Josie's bubble-lettered, girlish scrawl:

My sweet little Faun,
Oh what a GIFT it was to get your (or may-be our?) magazine. My
"roommate" says she thinks I'm a celebrity but I've been telling her
I'm just a regular girl . . . which of-course she didn't believe when the
magazine arrived ha ha! I read it front-to-back and I want to say
THANK YOU. I was worried may-be you did not like me anymore
(or that you were just pretending to. Lots of time to overthink in here.).
I'm sorry for not writing back sooner. I'm a bit too grumpy these days
I guess. Give me your telephone #? We can talk about our very very
deep and interesting feelings. My calling hours are 7–9 your time in
the morning. I don't have much news but I want to hear yours!

Love love love LOVE,
Josie

Added, in squished-together letters, at the bottom:

Sorry for short letter—only got 1 paper

I let out a breath. I put the letter on a dry towel, keeping it safe, before sliding under the bubbles in the tub. I ran my hands through my hair, billowing and weightless underwater, and when I came back up for air, I was crying. I went back under the water, relief rinsing over me.

Yvonne's jaw dropped to see the letter. "Truly," she said, "I thought she hated you. I would, if I were her." I thought the same.

I wrote Josie back with the motel room's phone number an hour later, dashing to the post office before it closed to send it as soon as I could. "How long does a letter take to get to California?" I asked the postal clerk, tapping my nails on the laminated stamps.

"A week," the clerk answered. He stuck a pencil behind his ear and asked, good-naturedly, "Sending a Christmas card?"

"Oh, just a letter," I said.

He looked down at the address, his eyes widening. "Right," he said. "Yeah, about a week."

So I waited. Each morning, no matter how late I'd been out shooting or sucking up at the Palladium and the Roseland Ballroom, I'd wake up early in wait for Josie's call. Everything came back to waiting for someone to beckon me. Waiting for someone else to move their piece so I'd have a turn.

Once, Yvonne and I stayed out dancing at Studio 54 until five A.M. We stumbled out onto the street together, laughing and meandering because we could. We were free. Yvonne spotted a diamond earring in the snow and picked it up, polishing it with the sleeve of her jacket. We hopped onto the hood of a parked car and leaned back on the windshield, steadying our drunken frozen breaths. She took the earring out of her pocket and called it a treasure. My head on her lap, my smile wide, I asked her to stick it through my unpierced ear. She did. It barely bled. It was beautiful.

"I've realized," she said, "we can do anything. Within reason."

"Not within reason," I said, laughing. "No reasons at all."

We rode the subway home to the motel, poking each other when our heads lolled or eyes fluttered shut. Yvonne vomited when we got back, occupying the bathroom until morning light, but when she finally fell asleep, she was smiling. I didn't join her. I still waited for that call from Josie.

When Josie did call, I had one stocking on and my toothbrush in my mouth. I spat into the sink, barely rinsing my mouth, and slammed myself down into the desk chair. I picked up the receiver and accepted the collect call. The line connected, ambient footsteps and clatter bristling. I cleared my throat and said, even though I knew, "Faun and Yvonne, who's this?"

"Faun!" Josie said across the line, her voice hitching. She giggled. "Oh, how good it is to hear your voice."

"I missed you so much. So much," I said.

"Thank you for the magazine," she said, very slowly. "Thank you, but—"

"But?" I asked, incredulous. "Josie, what?"

"Thank you, but I don't think you should send me anything more about myself." She paused. "A lot of the girls here are mean. Some are nice, but a lot are mean. Nobody likes me."

I pulled my second stocking up over my leg and propped my feet up on the desk. I ran my hand across the coiled cable, liking the slick cling of the plastic. "Why?" I knew now that not everyone loved her, but it was a surprise every time just the same. The way a cold shower shocks you even though you're the one who turned the water on.

"They think I'm bragging about being 'famous' or whatever they call it. And I don't blame them . . . a lot of them have had it way worse than me." She lowered her voice. "But I like the magazine. I love it. It's sweet and kind and some of the photos are fabulous. But—oh, I don't know—maybe I have to put all that behind me. All the glamour. That whole life."

"Right," I said, trying to understand. "The magazine can be your . . . I don't want to call it a finale, but—"

"Not a finale to *me*. Just a finale to Josie Holiday. Angel of the Sunset Strip." She laughed and laughed, then gasped, suddenly in tears. She wept across the line, and I cooed soft noises to try to calm her. If only I could hug her, pat her head, and push her hair behind her ears in tiny circles. Josie took a deep breath and said, even quieter, "I got a letter from some studio exec. He said they're turning my 'story' into a TV movie and wanted me to approve it. I told him to fuck himself. And he said, 'Oh, well, we'll be making it whether or not you want us to,' and I hung up. God, Faun. God. Everyone knows who I am, huh?"

"Yeah," I said, sorry to be breaking the news.

"I wish nobody did."

"Me, too. I'm sorry."

"Not your fault," she said. "If it's anyone's fault—"

"Yeah."

"Yeah."

The conversation turned lighter. We laughed back and forth, making jokes about the good old days, wondering if someday we'd feel tall and happy again. If we'd stand up straight. Smile at strangers. Smile at the day ahead. Nothing would be normal, but now things were neutral. Canvaslike and clean.

After an hour, Josie wrapped up our call. "Write me again?" she asked. "Write me all the time."

"I will."

She hung up and I went to sleep as Yvonne woke up to vomit.

YVONNE AND I had an eggs-and-bacon breakfast at a corner deli, and I wondered if maybe now Josie could stop being all I cared about. I planned to write her, sure, but I couldn't bear to have her on my mind every second of every day anymore. My preoccupation with her was starting to exhaust me. "Does that make me a bitch?" I asked Yvonne.

"No," Yvonne said, considering. "Who cares? I'm a bitch."

"You're not."

She shrugged, unsure whether to take my word for it. She sipped orange juice. "Life goes on."

It did. Tragically, happily, essentially, it did. "Are you going home for Christmas?" I asked.

"No," she said.

"Me neither." I didn't have to say this. I didn't have a home, and Yvonne knew.

She laughed. "You better get me a good present with all that photography dough."

I nodded and dug into my breakfast, happy to not be worrying about how to pay for it.

A year since Goody's Christmas party. A year since sitting on Floyd's lap. A year since Josie and Cal's engagement. Why did every moment only exist in terms of its relation to the past?

Yvonne and I talked about resolutions. Next year, I said, I'll get myself an apartment. I'll learn to do macramé and decorate the walls. Frame photos for end tables and stock my fridge with avocados and fresh eggs. Maybe Floyd could come visit when he was done touring Europe. I could have friends over for Thanksgiving and we could carve the turkey together. I could get a cat and cuddle it on rainy nights. I could get a Christmas tree. I could have a solid, real home that was mine and no one else's. Pure domesticity with a few forays into rock and roll whenever I took photos. It could be lovely or it could be lonely.

And I hated loneliness more than anything else.

But I had to chance it. Life wasn't waiting. The world wasn't waiting. I couldn't either.

I HAD JUST come back from an assignment at a Goodnews Brothers concert, where I'd taken tasteful backstage photos and tried to forget all the grody things I knew about them, when Yvonne asked, "I booked Baby Stout a tour. They're opening for Northern. I met their singer a few years back. He likes me. His name's Wilmer. I called him up and asked if they wanted an opener and they did. We're going all across the country. Tour starts next month at CBGB's. What do you say to being the tour photographer?"

Once again, I said yes like it was breathing.

I WROTE TO Josie with my good news, telling her I'd be off on a grand exploration, working hard and seeing sights. I told her Yvonne had gotten me the job—that we both had real-actual jobs—and that everything was falling into place.

She wrote me back, enclosing a late hand-drawn Christmas card in the envelope colored with ketchup and tinted soap. The letter ended with this insistence:

I'm proud of you! I'm proud of Yvonne! I'm happy for you. I REALLY am.

Her writing was stiffer and choppier, with jagged edges. I couldn't tell much through handwritten text except for when the words on the page were a lie. I wrote back promising to visit when I could. I took a PO box so Josie could still write. Now she'd be the one sending letters and getting nothing back. A cruel twist, but a temporary one.

Yvonne took me to the show at CBGB's. Before we knew it, we were on a tour bus, heading down to D.C. and touching the pretty broad shoulders of Northern's band members and playing poetic with Baby Stout.

I called Tzipporah from a pay phone asking if I could send her photos from the road. Tzipporah asked when I was leaving, and I said I was already gone. No surprise in her voice, she told me she expected good photos when I got back. Life turned back to the relentless whirl of spitting blood and happy-crying mascara that I'd learned to find comfort in. But it was calmer now. More organized because I had a job to do. Parts of me wished it could be crazy again.

Yvonne stopped threatening to jump off balconies. I still blushed every time someone kissed me and grew used to the way that made everyone laugh. I worked hard and took a hundred pictures every week, of landscapes and skyscrapers and birds and, of course, the bands. I shook so many hands, all of them belonging to people who already knew my name. I'd made it—I got calls at each hotel from local celebrities who wanted their Polaroids done by Faun Novak herself.

I'd meet groupies backstage in every city. They drifted in because of their half jobs or free time. Some of them didn't know who Josie was. Some of them only knew me. I swore I saw Kitty once backstage, but it was just another teenager with a grown-up haircut and the whole sky in her eyes. I wasn't their kin anymore. They stood back from me with the same intrigued apprehension that I'd held for press and professionals way back when.

When the tour made it to L.A., I tried to schedule a visit with Josie. She stayed stoic over the line, pretending to not mind that all her visiting hours were used up. "I'm appealing my sentence," she explained.

I wished her good luck, but it didn't work. It became hard to keep up with a friend I could never see. A friend who existed only through letters. Once inseparable, now infrequent pen pals. I dyed my hair and realized that in a few years, Josie would hardly recognize me.

Halfway through the tour with Baby Stout and Northern, I clicked with a different band that I met at a bar party. I called Tzipporah to ask for approval before hopping their bus and following them through the South until I moved on, on assignment or impulse. My photos accompanied splashy full-page interview spreads and reviews. Some of the bands thought I wanted to sleep with them or steal secrets. Sometimes I'd bend to their desirous fears, but it never felt right.

The music was what kept me going. This job couldn't be eternal—it was too loud and straining on the mind. It was tough on my body to always be traveling, but I kept at it. So did Yvonne. I had a career, but I still craved that invisible something that I'd been searching for all the while. That urge for incredulity gave me great photos.

The new groupies thought I was foreign to them, but I knew we'd always have things in common. We'd chased magic and danger and, sometimes, death. We'd let our hair grow long and unpermed past our eyes. At every concert, we'd stood closer to the speakers, feeling the drums in our hearts and the bass rattle our eardrums. More, more, more. More drinking. More music. More fucking. More adoration. Train-track walkers waiting, always, for the final slam of something absurd and incredible. I'd never found what I was looking for, but I tried. I'd turned up the music a little louder and wished a little harder.

Life remained bittersweet. It always would.

YEARS LATER, I saw a video of myself on a behind-the-music show documenting the last great year in Holiday Sun–land. The broadcast called it an era of triumphant terror, but no one had been afraid. The video was grainy, but I could still recognize every inch of the Troubadour's backstage. I was sitting on the edge of a couch, clutching my Polaroid camera for dear life, Darlene and Wendy just out of frame. Someone called over, "Faun, did you like the show?"

I answered, my voice so much higher than I remember it being, "I loved it!"

From off-screen came a laugh, uncomfortably clear through the static hum of the video. Josie. Sure, she lived on in prison. Sure, Cal was the one who was dead. Why, then, was she the ghost?

All the girls left ghosts behind, not just Josie. You can see us haunting pictures, ones I took and ones I didn't—we're a tiny hand on a shoulder, a tuft of crimped hair, a sparkling hemline that's always nearly out of sight. We're references to "girls like this" and "little girls" in songs. Inside jokes and aesthetic pleasures. Fake names. Beating hearts.

We were the ones the world wanted to exorcise the obsession out of. The ones who would bleed, and *did* bleed, just to feel the touch of someone special.

Maybe we knew exactly what we were doing, turning ourselves into specters, leaving pieces of ourselves behind, in search of something new. Promising ourselves that if we went to one more concert or kissed one more famous face, that this time, it'll really be good.

This time, it'll really be perfect.

Acknowledgments

THANK YOU TO MY AGENT, MARIAH STOVALL OF TRELLIS LITER-
ary, whose belief in the potential of this book never faltered. She is
one of those rare, brilliant people who can say in one sentence what
others would take paragraphs to write. Her continuous encouragement and sharp creative eye helped me persevere. Thank you, too, to
Howland Literary interns Cheyenne Jackson and Zoe Howard, who
enthusiastically read drafts.

Thank you to my editor, Asanté Simons, whose passion and clear
vision carried this book to publication. Her attentiveness and excitement kept me going through the terrifying process that is putting out
a debut book. I knew during our first phone call together, which was
filled with laughter, that she was someone I'd adore working with.
Thank you as well to the entire team at William Morrow for their
hard work and proactive attitude.

The beta readers for this book, especially Elizabeth Wolfe, picked
and prodded relentlessly at early drafts.

I am deeply grateful for all the teachers who enabled me to write
openly, honestly, and happily. Jennifer Simpson, who taught the wonderful twelfth-grade writing class I wheedled my way into in eleventh
grade, showed me that writing could be more than a hobby. Rawi
Hage, who led a fourth-year creative writing seminar at uOttawa,
taught me growth through kindhearted criticism and specificity. Many
others—including Lindsay Laviolette, Richard Linke, and Andrea
Vere—instilled me with the value of learning.

My mother, Cecilia, read this book in every incarnation. She in-
spired a love of reading in me and provides unfaltering encouragement.

Having true, supportive friends has meant the world to me through-out the process of writing and publishing this book. Anna Ranger was the first person to read it and say the characters' names back to me. Elliana Kleiner crossed her fingers under her pillow every night for me while this book was on submission. Others, too—including Julia Hubert, Helena Pentick-Weichert, KC Hoard, Susie Banks, Isabel Glasgow, Cynthia Oxley, Ana Paula Sanchez Garcia, and so many more—are people I will always be grateful for.

Finally, thank you to Peter Wiercioch. He already knows how much I love him.